THE SOCIETIES BOOK 1

I0616009

ASSIMILATION

SYDNEY REAMES

Ebook ISBN-13: 978-1-961057-05-0
Paperback ISBN-13: 978-1-961057-04-3

Cover design by: Deranged Doctor Design

CHAPTER 1

The day I found out I'd be leaving Earth began innocuously enough, with me sitting in front of the television alongside my best friend. Instead of our usual old movies, though, we watched live coverage of an actual alien invasion. And not from just one planet, but seven.

The worlds participating in the united group called themselves the Societies, and they'd each sent their own representatives. They looked nothing alike, aside from appearing humanoid, and even that description was a stretch for a few of them. At the insistence of Earth's otherworldly guests, some sort of televised discussions were required, and life in every continent ground to a standstill as the population sat glued to a screen to witness speeches and talks between the leaders of Earth and the Societal delegates that made up an interplanetary governing body, which they called the Coalition. Their leader, Magistrate Warrick, stood at the podium as we watched.

"Prior to our arrival here, and before the apparent loss of our shared histories, Earth was once a potential Society. The individuals originally selected to settle Earth led an unfortunate and ill-fated rebellion, for reasons we have never been able to fully uncover. During these events, they cut themselves off from the Hub, our central station and transport point between the Societal planets. As a result, their descendants have missed the opportunity to go through our coming-of-age process, the Choosing, and subsequent Assimilation."

As Warrick delivered the message, the scales that covered his face, the hue of red dirt, glinted onscreen. He was a resident of Rover, a desert Society. His short, pointed teeth and forked tongue gave him a reptilian countenance.

"What a load of garbage!" A pillow flew through the air toward the television, thrown by Hale, my oldest and best friend.

I imagined most of the planet was experiencing collective shock following the magistrate's pronouncement. Not Hale and I, though. Having been raised within the conspiracy group Verkent, we had been aware that everyone on our planet descended from another alien race, a knowledge passed down for generations. That race had callously stranded our ancestors on Earth, although it seemed the Societals wanted to tell a different version of events.

Hale scowled, his hazel eyes glaring at Warrick.

"Kena, you know he's lying. We both do. When your uncle sees this ..." Hale huffed and blew a wayward strand of ashy brown hair out of his eyes.

I could easily finish that thought. My Uncle Juliard probably was thrilled to see our visitors. As the leader of Verkent, he'd been hoping and preparing for such an event all his life. Our relationship was complicated, but I was certain we would be equally excited over the Societals making a long-awaited appearance. Verkent had existed for generations with nothing more than memories, books and illustrations to keep faith in the Societals alive. For many years our family had led the group with nothing to show for it but aging artifacts.

Onscreen, Warrick stepped down and the next speaker moved forward. I noted that each Society had different features—some with wings, talons, claws, or even gelatinous skin. It was difficult to believe Earth's inhabitants were at all related.

The next speaker wore modest attire that covered him head to toe, including a cape with the hood pulled up over his head. Glowing sapphire eyes visible from its depths were the only feature that gave away this delegate as something other than human. That would make him a Riftian, I knew. Of the seven Societies, Riftians were those we had the least information about. In our illustrations they had luminous eyes, but everything else was covered by their body-shrouding clothing. As he stepped to the microphone, I knew he was merely speaking to a camera, but it felt as if his eyes locked directly with mine. I felt a near-physical compulsion to keep watching as his crisp, clear voice boomed through the screen.

"I am Bayard, head delegate of the Rift. We thank you for your welcome. Throughout these last few days, you have heard us referencing the various Societies we represent. This Coalition is formed of an alliance among our Societal planets. As shared by my fellow delegates, each individual in the Societies begins life looking similar to all of you. We believe our character builds as we become adults and during the physical alterations we experience on the planet on which we end up residing. Until that point, we refer to our youth simply as Blanks. It is after the Choosing, when Assimilating to their new homes, that individuals experience the differences in abilities and appearance you have seen in us during these speeches."

"We know this already!" Hale chucked another pillow at me, but I snatched it from the air and tossed it back, hitting him squarely on the forehead.

"*We* do, but not everyone on Earth grew up in an underground conspiracy group. We're lucky they're handing out this information at all. If the Societals hadn't made global viewing of these talks a condition of their negotiations, do you think anyone in power on this planet would have been running to supply information on an alien invasion to the general masses?"

He rubbed the spot on his forehead where I'd hit him, scowling in my direction.

"You're mean when you're stressed, you know that? I could have been gravely injured just now." His face broke into a teasing grin as he climbed onto the arm of my couch. Bayard continued.

"It is participation in the Choosing process that we would like to offer Earth. Per our conversations with the task force of leadership your planet has assembled, we will allow fifty Earthers to go through the Choosing. The outcome of this may determine whether Earth will be considered as a future Society. Furthermore, we are of the belief that to ascertain Earth's potential we need to observe the Assimilation of your kind on a continuum. Societal Blanks all go through this process as teenagers, and we will need information as to what happens to those who never had such an opportunity. Therefore, we will be taking not only Blanks of the typical age for Assimilation, but accepting participants of all ages."

"What?" Hale fell backwards off the couch, arms wheeling. It was huge news, and the moment Bayard made the statement I envisioned myself traveling to the Societies I'd only dreamed of. I reached down to help Hale back up, as Bayard stepped down to allow the next speaker to come forward. I clasped under his shoulders and pulled.

"Oh my God, Juliard!"

I nearly dropped Hale again as he yelled, the sound ringing painfully in my ears.

"Yes, he'll be eating this whole thing up, I'm sure. I suppose I'll have to make a vis—"

"No, Kena. *Juliard!*" I followed Hale's gaze back to the television and promptly dropped my friend back off the couch, a grunt escaping him as his rear hit the floor.

Standing at the podium, his grey eyes reflecting the flashes of reporters' cameras offscreen, stood my uncle.

Juliard and my father had essentially run Verkent together. My dad had always been more interested in possibilities. He loved reviewing the abilities and features of different Societals, and the applications of each. He'd come up with hundreds of uses for the sprawling wings all of the Kites possessed; our illustrations of that particular Society were primarily soaring beings in a soft green sky. Juliard had been far more intrigued by how Earthers had been stranded here in the first place. He'd longed to know who specifically was responsible and had his own thoughts on how Earth should react if the Societals ever showed up again. Given that Verkent believed they'd abandoned us all, joining a task force to welcome them hadn't been on the top of the list. Yet there he stood, speaking as part of a committee of Earth's richest and most powerful leaders.

When my father was still alive, he and Juliard had been fiercely loyal to each other, despite their differences. They'd both done their very best to raise me after my mother left. When she'd first met my father, she found the idea of Verkent edgy and mysterious, rather than strange. The reality of maintaining an actual relationship and caring for a child wasn't what she'd had in mind when joining a fringe group like Verkent. She chose to run off and leave my father with nothing but a bad memory—and me, mirroring her looks, with green eyes and sandy hair. In part, her abandonment spurred my own fierce interest in the group. If she didn't love me along with Verkent,

I was determined to love it enough for both of us. I ignored the pain that always accompanied memories of her. After spending fifteen of my eighteen years without her, I'd become accustomed to swallowing down my feelings. My uncle was a different matter.

On screen, he finished an introduction that revealed our very private group to the world and then moved straight into discussing the plan, as though he were in charge of the whole process.

"The task force and myself anticipate widespread interest in this opportunity. Given the limited number of spots, we're accepting applications. In the spirit of fairness, there will be a randomized selection to determine the final fifty individuals who will be leaving for the Hub in two weeks' time."

"How?" Hale's question hung in the air as Juliard fielded questions from reporters.

"He must have shown them Verkent's records. The books, the papers, even the planetary maps. If he'd tried anything like this before their arrival, he'd have been dismissed as a liar, or insane. But with the Societals here in the flesh to confirm his claims, the world's leaders must have been more ... open-minded." It was the only explanation I could fathom that made any sense. I couldn't imagine he'd won them over with charm.

Juliard was serious about his relationships within Verkent, but he'd never had much use for the outside world, save a few exceptions. He had the ability to be an excellent negotiator when necessary, but that didn't make him likable. My father had been the personable one. Whenever someone new did happen to stumble upon our private, but not officially secret, group, it had been my father that saved us from looking completely unhinged. Juliard could overwhelm others with his impassioned speeches about the Societies. Dad had captivated people as he showed them all our artifacts, including a saucer-shaped disc he'd always believed to hold important information about the Societies. We had no technology that would allow us to view it, but it had always been my favorite item. At least Juliard couldn't have shared that with the world, because it had been in my possession since my father passed.

After he died, I tried to fill his shoes, taking on a leadership role for the group. Juliard had taken the opportunity to push his own interests—namely his desire to lead the group himself. Without my father to temper him, he'd turned even more toward viewing the Societals as a potential adversary, and we'd argued about it. The fight had left our relationship on shaky ground for the past few years. Even so, I wasn't going to let our feud get in the way of a potential opportunity to join the Societies. Random selection or not, I had every intention of being chosen. Which meant a visit to my uncle. I turned away from the speeches to find Hale staring at me.

"I can tell just by the set of your jaw what you're planning. As long as you're there, see if you can put in a good word for me as well, huh? Could be fun to go on a bit of a space adventure."

"*A bit of fun?*"

While I had been a serious devotee of Verkent growing up, Hale had been very clear that he had no idea whether the Societies were real or not. His doubt was a radical attitude for our group. What it had always represented for him was an opportunity for adventure if they did exist, and a great story if it didn't. As a kid, Hale's eyes had lit up, his whole body leaning forward, whenever my father's stories turned toward the Crew. Verkent's tales about that Society made them sound like a bunch of seafaring pirates, and Hale was obsessed. I had no doubt which Society he'd pick, if given the opportunity. But before that, I needed to patch things up with my uncle. Luckily for me, I had a pretty good idea where I could find him.

The next morning, I stood before the solid wooden doors of a church. Of all the places Verkent could have held meetings, it seemed curious that the basement of this church had served as the setting for our monthly get-togethers for as long as I could remember. What made it even more odd was that the church congregation knew exactly what our group was about. Though our belief in the Societies essentially flew in the face of everything they adhered to, they'd graciously lent the space to my father and uncle decades ago.

None of the church members attended our meetings, of course, but the sweet old ladies who orchestrated the congregation's potlucks left out cookies or other baked goods for us sometimes. As their attendance and finances dwindled over the years, ownership of the building had transitioned to Verkent. My father purchased it with Juliard just a few years before he passed. They allowed the church to continue holding their weekly services on the main floor. Verkent had kept itself largely relegated to the basement.

As I crossed the threshold, the rundown nature of the building made itself known. The windows held a thin layer of dust, and deep green carpet hinted at a taste in decor that had faded from popularity decades ago. My steps were slow as I moved down the aisle of the sanctuary, the colors from the stained glass dancing across my skin. The space held a calm sort of quiet. Peaceful, as I was sure its creators intended it to be. I knew there were many who saw churches as a source of stress, but I felt a sense of belonging here, even though my beliefs sat in the basement and not among the pews. I walked the steps up toward the pulpit and continued through a door behind the organ, into to a small hallway that held the church's offices. Part of me longed to linger in the welcome tranquility of this space, but I was determined to secure a spot at the Hub.

The smell of dust that could never quite be cleaned away lined the wood-paneled hall. I came to a stop outside the third door, my feet shifting on the aged orange shag carpeting outside my uncle's office. It took three shaky breaths before I had the nerve to twist the worn golden doorknob. While I knew I was fully capable of going toe to toe with my uncle, I certainly didn't look forward to the experience. I reminded myself what was on the line. A permanent move to the Societies my father and I had dreamed of our entire lives. The thought gave me the courage to enter. Inside was more shag carpeting and built-in shelves of natural wood, filled with outdated hymnals and religious pamphlets intermixed with Societal texts and artifacts. I circled the room, letting my fingers brush over the covers of these items as my thoughts drifted to my father again.

I'd just turned fourteen when he died. In my grief, and following my fight with Juliard, I'd largely stepped back from Verkent. If it weren't for Hale constantly gossiping about the group, I would have had little idea what they were up to. That had been years ago, though, and I had no intention of bowing to my uncle again, or being run off. He'd intimidated the grief-stricken girl, but I was determined not to let him defeat the eighteen-year-old who was so close to achieving her greatest dream.

I pulled a book from the shelf and thumbed through it. It was one of Verkent's journals on Dagan, an underwater Society. They had the ability to breathe in the sea or on land, moving through the dark, harsh oceans of their world with speed and grace. As Bayard said, each Blank picked a planet during the Choosing. The most interesting part came afterward. Assimilating, as the Societies called their faster version of evolution, involved all kinds of physical changes. Depending on where they lived, they could grow fur, or fangs, or even wings. These special features allowed them to survive the various planets they inhabited. I'd grown up dreaming of going through the process myself, as my father told bedtime story after bedtime story about the seven Societies and their amazing traits.

I thumbed through the book as a familiar voice broke into my thoughts.

"If it isn't my wayward niece."

CHAPTER 2

Juliard's deep gray eyes were locked on me as he walked across the room. I wasn't prepared when he reached out and pulled me into a tight hug. He pulled back and turned his face away. I wondered whether his eyes had been watering as he motioned me over to a set of chairs in front of his desk. The whole greeting threw me off. Juliard had never been a hugger. The only other time I could remember him offering one was after my mother left.

His eyes stared into mine until I took a seat. My father's eyes had been just the same shade as Juliard's, a color that reminded me of a stormy sky. Growing up, when either of them was mad, I could almost swear I saw clouds swirling, lightning threatening to flash, behind that gaze. As they were identical twins, it was far from the only feature they shared. Juliard's resemblance to my father only added to the hurt when we fought. They even had the same habits.

"I wanted to meet with you before the rest of Verkent arrives for a special meeting I've called today."

"You didn't ask me here. I came looking for you." I managed to keep some of the bite out of my tone, but just barely. He waved his hand dismissively, but I caught him flicking a strand of hickory-colored hair from his face. My father had done the same thing when agitated.

"Semantics. If you hadn't shown up, I would have asked you here. And I knew you wouldn't be able to keep yourself from coming once you saw me. Verkent is right at the forefront of involvement in all this, and I'm going to be relying on you."

"How could you have known that?"

"Oh, niece, if you could see your face right now. As if your actions were a surprise to me. You forget, not only have I been around you for all your eighteen years, I was around your father for a lifetime. Barging in here with a wordy speech as to why he ought to be included would have been just like him. That, followed by an angry and equally well-worded tirade if I refused. I'm saving you the time, and me the discomfort of being on the receiving end of your temper."

I hated to admit to myself he was spot on. It was just what I'd planned.

"Now, if I'd been dealing with your mother, it would have been different. She was always cold and indifferent. You, on the other hand, take after your dad and myself. Peacekeeping and nonconfrontational as a base, with a fiery temper that singes others when you're pressed too far. Not your best quality, but who am I to judge?" He shrugged.

I felt the very anger he referenced rising up at the mention of my mother. But I squashed the feeling down and focused instead on what really mattered.

"How did you get yourself a spot on Earth's task force?"

"Simple. I started calling and writing to any government official I could find, the moment the Societals landed. We're the only people on the planet with any inside information that's not coming directly from them. I couldn't let Verkent miss out on such an opportunity. They were hesitant at first, of course. Thought I was trying to cash in on the whole thing somehow. But I showed them our books, and once they confirmed what was in them with information they were able to get from the Coalition, they realized we were the real deal. They were pretty eager to pay me off in exchange for our information, but I'm a tougher negotiator than that."

"What do you mean?"

"Those fifty spots? I secured ten for Verkent." It seemed that at least part of the selection process wasn't going to be as random as my uncle had led the world to believe. I was surprised to know he'd lied outright. He was a twister of the truth, but not typically given to full-on falsehoods.

"Funny you should mention that, because that's exactly what I wanted to talk to you about. You and I have had our differences, but you know my father intended for me to help lead this group. I have just as much a right to one of those spots as anyone here, and I'm not going to let y—"

"Listen to you, launching into the speech I'm trying to help you avoid. Of course I'm giving you one of the spots. I told you, I need you in this process. I need someone I can trust amidst the other task force picks. For the rest of our spots, I've got a good idea of who may want to go, but we'll decide that once everyone's arrived. With my being on the task force, I'll have some pull, but there's bound to be some political and private influencers. Those other Earthers will be looking for all kinds of information from the Societies. The way they figure it, the Societies are trying to do a bit of an experiment with us, so why not do some digging back?"

The joy when he'd mentioned I'd be going was overshadowed by the other portion of his spiel.

"I'm sorry, but is *any* of this process actually going to be random? All these people around the globe applying, do they really stand a chance of being picked?"

"Given the millions of applications we've already received, I'd say they wouldn't have stood much chance anyway. And really, we should be careful to put our best candidates forward. After all, we're already an anomaly to the Societals. Strange simply for the fact that adult Earthers look the same as their Blank adolescents. No idea what they expected after abandoning us here generations ago, but I don't think this was it. They don't just want to see if we could go through their Assimilation process to test our worthiness as a potential Society; they want to see if there's some sort of age cut-off. You can bet they'll be watching you like samples under a microscope. And Earth has its own questions. They're thrilled not to be entrusting that job solely to a bunch of teenagers."

Unease crept over me. The Societals had been like heroes to me, growing up. The last thing I wanted to do was treat them with distrust. I struggled to think of how to bring it up and swallowed down my own guilt at the same time. After all, the whole point of my visit had been to secure myself a spot, no matter what it took. In my mind, it made sense to have Verkent go, since we were already familiar, but I didn't relish the idea of further subterfuge.

"Are we actually going through any of this process honestly, or are you sending us all up there just to spy?"

"No, no, of course not! At least, not me. The other task force members might have their own thoughts. I just want you to be aware of the different motivations at play here. I've already heard in the meetings with them that some members are very excited at the prospect of advanced weaponry they expect to find. They've got scientists champing at the bit to explore how the Societals can move from 'human,'"—his fingers made quote marks in the air—"as they refer to the Blanks, into the Assimilated forms so quickly. I personally am interested strictly for educational purposes. That's all."

"I don't know that sneaking behind the backs of our hosts to gather information is going to foster good relations with the Societies. And why are you being so accommodating? Dad was always the one who was more curious, and you were always more ... vengeful."

He flicked his hair again, then placed his fingers to his temple, pressing down.

"Perhaps I've had the opportunity to grow a bit these past few years, to think on my mistakes. After all, they cost me our relationship, and this is me trying to right it. You have to understand, Kena. Years of questions potentially answered! Our records are fascinating, but they're just a minuscule amount of what you're going to find out. Everything your father wanted to know, you'll get the chance to experience firsthand. In fact, I was hoping you could keep an eye on the other Earthers, make sure they don't get themselves into trouble."

I knew my uncle well enough to suspect he was up to something more than he let on. I also knew he wouldn't open up if I pressed the issue. That's what had led to our falling out in the first place. I decided to bide my time.

"I'm in. Of course I'll help you."

"Excellent!"

We spent the next hour or so hauling items down to the basement for Verkent's meeting.

"Well, that's everything! I think I heard a car outside on my last trip down to the basement. Everyone should be arriving." Juliard wiped his hands together, smiling at shelves that had been emptied of everything except hymnals.

He ushered me toward the stairs. As I stepped into the basement, I was enveloped in a tight hug.

"Kena! I know Hale told us you'd be here, but I honestly didn't believe it until I saw you!" I looked up to see Pim, who at seventy-six was our oldest member. His face was crinkled into a smile that reached up to his soft blue eyes. His wispy grey hair had thinned further since I'd last seen him. A wave of guilt hit me as I realized that in trying to cut off the negative emotions after my dad died, I'd cut off the people closest to me in the process. Of course, Hale had told them. He and I still got together at least once a week, and he kept me caught up on what went on in Verkent. I knew it wasn't the same as being there myself. If I wanted to repair those relationships, I'd have to open back up to the others in Verkent.

"Attention, everyone! I know we're not always the most organized group, but I'm going to need us to be today. Everyone take a seat quickly!" Juliard shouted across the room.

Most people listened while a few continued bustling around the table of snacks we always had set out, chatting.

"Seats! Now!" Juliard's voice boomed over the conversations. As the stragglers sheepishly made their way to the chairs, he swept his gaze over the crowd.

While Juliard ran through what he'd already told me about our allotted spots, I watched everyone's faces. Most had the expected blank look of shock, eyes wide. Hale reached over and squeezed my arm so hard it hurt, shaking me.

"Did you know this?"

"Only about an hour before you." I pried his hand off my arm.

"Now, we're going to have to make some quick decisions here, people. They want all the participants for the Choosing selected within the next week. Then there's several days after that for everyone to pack, quit jobs, get transported to a central location, and basically extricate themselves from their lives here."

It was all a mere inconvenience, given that I'd dreamed of such an opportunity all my life. Still, the severity of what I'd agreed to hit me. I had plans for college in the fall. While that no doubt paled in comparison to a new planet, I realized what I'd agreed to give up. No coffees with friends under the trees in the quad. There would be no degree, even though I hadn't settled on a major.

At the end of his spiel, Juliard opened the floor to comments regarding Verkent's nine remaining spots. The fact that not one person balked when he told them I'd already accepted one made me feel both loved and even guiltier over the distance I'd been keeping.

The first volunteer was a surprise. Sybil, a petite woman in her late sixties with graying brown hair and a shuffling walk, made her way to the center of the group.

"I'm not sure how far they're willing to stretch that age limit, and I certainly don't want to take a spot from someone else. But I'd, I'd like to go." She fiddled with her hands as she spoke.

"And I'm going as well!" Pim strode into the circle after her, wrapping an arm around her shoulders. When I'd left Verkent these two, both widowed, had seemed on the verge of finally admitting they liked one another. According to Hale, they'd been an official item for the past year. Pim swept a challenging gaze over the group, even though no one had contradicted him.

"What else am I going to do with my time? Keep watching reruns of shows I've seen a thousand times? Watch the rest of my card-playing crew pass away? We've got an opportunity to do something spectacular here!" Sybil reached out and squeezed his hand. He smiled down at her. Since I'd left Verkent, Sybil had retired from her teaching position, and aside from being an avid gardener and reader, I wasn't sure how she spent her days.

Hale's hand narrowly missed my cheek as he pushed his way out of his chair and to the center of the group.

"I'm going, too!" I hadn't really doubted he would but even so, I felt relief as he stood beaming next to Pim and Sybil. Hale had been in my life since birth. I couldn't envision a world in which he wasn't around.

"What about the actual teens? Are we allowed to go? What's the minimum?" A skinny, straw-haired teen named Thomas locked eyes with Juliard as he posed the question, his mother's face paling as they awaited the answer.

"Technically, you can go at sixteen." I sensed a *but* coming from Juliard, and perhaps Thomas did as well, because he stood quickly and moved towards the center of the group.

"Excellent! I'm seventeen. I'm going!" His mother, Judy, wore a somewhat panicked expression, eyebrows rising nearly into her hairline. She didn't raise her own hand. I knew from Hale that she had an infant at home.

Spots quickly dwindling, a raven-haired teen named Veronica stood up next.

"I'm eighteen. Legally an adult. I'm going." Arms crossed in front of her, she stared around the circle with heavily lined blue eyes, but no one argued. Her mother and father sat in chairs next to her, beaming. They'd been die-hard Societal believers, and I was a bit surprised they hadn't volunteered themselves.

As Veronica joined her fellow volunteers, a voice rose from the back of the room.

"I'll go."

Silas made his way to the center of the group. He was just over six feet of muscle, with more than a few scars, and I was surprised I hadn't noticed him entering late. He was thirty-eight to my eighteen. He'd always had a serious demeanor and a resemblance to a real-life action star. He'd been a seemingly odd addition to our little conspiracy group. His mother was a devoted member, and he kept coming after her death when he was a teen. I never knew how much stock he really put into the whole Society thing, or if he simply carried on in her memory.

Silas towered over the others in the center of our group. Rumored among some Verkent members to have been a member of Delta Force, he had been absent from meetings for long stretches of time through my childhood. He lost part of his leg in an operation he wouldn't discuss, a couple of years after my dad died. He'd worn cargo pants to the meeting, but I knew his left leg ended just below the knee.

I'd gone to visit him in the hospital several times. He'd always been closed off enough that I didn't think anyone truly knew him, even in Verkent. Still, I felt a kinship with him in our mutual experience of losing our only parent at a young age. I brought in card or board games and we played, mostly in silence, after his surgeries. I never brought up his physical therapy, which had gone poorly the first several months, and he didn't bring up Verkent or my dad. After about a year he was back to a routine more reminiscent of his old self, in the gym constantly. He found an office job I couldn't picture him settling into. Once he went back to something akin to his former life, we sort of grew apart again. I was happy he was going to the Hub with us, though.

I was snapped out of my nostalgia as a second man waved an arm wildly and walked to the center.

"Me too! Sounds fun. Why not?"

The first surprising thing about the volunteer was that I hadn't met him before. Verkent didn't exactly go around advertising its existence; thus we had a fairly small and close-knit circle. The second shocking factor was the man's sheer size. He was taller even than Silas by a couple of inches, but it was his mass that made him stand out. Silas was muscular, but this man looked like a tank in human form.

His muscled shoulders and arms seemed almost at odds with the grin on his face, which would have looked more fitting on a Labrador than a bodybuilder. He had close-cropped hair that was starting to gray, although I wouldn't have guessed him to be much older than Silas.

When Silas clapped him on the back and smiled, I had a good idea of who he was. Hale had mentioned that a man named Dex had started coming to meetings. At least according to Hale, Dex had happily shared at his first Verkent gathering that the two knew each other from work. As I saw him for the first time, I doubted it was from the office job.

When only two spots remained, Rory and Kimberly stood up. The couple had been whispering together since Juliard's speech ended, Kimberly's auburn curls falling over Rory's shoulder. The two had lost a child a year before I lost Dad. I knew for a fact they visited him weekly.

"We'll go." Rory patted Kimberly's hands as a tear made its way down her cheek. It reminded me that, even with everything to be gained, every one of us would also be leaving something important behind.

The meeting tapered off soon after that. Juliard asked those of us going to stay behind. The remainder of the evening consisted of Juliard presenting everyone with checklists he'd printed off from the task force on what we'd need to do to prepare. As he read through and clarified each item, my anticipation grew. In two weeks, my life would change forever.

CHAPTER 3

After our initial meeting in the church, I'd hoped Juliard and I might spend some time together prior to my departure. I wanted to know more about his motivations. Since I no longer needed to pack and prepare to move into a dorm, my time was free. Juliard's time, it turned out, was anything but. Overnight, Verkent had gone from a fringe conspiracy group to a wildly popular organization that many saw as their golden ticket to get to space. Juliard's face was constantly on screens, reiterating the application process for the Choosing.

When my dad passed away, I'd remained in our home, with Juliard listed as my official guardian. He'd largely left me to my own machinations and hadn't entered the house in over a year. Given that, I easily could have remained there until we left, but I'd taken up temporary residence at the church. They had a couple of small rooms with a shower attached that had occasionally been offered to those in need. I figured I'd stand a better chance of catching my uncle that way, but he was in and out daily. He typically left as quickly as he arrived, but I did get small snippets of information. My second night at the church, he told me that he'd been correct in thinking the other forty applicants had been predetermined. On day four, he shared that the task force had secretly commandeered an arena. They intended to move all the applicants there to process before we left for the Choosing.

Occasionally I watched my uncle's televised appearances. Juliard had always possessed the conviction, but it was my father who had the words. They both had a lot of natural charm, but they wielded it differently. It was strange seeing Juliard field both roles at once. He was pushing me to the side again, but I knew it was only temporary. I didn't fully buy his claim of regretting our distance. Whatever the reason, I'd kept to myself the artifacts my father had stored. Whenever I felt particularly annoyed at Juliard, I would take out the disc my dad had kept from the Societies and turn the silver case over in my hands. I hoped to find a way to view it once we reached the Hub. On the night we were all set to leave for the arena, Juliard surprised me by asking for a private meeting at the church.

"Won't they need you there with the task force?"

He waved dismissively. "The important piece of the job is done for now. I got you all in, and through my pushing and prodding I was able to get several other individuals through who I think could be very helpful to us."

"Helpful how?"

"I just mean, a lot of these task force members are privately motivated by greed in some way. I was able to stack the numbers with at least a few people I think are genuinely interested in the Societies, like we are. You won't be able to contact me for a while once you go, but I'd like you to take notes on everything interesting you see. I'm gutted I'm not going myself."

"Why aren't you?" It was the first time we'd been in the same room together long enough for me to ask the question that had bothered me since he'd announced our participation.

He stopped his characteristic pacing around the office, his posture stiff.

"Well, I'm needed to support the task force, naturally."

"I thought you said the work was done for now."

"The work in selecting applicants, yes, but there's quite a bit more to it than that. Lots of big things are coming. I can't share it all with you, but it's going to be very exciting."

"But this is your life's passion, isn't it? Surely now that everything's organized, they could let y—"

"Kena. Drop it! Now."

I ground my teeth to keep from snapping at him. I'd learned the hard way that a toe-to-toe debate with Juliard wouldn't win him over. If I wanted to figure out what his motivations were, I'd have to do it indirectly.

"You're right. I'm sure you have your reasons. I'll just miss you up there. I always imagined if this happened, the three of us would be going together."

His body posture relaxed, and a smile lit his face as he walked toward his desk.

"Your father would be very proud of you."

A short car ride later, we'd made it to the arena. As we walked onto the turf, which was typically the focus of thousands of football fans, the size of it seemed almost comical. Everything set up for the applicants and task force members took up only a small portion of one end of the field. Everyone milled around inside a roped-off section. It was interesting to think that some of the most powerful people on the planet were gathered in the same place, and for once all of us were literally on a level playing field.

As Juliard left to join the other task force members, I managed to spot Hale's gesticulating hands and followed his direction to a small semicircle of Verkent members. He was chatting with Silas and Dex as I walked over. Rory and Kimberly were off to the side, in conversation with Thomas, who was fidgeting. Veronica was nowhere to be seen.

"Kena! I'd like you to meet a recent acquaintance of mine." Pim's voice rang as he all but shoved a figure in a hooded zip-up into my path.

"This is Digit."

The woman he'd pushed in front of me held out a hand to shake, and I noted, peeking from the edge of her rolled-up sleeves, a blue circuitry tattoo.

"I'm Kena. How is it you know Pim?"

"We're very recent acquaintances."

Pim stepped up next to her.

"She's into technology as well! More formally than me, of course. It's about time someone around here shared my interests! Oh, but there I've interrupted. My apologies." Pim couldn't seem to stand still and was dancing from foot to foot. An accountant by trade, he had taught himself coding for fun prior to retiring and had become very involved in it since. He'd always enjoyed tinkering with whatever the latest technological gadgets were, but no one else in the group had shared his passion. I looked back over at Digit, whose chestnut hair was poking out the sides of her hoodie. In the male-dominated field of tech, she wasn't what I would have expected, although she reminded me of someone.

"You remember that hacker that used to call himself Digit in his videos? The one that froze those trafficking websites?" A social justice warrior with a keyboard, Digit had made quite a name for himself before allegedly being caught.

"So you've heard of me!" She smirked, pulling down the hood.

"Hacker? But that's illegal!" Pim sputtered, shaking his head.

"Very. It's also how I got busted. Seems the task force is very interested in potential alien technology, though. They gave me a choice: participation or prison. Easy call, right?" She shrugged.

Digit hooked Pim into a side hug as he spluttered. Pim was a sweetheart, but a bit old-fashioned when it came to law-breaking.

"That was really you? No wonder he ... you ... always altered your voice in videos."

"Yep, not many people suspect a woman." She winked.

"What exactly are they wanting you to accomplish up the—"

"Oh, Pim told me about you! You helped all those innocent people. How wonderful! Tell us more." Sybil linked her arm with Pim's on the other side, pulling Digit into conversation before I could get any questions answered.

"Met the resident computer hacker, did you? Shame you told Pim who she was. I was going to let him continue on for a bit before I warned him he's made friends with a dangerous outlaw."

Hale waggled his eyebrows, laughing at his own joke. I just shook my head at him.

Near the end of the field, someone stepped up to a podium, asking everyone to gather together. As we all moved ourselves in front of a small stage, I realized there were some notable absences: the media, or any Societal members. Juliard sat in a row of chairs behind the speaker, amid several other task force members.

The first man to step up to the podium was somewhat reminiscent of Silas or Dex. Rugged, tall, muscled. He also seemed to be leaning heavily into a military look. He wore a set of stone-blue cargo pants and a matching jacket and sported a severe crew cut.

His belt was full of bulky accessories that seemed more fitting for a battlefield than a near-empty football stadium.

"All right! Everyone settle! I'm Kaiser, and I'll be prepping you for this mission. There are some important things you'll need to know to prepare you for what might be up there. First, we're keeping this whole transport of you all very need-to-know. I don't have to tell you that millions of people vying for fifty spots could easily lead to a riot on the spacecraft if we're not careful. Even with the security we've got in place, it's possible people could try and make a run on the stadium." He swept his gaze across the turf, as if looking for a crowd of people to appear.

"You'll also notice none of those *things* are joining us tonight, either. This is a strictly private briefing for Earthers only. They may think they're running the show up there, but we have a plan of our own."

"Oh good, he's crazy," Hale whispered through his teeth as he smiled up toward the podium.

"The official line is that Earth is giving this whole *Choosing* thing a sporting chance. You'll follow the routine once up there and go through the procedure. But you'll be tasked with collecting information and reporting it back to us. They hold something they call a Coalition meeting between all their leaders a couple of months after their precious little ceremony, and this task force will be in attendance. That means anything you find out about armies, weapons, technology and the like should be mentally cataloged. It also means you'll be up there long enough to acquire some of their physical features." His nose wrinkled. "Don't worry, though. It'll be a worthwhile sacrifice. And we'll be down here, doing everything we can to make sure you'll all be able to be extracted once we have what we need, if things go south."

"*Extracted*? What does he mean?" I hissed back at Hale. He gave an infinitesimal shrug.

"Do you think Juliard knew about this?" His hazel eyes searched my face for an answer I couldn't give him.

"Which brings us to one of the key components to this whole affair. Societal Assignments. We've placed you based upon your skill sets, or the information your financial backers are hoping to obtain. Therefore, you will all be required to *Choose* the Society you are given here, without mentioning it to the space freaks."

Behind Kaiser, my uncle cleared his throat. The man at the podium let out an exaggerated sigh before turning back to the microphone.

"Right. All but you Verkent members. You'll be picking your own Societies, for all the good that's going to do anyone. The rest of you, we've placed information packets in each of your bunks regarding your new Society. We've been at a disadvantage so far, with only the information Verkent and the aliens themselves have provided. Keep this in mind. Those individuals up in their precious Hub, or whatever they call their space station, sat out there for who knows how long, observing us, scrutinizing us, and judging us. And you can bet they've been gathering as much information as possible during their little excursions down here. It's about time we even the playing field." He stepped down and stalked toward one of the chairs on stage as Juliard strode up to take his place at the podium.

"I'm sure we all appreciate my colleague's very informative speech." Kaiser's dark eyes glinted as he glared back at my uncle. His sheer mass on the folding chair would have been comical if it didn't make him look like a caged animal about to lash out.

"He is correct. The Coalition is under the impression we've agreed to go through this process by the book. Now, as much as we'd all like to foster friendly relationships, there's always the chance that won't happen. Your participation in the Choosing is partially a test to see if the Societies would like to continue more permanent relations with us. And with that, exchanges of technology and information they've thus far kept to themselves. Having you all go up there and preemptively gather some useful intel will be helpful regardless, but especially if this ends up being a very short-term event."

It was Kaiser's turn to clear his throat.

Juliard ran a hand down his face.

"If that is the case, we have a whole team of very experienced scientists here who will be available to attempt to reverse any physical changes if you need to reintegrate to Earth."

"So, they're going to experiment on us?" Hale kept his eyes firmly on the podium as he whispered.

"I'm guessing the answer would depend on whether you asked Juliard or Kaiser."

"This is certainly a no-risk-no-reward situation. You've all been given a great opportunity, not just for yourselves, but for your planet. We're depending on you." Juliard finished. After my uncle stepped down, we were released to the tents.

I knew I'd have difficulty sleeping, given the enormity of what awaited us. I was pacing when Juliard entered, a stack of files in his arms.

"Brought you these." He dropped them on my cot, and I felt myself tense up. Had he been wrong? Were we being assigned after all?

He held a hand up.

"Don't worry, they're files on the other applicants. If the task force is set on digging for information, I figured we could gather some of our own. I've been making notes and copies when no one's looking. Split the pile up and share it with a couple of the others. I'd caution you against Hale. The boy's all right, but he's a blabbermouth. I might suggest Silas as a good choice, or even Dex. They're both used to keeping secrets."

"What happened to not spying?"

"I specified we weren't looking into the *Societies* with the same motivations as the others. Can't hurt us to know who else is going up there. Plus, some of them could be helpful if they were more sensitive to our information-gathering methods."

"As opposed to?"

"Whatever the task force is hoping to accomplish. Some of the others going are just relatives of well-off task force members or their friends. Spots were offered up to gain favor. Others, though, are going for specific reasons, like that hacker Digit. They figure if they send one of our most advanced tech people, they're much more likely to get into advanced Societal systems. They've got some ex-military similar to Silas and Dex."

"Kaiser's not going, is he?"

"No, he's staying down here to bug the rest of us instead. He didn't care for the Assimilated features. You should still watch, though. Not everyone we're sending up is exactly above-board. There's a set of twins whose father is a disgraced dignitary of some sort, very unsavory business."

I sat on my cot and picked up the first file.

"I'm not going to be there, Kena. Verkent was founded by our family. The task force may have an angle going into this, but we're the ones who have been hoping for this moment for a lifetime. I need you to lead the group in this."

I nodded, but I couldn't manage any further response. He was conceding to me the leadership I'd been after, but I knew he wasn't doing it without his own motives. What I wanted was to get us through the Choosing as it was intended. I didn't have any interest in whatever political games the task force or my uncle were playing.

Juliard was already walking out of the tent when I looked up from the pile. One hand already lifting the flap, he stopped and made his way back over to me again.

"Your father and I, we made a lot of mistakes. *I* made them after he was gone, but I love you, Kena. Never doubt that."

He didn't wait for a response before he turned and left. I had enough memories of growing up with him to know he did care, but that didn't mean he wasn't out for himself. Years of resentment warred with my remaining affection for him. I figured that, once we were at the Hub, it ultimately wouldn't matter. I'd have the life I had always dreamed of having with my father, and Juliard could help or oppose the task force all he wanted.

CHAPTER 4

The next morning, they loaded us all onto buses and drove to a remote area outside town. We were all going to be loaded on a small transport vessel that would take us to the Hub, our home until the Choosing. I was eager to see what had to be a massive space station, if it housed as many Societals as we'd been led to believe. The sun wasn't even fully up as we neared our destination.

"There had better be coffee up there." Hale groaned as he pressed a thermos into my hands.

"If not, I'm glad one of us thought to bring it here. To our potential last cup of caffeine." I held my thermos aloft and he tapped it with his own.

Hale shifted his feet back and forth, taking several loud slurps before he spoke again.

"So, how are you feeling about everything?"

"I'm ... fine. Really." I held the coffee thermos in a death grip as my answer squeaked out.

He snickered.

"Yes, I can see that." He nudged me companionably as he downed the remainder of his coffee.

Truthfully, I was still worried about Juliard's sketchy behavior, and whatever Kaiser and the others were up to. I was also finding myself especially nostalgic this morning, my memories shifting to my father. He'd dreamed of the Societies just as much as I had. I blinked, holding back tears at the thought that he had missed the chance to see them. I turned to Hale to say as much. But as we crested a hill, instead of opening up to my friend, I dropped my coffee on his lap.

"Geez, Kena!"

We'd made it to the ship. Out the window I could see something that was neither a NASA-style rocket nor a saucer-like contraption. It was more of a lopsided oval. Every bit of it was sleek and a muted grey. It was huge. If that was the temporary transport, it was hard to fathom the size the Hub had to be, given it housed permanent workers and all the Blanks preparing for the Choosing.

After we'd unloaded from the buses, a ramp extended itself from the ship, and Society members began walking down. As they stopped in front of our group, I strained my eyes trying to take in every detail. The rust-scaled magistrate, Warrick, made his way to the front, voice projecting across the field.

"While there is a complicated history between Earth and the Societies, we are happy to have this opportunity to mend relationships and build new ones. Today we will be traveling to the Hub. Think of it less as a space station and more as an additional mini-planet. It houses many of our research centers and the

Coalition members representing each Society." He waved a hand at the delegates behind him, and a second set of eyelids blinked across his amber iris.

"As you may imagine, this kind of travel is taxing on the body. You will be sedated for the journey, and by the time you awake we'll have arrived at the Hub. You'll be given lodging assignments with the other Blanks during the pre-Choosing process. All Blanks go through Societal visits and education, but you will also be provided some extra sessions to give you background on the Societies."

A strand of hair a shade or two darker than his skin blew in the breeze, and he swept a clawed hand over it to tame it.

"You will each be systematically seen by our menders prior to departure, to administer the necessary medication for the journey. As it is much better tolerated on a full stomach, we will be eating before departure. Please use this time to introduce yourselves to one another."

The other delegates began mingling with the crowd, but Warrick turned around, disappearing through a door in the ship that sealed itself quickly behind him.

"Guess he won't be joining us, then. Oh well!" Hale rubbed his hands together, scanning the crowd.

"If you're looking for the food, it's in the tent back there." A talon-edged finger pointed past us. A woman with sharp canines smiled down at us.

Hale stared for a second longer than necessary, and it was my turn to elbow him.

"Right. Thanks. I'll just ..." He turned and wandered toward the breakfast spread.

Off to my left was a man with flared wings that faded between shades of brown, orange, and amber. Next to him stood a woman covered head to toe in a substance that looked like an inky oil spill with neon patterns painted on it. To their right stood a tall man with what appeared to be hooves holding up his hooked goat-like legs. It felt like I was seeing every celebrity I'd ever idolized all at once. I took a shaky breath and reminded myself I would be one of them, if things worked out.

I took a step forward, bumping into a cloaked figure as he brushed by.

"I'm so sorry! I didn't mean t—. Hey, I know you!"

He lifted one eyebrow over the glowing sapphire eyes I'd seen on screen. I felt like an idiot.

"I mean, not *know*, obviously. I've seen you. On television. You're the Riftian delegate."

He continued to stare with an intensity that was unsettling. When he was onscreen, I'd felt compelled to watch him, and with him in front of me I experienced a similar sensation.

"I'm Kena Eckhoff. One of the Earthers. Well, of course you can see that. I'm a member of Verkent, that group that knew about you all before. My Uncle Juliard is on the task force."

He extended a hand and shook mine. His grip was firm but gentle, and slightly chilled.

"I am Bayard. I've seen your uncle at some of the meetings, although I've not yet had the pleasure of speaking with him myself. Is he here?" His glowing eyes glanced side to side across the gathering.

"Well, no. It's mainly just the participants and a small esco—"

"They're not knocking me out for this entire trip!"

"Would you calm down!"

"This is starting to feel like an alien abduction. They're not pumping me full of anything. I'm calling my father immediately!"

"If you back out now, you could ruin things for all of us!"

The chorus of alarmed voices grew louder behind us. Bayard stepped away, but instead of going toward the ruckus he walked back toward the ship. So did the other Societal delegates. As they cleared away, a small group of arguing Earthers became visible. No one intervened, though. It looked like Kaiser was right about at least one thing. They planned to observe us.

"Volatile, aren't they?" a winged woman whispered to her companion as she swept by. I wanted to sink into a hole with embarrassment.

In the center of the Earther crowd stood a pasty teen, who sneered at two taller adults. Their features were so similar I was certain they were the twins my uncle had remarked upon, and I would have guessed them to be somewhere in their mid-twenties.

"Everyone, please, for this to work we need to remain calm and organized." Pim waved his arms as he tried to get everyone to listen.

"Nobody asked you, old man!" one of the teens at the center of the argument yelled, scowling at Pim.

"That. Is. Enough!" The others turned toward me as I yelled. It didn't bother me that some of the Earthers were concerned. They hadn't grown up anticipating the same things Verkent had. The disrespect to Pim, however, sent me over the edge. I looked out across the group of faces in front of me. It seemed that if I really wanted the chance to be a leader, I was already being presented with an opportunity.

"I'm Kena, one of the leaders of Verkent." None of my fellow conspiracy group members contradicted me, and I barreled on.

"I understand people are nervous, but we will never get a chance like this again. If that ship leaves without you on it, there is no amount of money that could buy your way back on. The Societies once cut off an entire planet and left us here. I doubt they'll give a second thought to leaving one or two individuals behind now. Millions of people would have killed for these spots, and they're sending us. We're exploring not just one new world but several. I for one am not going to let anything stop me from getting on that ship. What about the rest of you?" For a few tense seconds of silence, I stared them all down.

"Well, I'm not going to say no after that speech." Silas headed toward the onlooking Societal delegates and up the ramp.

"Definitely not!" Dex started after his friend.

Pim offered Sybil his arm as they followed the other two, and soon the majority of the crowd moved toward the ship and disappeared through the doors.

The teen I'd yelled at glared out the side of his eyes as he slunk past, and the two near-identical individuals he'd been yelling at made their way up to me. Their eyes were a shade or two lighter than their rich, umber skin, their gazes searing into the back of the retreating teen. The woman spoke first.

"I am Cassia, and this is Cassius. My brother and Derek do not get along. We would have certainly been able to handle it, but we appreciate you convincing everyone." Cassius himself said nothing as his sister spoke, but glared after Derek. Cassia nudged him in the ribs.

"Yes, well stated."

"We are both interested in hearing more about our new hosts. Given your position in Verkent, you must have knowledge of these Societies?" Her gaze locked on mine as she posed the question. I nodded.

"Good. Then it's settled. We will discuss things more once we've arrived at the Hub." The two turned in unison and walked toward the others.

"Way to go, Kena." Hale slapped me on the back. "Although I personally would've preferred to stay awake on this trip. All this caffeine, wasted." He stared at his empty coffee thermos with a frown.

When we joined the others, there was a crowd at the entrance of the ship. A "mender" checked off names before everyone boarded, the dull purple scales on her arms reminiscent of a crocodile.

"Eckhoff, Kena."

"That's me." I was directed not to a seat, but rather a small, wheeled cot. A second Societal, this one with curling horns atop their head, walked up holding a needle. Before I could ask how long the journey would take, I felt a pinch on my neck, and everything faded out.

CHAPTER 5

"Kena ... Kena." I turned groggily toward the voice. As my eyes opened, I saw a nose not even an inch from my own. I scrambled back up in the bed and reflexively threw a pillow at whatever or whoever it was.

"I just wanted to see if anyone else was awake yet." Hale, who had dodged the pillow, grinned at me.

"Where are we? Did we make it?" I could see a row of beds that continued on both sides of my own.

"We're in some kind of hospital wing. I woke up first, and they said when we're ready we can head down to the Blanks' lodging area. Actually, I've been up for a while. I got bored, so I've kind of been poking you in the face until you woke up." He plastered a sheepish smile on his face.

I swiped at him again with my pillow, missing him by a few inches.

"Hey! It's no fun being the only one seeing this! Do you think maybe it was all the coffee I drank before we left?"

"We don't have any idea what they gave us! What if it's supposed to wear off on its own?"

"Either way, you're up now, and besides, I—"

An individual stepped forward and approached the beeping screen attached to the side of my bed. This one was covered in a dark slime, broken up by a series of swirling neon pink shapes lighting up the arms. That meant Dagan, the underwater Society.

"All appears to be in order. You can go with him to temporary housing if you wish." The voice bubbled up through the slimy features, swirling patterns of neon blue dotting the Dagan's cheeks.

I tried not to stare. There hadn't been many of this particular Societal on Earth. What Verkent knew of Dagan was that they lived almost entirely underwater, having Assimilated amphibious traits.

"Maybe I should stay and wait for some of the others to wake up." I looked around, trying to locate the other Verkent members.

"That isn't necessary. We've got it under control here; they'll all be fine. Also,"—the slimy Societal leaned in conspiratorially—"it would be a great help if you took the other Earther with you. He's been up for hours, and all his questions are making me want to eat an asteroid." The Dagan pulled back and smiled, or at least that's what I judged the attempt to be. Between the needle-like teeth and clouded eyes, it came off a bit terrifying.

"All right, then, time to go!" It didn't take much to convince me. I was eager to get a look at the Hub. I glanced up to see Hale carrying both our bags. As we exited the infirmary, we found ourselves in a sleek, metallic hallway of silver and matte grey. I had no idea where we were going, but I was much more interested in exploring than asking directions.

We turned left and saw another dripping Dagan individual, this one with neon orange and yellow swirls up the arms, working on a panel of buttons on the wall. As we walked down the hall, several Societals turned to stare, but no one stopped us. While I had tons of questions to ask all the Hub residents, I was content to observe at first. I had to hold myself back from an excited squeal as a Kite passed us, feathered wings tucked behind, so long they swept the floor in a purple train. Hale laughed.

"If you could see your face! I for one would never—"

"You two! Earthers, right? Go ahead and get checked in."

A heavily tattooed and scarred individual holding a tablet waved us over. Hale's eyes widened as he looked at the Crew member. It would come as a big surprise to me if he picked any other Society. I'd always held a soft spot for the winged Kites, but Hale had idolized the scarred and tattooed Crew members since he'd first heard the story of their seafaring adventures. As we stood in front of the man, his whole form wavered in the soft light of the hall. It was like watching a shadow blink in and out of existence.

"Each of you grab a bunk. Utilize the drawers in your section for personal belongings." Hale gripped my arm like a vise, and when I looked over, he was biting his lip.

"And put these on. We'll get you all a few more to change out each day." A tattooed arm held out a folded grey jumpsuit for each of us. The Crew member wore an identical one, as had all the Societals we'd seen in the hall.

As we stepped past him, we entered a room the size of an airplane hangar, filled with cots, a small bedside table next to each. The spaces around them were separated by thin walls, seemingly made of canvas. Not the most modern setup. In the room around us were the Societal teens. It was our first real opportunity to see the

Blanks we'd be spending time with during the process. I'd grown up knowing they looked like Earthers up until the Choosing, but it was still jarring to see it in person. They were identical to us, at least in physical appearance.

Hale tossed our bags into two adjacent stations. I was eager to get back into the halls. As we exited, I found myself face to face with the magistrate himself, his red hair and coppery skin clashing. Unlike the others, he wasn't wearing a grey jumpsuit but long robes. They were yet a third shade between orange and red. He leaned down, tongue flicking past his teeth as he smiled.

"So, our Earther guests are up. Excellent! And if I'm not mistaken, you're both Verkentian, yes?"

"Yes. And you're Magistrate Warrick."

"Indeed. A pleasure to meet you, Ms. Eckhoff. And you are Hale Ochter, correct?" Hale squeaked out an affirmative response. The magistrate took a step back, pulling himself up to his full height before slamming his fist on his chest twice.

"On Rover, that is how we would greet one another for the first time, but I believe you prefer to shake hands?" He extended a coppery claw towards us. He beamed, pointed teeth once again visible as I reached forward and took his hand.

"I'm quite interested to get to know Verkent, and particularly you, better, Ms. Eckhoff. But perhaps another time." His eyes moved over my shoulder, and I turned to see several of the other Verkent members headed toward us. He dropped my hand and swept down the hall.

"Was that the magistrate?" Pim stared at the retreating leader. Hale answered for me.

"Yes, and he seemed oddly interested in us. Kena, specifically."

"That does make sense. She's essentially in charge up here." Silas spoke, next to Pim.

I was flattered that the magistrate seemed to view me as a representative for the other Earthers, but it was a bit disconcerting that he'd known each of us specifically. There wasn't much I could do to gain knowledge on Warrick, but it was possible to learn more about the other Earthers who would be with me. After showing them to the cots, I gathered Pim, Silas, Hale, and Dex together.

I filled them in on Juliard's files. I hoped sharing the task with Pim and Silas would move me toward my goal of reconciliation with the two Verkent members. Tacking on Dex seemed smart, given his proximity to Silas and his (probably) previous line of work. As Hale was my best friend, I would have told him about them no matter what. It bothered me that Juliard had suggested hiding the information from him.

As tempting as it was to head straight back out to explore, it was already late, so we spent the remainder of the evening screening files. It seemed I'd had the right idea about Derek from the first. It didn't look like he had any discernible skills. The file made him seem like the very spoiled teen of an incredibly rich businessman. If anything, some information Juliard had scrounged up regarding some sealed juvenile files was a bit concerning. There were several other privileged teens, although none with Derek's kind of background.

"Looks like he's got a history of picking fights and then using his family's money to avoid consequences," Silas commented when I showed the others.

The twins' files were sparse, but I wasn't surprised, given their father had been a high-profile politician. Several of the individuals had very little confirmed information, but Juliard had written in guesses. He seemed to think the task force had slipped in not only some military members, but also a few scientists to harvest Societal DNA, a zoologist to look at the animal life, and some sort of consultant to study the sociopolitical structure of the whole system.

The following morning found us waiting in line for trays at breakfast alongside all the Societal Blanks. Kaiser's speech from the stadium seemed even more absurd as I took in the crowd. It was harder to think of a group as hostile alien invaders when they looked exactly like the Earthers and were all milling around a room reminiscent of a high school cafeteria. It also left me with a gnawing feeling that I was similarly being watched and judged. Despite our matching clothing, the Societal teens openly stared at our group. I made it up the line and saw there was a wide spread of food options, including quite a few that were wholly unfamiliar. Still, it all smelled safe enough.

After my tray was loaded down with what appeared to be some sort of fish, leafy greens, and a vegetable that looked like some form of corn, I found a seat over by some of the other Earthers.

Dex and Silas took the seats to each side of me, both trays loaded down with more than twice as much food as my own.

"You do realize this is breakfast, right?" Dex stared down at my fish.

"Space fish. Don't judge me if I don't try it anytime soon." Hale stuck his tongue out towards my plate as he set his own tray across from mine. I was surprised that between the three of them they hadn't cleared out the buffet.

I didn't come up with a retort. I was distracted by what was going on in the center of the room. A few men from the Hub shuffled into the cafeteria, carrying a rather large and unwieldy looking platform between them. Once they'd set it up, a severe-looking woman stepped up to it, seemingly indifferent to the fact that she was blocking anyone else from retrieving a dining tray.

It was clear which Society she was from. Large wings folded behind her back marked her as a Kite. Hers were a flat grey that visually blended into the walls of the Hub. Her eyes were grey as well. They didn't spark like my uncle's, or bring to mind a wintry day, like

Silas's softer grey ones did. Hers were dull. She tapped the podium for attention, talon-like nails rapping against the wood.

"For those unfamiliar, I am Iduna, one of the instructors for the Blanks. I have worked with many of you for years as you diligently prepared for the Choosing. Today, you will begin tours. If you turn over your trays, you will each find a medallion with the signet of one of the Societies on it. This represents the location you will visit today. You will go on these excursions with the same group until the Choosing. All will be given the opportunity to visit all the Societies." At that point she paused, the left side of her lip and one beak-like nostril curling upwards as though she'd smelled something foul.

"This does not, of course, include Earth, as it is not and perhaps never will be an official Society." It seemed not everyone was happy to have us at the Hub.

"In addition to the excursions, those visiting from Earth will attend evening sessions to fill in the woeful gaps in your Societal knowledge." She stepped away from the podium, moving to converse with some of the other Hub workers.

The Blanks across the cafeteria turned over their trays. As I flipped my own over, I saw an orange emblem depicting the top half of a bird rising into flight. The Kite symbol.

"What'd you get?" demanded Pim from across the table.

"Kite."

"Good. Someone can keep an eye on Sybil and make sure they're treating the older Blanks okay."

I looked over at Sybil, who was comparing her orange emblem with a green and gold one Cassia held. I was more than happy to agree. It was an opportunity to build back my relationship with another Verkent member.

"What'd you get?" I leaned toward Hale.

He held out a medallion stamped with a slate background. On the outer rim, a blue ribbon of color encircled the blackened tree in the center. The Riftian symbol, and an odd choice for a Society that dwelled in caves, as far as our writings had described them.

"Darn. I would have rather we had gone together."

"No problem! Watch!" His head scanned the table and landed on a group of younger Earther Blanks huddled together. He walked right up to one and snatched a medallion out of his hands. He gave him his own and walked back before he could react.

"Thanks very much, Mancio!" He waved over his shoulder as he strode back over.

"Read his file—seems like a bit of a brat, to be honest," he whispered as he sat down.

"You're not supposed to be trading them!" I hissed.

Technically, the sour-faced Kite had said no such thing. Hale raised an eyebrow at me and waited a few seconds. When I raised no further objections, he broke into a grin.

"That's what I thought." He pocketed the medallion. I couldn't help but smile back. In a matter of hours, we were set to visit what I suspected would be my favorite Society.

As Blanks around the cafeteria began to rise from their seats, a harsh rapping noise rang out. I turned to see Iduna back behind the podium. She didn't speak immediately but glared down at the Blanks until everyone sat back down.

"What a piece of work." Digit rolled her eyes next to Pim. Her circuitry tattoo was on full display, with the sleeves of her grey jumpsuit rolled up. The design made sense, given her former vocation.

"I've seen worse." Silas didn't bother to elaborate, but I noticed he reached down to grip his left leg where it ended. Iduna cleared her throat, sweeping a final gaze across the crowd before she spoke.

"Just one final bit of information I've been asked to share with the newer participants. Unlike some planets, each of the Societies are very careful with our resources. We believe in responsibility.

Therefore, please be advised we take steps to ensure population control. We do not risk overrunning the available space we have allotted. It may come as a surprise to hear that, following the Choosing, not all candidates prove capable of Assimilation. While unfortunate, this provides a simple solution to prevent overpopulation. Every five years, two months after the Choosing, there is a Coalition meeting. In addition to discussing future plans and improvements of the Societies as a whole, it is at that time that any who have not Assimilated are handled. Those who have not managed to undergo any physical changes by that point are disposed of. As luck would have it, they've moved the meeting up a year to accommodate the Earther representatives. Therefore, you will have until that point to prove you are capable of actually Assimilating. If you aren't able to accomplish that, you will be eliminated. Good day."

Several screams rang out from the Earther tables, followed by the sound of sobbing. The Hub workers moved to take down the podium as if nothing unusual had happened. Around us, the Societal Blanks moved toward the doors. I couldn't believe what I'd heard. I refused to. First, what Iduna referenced hadn't been mentioned anywhere in Verkent's writings. The Societies, other than cutting off Earth for unknown reasons, weren't violent toward each other. I got up from the table. Iduna's back was toward me, wings trailing her. I didn't care that it might be considered rude as I reached out and grabbed her arm.

She turned to me with a scowl and shook my hand off.

"What?"

"There has to be some misunderstanding. You're not actually saying that if we don't manage to Assimilate, the Societies will kill us?"

She swept a look behind me at the Earther tables. When she spoke, her voice was loud enough to carry across the room.

"You are placing blame in the wrong place. If you fail to Assimilate, *you* will be responsible for having killed yourselves."

CHAPTER 6

Iduna's grey wings flapped open behind her, making her look even more ominous—like a bird of prey ready to consume us all. Even her beaky grin as she met my gaze made her seem like she was prepared to bite.

"I'd get your group moving, if I were you. Failure to participate in these tours constitutes an inability to complete the process. No tours, no Choosing. No Choosing, no Assimilation. No Assimilation, and I'm afraid that would mean no more Earthers. Better hurry."

I pulled at my hair as she swept out of the room. I hated her. I loathed her callous attitude. To say nothing of the fear her words invoked. I longed to wipe the sneer off her face. But none of that mattered if we didn't even make it out of the Hub. I turned to one of the Verkent members I knew I could count on.

"Silas. We've got to get everyone ready for these tours. If we don't—"

"I heard the old harpy. Don't worry, these Earthers won't miss a single Societal tour, no matter how bad they try to rattle us."

With Silas's help, I managed to get everyone out in the hall to follow the other Blanks. I wanted more than anything to turn around and find a way to contact Juliard and the others for help. One thing at a time, though. The crowd entered a cavernous, domed area bustling with activity in its round center. In addition to the entrance we'd come through, there were seven decorative archways around the circumference of the room. Each held a closed metal door with a multi-spoke handle.

"Kites, over here!" I stowed my fear and grabbed Hale's hand. We walked toward the voice. Each arch had its Society's sigil emblazoned on it. Thankfully, rather than Iduna, a winged delegate I didn't recognize stood in front of the metal door belonging to the Kites. Once he had our group gathered, he spun the spokes and pushed it open. The guide ushered us all into a small tunnel illuminated by lights in the floor and ceiling. He heaved the heavy door shut behind us once everyone was in.

There were dozens of Blanks fidgeting in place, craning their necks. With the advantage of being taller, I was able to look to the end of the tunnel, where a large frame, something like a metal detector, stood. The space where one would walk through shimmered slightly as I moved my head, trying to see past it. The process of traveling among Societies was something Verkent actually didn't know much about.

"Do you think that leads to a ship?" Sybil's voice trembled. I hated that she sounded scared. There had to be a way to fix things. I needed to make contact with the task force. Surely they hadn't known about the deadly nature of the trip. Surely Juliard hadn't known. Doubt ate at me. My uncle had warned me that the task force badly wanted information on the Societals. I had to at least consider that they'd been prepared to sacrifice some of us to get it. Our host unfurled his wings and snapped them out to the sides, garnering instant silence and attention.

"All right, everyone, you know the drill. Orderly line starts here, please. No pushing or shoving. Stay close to the pad when you arrive and wait for all of us to get through. We've got people waiting who can help you get weighed down."

The others formed the line and started moving toward the metal detector. The first Blank who stepped through it vanished.

"Did you see that?" Hale, beside me, had gone a bit pale, his eyes wide.

"I did. Where do you suppose that thing lets out?"

We neared the front of the line, where our host stared down at us through amber eyes, head tilting at us when we hesitated to walk through. He was the delegate I'd seen back on Earth with the tri-colored feathers.

"Um, do you mind telling us how to ...?" I waved halfheartedly at the detector. He blinked.

"The Doorway? No one's bothered to fill you in? Hardly the mark of good hosts. The concept is simple enough. You just walk through. Although really, it would have been better if they'd prepped you at least a little. It can be disconcerting the first few trips."

"Good hosts. Yeah, right. Sourface was too busy threatening to murder us all to teach us about Doorways," Hale muttered beside me as I turned back toward our delegate.

"I'm sorry, but I still don't really understand. How does this get us from here to there?"

"Well ... I don't think this is the time to get into the science behind it all. You'd be best off asking someone at the Hub about that.

Think of it as a sort of protected wormhole, if you will. The Doorway sort of ... picks you up here, and then drops you out in another spot elsewhere. See? Simple."

It did not sound simple, but our options were to chance it or turn around.

"I'll go first." Hale set his mouth in a hard line and stepped through.

"Excellent," our host said, rubbing scaly, taloned fingers together. "Who's next?"

I swallowed my fear down deep and strode in after Hale. Darkness enveloped me, but the sensation wasn't bad. It was like being tugged along by a gentle current. I began to think it wasn't nearly as frightening as I'd expected when I started to fall.

I landed firmly on my butt. As I stood and rubbed my sore tailbone, I came face to face with a wall of winged Kites, all staring. The morning had left me devoid of enthusiasm. Instead of moving to introduce myself, I joined Hale off to the side.

Looking around, I saw we were in a tinted dome that obscured whatever lay outside. Our host emerged from the Doorway, then held a hand out behind him and caught Sybil. He set her down gently next to him. Once she was settled, our host stepped back to the center of the landing area, snapping open his wings. A few of the Earthers in our group startled at the sudden movement, which led to snickering from some of the Societal Blanks and surrounding Kites. The underside of the wings had stripes of alternating black and cream, and around the edges and back, slashes of rust-colored feathers. His hair was black but also glinted with flashes of rust when he moved. I wondered how much of his appearance was Assimilated.

"I am Keldrin, one of the acting delegates between Kites and the Hub. In addition to those of us who serve as part of the Coalition to represent our homes, each Society has a planetside ruling system. Kite has a queen. Nimue, however, resides on the opposite edge of our planet. Today we will be touring Tarsatius, our main area of trade. For those who are first-time visitors, you will each need both weights and a flight system while on Kite. Remedied quite easily if you choose to Assimilate here and get your own set of wings." He preened, fanning his out.

"You will each be paired with a flight partner. We don't want any accidents or people falling out of the sky. Far too much paperwork when that happens." He kept a straight face, and I couldn't tell if he was kidding.

Kites meandered through the Blanks and attached small weights to everyone's wrists and ankles.

A woman with magnificently orange monarch wings and umber skin stepped up to Hale. Glancing at Sybil, I saw Keldrin himself helping her. A few winged inhabitants passed by some of the Earthers, scowling, before helping the Societal Blanks. A man walked toward me holding one of the sailing devices. His mouth spread into a dazzling white smile as he held out a hand in introduction. I noted that, unlike the others, his wings didn't protrude from his shoulders but were attached all the way up his bronze arms.

"What's your name, Earther?" He shook my hand with so much enthusiasm I was nearly thrown off balance.

"Kena. And yours?" I extricated myself from the handshake as I placed the weights he'd given me on my wrists and ankles.

"Ryshal." Up close, I saw that his wings were leathery but lightly furred.

Once everyone was strapped in, we followed Keldrin out of the dome. The reality of being on an entirely different planet struck me. The Kites' realm was wondrous. The whole planet seemed encased in a soft, green-tinted glow, like sunlight shining through glass. More than one small sun provided light from above, and even more interesting was that a clear cutoff could be seen between the light and the darkness of space beyond. Even with the announcement from that morning hanging over me, I couldn't help feeling joyous awe as I looked at it.

"While Kite technically has the smallest land mass, if you look at the spherical portion of the planet itself, we tend to spend a great deal of our time on what we like to call the extensions of the planet." Keldrin motioned overhead.

The extensions consisted of large boulders, some attached via vines and some floating freely, with greenery spilling off the sides. It was hard to tell whether these green connections had grown downwards or the roots were coming from the planet and tethering the rocks in space. It was one thing to pore over illustrations of floating waterfalls in Verkent's books, but quite a different matter to actually see one spilling off the side of a giant rock above us.

"Let's head out. Everyone, please follow your guides." With one press of his wings downwards, Keldrin shot into the air.

I sidestepped to my left as Ryshal fanned out his wings. He took a few running steps and then launched himself into the air. He yelled down at me.

"Just get a nice quick start, and then spread your arms and leap!" He grinned as he flapped.

Steeling myself, I started to run. As I leapt into the air, I began to float. Opening one eye, I squinted to see what was in front of me.

"I'm flying. I'm actually flying!" I whooped, flapping harder and pressing upwards in my excitement. I was elated. I had often dreamed of what it would be like to fly. I could only imagine what it would be like with real wings.

"Bank left," Ryshal instructed with a grin as we flew around one of the long-vined extensions. I mimicked his motions.

I continued to follow his direction as we flew around several extensions. We stayed within eyesight of the group, but Ryshal seemed to enjoy watching me mimic his maneuvers. He grinned wider every time I managed to execute one of his instructions.

"Pull back here!"

I did as he asked, and we came to a floating stop next to an extension that had small flowers in shades of cream and orange cascading off the side. Winged creatures reminiscent of hummingbirds buzzed amidst the blooms, their iridescent wings glinting.

Ryshal seemed genuinely interested in Earth and asked several questions as we slowly wove higher and higher. After I'd answered several, I posed one of my own.

"Your wings are different from the others. I know they're all unique, but yours stand out."

"Is there a question in there somewhere?" I glanced over, worried that I'd offended him, but Ryshal's eyes glinted as he continued to smile.

"The wings I've seen in the Hub have protruded from Kites' backs. The same with Verkent illustrations. Yours connect to your arms. I just wasn't certain ..."

"You're wondering whether this is normal. Every set of wings is unique. They can protrude from the back, or connect to our arms partially or fully. Neither is abnormal, although this particular type is certainly rarer. That just makes me even more proud to wear them. Do they resemble the wings of anything you're familiar with?" He tilted his head with the question.

"Yes actually. A bat."

His face scrunched in confusion.

"Hmmm. I've heard about some of the animals you all prefer to keep as pets, but not that one. Is it similar to a cat or dog?"

"I think they look like cute nocturnal sky puppies," I volunteered.

He laughed. "Nothing wrong with that! Nocturnal?"

"Yes, bats prefer to hunt at night."

"I have always been partial to nighttime flights underneath the stars. I wonder if there's anything to that."

Keldrin signaled us to land on one of the larger extensions. It could have fit my childhood neighborhood easily. A creek ran through the center and fell off the edges. It was anyone's guess where the water supply came from.

"Our current location is a favorite recreational retreat of local inhabitants. You'll find Kites are generally most comfortable near the sky. If you should pick this Society, the weights you currently wear would not be necessary for long. The formation of wings is a personal and private process. You'll find similar secrecy around certain items on most planets, some more than others. While this is a sought-after Assimilation, it's worth noting that the success rate for wings is about seven out of ten. Please keep that in mind when making your decision."

The reminder dulled my enthusiasm again. In an entire lifetime of fantasizing about the Societals of the sky, I'd never envisioned a failure rate for attaining wings. And I certainly never would have guessed at the deadly consequences. Keldrin continued with information about Kites being largely agricultural, the floating rock and vine-to-planet system creating some unique growing opportunities. It was hard to pay attention. Afterward, when we'd made our way back under the dome, Ryshal helped me remove the weights. Looking behind him, I noticed a few glares coming my way from some of the Kites and Societal Blanks. One of Ryshal's wings whipped out in front of my face, blocking the view of the others.

"This should help shade us from the suns while I finish this up." His voice was overly loud. He switched to a whisper as he leaned in close.

"You've no no doubt heard what happens to those who don't Assimilate. The Choosing does allow you some control. You can pick anywhere you want. No Societal is meant to intervene in that, but don't be surprised if some nasty tricks are pulled in an attempt to intimidate you into certain options. Not everybody wants Earthers up here."

"Why not?"

"Your separation, for one. Your ancestors led a bloody rebellion against the other Societies and the Hub."

"That's not exactly our version of events, but even so, it's so long ago, what does it matter?"

"The rumor is that the leaders of Earth took something before they were cut off. Research that held the key to the Societies being able to settle new planets. Without it, we haven't been able to expand since. That's why they introduced the population-control methods we have in place now. I don't suppose Verkent ..."

I shook my head, and gave an honest answer.

"I've never heard of any information like that existing. If it ever did, it's likely it was lost generations ago." It was still unfair, but at least it explained some of the animosity.

"I'm rooting for you all. We need other points of view. Maybe having you all join the Societies could help. Still, not everyone feels that way. You're all descendants of those original Earthers, but don't be surprised if Verkent gets some extra negative attention. There are those who are convinced your group is directly responsible for our current predicament."

"That doesn't make any sense! Trust me, if giving the Coalition information on how to settle new planets again would save us, I'd hand it over. But I've never come across anything like that."

"Maybe so, but those who are still grieving loved ones who didn't manage to Assimilate aren't exactly seeking a logical explanation, just a scapegoat."

"And you?"

"I'm smart enough to realize none of you are directly responsible. You and the other Blanks are all in the same boat now. I'll certainly be pulling for your success. If you end up here, perhaps we could be friends?" He held an arm out in offering, and I shook it.

His warnings echoed in my head as we moved back through the Doorway to the Hub.

CHAPTER 7

I was emotionally, mentally, and physically exhausted. After the tour we'd returned to the cafeteria. Some of the Earthers sat in front of empty places. I didn't blame them for losing their appetite, but I decided that at least eating would feel like a familiar routine. While I scooped something covered in cheese onto my plate, a commotion several trays down the line caught my attention.

I looked up to see a couple of Societal Blanks push their way in front of an Earther in line. I remembered her name, Su Jin, from her file. She said something quietly before one of the Blanks knocked her tray onto the floor. I ran over as her eyes teared up.

"I don't care if you were in the line first, Deserter!" the first boy spat at her.

"You're also the first planet to rebel against the Societies. What's the matter? You thought you were too good for us? You didn't belong with us then, and you don't belong here now!" the second shouted as I reached Su Jin and put an arm around her.

"Leave her alone!" I seethed at them, furious at their misplaced anger.

"Or what? You think we have to listen to you? You're just an overgrown Blank. A gigantic no one who never Assimilated, and yet you get the chance to go through this process. You'll get what's coming to you soon enough."

He lunged forward, and I threw my free arm out to shield us. It caught the Blank squarely in the nose.

He clutched at it with one hand and made a fist with the other. He pulled his arm back to swing, but then dropped it. The second Blank gulped, and both Blanks' eyes went wide.

"Problem, *kids?*" I turned to see Cassius, his arms folded in front of him. He presented a formidable wall of muscle. His twin sister mirrored his lethality as she placed a hand on her brother's shoulder, sliding in gracefully beside him.

"Now, brother, no need to get upset. They were just leaving, right?" She raised a questioning eyebrow at the boys, who nodded.

"I thought so. You must have gotten lost on the way to the door. You've lost your appetites."

They scrambled toward the doors.

"Wow. You two have got to teach me how to get that reaction from people."

"The first step is, you have to be willing to back up your words with action if needed. People can sense that. You seemed to be doing fine, though." While Cassius answered, his sister scooped food onto Su Jin's tray.

"Secondly, you have to know who you're up against. We're at a bit of a disadvantage here in general, but those two were easy enough to figure out. They're mad at us for what they see as taking spots away from their family and friends. The ones who didn't Assimilate anyway." It wasn't a bad theory.

Su Jin muttered a thanks to Cassia before heading toward a table with some of the others.

"My brother and I would like to sit down and discuss Verkent's knowledge of the Societies. Reading a summary from the task force and talking to someone who grew up with it are separate things. Especially given our current predicament, it can only help. In exchange, we'd be happy to assist with whatever Verkent's trying to accomplish up here."

"Why would you assume we've got some sort of pl—" I shut my mouth when Cassia held up a hand.

"Let's skip the part where we pretend those task force members didn't all have some ulterior motive. My brother and myself were sent up here for redemption. Your uncle must have sent you for something specific as well."

"He didn't send me. I volunteered of my own accord. I have my own goals here."

"Then allow us to help with those."

I assessed the twins. In my brief encounters with them, they'd been very direct. I respected that. I also knew exactly what I wanted to accomplish, even though I wasn't sure how. I filled them in on my decision to try to make contact with my uncle as we walked toward one of the Earther tables.

As we sat down, another group made their way into the cafeteria. It was clear from the tinged skin and sand clinging to some that they'd been visiting the Rovers' desert lands. As the Earthers from the group sat down, I noticed a sunburned and freckled redhead named Sarah crying quietly, while a girl named Thea with dyed burgundy curls comforted her. The Rovers' world had to be a far cry from the expensive private college they'd attended previously, according to their files.

"You know Sarah's assigned to the Rovers." Hale leaned in. I felt silently guilty and relieved at my own freedom to pick a Society. We were all at risk of not Assimilating, but at least the Verkent members had the freedom to pick for themselves and hopefully increase their odds of success. A pampered heiress trying to Assimilate to a rugged Society like the Rovers seemed like a recipe for disaster.

"I don't know why she's the one crying. It's Thea who got thrown in a damned hole," Dex grumbled as he sat down with our group. Sand cascaded onto the table as he wiped his arms off.

I glanced at Thea, with her arm around her friend. Sarah's burnt skin clashed starkly with her red hair.

"A hole?"

"Yeah. When our guide wasn't looking, someone shoved her off one of those endless damned dunes into a convenient pit of sink sand. I got her out without much incident. It was still a nasty trick to pull. If she'd been by herself or lingering at the back of the group, she could've been sucked down before we even noticed." Dex glared.

I blanched a bit at that, wondering if the intent had been intimidation or something more sinister. I shared with the group what Ryshal had said about how some of the Societals viewed us.

"That's unfair! They're the ones who cut us off and then showed back up, asking us up here!" Hale fumed.

"Not according to them," Silas reminded him. "They all think we're the ungrateful descendants of rebels who tried to destroy their precious system. It makes even more sense if they believe we're also the reason some of them are being killed. Doesn't sound like there's an easy solution, either. I grew up in Verkent and never saw any of our texts reference settling new planets."

"We represent an unknown factor." Digit slid over several seats as she joined the conversation.

"One that might just be able to help them, if someone really does have that information they're after," I countered.

"Yes, but according to you, no one has any idea where that information might be. Wouldn't you or your uncle be the most likely individuals to have it?"

"It's understandable, but also regrettable that some of them are responding this way." Pim was all logic, but he squeezed Sybil as he spoke.

By the time dinner was over, I was more than ready for rest. As people started to pick up their plates, someone cleared their throat at the end of the table. I turned to see a tusked man whose wiry, dark hair stuck out at all angles.

Cassia leaned in.

"He's from the Canopy. My assigned Society."

I turned to her brother.

"Yours, too?"

"Nope, I'm getting wings."

At the edge of the group, the man spoke.

"I am Nien and I will be your Societal Educator. If you will all follow me, we can get started." He beckoned us with arms that were plated along the outer edges.

I wasn't the only one who groaned. Given everything that had transpired, I'd managed to forget we had extra lessons in the evenings. Nien furrowed plated brows at us, his eyes sporting wide bands of orange and gold reminiscent of a sunburst. He let out a sigh that sounded very much like a snort.

"I do understand it's been a trying day for you, but these lessons are a mandated part of your participation here. So, if you would all please follow me."

We were all led to a large classroom. While the steel tables and chairs facing a board and desk were reminiscent of Earth, the similarities stopped there. The space was sleek, minimalist, and modern in the way that underfunded Earth schools tended not to be. Each table had several tablets on top, silver stylus pens next to them. After we'd all chosen seats, Nien clapped his hands together at the front of the room.

"Let's go ahead and get started! You're welcome to take notes on anything you learn on the devices you've been supplied. Please do keep in mind that whatever you write could be easily accessed by any instructor at the Hub, or any delegate on the Coalition." I appreciated the warning, and it placed the instructor on my list of potentially trustworthy Societals.

"In these lessons I will attempt, to the best of my ability, to fill the gaps in your knowledge of the Societies. That being said, I fully anticipate you will ultimately be making this decision based on piecemeal information. Today I will be providing an overview of our different Societies. There are seven."

Nien's voice was somewhat monotonous. He rattled off the names like someone who was better at dealing with data than people. I didn't mind. After what had been a hectic day, his rhythmic words were comforting.

"Dagan, those who live primarily beneath the sea. The Crew, nomadic ship-dwellers who live primarily on it. The Clan, those who dwell within snowcapped mountains and in mines. The Rift, modest individuals who live within the caves. Rovers, nomads of the deserts and oases. Kites, winged Societals who inhabit the skies. Lastly, the Canopy, perhaps the most beautiful of all Societies. Home to jungles, rivers, and the widest variety of animal life." He clearly favored his own planet, but that wasn't surprising.

"We are currently residing in the Hub, which is our station that houses the Doorways between each of the Societies. Blanks live here, alongside permanent workers. This includes the delegates representing each Society and our magistrate, all of whom make up the Coalition, which governs everyone as a whole. That being stated, each Society also maintains some form of planetside governing system. Only fully Assimilated adults may work on the station."

The remainder of the lecture was primarily a short overview of our pre-Choosing process. Near the end, Nien opened the floor to questions. While Nien chatted with some of the others, I turned to Silas, who filled us in on his day visiting the Rift.

"It was less exciting than any of your days, to be certain. No one tried to kill me, for one. We spent the whole visit in a giant cavern, listening to a rather vague lecture."

"It's the most mysterious of all the Societies," Pim piped up, looking up from his conversation with Sybil.

"That just means we have an even poorer chance of guessing whether we'd survive choosing it," Hale grumped.

"For all we know, that could be our best plan. It might also benefit us to build some relationships with the individuals who work at the Hub," Silas countered.

"I'm planning to ingratiate myself to the Hub occupants in hopes of gaining an eventual spot working here with the tech systems. That is, if we end up here that long." Pim leaned in as his voice got quieter.

Silas moved the conversation back to the Riftians.

"They've got a large lake in the cavern where their Doorway lets out that's simply called the Lake of Death."

Up front, Nien answered a question regarding the governing systems across each of the Societies. The Kites had their queen, while the Clan had a series of lords. Normally I would have been interested, but I was thrilled when he wrapped up the speech and we were dismissed.

"Hope the days aren't all this exhausting!" Hale slumped as we moved toward our cots.

"Maybe it'll be different once we get to the Choosing." I tried to offer what comfort I could.

"Perhaps. But do we think that event will represent a beginning, or an end?" Silas's question as he moved past us was fair, but that didn't prevent fear from following his words.

CHAPTER 8

The next morning, we were directed back to the Doorways after breakfast. The tension and noise were heightened from the day before. My group was set to visit Dagan, one of the two sea-related planets. It was also home to the least human-looking beings. Something about their form just seemed a bit less solid, and a bit more fluid, like the water they resided in. All of the Dagan had a sheen of something across their skin that made it glisten darkly, like spilled ink.

Verkent knew the coating over their skin helped them blend with their darkened environment. Each Dagan also had a series of vibrant neon patterns on their bodies that increased in brightness in the deep waters of their planet. Our host for the day led the group through a dark tunnel toward the Doorway. When we landed, we weren't on an open-air pad. We were inside a transparent tunnel, with nothing but waves of darkness splashing eerily against the walls. Lights dotted each archway of the tunnel, providing limited visibility into the waters beyond.

"What's that?" one of the Societal Blanks shrieked as a large serpentine tail passed over us. It was somewhat comforting to realize that even the Societals hadn't seen everything. Our host glanced up through clouded eyes at the vanishing finned creature, but didn't respond.

"I am Iknan, your host for today. Welcome to Dagan." Long, spiny teeth protruded from Iknan's bottom jaw, and the webbing between the host's fingers spread as they gestured towards the rest of the tunnel.

"As you exit the airlock chamber, we will be providing you with a reed, which is a compact breathing apparatus for our visitors without gills. It will also assist with pressure equalization while underwater. I must insist you keep it clamped firmly between your teeth, and do not take it out until we are on the surface."

As we lined up and moved toward the exit of the air-filled tunnel, two Dagans held baskets of small wooden reeds, handing one to each Blank. The one on the right pulled the basket away as Hale reached the front of the line.

"No Deserters," the Dagan hissed at us through needle-like teeth. Luckily the one on the left didn't seem to have such biases, and nudged their basket toward Hale. I gently guided Sybil to that side of the tunnel. Terrified at the thought of not being able to breathe so far underwater, I clamped down hard on the reed I was provided. It wasn't very comfortable. I assumed it provided enough oxygen to survive, but it was a lot less than open air, and the sensation made me desperate to open my mouth and suck in oxygen. I resisted the urge.

"With all their advanced tech, you'd think they could come up with something better than these scrawny reeds. I can barely breathe with this thing!" Hale grumbled next to me before shoving the reed back in his mouth. Beside him, Sybil took measured breaths in and out in a steady rhythm, her eyes wide.

"Remind me again why *our* Society should take seriously the opinion of a Deserter? Someone coming from a planet who willingly cut themselves off from advancements such as this?" The haughty tone belonged to one of the Societal Blanks, shorter than Hale, with light purple eyes. Hale leveled a glare at the Blank but didn't take his reed out.

As we passed through the first section of the airlocked tunnel, the door closed behind us and we found ourselves in a second chamber that began to fill with water. It took everything in me not to hyperventilate at the claustrophobic sensation.

"We do not take chances with our guests. We will move through four chambers to slowly adjust to the atmospheric pressure." Iknan's voice buzzed in the air but took on a bubblier quality as the water reached his gills. It struck me as ironic that they were so careful with their guests, given what they were willing to do to Blanks who didn't successfully Assimilate. Resentment had quickly replaced my initial fear. That, and a sense of determination. I'd spent my entire life hoping to see the Societies, and the joy of it had been removed within a day. Either I'd find a way to successfully get everyone through the process, or I'd get them back home.

In the last chamber, the lights went out. Iknan's body lit with blue and yellow neon swirls, and I could faintly make out Hale's eyes, pupils dilated in the surrounding darkness. I clenched my teeth even tighter and again fought the urge to gulp in extra air. With a faint popping noise, the final door opened, and we were left staring directly into the sea.

Iknan motioned us forward, those clouded grey eyes turning toward our exit. Pim had visited the previous day and informed us all that the Dagans' clouded eyes helped them filter the light at the bottom of their oceans. I planned to stick as close to our guide as possible, since I wouldn't be able to spot whatever creatures were swimming around. As we swam, we were neither crushed by pressure on the seafloor nor buoyant enough to float to the surface. I wondered if that was the effect of the reed, or if it related to a completely different atmosphere. Iknan motioned for us all to circle around them, and we hovered, treading water as he spoke.

"We are currently outside of the central dome, which encompasses our largest city. It boasts the highest population of any of our dome units, with each having a centralized vocational area encircled by residential dwellings." As he spoke, we swam past a massive dome housing a multitude of buildings whose lights permeated the ocean beyond.

"These serve as protection from some of the planet's animal life, which tends to be drawn in by the noise and light. We have very little need for air, although we maintain a tolerance for it. Some of our more adventurous residents choose not only to work but to also maintain homes in the open water." In all the years I'd envisioned myself joining the Societies, I'd never pictured residing deep under the surface of an ocean.

We passed several more domes, with Iknan providing a brief description of the purposes of each.

"I will be taking questions once we reach the surface. While we spend the vast majority of time underwater, there are some large land masses we make use of there. Should you successfully Assimilate here, you would be provided temporary, oxygenized housing for the short time it takes to grow gills. I can promise the convenience is well worth the excruciating pain. Now, if you will please follow me."

As we continued, it became clear just how far down we had truly been. It took several minutes of effortful swimming before my mouth broke the surface. Even though my head knew I wasn't drowning, my body clearly didn't care as I heaved air into my lungs. I looked over the sloshing waves and saw Iknan watching us all. While Dagan features were hard for me to read, his head was cocked to the side in a way that suggested curiosity.

The skies above us were filled with saturated purples and oranges that might have made a pretty sunset if it weren't for the roiling black clouds being swept by a furious wind. Arcs of blinding lightning shot between them and down toward the sea. As the group treaded water, a grey rain started to fall from the sky. No longer distracted by the discomfort of limited oxygen intake, my other senses kicked in and I became aware of the water spraying in my face from the churning winds. Thunder echoed around us.

"At least there aren't massive waves." Hale's smile wobbled a bit as he yelled over the wind.

"Skrill!" one of the Societals cried before I could respond to my friend. Then they dove. Iknan disappeared below the water as well. A massive buffeting air hit my face as I watched enormous wings sail past. I rubbed my eyes, saltwater stinging them. Above us, pterodactyls, or at least something that looked eerily similar to them, circled the skies. I strained to get a better look through the water being flung in my face. At least from underneath, the head, belly, and wings of the creature were a deep purple.

"Move, Deserter!" A Societal Blank pushed past me. It was the same teen who had insulted Hale. As the heads of the others popped back above the surface, they all started swimming toward a blurry shape in the distance.

Above us, the skrill let out a cry that didn't sound like any reimagined dinosaur I had ever heard. I would have placed it somewhere between an amplified buzzard and a blood-curdling scream. I kicked my legs frantically, determined to get as far away from the noise as possible. Back on Earth, I swam for exercise frequently, but fear locked my limbs into jerky movements as I struggled through the waves.

The shrieking of the creature echoed across the sky; a perverse melody set against the rumbling thunder coming from the clouds. I kept moving toward what had to be an island in the distance, until I felt a small wave propel me forward. It was so at odds with the chaotic movement of the choppy waters that I broke my stroke to look behind me. A massive, whale-like creature breached the waters, its bone-pale flesh blindingly bright against the sky. Three skrill dove at it, one after another, until the whale managed to slap one with its massive tail. The winged creature was thrown under the waves.

I reached the sand and noticed the grains were grittier and much larger than any beach we had back home, sparkling gold flecks. I stumbled onto the land and sat down in a less than dignified heap. The sound of my own frantic breathing echoed in my head as I scanned the area for Sybil. I had promised Pim to watch her. She was being helped ashore by our host.

"Welcome to Dagan. It seems they're not even going to wait for the Choosing to try and get rid of us." Hale's tone oozed sarcasm as he shook seaweed off his arms.

Back in the waves, the massive body of the whale curved like a half-moon. It was being held up by the claws of two of the giant skrill as they began to feast.

"Where's the third?" I asked no one in particular. I hadn't seen it reemerge from the waves.

"The omnidon sank it with his tail," one of the Blanks volunteered.

I shuddered at the thought of being back underwater and coming face to face with a tooth-filled beak larger than my body. Dead or not, I had no interest in seeing a skrill up close.

"Scared, Deserter?" The same annoying Blank from earlier sneered.

"As a matter of fact, yes. Either one of those animals could have been deadly. They're large, toothy, dangerous predators. Giving them a healthy level of respect and space is the intelligent thing to do. If you don't realize that, I doubt you'll last very long, whether you Assimilate here or anywhere else." I advanced on him, stopping when my face was inches from his.

He stared open-mouthed in the face of my tirade. Behind him, the rest of the Societals showed mixed reactions. A few were scowling, but several had small grins or had even started to laugh. Perhaps not everyone agreed with the Deserter garbage. I was torn between pride at having stood up for myself and a feeling that I should have held myself back. I was angry, but it wasn't the fault of a misinformed teenager. My rage should have been directed at whoever had implemented a system that killed its participants. I was back and forth on whether I was upset with the task force. I needed to confirm whether they'd been aware of our predicament.

Iknan was off to the side. He seemed to be purposely ignoring the entire ordeal, talking louder than necessary to Sybil about coral that lined the islands. Maybe he was warmer than he'd initially let on. Or maybe he just didn't want to get involved.

"You don't deserve the chance to Assimilate into any of the Societies," the Blank sputtered. "You should have stayed on your own useless planet."

"Hey *kid*, what's your name?" The Societal Blanks weren't much younger than us, but nevertheless Hale stared him down.

"Bo." I was a little surprised when we got a response.

"Well, Bo. Let me give you some helpful advice. Shut. Up. I'm not listening to this trash on every Societal tour. The next time I hear it from you, I will personally shove this reed so far into your throat you'll need it surgically removed to be able to insult us again."

Bo stalked away. I walked over to Hale and put a hand on his arm. He sighed.

"I know. Too harsh. It's just ..."

"Too much. I agree."

"It's like we're being shown our greatest dream and worst nightmare back to back, and they're expecting us to go through this whole process like none of that's happening." He'd voiced the problem perfectly. We couldn't afford to have an intense reaction and risk getting ourselves removed from the process. Our lives depended on it.

Iknan walked back over to the group. The remainder of the tour was uneventful in comparison, as he took us back to the Doorway on a path that did not involve swimming by a dead skrill.

Once we'd returned to the Hub, my clothes and hair were dry but crusty from Dagan's seawater. I wondered if the oily substance that coated them also helped with their constant exposure to saltwater. I needed to talk to the others but decided to head to the showers before the cafeteria. I sighed contentedly as the warm water washed away the grime. The day's events had not endeared me to the idea of living on Dagan. After toweling off and donning yet another grey jumpsuit, I walked back to my bunk. Hale sat on the edge of it, with two sandwiches in his hands.

"Thought you might be hungry after choosing your beauty routine over food." His expression and tone were serious, but I knew better after a lifetime of friendship.

"Yes, and now I will be comfortable sitting through Nien's class, *and* I have received delivery service." I smirked, swiping the smaller of the two sandwiches and taking a large bite. The familiar banter helped calm me down a bit.

"You won't be the only one. Hold this." He shoved the second sandwich towards me and pushed himself off the bed.

"And don't eat it!" He waved a finger at me before heading for the showers. In all the time we'd been friends, he'd been exponentially guiltier than me of food theft. Just to spite him, I took a small nibble out of the edge. I set it carefully on the bedside table while I combed out my hair and checked the results in a small mirror. My green eyes stared back at me as I wondered what changes would be wrought on them in the near future. Like many of the girls I'd gone to school with, I'd been a bit insecure about my looks for years. My hair never sat quite right, and I'd always wished it was more golden and less straw-like. Some of the others might have worried about the physical alterations of Assimilation, but I looked forward to them. That was especially true given what awaited me if I didn't manage to achieve them.

"Told you I'd have time to eat." Hale shoved the sandwich in his face without acknowledging the bite I'd stolen as he returned.

When he was done, he shook his head like a dog, water droplets flying everywhere. I ducked, laughing.

"Good to see you both in positive spirits." Pim joined us, arm in arm with Sybil.

"Truthfully, some laughter in the face of what's happening to us isn't a bad defense strategy." Silas followed them, alongside Digit and Dex. It seemed like a good opportunity to let them in on my plan.

"Actually, I have an idea to possibly help with that. We're not supposed to contact Earth's task force until we see them in person at the Coalition meeting, right? That's weeks after the Choosing. By that point, it'll be too late; our fates will be sealed. I want to talk to them now. If I could reach out to Juliard, maybe he could convince them to help us."

"You realize they may have known before sending us." The twins came into view from behind a nearby canvas divider. Their heights and features were similar, but Cassia kept her hair in long braids, while her brother had closer cropped twists with a fade on the sides.

"I don't feel it's likely that Kena's uncle knew. He's not the most affectionate man, but I grew up watching him dote on her. It's a stretch to picture him putting her in harm's way. Especially when I can't see how her death would benefit him." Silas continued as if our two newest members had been there all along.

It wasn't the most touching reason to look out for my well-being, but I agreed. My uncle had always been cunning, but I'd never seen him engage in violence.

"Kaiser mentioned extricating everyone. Just from his demeanor, I'd wager his version would be aggressive. But maybe we could use whatever he has set up to our advantage. If Juliard could find out what he has planned, maybe he could put together a way to safely transport any non-Assimilated Earthers with him after the meeting."

"You know, the Hub has a communication center to relay messages between all the Societies. It's likely they've got something set up to contact Earth as well. Their tech people have been quizzing me ever since I arrived. They like the idea of getting to know a real Earther outlaw. At least the ones who don't want us dead. If we can get into that area undisturbed, I could probably figure it out." Digit smirked as she offered up the plan.

It wasn't a fully thought-out idea, but time was a luxury we didn't have. We decided to go by the communication center after Nien's lecture. Hopefully a few members of the group could distract the workers long enough for Digit to work her magic, and for me to contact my uncle. I felt more settled with even a poor plan in place.

"Today we will be covering a few basics regarding plant life of the different Societies. Specifically, what to eat and what will kill you." Nien rubbed his hands together, grinning around his tusks at the start of the evening's lecture.

"Which is the longer list?" Hale questioned.

"Truthfully, it depends upon the place. It may interest each of you to know that we try and use as much as possible from the planets when we start a new Society. Only with careful scientific consideration do we introduce new animal and plant species that may benefit the environment and its inhabitants. On Rover, they introduced trees that actually mist water when the air surrounding them is hot enough. This provides hydration and shade."

We took notes as he continued the lecture, Society by Society. Even though I was interested, I struggled not to squirm in my chair, eager to enact our plan.

"The Canopy had so much variety that no new animal or plant species were introduced. It really has to be seen to be believed, though, and since you all haven't had the chance to visit, I've brought a holofilm."

My attention was piqued as he held up a sleek disc. Though much smaller in size, there was no denying its resemblance to the item from Verkent I'd brought with me. My desire to find a way to view it had been overshadowed by everything else, but I was thrilled to realize I'd probably find a way to see what it contained. Nien inserted it into a device he called a holocorder. It did exactly what its name insinuated and projected a clear and crisp video directly above itself. It didn't even require a screen. We watched as vibrant plants were displayed in front of us, while the instructor listed off their names.

Once he wrapped up the lesson for the evening, our group made our way toward the communication center. Fortunately, Digit and Pim had been eager enough to meet the Societal techies that they'd already been and were able to direct us. I'd anticipated suspicion or resistance, but Pim drew the two Hub workers away without difficulty. He simply mentioned some gadget he'd brought with him from Earth, and they followed him down the hall. As soon as they were out of sight, Digit slipped into one of their chairs, while I took the other.

"Darnit."

"What?" I was worried we'd hit a snag.

"Just look at this! Everything is neatly labeled. All we've got to do now is essentially turn the system on. It's even got two options listed: the task force's main headquarters or Verkent's office."

"Why is that bad?"

"Because I like to put my skills to use! Anyone could have accessed this. Honestly! The lack of security some people have, and they thought I was a criminal." She shook her head as she pushed a series of buttons and switches that I personally thought looked anything but simple. I was about to ask how we would know if it worked when a holoscreen projected in front of us, and my uncle's face appeared in the air.

CHAPTER 9

"Kena?" Juliard's eyes widened, then shifted to the side. "And friend. What a surprise. You do both realize you're breaking the terms of our agreement with the Coalition by reaching out to me? Then again, it's just the sort of thing your father or I would have done, just for a laugh." He smiled.

"Unfortunately, this isn't a happy call. I think we're limited on time, so I'll just get straight to it. Did you know the Societals are going to kill us if we don't Assimilate?"

His brows shot up again.

"What? That can't be right! There has to be a misunderstanding. We weren't told anything like that."

"No misunderstanding. They were very clear about the consequences, should we prove to be poor candidates for this process. We've got until your meeting with the Coalition to show some physical signs that we fit in wherever we pick, or we're done for." Digit leveled an unblinking stare at my uncle as she spoke. He turned toward me as he responded.

"Kena. You have to know I never would have sent you up there if I'd known anything about this." Technically, I had been determined to go, but arguing over whose plan it had been wasn't important.

"You need to fix this, Juliard. The task force needs to step in here. Even if ... even if it means pulling us all out before the Choosing." I hated to even voice the option, but if that's what it took to get everyone back safely, that's what had to be done. If I'd been asked, growing up, what I was willing to give to see the Societies in person, I'd have said the answer was anything. It turned out that wasn't the case. It grieved me to even consider giving it up, but I was willing to do it if it saved lives.

"I'll talk to them, of course. But I don't think they'll go that route. At the Coalition meeting we'll be discussing Earth's long-term relationship with the Societies. Are we going to join them, can we access their resources, what can we each offer the other, and so forth. They were very clear that any reneging on our end would be viewed very negatively. Now I understand why. The stakes were much higher than they let on."

Out in the hall, a voice rang out.

"Oh, so *that's* how they keep track of everyone in the Hub. How *interesting.*" Pim practically yelled. It was time to go.

"Juliard. We've got to leave. Try to figure this out, please. And if you can avoid involving Kaiser, do."

"As if I would leave something this important to that war-hungry oaf. *I'll* fix this. If nothing else, we'll come up with a way to get anyone in danger out after the Coalition meeting. I'll find a way to reach out to you then. Kena, one more thing, there's a—"

The screen shut off and Digit pulled on my arm.

"Time to leave!"

We made it into the hall just as Pim and the Hub workers rounded the corner. Pim held his arms out and plastered an exaggerated smile on his face.

"Kena, Digit! So nice to see you. Would you mind accompanying me to the dining hall? I've got a craving for a snack." I could feel the stares of the Hub workers as we left, but no one stopped us.

We'd actually managed it, but I wasn't sure it mattered. Juliard said he hadn't known anything, but I found myself doubting him. I wanted to know what he'd been cut off from sharing as well. We still had no real plan. It seemed like we needed to be prepared to see the Choosing through, and just wait to see if they could get us out later if it became necessary.

Our second week at the Hub started with a visit to the Rovers. I stood by my bunk afterward, shaking sand out of yet another grey jumpsuit. The planet had been dry, barren, harsh, and hot. Our host, Etok, had stood comfortably in the heat, leathery teal skin glinting against the sun's rays while he extolled the virtues of the desert planet. For one, they had the Assimilated ability to withstand searingly hot temperatures. It made me pity Sarah, whose sunburn had started to peel.

"At least those oasis areas with the soft-pink pools were gorgeous. Do you think Societals vacation on each other's worlds?" I gave my boot another shake, sending grains of sand flying.

Hale scoffed.

"Did you forget the part where that flying scorpion thing landed on Bo and he screamed like a four-year-old? It was funny, but not my idea of a vacation. I still can't believe you just let that snake slither right into your hand!" He huffed.

"Etok said they were harmless, and it was kind of cute."

That, and the small copper snake had been by far the cuddliest creature we'd seen. My least favorite had been the sand scuttlers. Etok's golden eyes had gleamed as he described the way their pincers could tear at flesh, while several of the Blanks cringed. Rover residents were quite literally thick-skinned, and it seemed there was a good reason for that.

"I thought the regular scorpions were almost worse than the flying ones." Pim joined the conversation as he walked up, arm linked with Sybil.

"*Regular* scorpions? Just great! We didn't even see those." Hale fell onto my bed in a mock faint.

"Well, I agree with Kena. I liked the snakes. Etok told us they've also found the creatures have a heightened immunity, and their blood has helped the Rovers develop some antidotes in case a bite or sting does occur. Then the residents help the snakes by deterring large predators." Sybil grinned as she relayed the information. Following a trip to the dining hall, we all walked to the classroom. After seeing how simple it had been to get into the communications center, I had another idea I wanted to pitch to the others after the lesson.

"Today, I will be discussing history. As you are aware, representatives from each of the seven Societies make up the Coalition, which governs everyone from the Hub," Nien began.

"What even existed before the Coalition?" Sarah's hand rose as she spoke. I noticed her sunburn had started to fade.

"An excellent question, and a history that I must remind you Earthers share as well. Prior to the existence of the Societies, the Ancestors resided on one planet. Its original name is now only a painful reminder of its fate; it is referred to simply as Lone. Interestingly enough, Lone shared many of the same features that make Earth so habitable. Large land masses separated not by massive oceans, but by rivers. Initially, the residents there existed with the same respect for their surroundings as Societals do today."

Nien's expression changed, and he frowned over his tusks as his eyebrows knit together.

"Unfortunately, after a time the relationship with the planet changed. Instead of Lone supplying provision and being supplied with care in turn, the number of people on the planet began to outpace what it could provide. Rather than banding together as space became crowded and resources became limited, fights broke out and raged for years, becoming increasingly violent. With the help of scientists and teams of searchers, a solution was found. At that point we had not yet mastered the near-instantaneous travel methods we currently have via the Doorways, but we had still made advancements far beyond what Earth has achieved in terms of travel in open space."

"So, you've always been okay with murdering people, then," Derek's voice rang out. I was interested to see how Nien responded. He went on with his speech, not acknowledging the teen.

"The Ancestors were able to locate three suitable alternative planets that could support life for us off of Lone. With violence escalating, the first Choosing was born out of necessity. There was a large faction who decided to remain behind, warring over what was left. Knowing this mentality would bring problems to new planets, and hoping to avoid a similar struggle, two things were determined. The first was that there would be no second opportunities. Everyone had one choice: to leave Lone, or to remain. Those who stayed eventually perished at each other's hands or as the planet became devoid of resources. Since that time, the planet has remained empty. The second agreement was the formation of the Societies. That even across multiple places we would remain united under a Coalition of representatives. The original three Societies were the Canopy, Dagan, and the Rift."

"What is the point of this? Who cares?" Derek let out a sigh. I waited to see if Nien would say anything, but he wasn't the one who stepped in.

"Sit properly and be quiet before you are made to do so. We need to learn all we can if we hope to survive here." Cassius glared at the teen. The other giggling individuals at Derek's table grew quiet.

"As if anyone asked me if I *wanted* to come in the first place," Derek muttered under his breath, but he turned back toward the front of the room. I didn't care for him, but I understood his frustration. The situation was bad enough for those of us who had volunteered, let alone those who had been pressured or threatened into it.

"One of the ways our Societies remain united is in our celebrations of life, and of death. The Canopy took on the responsibility of celebrating births. The Rift took on the responsibility of handling the dead. Only the Riftians know all the details, as they inherited the remainder of the abbots from Lone who performed such things. With any death where a body can be recovered, they see to it that last rites are provided in the way of our Ancestors. Their Lake of Death—though I'll always wonder how no one came up with a more respectable title—is of the utmost importance to this process. Several of you have seen it on tours, as it takes up most of the cavern where their Doorway lets out."

"Earth is like Lone. Not just the planet, but the inhabitants as well." Nien's gaze whipped in my direction as I changed the subject. He didn't snap at me for the interruption. Instead, he dipped his chin in my direction before continuing.

"Yes. I believe that part of why there is apprehension about Earth is the recognition by some that you have followed a similar path.

You have a history of living in destruction with your planet and each other. It is possible, depending on the results of this Choosing, that the inhabitants of Earth may be offered what the Ancestors were, a singular Choosing. If that happens, it will be entirely in their hands what becomes of them." Nien and I stared at each other for several seconds. I refused to break eye contact, trying to glean from his expression whether he thought we would fail or not.

"It is of course also possible they end up a fully fledged Society with a permanent place here." He turned away as he spoke, breaking the tension. Once he finished, the classroom cleared quickly. Only our small group remained.

"Juliard said something that made me think. He told me the Coalition must have been withholding some information. We've already figured out what the stakes are, and that not all of the Societals want to see us succeed. If we want to give ourselves the best possible chance, we should gather as much information as possible. And not just what's being provided freely in class. We can't take chances on more important details being kept from us."

"So, what are you proposing?" Dex questioned. Instead of answering right away, I turned to the others.

"Pim, Digit, have you continued working on the Hub techies?"

"I'm happy to say that through compliments and skills we've been able to ingratiate ourselves to the Hub programmers. We know they monitor the entire Hub through a series of cameras. I also think we have a good idea where to look for your secret information. Coalition Hall." Digit smirked.

"It's where the offices of each of the delegates are, and a library of information related to the Hub and Societies," Pim clarified.

"And they just told you about that?"

"Told us, allowed one of us to find out because they have lax security, what's the difference really?" I liked Digit more and more with each interaction.

"That's the play, then. We break into the hall and find out everything we can. My vote is sooner rather than later. I think we should go after our next tour." Silas leaned back against his chair, appearing relaxed in the face of what he'd proposed.

"He's right. If we wait too long, we miss the opportunity. We stand a much better chance working together while we're all here than after they've split us up."

We came up with a rough plan that essentially involved shutting down security cameras while ransacking the offices.

"With the level of security set up in Coalition Hall, it's near impenetrable, but they rely too heavily on technology. If we take the system down, there's no actual Societals watching the area after the delegates have left for the day. I should be able to hack it and register a malfunction in the code. That would force it to reboot. You all would be able to sneak in while the system is off and doors are unlocked." Digit made it sound a lot simpler than I anticipated it would be in practice.

"The more errors we cause, the longer you'd likely have. Although generally, the more that goes wrong, the more likely someone will show up to fix it. The programmers do get alerts for things like shutdowns. A small malfunction here or there won't look suspicious, but we shouldn't do too much." Pim expanded on Digit's statement, his pale blue eyes sweeping across the group.

"How do we know when to get out?" Silas asked a question I should have thought of.

"The lights. The ones that run along all the hallways. In theory, emergency lighting should kick on while the system reboots. Those will be much softer, to save energy. When you see the regular lights blinking back on, that's your signal to book it out of there." Digit waved a tattooed arm as she mimed our exit from the hall.

We headed back to the bunks with a plan in place. The others' support meant everything to me. For the first time since my father died, it felt like my family had grown instead of shrinking. I planned to do anything necessary to protect them and to ensure it stayed that way.

CHAPTER 10

The next day was our visit to the Rift. I was more curious about them than any other Society. Hale and I had gone through our usual breakfast routine with our group and were standing to leave when two Societal teens knocked into me with their trays. Bits of food spilled onto my jumpsuit.

"Hey!" Hale yelled after them when they failed to stop. One teen turned to look at us and put on an exaggerated expression of surprise.

"Oops, didn't see you, Deserter. Maybe it's because you shouldn't *be* here."

Hale lunged at them, but I grabbed his arm, pulling him back.

"Those two owe you an apology!" he fumed, waving after them.

"I appreciate it, but we've got enough to worry about today. You go ahead to the Doorways; I'll go change and meet you there."

"It's what you would have done if they'd bumped into me." He huffed. He was right. I'd always been better at defending others than myself, though, and we had more important things to focus on. Hale shot another glare at the backs of the two teens before he headed toward the Doorways.

I sprinted down the hall to the bunks, hoping to change one grey jumpsuit out for another and make it back in time. As I rounded the last corner to the door, I saw a large figure exiting. I threw my hands out in front of me to stop myself but couldn't help bumping into the person.

"I'm so sorry! I really didn't mean—" I blinked as I realized I'd just run into the magistrate himself. As he looked down at me, the scowl on his face quickly morphed into a smile. He held out his hand.

"Miss Eckhoff, it's quite fortuitous running into you here. I'd been looking to see if you were still in the bunks." As he gestured behind him into the room, I could just see the edge of my cot.

"Me? Why?"

"Your position in Verkent, of course. It reminds me a bit of our structure here. Your uncle in charge on Earth, and you acting as a delegate here. And do tell me, how *is* your uncle? Since you've last seen him on Earth, of course. You know, I spent such a brief time with him, but he seemed truly fascinating. I had so hoped to discuss with you some of the topics he brought up regarding Verkent." His forked tongue slid out as he spoke, head tilted as he stared at me with unblinking eyes. I tried not to panic at his line of questioning so soon after our unauthorized call.

"I really would like to, honestly, but I'm running late for today's tour."

He waved dismissively.

"I'm sure we can arrange an alternate tour if you'd like. After all, my schedule doesn't open up often, and I would like to hear more about Juliard and Verkent." As he reached an arm out towards me, I pulled back. Warrick frowned, and a shadow fell over us.

"I apologize, Warrick, but with all the added Earther courses and extra Blanks for this Choosing, I don't think we'd be able to accommodate any additional visits. She'll simply have to meet with you another time." The Riftian delegate, Bayard, stood next to me. My mind hadn't remembered accurately how striking his glowing blue eyes were. That same compelling pull that seemed to happen each time he appeared swept over me. It made me feel, without actually knowing him, that he was trustworthy. I shook off the odd sensation. Warrick scowled again, a slight hiss escaping with his tongue. Within seconds he'd put his smile back in place.

"Of course, Bayard. Another time then. Miss Eckhoff." As he walked away, I caught sight of the edge of a reptilian tail flicking out the back of his robes.

"Your Earther friend mentioned you had to stop back by the bunks. I wanted to make sure we had everyone in the group before leaving." I thanked Bayard, then moved quickly to go change. The delegate was silent as we walked. I joined Hale at the Doorway.

When we exited on the Riftian side, we stepped directly into a cave of some sort. There was a cool and pleasant breeze weaving its way through the group. As my eyes adjusted to the darkness, I saw a few other people shiver as the soft winds washed over them, but I found the sensation rather refreshing. Bayard had already begun walking toward a dim light illuminating the exit of the tunnel.

"He's not even speaking to us—not the most gracious host," one of the Societal Blanks whispered to the others.

"The Riftians just think they're better than everyone else. They look down their noses at us."

It was the first time I'd heard the "us vs. them" mentality in relation to another Society instead of Earth. It made me even more interested to learn what the secretive planet contained.

"They're renowned for their intelligence, not their upbeat personalities," a third Societal chimed in.

"They're being a bit harsh, considering we've been here all of thirty seconds,." I whispered to Hale.

"Actually, I tend to agree with them, although please don't mention that to Bo. Even Verkent didn't have much on them. It's always bothered me. Even more, now that we're here. Considering how difficult it could already be to Assimilate somewhere we know about, how much more dangerous would it be to have to pick somewhere like this? We don't know anything about them."

"You could always choose the Rift and find out those secrets for yourself. You've always been the adventurous one."

He laughed into his hand at my suggestion.

"I like action, but I'm not stupid. I have no interest in spending our potentially limited time inside a damp cave."

A muted light washed over us as we emerged from the tunnel into a yawning cavern. A natural hush fell in the echoing space until all that remained was the soft drip of water off of stalactites and the lapping sound of waves. The vast area was largely taken up by the dark lake that disappeared even further into the back of the cave. I assumed it had to be the Lake of Death Nien had mentioned. It wasn't nearly as ominous in person as he'd made it sound. The whole setting was rather peaceful.

In front of the water stood several Riftians. The darkness of the cavern only made their glowing eyes stand out all the more. Shining greens, blues, and even magenta peered out at us from beneath a series of hoods on their cloaks. I wondered what else was hidden under their robes. Surely, they had some Assimilated features other than shining eyes. If the Dagan's neon marks served the purpose of deterring predators and providing vision in the depths, perhaps the Riftians' eyes helped them in the dark caverns they called home.

"Are you feeling a bit ... odd?" Hale leaned in close.

The sensation I always had around Bayard had grown. It seemed as though all the Riftians around us were giving off the same notable aura. A surge of feelings swept over me, like a nostalgic memory that stirred emotions of both happiness and a longing for something I couldn't get back. It had to be some Assimilated feature that allowed them to invoke such a response, but everything I'd ever read indicated that the qualities people gained after the Choosing were strictly physical.

"Welcome. We are not going to be embarking upon a typical Societal tour today. Instead, we will be limiting our tour to the cavern in which you are currently standing, and the small antechambers which are directly accessible from it. That is the extent of the Rift visible to those who have not chosen here." Bayard walked as he spoke.

He moved so fluidly that I had to glance down to ensure his feet were touching the ground underneath him and he wasn't simply floating. As the bottom of his cloak swept the rock, it was impossible to tell for sure.

"You have no doubt noticed that Societies each have aspects of their planet and their customs they prefer to keep to themselves. The Rift holds our privacy at a very high value. Please follow me toward the first stop on today's tour, the Main Hall." The other Riftians shifted silently to attention as they began to follow Bayard. Before we could take more than a few steps, a freckled Societal Blank stopped him with a question.

"Wait! Aren't you going to say anything about the lake?"

Bayard paused.

"As we exit, you will note the majority of the posterior cavern wall contains the Lake of Death. You can see that it seemingly disappears into the darkness of the caves beyond. While we have Riftians that work around it, not even our people know all its outlet points." Vague description finished, he moved on.

"Nice try, Saf, but a waste of time to try and pull answers out of a Riftian," Bo whispered to the crestfallen girl.

"I should have known better than to ask anything of a Riftian. This whole day is a waste of time. Who would live in a Society with a creepy death lake as their welcome mat, anyway?" Saf's teal eyes glared at Bayard's back as the delegate led the group onward.

One of the other Societal teens, a shorter girl with coffee brown eyes, cringed as Saf spoke. Her hair was several shades deeper than her light brown skin. I didn't like seeing people picked on, whether they were Societals or Earthers. I walked up and linked my arm with hers.

"I like the Cavern. It feels peaceful. If you ask me, that lake doesn't look like anything sinister. This whole place is a lot more welcoming than some of the other Societies." I projected my voice as Bo turned around with a sneer.

"You *would* think something like that, Deserter." He started toward me, but then paled a bit and changed course, dragging Saf with him.

I turned and saw Hale glowering beside me.

"Th-thanks for defending this place. I'm Ariadna." The brown-eyed girl held out a hand, jumping just a bit as I grabbed it to shake. I had to try to remember they did that for our benefit, and it wasn't a natural greeting for them.

"Kena. And I meant it. Is this where you're planning to Assimilate, then?"

"Yes. M-my sister lives here. We were very close growing up, and I miss getting to see her. Even though she won't tell me much about things here, I-I can tell she's happy with her Choice."

"Ariadna, if I may ask, where do Blanks grow up here? Do parents ever come from two different planets?" I couldn't believe we hadn't touched on it sooner in Nien's class. It was a topic not addressed in Verkent's writings, either. I'd hoped the answer might clear up how they could treat their young so callously.

Her eyes widened a bit.

"Um, I can give you the summary. Wh-when kids are really little, families can choose to stay on the planet of the parents for a while or just live at the Hub. The Rift has spaces like that for families in one of the Cavern's antechambers. At a certain point, all kids transition to the Hub for education. Some people live there on their own, and there are plenty of adults whose job it is to help the kids. Others move their whole family unit until kids go through the Choosing. Th-the housing wing at the Hub is pretty enormous, actually."

"And their parents? Are couples always from the same Society?"

"W-well, technically there's no rules around it. Although the majority of parents are from the same Society. When that's not the case, they can live on either individual's planet until it's time for the kid to move to the Hub. It doesn't happen very often, though."

We caught up to the group as she finished. We stood in another very large room of stone, this one set up as a banquet hall.

"The Main Hall is where we host the majority of events, or visitors from other Societies. Whether you Assimilate here or simply choose to come see someone who has, you will likely spend time here. We do our utmost to make sure our guests are comfortable."

The rest of the tour moved along similarly. A series of antechambers connected to the main cavern, which served various purposes. Unlike some of the other tours, we didn't see any living quarters, but I imagined they looked much the same. We did see a library, a games room of some sort, and even a garden inside one cavernous chamber, although it was clear all the plants had been brought in from elsewhere. Bayard did most of the talking, with the other Riftians chiming in briefly in specific rooms. It was perhaps the least social but most professional tour we'd had. We finished up back in the cavern, with Bayard addressing the group.

"The Rift, more than any other Society, asks for a lot of upfront trust. We do not dazzle with shows of gorgeous scenery or unique physical Assimilations. We operate largely on inner guidance. We ask you to consider whether you feel pulled to this Society, and if you do, to follow that voice." I certainly felt a pull around the Riftians, but I wasn't sure if it was the one he referenced.

As we were ushered back to the Doorway, several Blanks grumbled about the vagueness of the visit. The meeting with Ariadna had been nice. Her words about her sister also made me think there was more to the Rift than the first visit indicated. That evening, before the lecture I found myself once again in the cafeteria, enjoying almost-familiar foods.

"Everyone ready for another Nien lecture?" Sarcasm dripped from Hale's voice. I knew sitting in a classroom wasn't his style.

"I'm actually enjoying them." Su Jin's quiet voice barely registered above the general din. I hadn't spoken to her much since the Societals had upended her tray. Veronica had managed to pull her and the other girls away from Derek's side of the table for the evening.

"The visits are interesting, but I'm ready to get through the actual Choosing." Cassius took a large bite after he spoke.

"On the other hand, with each visit to a Society we get that much closer to Assimilating, or not Assimilating," Dex put in.

"Yeah, I'm not loving the idea of dying. And I'm certainly not happy about potentially getting killed over a Choice I don't even really make." Digit stared at her hands. I knew from her file that she was assigned to the Rift. It didn't really seem like a fit for her.

"I'm just mentally tallying pros and cons from each visit, and trying to be thoughtful with my decision." Sybil took a small bite of some orange vegetable.

"I'll admit, sometimes I'm envious of those of you who have a real choice. Then again, I am able to already put my attention solely on the Canopy." Cassia shot a look at her brother after she spoke. I imagined it had to be hard for the twins to separate, since he'd been assigned to Kite.

I tried to think of something supportive to say. Silas saved me from the necessity with his next statement.

"I'm planning to go to the Rift."

Everyone stared at him for several moments in silence while he continued with his dinner.

"Be sure to let us know what you find out once you're there, since they've shared nothing so far." Hale's expression was sour, but Silas just laughed as we all cleared away our trays and headed to our lesson.

Nien launched into a conveniently timed lecture that evening.

"We will dedicate the beginning of this evening's class to the Rift, and then move along to some information regarding the Hub and its technologies. Those of you who have visited the planet likely have noticed that while Riftians have limited physical differences from Earthers or Blanks, at least visibly, they do *feel* different to you. This is thanks to an Assimilated trait we refer to as projection, which is actually quite interesting, since the majority of Assimilated traits tend to be physical in nature. Riftians are all able, to varying degrees, to alter the perception of those around them. Whether this is conscious or subconscious is not something they share off their planet."

Putting a name to the sensation I felt around them made me feel a bit better about it.

"So, it's like mind control?" Dex slapped his hands to the side of his head, and I stifled laughter at such a large man looking so tense.

"Some of these discussions are not as simple as yes and no. They are shades of grey. The Riftians do not control your thoughts, but generate a feeling in others in response to themselves."

Derek rose from his chair to respond to Nien.

"That seems like cheating."

"You're being overly dramatic. So what if they can affect your first impression of them? The fact that you're judging them like this should let you know you *do* ultimately have a say in how you perceive them." Cassius stood, arms crossed, as he turned toward Derek. His sister added her own commentary.

"Also, this is the Choosing. That's the entire point. If you don't like the Rift, don't go. I myself would be very interested in learning their secrets."

Cassius nodded and thumped her on the shoulder. I tried to decide if she was being noble in referring to a choice she knew she didn't have, or if it were possible she had hinted that the others should make one regardless of what they'd been instructed.

"They're also the most respectful Society so far," I said, adding the detail that had been most meaningful to me.

"What do you mean? They didn't seem very friendly to me." Mancio's lip curled as he looked in my direction. Derek high-fived his friend as they both sneered.

"I didn't say *friendly*, I said respectful. Haven't any of you noticed they're the only place we've visited so far where not one single person from their Society has called us Deserters or lashed out at us in some way? It's the same thing in the Hub. I'm not sure how many of you are watching the facial expressions as we walk the halls, but they're not all welcoming. The Riftians are the only ones I've never seen look at us with a glare. Not even once."

"Not that you could tell. With those hoods up all the time, who can say how they're looking under it?" I wasn't surprised to hear Derek's voice contradicting me. Hale spoke up in my defense.

"Kena's right. We've been having small incidents everywhere but the Rift. They've been nothing but civil toward Earthers." The defense meant a lot, considering that I knew he didn't personally care for the Society.

Nien changed the subject.

"Let's move along to our next topic, which is the role of the Hub's workers and what technologies they're responsible for maintaining."

Pim and Digit were the only ones who looked intrigued. Nien pulled out the small holocorder he'd used in a few previous lectures. We spent the rest of the lesson watching clips from interviews with Hub workers as they briefly described their roles and responsibilities. After it finished, people began filing out of the room. Derek was looking rather sulky as he muttered something to one of the girls, who nodded emphatically. Hale hesitated at the door, but I waved him on. There was something that had been nagging at me.

"A question, Kena?" Nien asked without glancing up from his papers.

"In our last lesson, you mentioned a lot of decisions getting made during the formation of the Societies." Nien inclined his head, and I pressed forward.

"Who made all those decisions? How did the group choose who to put in control?"

"Excellent questions. The most powerful individuals ruled at the start. Primarily the ones remaining from Lone who had held influence there. Lone also had a council like the Coalition, with representatives from different regions. Currently we have a balance of planetside policies and the Hub. Here, each Society has several delegates, who reside on the station near full-time. You've been meeting them on your tours. At the head of the Coalition is the magistrate, currently Warrick. The delegates are elected by their planets, and the Coalition members choose among them who is magistrate. The Societies vary. They're allowed to exist as they will, but any issue impacting multiple Societies is handled by the Coalition."

I was going to have to be more direct to get the information I wanted.

"Does everyone have to agree with the decision to elect the magistrate? What about the people? Do they like him?" Warrick wanted something from me. I hadn't really engaged with him yet. He could be a powerful enemy or ally. It depended on his views and how much power he really held.

"A magistrate cannot achieve their position without a substantial majority of the Coalition votes. Such a vote is rarely unanimous, but we have a precedent of respecting the outcome. Are you merely someone who finds politics interesting, or is there perhaps a more personal reason for this line of questioning?" He continued to rifle through his papers, but shot me a look out the side of his eye. I didn't mention Warrick directly. I had no way of knowing if he and Nien were on good terms.

"I was just curious. Even with all the information Verkent had, I'm still trying to fill in some gaps."

"Kena, the Societies run on a balance. That being said, no system is perfect. It's part of why we value so highly the multiple perspectives of Societies. And for those of us who are wise, the perspective of our newest participants in the Choosing. If you have any thoughts you feel need to be shared, I am always available."

"So, you support the way things run here?" I was curious whether that decision, too, had been supported by the majority.

He sighed.

"The Coalition attempts to weigh the pros and cons of every decision. Some of those come at a high cost. It's not ideal, but Earth does the same."

"My system doesn't go around killing innocent people just because they couldn't fit the standard of perfection."

"Doesn't it?"

CHAPTER 11

"You're fidgeting with your hands." Hale smiled as we walked by a few lingering Blanks. I couldn't help it. Somehow, breaking into the Coalition offices and stealing information seemed a lot more serious than calling my uncle.

"Who knows what they'll do to us or the other Earthers if we're found out?" I had intended to help him see the severity of our situation, but Hale just rolled his eyes and pulled me into a side hug.

"We will not get caught. Pim and Digit said they would shut everything down, and we will find something to help everyone." He sounded more certain than I felt.

It was still our best option. It seemed more likely that we'd find useful information at the Hub than any particular planet. Pim was an old friend whom I trusted implicitly, and Digit was a genius with technology. Maybe Hale was right.

We rounded a corner and met up with Silas and Dex on their way from the cafeteria. We'd decided to all at least come and go from different locations. Shoulders back and head high, Silas appeared to be in his element.

"History may be written by the winners, but you can bet somewhere there's evidence of whatever really happened. There's a big difference between the victory as it really occurred and the victory as it was told to the masses, believe you me."

"You think we'll find something related to how Earth got cut off?" I asked him.

"I wouldn't doubt it."

As Cassius and Cassia fell in step with us, I thought of Silas's theory. My dad had been interested in that information. He'd died without ever figuring it out. I couldn't say for sure what his response would have been to finding out the deadly truth behind the Societies' Choosing, but I knew my own mind. I wouldn't have been surprised to find a violent secret at the heart of Earth's history.

The Coalition Hall was behind a set of dauntingly tall double doors. Wooden around the edges with opaque glass between, they stood out against the matte grey of the rest of the Hub. The tops of the doors were adorned with vibrantly colored circles of glass. I could tell they were meant to represent the Societies and their respective seals, but they reminded me of the stained glass at Verkent's church. As we approached, the blue lights that illuminated the entrance dimmed into nothingness and a faint hiss of air sounded as the doors slid open. Pim and Digit had been successful.

We made our way down the hall and fanned out. One rather large flaw in the plan was not knowing the exact amount of time Pim and Digit would be able to keep the system down. We needed to cover as many areas as possible. Cassius and Cassia ducked into the first two doors on the left, which belonged to the Dagan and Clan delegates. Silas and Dex started with the Crew and Rift, hoping to meet them in the middle. Hale and I walked further down the hall, intending to go straight to the magistrate's office. If I could figure out more about him, maybe I'd have a better idea how to deal with him.

Warrick's door created a dead end to the path of offices and mimicked the larger ones from the hall's entrance. As I began to push it open, I saw an ostentatious display of ornamental designs across an old wooden desk. Hale slipped through the door in an instant, moving to examine a pile of papers on the desk.

I had started to follow when a warm, soft light off to my right caught my eye. I turned toward it and saw a smaller door down a short and awkwardly angled hall that I hadn't even noticed when we first passed by. Acting on instinct, I abandoned Warrick's office and moved toward it. A small, unassuming wooden door greeted me at the end. It was already ajar. As I pushed it, my eyes found the source of the light: a small fireplace, with green wingback chairs set in front of it. I scanned the towering shelves of leather-bound books in the sitting area. I longed to examine them, but what lay beyond them held even more immediate interest.

Along the side of the wall and leading back into the cavernous dark room were rows and rows of holofilms. Darkened cases with basic labels lined the metal shelves like a warehouse. I thought of the film I'd brought to the Hub. I was betting if there was any holocorder old enough to play my disc, it resided within the library. I pulled myself away from the books and plunged forward into the shadowy stacks.

It didn't take me long to find a larger container on the first shelf with a holocorder similar to the current version. I was silently thankful they were lighter than their bulky appearance suggested as I hefted it onto the floor. I grabbed the closest holofilm and inserted it. My hand shook as I reached for the button to display its contents.

My breath stilled to nothingness as an image flickered to life in front of me.

"We are in the Hub's central technology kiosk today demonstrating the proper ways to clean out the wire boxes for your transmitting cube. By the end of this demonstration, you will have a clear understanding of maintenance ..."

I should have realized that at least some of them had to contain Coalition information that was useless for our purposes. Slightly disappointed but undeterred, I flipped over the container on another holofilm, finding a label that read "Scientific Significance of Skrill Droppings." The sheer number of rows was daunting. I asked myself: if it had been up to me to organize, what would I have done with any secretive or important tapes? Either put them in seemingly innocuous cases, or shove them so far in the back no one would be likely to get to them. The first option risked someone finding them by accident. That, and I'd be left opening every case, hoping to find something. I reached a decision and made my way to the back of the room.

After scanning a few shelves, I noticed another holocorder that looked much worse for wear than the first. A few more rows, and I made it to the back wall, where, instead of another shelving monstrosity towering over me with metallic sturdiness, a small bookshelf sat alone. It only came up to my shoulders and was sparsely occupied. A few of the holofilms were a different shape than the rest and shoved together in an opened box. Sitting on the floor next to them were a few more holocorder boxes covered in dust. The first held what I'd been looking for. Dinged-up in places and showing age, the silvery object gave me immense hope. I knew, no matter the risk, I had to bring my disc-shaped film back somehow. The Hub had a way to play it.

I spent only a moment regretting I hadn't brought Verkent's disc with me before I pulled a different one out of the assorted box. I had to wipe a thin layer of dust off the label and did a double-take when I saw "Lone" scrawled on it. The writing obscured whatever original title had been beneath it. I quickly located a holocorder that matched it, eager to see what I could of the planet the Societal Ancestors came from. As I pressed the button to play the film, an image flickered to life. A soft crackling noise competed with the soft sounds of plant life caught swaying in a breeze as the image cleared. It seemed a bit off-kilter, and I reached out a hand instinctively to tilt the holocorder before realizing the film itself was crooked and moving. Current holocorders weren't affected by operator motion.

At first, the only sound audible over the crackling was the huffing of whoever was operating the holocorder as the person ran through a series of huge fronds. When they emerged from the edge of the plant life, the image jumped into sharper focus and the tilting ceased. The person recording scanned the holocorder downward, toward an embankment in the valley below. Hazy smoke rose from a cluster of homes. It was centered in one area but appeared to be growing. The holocorder lurched forward again into the tall brush. All that was visible for the next minute was stalks and leaves. I jumped as screams rang out. As the operator moved forward, a crashing sound increased until another body nearly collided with the holocorder, running from the haze.

The operator stopped, and tall brush filled the sides of the screen. It looked like they were crouched down somewhere. From their close vantage point, the haze from earlier became billowing smoke, and I imagined heat hitting my face as I stared at fire consuming the buildings. The screaming had grown louder, and occasionally another blur would be seen on the periphery, running from the destruction. As the crowds that ran past thinned, the screams lessened and a methodical thumping took their place.

A horde of armored individuals marched into the area. Helmets covered their features. Some were riding horse-like creatures with four nostrils, thin elongated ears, and whip-like tails that were barbed at the ends. As the group came to a halt, several of them pulled logs over and sat down. Their postures were relaxed, seemingly unbothered by the fire and fading screams. They started to pull off their outer layers, and then their helmets. As the final layer was unwrapped from one of the faces, I gasped.

All the individuals onscreen were clearly adults, but their facial features marked them as Blanks, just like Earther faces. I had assumed that as the Ancestors of the Societies, Lone's residents would have had Assimilated features. It made no sense. We resembled the Ancestors more than any of the Societals.

As a voice rose in the film, I heard one of them speaking sternly to the others. Several of the soldiers glanced into the brush. My breath caught, thinking of the holocorder operator. The men started to fan out, and a rustling sound came through the holocorder as the scene disappeared into a pile of brush. A tree line came into view, and I heard the huffing of the operator's breath as they ran. As I watched, I willed them to get away. Without warning, the image toppled to a view of dirt as the holocorder dropped to the ground. Something heavy landed next to it with a thud, and I found myself staring into brown eyes, wide and fearful as they gazed at the lens in death.

"Kena!" I startled at the sound of my name.

"Kena!" Hale's urgent call came again from across the room.

"Back here! Hale, you'll never believe what I—"

"Time to go! Didn't you hear that beeping? The systems are coming back online."

Too late, I realized the library surroundings dampened whatever noise was audible outside, and the lighting hadn't changed at all. I quickly but carefully placed the holofilm back in its box and laid it on the shelf. We moved furtively through the shelves. With every step, I worried I was going to get us caught. When we reached Dex and Silas by the main doors, I let out an actual sigh of relief. Cassius and Cassia had already gone. We all made our way separately to Nien's classroom. We'd chosen it as the most likely place to review what we found without being overheard. As Hale and I walked in, I saw Pim and Digit sitting casually at one of the tables, poring over a book. I filled the others in as quickly as I could on the holocorder footage.

"And that was the end of it, just the dead operator staring at the holocorder. They've made such a big deal over Earthers; how did it not come up that the Ancestors looked like us, and not like any of them?"

"Surprising none of us even thought to ask what they looked like before Lone's destruction." Pim's gaze drifted to the side as he held a hand up to the side of his face.

"I'd assumed they'd Assimilated in some way, like they did with the new planets. Nien never indicated in our lectures that they'd had to learn how to do it over time. I wonder how they triggered it, if it wasn't natural?" Silas rested his chin on his hands.

If we could figure out what the Ancestors had done to trigger Assimilation, we could copy them and save the Earthers. Sadly, no one else had found anything related. The twins and Dex had come up empty, but Silas had noticed something interesting in Warrick's office, where he'd joined Hale in my absence.

"A crest that doesn't belong to any of the Societies. The border was a red circle, and in the center a white emblem of a spear. It was stamped into the underside of his desk, between two drawers."

"Couldn't it just be the maker's mark?" Dex questioned.

"Unlikely. It had the same circular border as the Society crests, same art style as well."

If Silas found it noteworthy, I did as well. No one really knew what to do with the information, though. Before we left for the dorms, we all agreed that, as foolish as it was, we'd have to try again before the Choosing if we wanted any solid information.

That night, I tossed and turned as I had a nightmare about the library. In my dream, one of the soldiers picked the holocorder up from the dirt next to its poor, dead operator. He removed his helmet, and Warrick stared down into the camera. The same scene kept repeating. Each time, as the helmet lifted, a new face stared back. Bayard's, Nien's, Kaiser's, Juliard's, and finally, my own. I woke up in a sweat, and instead of going back to sleep I rifled through my bag to make sure the disc I'd brought was still there. I placed it in a small pack I could carry along on the tours. I no longer felt safe leaving it in the Hub.

CHAPTER 12

I was tired and distracted the next morning as we exited the Doorway on the Clan's planet. For the second visit in a row, we found ourselves in a cave of sorts. The Rift's cavern had held a certain coziness, but the Clan's caves, massive and dark, lacked that trait. The residents lived inside the mountains. They had mined the caves, and the entrances to darkened tunnels could be seen in every direction, veering off from one another haphazardly. With every step we took deeper into their home, loud clangs and metallic noises echoed around us.

I lowered my voice before I spoke, worried my words might echo in the yawning darkness.

"Do you think it's ever quiet here?"

"Unlikely." Hale leaned over and peered into a hole off the side of our path. The clanking continued as I looked over his shoulder, unable to see anything but shadow.

Ahead of us, our host for the day, Ugdol, addressed the noises.

"You'll get used to the sounds, even if some of our visitors claim it can be jarring. I'll tell you now, it's better than being outside the mountain. Out there, you never know for sure if it's the wailing winds or a snow beast howling as it hunts you." He had a patch over one eye and a scar running along his lower lip. This caused a pointed tooth to jut out and made me think he might have first-hand knowledge.

"Today, when we see the outer rim of the mountains, you'll witness calm, soft snow. Typically, it's howling outside, with all manner of creatures being camouflaged by the white winds." He turned away, hooves clacking and echoing against the stone floor as he led us deeper. The main hall we wandered through was lit by dim torches. Unfortunately, they gave off no heat. I was shivering by the time we reached the next hall, and it had no lights at all.

Ugdol handed out small headlamps to each of the Blanks but didn't keep one for himself. His yellowed eyes reflected the lights of our headgear like those of a cat in the dark. I helped Sybil get hers adjusted before we set off.

"We'll be taking this shaft upwards until its eventual outlet at one of the peaks. On the way, we'll see several tunnels leading to our metal rooms."

I gaped as Ugdol began scaling the wall upwards. There was even more to the Clan than met the eye. For the rest of us, there was a metal ladder set into the stone. Despite the chill, I was sweating and huffing by the time Ugdol directed us through a side tunnel and we got a break from the elevation gain. There was hardly enough room for everyone to stand upright. I started to feel claustrophobic.

"Do you suppose it hurts when their legs bend like that?" Sybil's voice trembled a bit, and I followed her gaze to where our host walked ahead on his goat-like legs. Multiple Verkent writings described some of the Assimilations as highly uncomfortable, but I wasn't eager to remind her of that.

"Aw, Syb, I wouldn't worry about it. He seems tough. And you won't need to deal with it anyway. Surely you're not planning to choose this place?" As Hale swept a hand out at our surroundings, his fingers hit the ceiling. He sucked in a breath and shook his scraped knuckles. Sybil pulled them closer to have a look. It was hard to imagine our gentle gardener dwelling in the mountains, which seemed bereft of any plant life.

My breathing eased as we funneled into a small domed room at the end of the tunnel. I fought the urge to stretch just to prove to myself I wouldn't hit the ceiling. Clan miners, some holding pick axes and shovels, lined the room. Their faces bore any combination of elongated, furred ears, snout-like noses, and horns. A few had bovine tails whipping back and forth behind them. That wasn't what held my attention, though. Surrounding our hosts were piles of glistening gems. What appeared to be rubies, sapphires, emeralds, and diamonds were being thrown haphazardly to the side of the workers. I sucked in a breath at the massive amount of wealth sitting discarded in the room.

I looked to my side and saw Hale and Sybil equally transfixed, their eyes on the massive, glittering piles.

"Curious. It appears Earthers have an obsession with the colored rocks, similar to some of the other Societies." One eyebrow raised, Ugdol scanned the reactions of the Blanks.

"Well, yeah! Do you have any idea what all this is worth?" An auburn-haired Earther, whom I vaguely remembered being called Luke by some of the others, gesticulated, arms flailing as he waved them towards the glistening piles.

"To you, maybe. Clan inhabitants are interested in metals and minerals which can be utilized to make useful products. These are mere decorations. Some are sold to the other Societies for such a purpose, but there's far more product than demand. In truth, we store most of them in vaults, out of the way." Our host started to usher us out of the room.

We'd only taken a few steps back toward the tunnel when Luke yelped. I turned to see him clutching his head, a shining magenta gem on the floor at his feet. A cluster of miners laughed, while one individual at their center stood with his eyes locked on Luke, shoulders back as he glared at the Earther. He snorted through bovine-like nostrils, and steam rose in the cold air.

Before anyone else had the chance to step in, Sybil stalked toward him, finger raised in accusation. The Clan miner's eyebrows shot up, and he leaned away from her as she wagged a finger inches from his face.

"That was absolutely disgraceful, young man. Shame on you, waiting until someone's back is turned like that. We are here as your guests, and this is how you choose to behave? I must insist that you apologize immediately." Sometimes I forgot Sybil's former job as a teacher, but it was totally believable as she managed to look down on a man a whole foot taller than she was, who sported horns twisting out from behind his temples.

He shook his head, his shocked expression settling back into a glare as he stared her down. He took a step toward her before an arm shot between them and his gaze was redirected toward our host.

"She is right, Toth. We do not have to like these outsiders, but we are better than attacking someone when their back is turned. If you have a problem with them, have the decency to say it to their face."

Outsiders was a step up from Deserters, but I couldn't believe he had allowed that kind of thing. Ugdol stepped back from between them, and Toth smiled down at Sybil. The expression looked predatory.

"Your back's not turned now." Toth angled his twisted horns toward the older woman, and she began to back away.

I ultimately had no control as to whether the Earthers Assimilated, but I did have the ability to look out for my friends. I grabbed the nearest tool at hand and threw myself between Sybil and her attacker. I struggled to heft the pick ax I'd laid my hands on. To my mortification, Toth and the others behind him started to laugh. He leaned his massive head toward me, snorting out his nose. It hit my face like a wall of steam.

"And just what do you intend to do with that, Deserter?"

He clearly didn't consider me a threat as I trembled under the weight of the ax. Still, I managed to get it aloft. I felt a hand on my shoulder that, through years of friendship, I recognized as Hale's. Arms shaking, I gritted my teeth and managed to meet his gaze with a glare of my own.

"If you say one more unkind word to Sybil, I will swing this into your hide." In reality, I wasn't sure I'd have been able to manage it. Hale backed up the possibly empty threat.

"She means it, too! If you're dealing with me or Syb, you're going to get told off, or maybe just punched in the face. If you manage to anger Kena, she will ruin your life." He took a hand off my shoulder and stepped to my side. Toth glanced between us, and I felt tension building before Ugdol's voice broke it.

"Earther, put the ax down. We're all wasting time here. We've still got lots to get through. Blanks, back to the tunnel. The rest of you, back to work." He waved his hand, shooing the miners back to their shovels. I waited until I heard Sybil's shuffling steps receding before I put down the ax. As I passed our host at the door, I swore I saw the smallest of smiles as he dipped his chin towards me.

I was shaking as we reached the exit that led us out of the mines. Sybil grabbed my hand and thanked me several times.

"I really don't know what came over me, dear, truly I don't. We mustn't mention this to Pim. He'd be so worried about it. You don't think I've made our situation worse, do you?" She chewed on her lip as I assured her that I was much more likely to be the cause of commotion than she was.

We made our way out onto a snowy path that was just as picturesque and quiet as had been promised, and I plopped myself onto a drift as the others wandered around. I stared over the side of the mountain at the lower peaks below, and off into the distance at a vibrantly orange setting sun. Hale hung back with me.

"I'll be telling everyone in the group tonight about my two favorite warrior women." He beamed at me before he sat down and placed an arm around my shoulder.

"Hey, what's eating you? I know the guy was a bit intimidating, but you held your own. You should be proud."

I dropped my head into my hands, speaking toward the ground instead of my friend. I heard the crunching of shoes on the snow around us as I spoke.

"I can't decide how I feel. I couldn't stand the idea of him hurting Sybil, but am I a hypocrite? We're all mad, and of course scared by what will happen if we don't Assimilate. Then I go and threaten a Societal with violence. Does that make me as bad as them?"

"Of course not. It makes you smart. These Societals have all kinds of physical advantages, and they've been poking at us since day one. I think it's good if they know we're not so easily pushed around. Although, maybe if you Assimilate here you try to give Toth a wide berth, at least until you grow horns." He ruffled my hair and I watched his breath cloud the air as I tried to picture either of us with ram horns growing out of our skulls.

Being around the Clan miners had reminded me of running into a wild animal on a hike. As if each of them had been sizing us up, trying to determine if we were predators or prey. I knew which one I'd felt like since we'd first reached the Hub, and I also knew which I'd rather be.

I was too stressed to really appreciate the snow, although I did feel warmer outside in the sun than I had in the mines. As the tour ended and Ugdol led us back along the twisting paths to the Doorway, he stopped the group at the tunnel from our earlier incident. I was relieved when he asked us all to wait as he went to check in with the miners. I had no desire to face Toth again. Ugdol said little when he returned, and we made our way back to the Hub.

When we were back in the main lobby of the Doorways he asked Luke, Sybil and me to stay back. Ugdol asked each of us to hold out our palms before he pulled out three gems. Unless I was very much mistaken, Luke ended up holding the same magenta gem that had been thrown at the back of his head. Sybil received a translucent turquoise-colored stone nearly the size of her palm.

"An apology from our Society. The others do not have to like you or approve of your participation. We are supporters of independent opinions in the Clan. We do, however, have strict morals. If we are going to disagree with someone, we do so to their face, on an open field. We are not cowards. Assimilation will decide things for the Blanks, and after that, if they still have a problem with you, they can face you directly. While the gems mean little to us, aside from aesthetics, they may be quite valuable to you."

Sybil and Luke joined the others, and Ugdol waited until they were some distance away before placing a rose gold gem into my palm.

"This one is rare even within the Clan and, unlike most of the gems, quite useful. It is yours to use freely, although I would suggest keeping it to yourself for now." With no further explanation he walked away, and I was left to wonder at the significance of what I'd just been given.

That night, Nien spoke about the process the Hub and Coalition went through to locate areas where new Societies could be planted.

"For the Societies, finding new potential planets is an incredibly important piece of our shared culture. Not only does this benefit the existing planets and their inhabitants by preventing a lack of resources due to overpopulation, but it opens us up to new possibilities as well. Each new planet brings discoveries of different materials and elements we can utilize, new animal and plant life, and the evolution achieved by Assimilating and gaining new abilities and perspectives to bring to all Societies as a whole."

As Nien fiddled with a holocorder up front, Derek scoffed.

"So, it's just like Earth's leadership suspected. A power grab. You farm these planets for resources and ways to get an edge. What's going to happen when you decide you want whatever we have on Earth?"

"That is the most idiotic thi—" Cassius stopped as perhaps the only person he allowed to interrupt him spoke.

"The pursuit of additional intelligences, resources, and perspectives would be an asset to all of the Societies, not a deficit. If you considered your thoughts for one second before speaking, you might have realized that they already had access to our resources once, and whatever they were, the benefit of cutting us off outweighed any contribution the planet made to their system. You would do well to keep thoughts like this to yourself and let the rest of us at least try to gain information which might help us Assimilate." Cassia stared down her nose at the teen.

Derek glowered at her in response. The legs on his chair squeaked as he fell back into it, arms crossed.

"*Cutting us off*? The same way your father got cut off from all those lucrative friends of his when they realized he was useless as well? I don't even know how you two managed to make it into this group. The rest of us have class, pedigree. I wouldn't have trusted you to pack my luggage for the trip here."

I sucked in a breath at the insults. The twins' file had been vague on their father's fall from grace, but it hardly mattered. Derek's father was highly respected in the business world, and that clearly hadn't translated into producing a son with good character. Cassius leaped out of his chair and had Derek in a headlock before the teen spoke another word. No one moved to stop him.

Nien, still fussing with the equipment, appeared blissfully unaware of the entire exchange, muttering to himself about "all this advancement and can't get a regulation holocorder to start up," as Su Jin held the item aloft so he could inspect it to find the source of the error.

Derek kept digging a hole for himself, his voice choked to a strained whisper as Cassius tightened his hold.

"It's. Just. The. Truth! Everyone knows he—" Derek was reduced to wheezing and clawing at Cassius's arms, his eyes bulging.

By that point it seemed clear Nien was ignoring the whole exchange on purpose, his back turned to the group. Silas and Dex stepped towards Cassius.

"No one's arguing that he's an idiotic jerk ..." Dex set a hand on Cassius's shoulder and tugged his arm open. Derek sucked in air. "But it's best if you put him down." Silas pried Derek away from Cassius, the former slumping on the floor as he held his neck.

Cassius had started back to his chair when Derek opened his mouth again, his voice hoarse.

"No wonder they assigned your sister the Canopy. You're animals, both of you. You belong here with all these Verkent and Societal freaks."

Dex, Silas, and Cassius all lunged toward Derek. Dex's hands were inches away from Derek's cringing face when Nien stepped between them. The speed and stealth with which he'd moved had to be an Assimilated perk. Nien hauled Derek back to his seat and sat him in it without so much as a deep breath. Derek grimaced as Nien's fingers pressed into his shoulder.

"You would do well to remember that you now live among all of us *freaks,* and that you will very soon be one. If you are lucky." The pointed teeth behind his tusks were on full, terrifying display, with his lips twisted into a snarl. Derek paled. Our instructor was quite intimidating when he wanted to be, it seemed.

Nien's features fell back into place as he walked to the front of the classroom with a smile. With more glee than I would want to admit, I remembered that Derek was going to the Clan. I wanted to feel sorry for him, but I couldn't quite manage it.

"Since our holocorder isn't being agreeable anyway, perhaps some additional information on settling new Societies. Evaluators are constantly looking for potential planets. They work from a list of requirements. First, does it have any current advanced lifeforms? If so, it's not a possibility. We have no desire to pull resources from another group or risk aggressions. Then, does it have the basic atmosphere needed? After that, questions such as, what are the local plants and wildlife like? How will our presence impact that system? What Assimilated traits would we need to thrive, or do we anticipate would be likely?"

"And when in this process do you actually put people on the planet?" Dex leaned in.

"That is where settlement comes in, or did back when we were able to achieve it. Adults who are fully Assimilated elsewhere offer to go to new potential Societies as semi-permanent or permanent residents, to get things set up. It can be a risk because there's no way of knowing for certain what will happen until people actually Assimilate. While we can guess, there's no way to know with certainty what features or abilities Societals will gain to help them survive in their new home. Even though we haven't been able to settle a new planet since Earth left us, many Hub workers dedicate their whole lives researching potential new Societies. This way, we are ready if it ever becomes a possibility again."

"What went wrong on our planet? If this system is so foolproof, why don't we have horns, or wings, or cool abilities or glowing eyes?" I was a bit shocked to see Thea speaking. She generally kept her conversations to hushed tones among Sarah, Su Jin, and Derek.

"Maybe they never meant for us to Assimilate to Earth at all, and it was just a way of dumping their defectives. They clearly don't mind killing us off. They just came back to finish the job." Mancio tilted his head, casting a side-eyed glance at Nien.

"As you are all well aware, the official Hub statement is that Earth purposely cut *themselves* off from the technology and aid of the Societies, for reasons known only to your predecessors. There is a lot riding on all of your shoulders. Prove to them that you are capable."

I hoped he was right, for the sake of all of us.

"Nien, why continue to look for these planets? If they haven't been able to settle one since Earth, shouldn't the effort have been on figuring that out? If they couldn't solve that problem alone, why not return for us sooner?"

He sighed but didn't dodge my questions.

"The Coalition is always working to avoid another Lone disaster. The delegates and leaders of each planet are constantly tracking their numbers. Every Society has a maximum amount of inhabitants before we start having a negative impact on the environment. At that point, we start to have problems Assimilating. Currently, we control the population, or we risk everyone. Surely you all have gleaned from your tours that it would be exceedingly difficult to reside on most of these planets without Assimilation."

"Do you mean to say this ridiculous kill-off-the-youth protocol doesn't have to exist? If you had somewhere new to settle, we'd be safe?" I knew my words bordered on disrespectful, but I was fed up.

"Yes, but all the files we had with that knowledge were lost on Earth. As for not returning sooner, we couldn't find you. When we initially go to these planets, we have to do it the old-fashioned way. Doorways have to be placed once we're there, and Earth's was destroyed in their rebellion. Afterward, it was discovered they'd taken or deleted any information pertaining to their location or settlement. Scanning all of space to find one planet is more difficult than you'd think."

CHAPTER 13

After what Nien had said, I was even more convinced we had to find a way back to the library. It was possible whatever they were looking for was on my holofilm. We were quickly running out of tours—and time.

On the day of our Crew visit, I started my morning off with the Hub's coffee substitute being wafted under my nose by a very enthusiastic Hale. "Today's the day!" he crowed, practically dancing around me as I stretched. He perched himself on the end of my bed with a grin.

"Is there any reason why my best friend has chosen to torture me by planting his overly excited self on my feet while I'm trying to sleep?"

"What about the fact that I brought you coffee, saving you a walk all the way down to the dining hall?" He shoved the cup toward me. Unable to resist, I swiped the mug from his outstretched hands and took a long sip.

"You're forgiven." I sighed contentedly as the drink warmed me.

"So why the excitement over seeing the Island planet? You weren't this excited for Dagan. They're both sea-based worlds, right?" I hid my grin behind a jumpsuit. I knew it had been his favorite growing up, but it was worth the teasing to see the way his eyes flashed, coffee spilling as he waved his arms.

"Are you joking? For starters, the Crew looks incredibly cool with all their tattoos. And they're basically pirates. That doesn't sound like an adventure to you?"

Composed entirely of solid black and white ink, every Crew inhabitant I'd seen walking through the Hub sported an astounding collection of tattoos. It held a certain appeal. Then I thought of trading the overcrowded dorm areas for an equally crowded ship, unable to ever truly get away from people.

"Not really, no."

He waved me off.

"You say that now, but I'll bet you'll be singing a different tune once we've visited."

"What about their ... wavering?" I was unable to come up with a better term for it. While the Dagan had the undulating and oily texture, the Crew had an odd, wispy nature to them.

"I'm sure we'll get an explanation today. The Crew seem very straightforward, unlike some Societies I could mention." He'd made several digs at the Rift since our visit.

"Not that it matters, because you've been eyeing a set of feathers." He flapped his arms and hopped from the edge of my bed to the floor as coffee droplets flew everywhere.

"Watch it!" I flung my arm up to block the spray of liquid that threatened to drench my jumpsuit.

At the Doorways, our Crew delegate wavered in place under the bright lights of the station. It was like he managed to be something completely unsolid, but in no way transparent. Watching him was similar to watching a holofilm in real time. It was as if he was caught in a constant breeze, his form refusing to stand still.

After we stepped through the Crew's Doorway, we landed in a receiving area of veritable chaos. Voices rose over one another and people moved to and fro between various vendors holding baskets of fish and fruit aloft. We made our way to a row of docks. Sea air hit my face as I stared up at row after row of towering ships.

They were a mix of metal and wooden hulls, each so well-kept, so perfectly symmetrical, there had to be some superior craftsmanship going on. I assumed there was tech within them that I couldn't even begin to guess at. Hale kept shifting from one foot to the other.

"Which one do you think we're getting on? They're all sleek, but I'd love to see one of the classic wooden ones, wouldn't you?"

I cringed a bit as I thought of an old carrier vessel turned museum I'd toured once. The deck had been impressive, the internal compartments cramped and hyperventilation-inducing. As Hale raced up and down the road, trying to take in the behemoth vessels from every angle, I recalled our sleepovers growing up. We'd both had parents who believed in bedtime stories, and the guest always got to pick. I'd leaned towards fantasies with fantastic new creatures and worlds. Hale had liked swashbuckling adventures. It was no small wonder he was thrilled. I vowed to myself to act enthused, no matter how cramped the interior of the ship was.

Our host for the day sauntered back over from a conversation with some others by the docks, arms swinging rhythmically with his steps. He was covered in a heavy blanket of black tattoos and had unruly red hair that looked like it spent a lot of time being buffeted by salty winds.

"Hello all. I'm Track, your host for the day. Let's get into it, lots to cover. We'll be boarding the *Nimitz* today. You've all been through a similar speech to this several times now, so I'll keep it brief. On that ship there's a whole hierarchy of command and experts in many different areas. None of you fits into that hierarchy, and no one here is an expert on anything yet. If anyone on that ship tells you to move aside, pick something up, or put it down, you do it immediately. Especially the captain. The head of any ship is the captain, and Everleigh is in charge here. We like to run a controlled chaos on these waters. We don't have as many unnecessary policies as a lot of Societies, but we do believe in listening to the people who know what they're talking about. Everyone good with that?"

An chorus of yeses came from our crowd.

"Good. In that case, on we go!" He led us up a massive gangplank to one of the wooden ships. I glanced over and saw Hale grinning.

The ship itself was bustling with activity the moment we entered. People rushed past with mops, buckets, and even trays of food. The constant thrum of motion made my eyes swim. I felt that if I lived with the Crew, I'd have a continuous buzz in my brain from the endless movement.

"We'll tour the ship and sail by several islands, although we won't be disembarking until we're back to Main Port. If you choose to Assimilate here, the majority of your time will likely be spent at sea. Now, if you'll follow me below deck, please."

"Sir, excuse me!" I threw my hand in the air like I was in a classroom. Track raised an eyebrow.

"Before we get started, could you explain the Assimilated feature you all have of ... the way your bodies waver ... or um, the texture they have that isn't really solid, but I mean, it is ..." Bo sniggered. Ariadna shot me a smile as I struggled with my words. I just hoped I hadn't offended our host.

I couldn't read Track's expression at all.

"Shadowing. That's what you're referring to. You're not far off; we do appear less than solid. I'd caution anyone against that assumption, though. Crew members are very much muscle and sinew, like everyone else. What you see is a defense against the elements on this planet. By shadowing we're protected from the sun, wind, and sea spray. You'll notice no one gets burnt, our tattoos don't fade, and while we appear to get blown in the breeze, our footing stays solid."

Ariadna caught up with me as Track led us down a stairwell.

"That was bold. The Crew aren't as secretive as some Societies, but it's difficult to tell what will set them off. They settle things quickly, and sometimes physically. V-very straightforward. If they're upset, they'll yell or punch you in the face. Sometimes their delegates struggle to get along with the others. A-at least that's what I've heard from my sister. He was as likely to knock you on your butt as he was to answer." She shrugged as she continued down the stairs.

"They do look and move like shadows, when you think about it. It's a fitting name," Sybil said as she joined me on the stairs.

"I still don't really feel like I understand. Some of the things like wings or snouts are fantastical, but I can see and touch them. Shadowing makes them look like they're two textures at once."

"You can't explain everything, Kena!" Hale's jovial demeanor continued as we made our way through the tour.

As suspected, there were technology areas in the ship containing screens and displays I couldn't guess the function of. The antique look only went so far. When we saw the living quarters, I was pleasantly surprised to find them much more spacious than I'd anticipated. I turned to Hale to comment on it, but he'd disappeared from my side.

I found him off to the side of the group, deep in conversation with a Societal. Not unlike the rest of the Crew, she had several tattoos, though judging by how much unadorned skin was left, she must have Assimilated recently. Her black hair was cut close to her head, with the exception of a long swath near the front. She had a pierced nose and amethyst eyes that looked like she'd lined them with charcoal. She was petite but something about her expression gave off a tough vibe. Hale wore an enormous grin on his face.

She turned with a self-assured smile as I got closer. Her eyes locked on me, and I felt like I was being sized up as I held out a hand. She stared but didn't take it.

"Kena, this is Nix. She's about our age, Assimilated here within the last few years." Hale glanced between the two of us.

"Very nice to meet you."

"And you. You're Verkent's leader, huh? How exciting." She kept the smile on her face, but I felt annoyed at her tone. Track called for the group to follow him back to the deck. As we made our way up the stairs, Hale gushed.

"Isn't she great? Just one more plus about Assimilating here."

"You've known her for three minutes!"

"Yes, and it took only that long to realize I want to see more of her." I rolled my eyes. I wasn't used to sharing Hale's attention with anyone, and even though there was nothing aside from friendship between us, it still bothered me. We were in the middle of a crisis and he was trying to play pirates and pick up a girlfriend. As we exited the stairwell, I was rendered speechless.

"The sunsets here are a personal favorite of mine. I'm biased, of course, but I think they're quite impressive." Track gazed into the distance.

Two small orange suns cast warm light across the water, and around them were bending waves in the sky of greens and blues. The crowded underbelly of the ship would likely drive me crazy, but if I could end each day staring silently at those lights, I might be all right.

Whistles echoed off the side of the ship.

"We're not the only ones who enjoy the lights. A few of the sea mammals come up and sing to them sometimes." Track pointed downwards.

As Hale and I leaned over the edge of the deck, we could see a whole pod of some sort of fuzzy creature singing toward the lights.

"Otter dolphins?" I glanced at Hale.

"Good a name as any, until we find out what they're really called." Hale shrugged and whistled back at them. In response a few flipped, sending water splashing into the side of the ship. Seeing how happy he was, I felt the annoyance from earlier ease. Hale wasn't at fault for the situation we were in, and why shouldn't he be excited for joining the Crew? The tour finished as we pulled back into Main Port.

"Where's Sybil?" I wondered aloud, glancing around as we disembarked.

"Talking to one of the older deck hands back there." He gestured back up to the ship.

"Amazing. She's done this in every Society. Her likability truly transcends worlds."

We waited for her before heading back through the Doorway. Later that evening, Hale tried to convince me to join him in the Crew.

"You might like it if you gave it a chance. I saw the way you looked at those lights." He leaned in, expression hopeful. I sighed.

"Yes, they were captivating, but those constant crowds aren't for me. I'm sorry, Hale, but I just don't think that it's something I'd get used to. I'd feel constantly on edge. Unless maybe they have an island paradise they'd be willing to drop me at for the weekends."

"I knew you'd say that, but I figured I might as well ask. You're going to get a set of wings, aren't you?"

"Wouldn't it be convenient if I could just fly you around when you came to visit?" I was happy for him that he seemed so certain of his Choice. I just hated to think of him being so far away. Whether we both Assimilated or not, the whole friendship was going to change. We'd never lived farther apart than a block, let alone a planet away.

CHAPTER 14

With only one tour left before the Choosing, there was more pressure than ever to get back into the Coalition's offices and the library. I sat in Nien's classroom on edge, as I clutched my bag closer to myself. It felt as if someone might suddenly decide to search it for the antiquated holofilm that lay inside.

At the table next to me, Su Jin gushed over the beauty of the Canopy and how lucky Cassia was to be assigned there. She herself was set to go to Kite. The assigned Societies were a key topic of discussion for nearly all the Earthers. Sybil joined the conversation, eager at the prospect of flight.

"Suppose that means you'll be wearing some wings as well?" Silas asked Pim.

"Aren't wings supposed to be one of the more painful Assimilations?" Hale bit into an apple as he joined the group, fruit flying when he spoke. Cassia shot Hale a glare as Sybil's face fell.

"What about you, Digit?" Hale turned away from Cassia as he changed topics.

"I'm assigned to the Rift." She shrugged but then winked at him. Given the consequences that awaited everyone, I had begun to have serious doubts about everyone going where they were supposed to.

Nien walked into the room, and the conversations quieted. While I suspected he had to be privy to at least some of Earth's secrets, he'd never said anything out loud. Once everyone's eyes were focused on him, our instructor disappeared. Gasps and a yell rang out in the room. Seconds later, he reappeared in the same spot.

"For our next to last lecture, I thought we could focus on something fun, the traits you Assimilate on different planets. What you just saw is a rather useful form of camouflage those in the Canopy possess. It takes time and effort to master, but if utilized properly you can blend into almost any surroundings." It was impressive and made me further question how many times he may have overheard things from the Earthers he wasn't supposed to.

As everyone in the room settled, Hale pulled a bag of biscuits and container of jam seemingly out of nowhere.

"What in the world is all this?" I pulled his bag towards me.

"I've finally won over the dining hall staff so I don't have to go hungry in between meals. They've decided I'm an incredibly sweet young Earther who is woefully uneducated on all their traditional foods, so they're plying me with all kinds of treats. Bless them. Shame I didn't do this sooner." I rolled my eyes and shoved the bag back to him as I turned my attention to Nien.

"I think one of the traits you all may be most interested in is that of lifespans. Considering the fact that you are used to an expectation of seventy to eighty years and Societals outpace that multiple times—"

"You mean we're not going to die?" Hale spat biscuit onto the table in front of us as he leaned forward. Nien curled his lip up as he glanced at the soggy food.

"We are not immortal. Consider what we've discussed of the Rift handling the dead. I have my own theories on it. Earthers have essentially been stuck at an earlier stage of development than Societals, which I think has had a negative impact on your aging." He placed a hand on his chin and paced the front of the room, his grey pant legs swishing with his steps.

"So it's just one more thing you think makes you better than us." I didn't have to look over to know it was Derek who spoke.

"Not exactly." Nien didn't elaborate.

"How long *are* we going to live, then? Assuming we're able to Assimilate." Hale had abandoned his snacks.

"It depends. Every Society has its own dangers. That being said, and taking into account slight variables in averages across the different planets, somewhere between three hundred to three hundred and fifty years, on average. By the numbers, those in the Crew tend to land on the lower end of that due to their risky choices. Riftians tend to live rather long lives. If rumors are to be believed, there have been Riftians who lived over four hundred years. I haven't personally seen the science behind that, though."

A lone hand rose into the air. It was Pim. As the oldest individual in the Choosing, I imagined the discussion was more meaningful to him than anyone else.

"What about those of us who aren't the age of an average Blank?"

"The honest answer to that is that we haven't a clue. That's part of what makes this an enticing experiment. In the initial three Societies, our ancestors Assimilated naturally to their new homes over time. We didn't really start tracking these things until other Societies were being established. While most of us hope for a different outcome, it is always a possibility that Earthers could fail to Assimilate at all. Maybe you'll only gain some traits and not others."

"Would *some* be enough to save us?" I asked. Nien turned his orange and gold eyes towards me.

"Perhaps. It's what I would support if given the opportunity." It wasn't nearly the affirmative answer I'd wanted, but it was more positive than some of his previous responses.

Hours later, Silas, Dex, Hale, the twins, and I prepared for a second break-in of Coalition Hall. Digit and Pim had kept their ears open for any gossip on the first incident.

"Some of their programmers think the Hub's system going down was intentional, but not all of them. There was also some talk of it being done by Societals, so all the suspicion isn't on us. After a second incident, though, I'd be shocked if they didn't hype up security." Digit scanned the hall, but no Hub workers walked by.

"We'll take the front offices. If anyone does show up, I can promise to put up quite a fight. Hopefully it would give you all enough distraction to get yourselves out," Cassius volunteered.

"I truly appreciate it, especially with the potential consequences. But if we get caught, I don't think any of us are equipped to take on Societals." I was thankful for the sentiment.

"You might be surprised, Kena. When he went after Derek, Dex and I held him back because he allowed it. It would have been incredibly difficult otherwise." I blinked in confusion at Silas's words. Cassia took a step toward me.

"Our father was a well-known politician who had plenty of enemies back when he was considered well-liked. My brother and I grew up with death threats against him and our family being the norm. He insisted we take lesson after lesson on self-defense. If those Societals try to get rid of us, Assimilation or no, they'll find it a harder job than they bargained for."

Digit and Pim were successful again. By the time the rest of us reached the doors to the Coalition Hall, they were unlocked. Cassias, Cassia, and Dex headed to the offices to see if anything had been missed the first time around. Silas and Hale followed me to the library.

My memory had not done justice to the magnitude of the room. Hale and I went straight back toward the older holofilms. Silas started checking the books to see if he could find a white spear symbol like the one from Warrick's desk.

It didn't take long for us to find a holocorder that fit the disc I'd brought along. It had been one of my father's prized possessions, and I had a feeling it contained something important. After a lifetime of waiting, I was finally going to see what secrets it held. My hand trembled as I pressed the button to start the film. A field of green greeted us as it began. Even though it was short grass and not tall stalks, the scenery reminded me of Lone. I suppressed a shudder as a sense of foreboding swept over me. The operator carried the holocorder into a canvas tent and set it down on a table in the center. Chairs lined the view on the screen.

Several individuals seated themselves in view of the holocorder, each wearing a red and white mask. Some were painted to look like human faces; others had animal features, and some swirling patterns. The man who sat at the head of the table wore a mask with a wolf snout. The same white spear symbol was stamped on the clothing of each one in the scene, over their hearts. I reached out a hand and shook Hale without looking away from the image. The symbol was an exact match for the one Silas had seen on Warrick's desk.

The holocorder spun around as the soft sound of canvas being pulled aside was heard. The man who entered wore a nondescript grey cloak. He had it pulled forward, shielding his entire face. The

Cloak made his way to the table and the Wolf gestured for him to take the other end.

"When we received a request for an audience with The Spear we were intrigued. The name of our organization is not shared outside our group. We thoroughly questioned a few of our newer initiates, admittedly without success. In exchange for this conversation, I would like to know how you found out about us."

The way the Wolf had stressed *questioned* made my skin crawl, and I pictured what must have been rather unpleasant scenarios for the poor initiates.

"Agreed. Assuming the conversation yields the requested information." The Cloak's voice was richer, even with his words somewhat muffled behind the cowl.

"Typically, we would insist on receiving our end of the bargain up front, but as a gesture of goodwill and in the name of being a gracious host, we'll wait. Now that negotiations are out of the way ...." The Wolf spread gloved hands towards the Cloak. It seemed everyone present had taken great pains to hide their Societal affiliations.

"I had rather thought you'd be able to guess the reason I asked for this meeting, and what information I might require." The Cloak steepled his hands and leaned forward, putting the burden of response back on the Wolf.

"Two possibilities have crossed our minds. One being tolerable. You may wish to join us. Unlikely for anyone from a group who has just been granted the honor of settling a new planet, but perhaps you would prefer to live somewhere else and realize you have another *Choice*." He spat the last word, as though it were something distasteful. My attention increased as he referenced *settling*.

"The less acceptable option is that you are planning to disrupt our plans. That would be regrettable, for you and your fellow settlers. I would so hate to see something mess up Earth's grand entrance."

I felt Hale grab my arm, his grip tight. At least the Cloak was an original Earther. For better or worse, I wanted to know what had happened to them, and who the Spear group was. The Cloak leaned back in his chair.

"You and I both know the settlers have no intention of abandoning Earth. Being here is an enormous honor. I would never ruin it. I'm here because we would seek to understand your motivations. I would like this matter brought to light and discussed openly at the Hub. From what we understand, you want to go back. We cannot figure out why."

The Wolf cocked his head to the side in response.

"It's a bit disappointing to have to spell it out. Can't you see the poison seeping through the Societal system? The whole premise is built on this idea of autonomy. But it's a lie. Everyone is subject to the overlords that are the Coalition delegates and their beloved magistrate. They make everyone to choose a Society and Assimilate. They force uniqueness on everyone and end up with no one being truly unique at all. They encourage sharing perspectives but end up compromising with laws that resemble no one's original ideas. They keep our hands tied with this idea of peaceful existence, to try and prevent another Lone catastrophe, but for what? Our lives, our very existence, are nothing more than a performance. By making us choose a mask to wear for our entire lives, they force us away from ever becoming who we might be together, from what we might accomplish." I found myself disagreeing on the part about peaceful existence, but then I remembered that hadn't happened until after Earth was cut off.

"Then your uniforms are meant to be ironic?" The Cloak gestured around the table at the menagerie of masks before him.

The Wolf stood up and slammed his fists on the table.

"That is not the point I hoped you would have focused on, but yes. Of course they are. They're also quite useful at concealing identities, which is an unfortunate necessity. If all goes well, though, we soon won't need to hide anymore. We can be ourselves once again. We can go home." What did he mean by *home*? Surely, he hadn't meant Lone.

"It's dangerous, and reckless, not to mention—"

A scream drowned out the Cloak's voice. The sound was ugly and violent. I cringed. On film, the Wolf took over the conversation.

"I see we're running right on time. You seem surprised. How delightful. I was hoping we'd have this advantage. You see, I never expected you to go along with our ideals. You all agreed to settle another one of these ridiculous experimental planets, which means you're too far gone for our purposes. You're too loyal to the Coalition and all their useless restrictions. No, I just wanted to get you isolated from the rest of your group. It's much easier to pick off the others when their leader is occupied."

Hale slammed his palm onto the floor next to me.

"He's twisted. This sadistic Spear group is nothing but a bunch of villains, out to butcher the Earthers."

On film, the Cloak turned back toward his masked adversaries.

"You may find we are not wholly unprepared. Many of the other settlers are armed and waiting, in case this meeting went poorly. You won't be able to get rid of us all. We will find a way to let the Hub know of this treachery." The surroundings shifted as the holocorder whirled back toward the Wolf.

"I don't doubt that you would. Conveniently for us, you'll never have the opportunity. We're not here for a slaughter; we're here to teach a lesson. These lives you've lost are the price you're paying for sticking your nose somewhere it didn't belong. As their leader, I think you should be around long enough to let the guilt of that responsibility eat away at your mind, don't you? That's why we'll be leaving the rest of you here."

With no evidence but my own intuition, I could swear the Wolf smiled under his mask.

"You can't mean—"

"Oh, but I do! We'll be cutting Earth off. I think that stranding you here on one of the Coalition's little science experiments is better than just killing you all off. A bit of an experiment of our own. What happens to these little seedlings from the Hub when there's no one to tend to them? Now, if you'll excuse me, I'd like to see how many settlers we did away with before we permanently relieve ourselves of this tawdry planet."

Several of the other Spear members laughed as the Wolf turned to leave. They fell in line behind him, and we, or rather the holocorder, were carried off with the Spear and outside the tent.

As the film emerged onto an open meadow of green covered by a spray of flowers, I saw the chaos of Spear members clashing with all manner of other Societals. Bodies bearing red wounds made a mockery of the beautiful landscape. I heard guttural cries as the holocorder swept past. The Wolf walked across the field, and I noted the settlers appeared to be losing the battle.

An inhuman roar rent the air as the Cloak burst from the tent, brandishing a sword. He moved toward the Wolf, cutting down any Spear members who stood in his way. As he did so, his hood fell back from the top half of his face, and I saw glowing bronze eyes alight with anger. He'd been a Riftian, then, before he'd chosen to go to Earth. He stood facing the Wolf, and I noticed he was tall and broad-shouldered. He was also brain-prickingly familiar, but I wasn't able to figure out why. With a yell, he charged.

The Wolf pulled a sword of his own, and the two began to fight. Behind them in the distance I saw the opening to a large, metallic tunnel with a spoked door.

Even on film, the noise of the fighting was thunderous, a terrorizing mix of screams and weapons meeting. One yell managed to rise over the others, and whatever had been said made everyone sprint toward the Doorway. As they clambered over one another, masks were wrenched from faces. The white sigil painted on their chests was the only thing that distinguished the Spear from the settlers.

The tunnel housing the Doorway started to emit sparks. I longed to yell out and warn them, but I was lifetimes too late. All I could do was sit and watch from the same Hub where Spear members must have waited to cut off an entire Society of people, leaving them adrift in a hostile solar system. Our view took us closer to the crowd, as the operator ran for the only exit off the planet.

The Wolf yelled behind them as he ran toward the Doorway, one arm bleeding.

"Not until I'm over! Don't let them close it yet!" No one paid him any attention as each group continued trying to fight and flee at the same time. An odd sputtering sound came from the Doorway, and colored smoke spilled from the tunnel's entrance.

"That's the signal! It's closing! Get to the Doorway!" The Wolf's sneering dominance was gone. As he ran, he was knocked to the side. Our view got closer to him, and the operator must have turned back towards his fallen leader. The Cloak stood over the Wolf, his searingly bright bronze eyes flaring. Weapons cast aside, they latched onto each other, rolling through the dirt as they clawed and hit.

Behind them, everyone shoved and pushed. I knew they wouldn't all make it through the Doorway, and yet I still held my breath and willed them to move faster. The bodies at the front tumbled through. A shout rang out as the Cloak wrenched the mask free off the Wolf's face. His eyes widened in a shock that I felt crash through myself as well. I didn't want to believe what I saw.

"No!" I screamed the word at the film, and felt Hale's arms catch me as I threw myself back from the images.

The Wolf stood unmasked, his eyes glowing with a golden Riftian light. He didn't speak. His eyebrows were knitted, his expression malicious. He reached forward and wrenched down the cowl that had covered the lower half of the Cloak's face, and I felt the floor start to spin beneath me. The two men's faces were identical, save for the color of their glowing eyes. I felt Hale's hands steady me as I tilted.

"It's going!" A panicked scream came from offscreen. Whoever was holding the holocorder jolted into action, as did the twins—for that is what the Cloak and Wolf had to be. They were too late, though. An explosion rocked the earth as both men were thrown back into the dirt. The image on the holocorder blurred, as if it had been damaged in the blast. After a few blinking shots that showed flames engulfing the Doorway, it started to fade. The last image was of a smoking pile of rubble where the Doorway had been, and it felt like the perfect representation of my emotions.

"The Spear must have managed to kill off any Earthers who made it through that Doorway." Dex's voice made me jump. Evidently, the others had joined us at some point.

"Warrick's office was locked tight. I decided to help in the library, but I couldn't find anything. Then we heard you scream." Dex's voice was soft.

Silas reached out to pull me to my feet. Hale gave me a hug before stepping back, his stare locked on mine. My voice trembled as I tried to hold back tears, but I had to put a voice to what I'd witnessed.

"How did I just see my uncle and father on that film?" Both those men had the same striking nose, the same deep-set eyes. My father's had been grey just like Juliard's, but I recognized their shape all the same. I imagined that if they'd styled it differently their hair could have looked identical as well. Even their builds were the same. I broke down, dropping to my knees and sobbing. Hale was with me in a second, arms wrapped around me from one side while Silas knelt on the other.

"Her father was a Societal? How is that possible?" Cassius's voice sounded from above me.

"It's not. But it definitely looks like she must be a direct descendant. Her father and uncle were identical twins, and an uncanny copy of those two."

I didn't know what to make of it. It felt like my mind was fracturing. If the film hadn't depicted something from generations ago, I would have sworn it was truly my father and Juliard fighting. I took a few breaths to steady myself.

"The Wolf got stuck with them. So did some of the other Spear members. Do you think the settlers spared them?"

"It's impossible to say. Strategically, if it were me, I wouldn't have. Still, what appears on that film took place before the Societals were as violent as they are now." Silas finished the statement as lights flickered on along the floorboards. The system was rebooting. He held out a hand and hauled me up. It was time to go. We ran, not stopping until we were in Nien's classroom.

Hale recapped the film for Digit and Pim.

"And then, well, the Spear leader, the wolf-faced one, um, he was fighting with the cloaked guy, the Earther and ... um ...."

I looked at Pim, the one in the group who'd known me the longest, aside from Hale.

"They were twins. Identical twins. And a perfect match for Dad and Juliard." His eyebrows drew together as he leaned forward to take my hands in his.

"That had to be shocking for you. Given your family's leadership of Verkent and their significant contribution of Societal relics, it's not too surprising to find out its founding members could have been connected to us relationally. Still, though, to see such a thing." He patted my hands.

We debated what to do. On the one hand, Earth was vindicated if we chose to share the information. We had absolute proof that the settlers hadn't conspired in any way against the Hub. On the other hand, my family was clearly responsible for cutting Earth off, and for trying to save it. I was convinced that, if I shared the information with the Coalition, they would assume we also had information on why they couldn't settle new planets. They might demand something I wasn't able to provide. Ultimately, we chose to keep it to ourselves, at least until the Coalition meeting. At that point, I planned to press Juliard for more information.

Aside from how the Societals might view things, I had my own feelings to deal with. We had no way of knowing what had been done to the Spear members left on Earth. Even though it was generations in the past, their appearance made me feel connected to the brothers. Hale and the others had said it didn't matter, but it mattered to me. I was directly descended from one of those brothers. But which one?

CHAPTER 15

Even the excitement that surrounded the very last Societal visit wasn't enough to fully break my melancholy. I did my best to put the film out of my mind, but it was difficult. I had briefly considered trying to reach out to Juliard again for advice, but that option was impossible. Pim and Digit had been correct in thinking that security around Coalition Hall and all the tech areas would increase after our second break-in. Extra grey-clad Hub workers seemed to be everywhere.

Our group went to the Canopy for our final visit. The lush plant life that seemed to cover every inch of our surroundings was like nothing I had seen before. All around were vibrantly pink leaves, deep emerald flowers, and aquamarine moss so saturated in color that I had to touch it to reassure myself it was real. A cooling mist rained down and kept the heat of the jungle-like planet at bay. Our host, Yivu, had furred arms and a long, swishing tail.

He'd walked us through a crowded market with bamboo-like structures and people milling about. A variety of large, predatory felines had stalked through the clearing alongside the Societals. Vibrantly colored birds sat on stands in an outdoor market area. There was a very hyena-like creature having what appeared to be a conversation with one of the merchants. Our host even provided a demonstration of camouflaging and had disappeared into the trees behind him.

The rest of the tour was a blur as I fell back into my thoughts, unable to stop replaying the holofilm in my head. It was only when Hale and I entered Nien's classroom later that evening that I was able to break out of it. We found Sybil in an animated conversation with the twins.

"And the colors! My gracious! I still can't get over them. Imagine the gardening you could do in a place like that. I honestly thought I'd had my mind already made up, but I won't lie and say I'm not tempted. The Canopy was just so breathtaking that it's really a toss-up at this point."

"Breathtaking and deadly. Is she forgetting the part where we walked by those poisonous plants that could *move* and actually bite you?" I elbowed Hale as his voice carried, but Sybil kept chatting away.

At least one of us had been able to focus on the tour. I was relieved when Nien arrived and announced that the final lesson would be just a brief overview of what to expect from the Choosing ceremony. I'd been so caught up since our arrival with the danger we were in, our jaunts through the library, and the film, that I'd failed to set time aside for a very important task. Actually deciding on a Society.

"Before we begin, I hope you'll indulge me as I address a question posed by Sybil. After all, it has to do with my favorite place, the Canopy. I was told you have witnessed the wildlife and people there conversing with one another. We do have a connection to the animals on our planet that is not achieved in other Societies. I wouldn't go as far as to say we talk to them, but we certainly do communicate." I thought back to the Rovers, with their companionable snakes, and tried to imagine a planet where that same bond was shared with all the animals.

Nien continued.

"There is a mutual respect at play. That is not to say there isn't a predator-prey relationship, but despite that, there is no animosity between species. We try to live with the animals and with the land, rather than pitting ourselves against it. In the same way you form different bonds with different people, we may hold a friendship with one animal in a herd but not others."

"What about how you look? Everyone in the Canopy is so different from one another." I tried not to be annoyed at Su Jin's question. I was curious, but I was also eager to get through the lesson.

"While all Societals can see the distinguishing features between them, I would say Canopy members vary the most. Many of the Assimilated traits from my home align with different animal species also present on the planet. You no doubt saw a variety of scaled, furred, or feathered individuals. Some have tails of varying lengths. Some individuals' anatomy may include limbs more adapted to running, jumping, and the like." Nien tallied the options, his short but polished claws gleaming. The conversation got further sidetracked when Sarah and her friend Thea started to ask about different animals from Earth, and whether they were present in the Canopy.

"Dinosaurs? We already saw what looked very much like a pterodactyl on Dagan."

"Not the Canopy, and Dagan does have some rather menacing-looking sea creatures, but nothing on land. However, the Rovers' planet actually does have some. Part of the planet has huge fissures on it, and deep at the bottom are some very large reptiles reminiscent of what you're thinking."

Sarah blanched at that answer, her already pale skin leached of color under her freckles.

"Elephants?" Su Jin gave Sarah a reassuring pat as she changed the topic.

"No! Those are actually just you. I have to say, reading up on your animals I was very excited. If this process goes well, I plan to visit Earth and see them myself. You will get to see a giraffe-like creature living amongst the Kites. Long necks are very useful for catching floating vegetation, you know."

I was antsy, but most Earthers around the room were smiling and engaged. At least the discussion helped ease the tension for some of the others. After an explanation of how three different Societies had some version of crocodiles, Nien clapped his clawed hands together.

"That was a lively discussion! Time to get to the real purpose of tonight's session, though: what to expect from tomorrow's ceremony. There are several key things you'll need to know, including your Societal salute."

"What's a Societal salute?" Derek had actually raised a hand in the air to ask the question.

"I suppose it would be beneficial to run through the schedule of events for the day. Now, when you first arrive tomorrow morning, Iduna or myself will be collecting your written decisions. These will be given to the magistrate, who will announce each of you as you enter the arena where the event is held. The space actually has quite an interesting story. Unlike the rest of the Hub, the floor of the arena is covered with dirt. It was collected from the soil of each of the seven Societies."

"Just great, old Sourface is going to be there on one of the most stressful days of our lives." Hale crossed his arms as he frowned. I recalled the grey-winged woman from the cafeteria who had looked down her hooked nose at us.

"You know what she reminds me of? A hissing, honking, evil-spirited goose." I imitated a bird noise, and Hale laughed. I was glad to be able to cheer him up.

Nien shot a look in our direction as he continued his speech.

"When you enter the arena you will make your way toward a marked spot near the center. The magistrate, Societal delegates, and some of the planetside rulers will be seated in their own box, but projected in front of you via live holofilm. When Warrick states your name, he traditionally announces your parental Societies first. In your case he will introduce you all as 'of Earth.' Once he announces your decision, you will execute the salute of your new Society."

He had us all line up at the sides of the room and stood at the front of the class demonstrating the salute for each Society. Then, one at a time, we had to walk between the other students as he announced us into each and every Society and critiqued our attempts.

"No, Dex, you're not meant to be punching yourself in the chest. You're just placing a fist over your heart. It's meant to show allegiance, not aggression." Dex tried the Rover salute again as Nien moved down the line.

"Very good, Sybil, if you go to the Canopy, they'll be very pleased."

"Why am I making this motion around my head?" Silas demonstrated the Riftian salute as Nien circled back.

"Because they frequently have their hoods up, but by lowering your nonexistent one you are essentially presenting to them the ability to know your true self. Riftians are notoriously closed off to all but their most trusted compatriots."

The idea of knowing my true self was something I was very interested in, but did anyone *really* open themselves up enough for everyone else to see it as well? There were parts of myself I wasn't comfortable sharing with anyone, except maybe Hale. And after what we'd seen on the holofilm I had a whole new worry—that I'd had some penchant for rage passed down through generations. I knew who I was before the Societies. A loving daughter, a devoted member of Verkent, and someone who had tried to have a moral compass. I wasn't sure those traits alone would get me through Assimilation, though.

Everyone had some level of difficulty mastering the Kite curtsy, which involved spinning in a full circle as well as some rolling arm motions. While the Rover salute was relatively simple, Nien had to correct a miserable-looking Sarah several times. Silas stood off to the side silently after practicing the Riftian salute, not bothering to learn the others. Pim and Sybil at least seemed happy and giggled over in the corner as he helped her spin for the Kite movement.

I practiced each salute with Hale over and over, thankful he was willing to help me after only learning the Crew's himself. It had involved a drawing and stabbing motion, as if he held a sword.

"You know," he reminded me after I went through the entire list a fifth time, "if you'd have decided this already, you'd really only need to practice one."

"Kena, could you stay for just a few moments to help me get everything picked up?" Nien held a hand up as everyone else shuffled out the door.

While I was anxious to get back to my bunk and try to work out what to do in the morning, I was intrigued as well. Hale left, promising to grab some snacks for me in the dining hall.

"I know you've observed, perhaps more carefully than anyone else in your group, the way the other Earthers are responding to this process. For all Blanks, and especially for Earthers, it has been stressful and overwhelming. You've been exposed to the reality of the Societies and largely taken it in stride. I do worry about how the Earthers will deal with things once you're separated and trying to Assimilate."

"I think we're all doing what we can to emotionally and mentally prepare for that. The stakes are high, and we can't control everything, but we're stronger than a lot of these Societals give us credit for."

"Yes, but that's not all of it. Earth being reconsidered for the Societies is one of the largest events in our history. Even so, it may pale in comparison to other things on the horizon." He ran a hand down the back of his wiry hair.

"What do you mean?"

"The Choosing is sacred to us, but not everyone wholly supports the current system. You've seen that there are problems with the way things are set up."

"I'd say that's an understatement, given what you're doing to those who can't Assimilate."

"All the more important, then, that you all take the Choosing seriously. In my years at the Hub, I have seen Blanks go where they were pressured to by family and friends. I have also seen some go wherever they felt at home. I can tell you that the successful ones made their own decision. Please encourage your group to make their own selection tomorrow, no matter what they've been told." He stared directly into my eyes, unblinking. I wasn't surprised that he'd figured out Earth's plan to assign people. We'd been careless around him with our conversations. I was lucky he was trying to help instead of ratting us out to the Coalition.

"I understand."

"It could be more important than you realize, for what's coming. I have something for you. Consider it a welcoming gift to the Societies. I hope it benefits you."

He held out a book. Embossed on the cover, I saw shapes stamped into the leather. The image appeared to be a map of sorts.

"Nien, what is coming? Something larger than just the Earthers being in danger, or our planet joining the Societies?"

"You'll have to find that out for yourself. You may be the only one who can." He walked out of the room, and I was left with several new questions and no answers. As I opened the book, I found it filled with a series of dizzying symbols scrawled across the page. I tucked it carefully into my pack, along with my disc.

I wanted to know what Nien had been referring to with *a larger problem*, but I'd have to save myself first. If I didn't Assimilate, none of the other problems mattered. Instead of heading directly to the bunks, I went to the dining hall to fill Hale in and get some Societal coffee before what would be a long night.

CHAPTER 16

As I entered the cafeteria, it became apparent I wasn't the only one who had decided an evening snack was in order. Sybil and Pim whispered to each other at the edge of a table. Sybil seemed to be comforting him, running a hand slowly down his back as he sat with his hands covering his face.

"You know it doesn't matter to me, Pim. I'll take any time we can get." It felt like I was eavesdropping on a very private conversation, and I scanned the group for somewhere else to sit. I spotted Hale walking toward me, his arms laden with food. He'd somehow managed to keep hold of two steaming cups of coffee as well, although it all looked rather precarious. He leaned toward me as he approached, and I just managed to grab both our cups before hot liquid spilled over the top.

"Figured you'd want to take everything back to your bunk. I know you'd rather brood over your decision in a quieter environment."

"How do you know I haven't already made up my mind?"

"Please! How long have we been friends? Don't insult my intelligence. I know for a fact you've put the problems that will affect others first. That can only mean you've put your own choice off until the last minute and will spend most of the night worrying over it."

I filled Hale in on my interaction with Nien.

"What bigger problems could there possibly be? Also, what's he expecting you to do with a book you can't read?"

"Both things I'll need to figure out. Although I was thinking on my way over here when he mentioned larger concerns ... so many things here have survived from the past. The Societies, their antagonism toward Earth. They expect that somewhere the secret to their settling of new planets has been kept safe as well. I'm wondering if the Spear isn't one more thing that's still in play. Warrick had their symbol on his desk, and we know some of them made it back to the Hub when Earth got cut off."

"Yes, but who knows how long it's been there? We can't exactly go around accusing him with no more evidence than that."

I shook my head.

"No, but I think it'd be a good idea to tell at least our group to keep an eye out as they join their new planets, just in case. And I'm not giving up on the magistrate. We may not be able to solve everything until after we've Assimilated, but I could still look into it afterwards. Assuming we make it that long."

As we entered the hallway, I expected to receive a reassuring response from Hale but heard a different voice.

"Kena. Just the Earther I've been looking for. I was hoping for a quick word, if you wouldn't mind a short trip to my office?" Red and silver robes swept around Warrick's legs.

"We both have time, actually." Hale stepped forward and positioned himself between us. Warrick raked a stare up and down my friend and his pile of food.

"I appreciate the offer of your time, Mr. Ochter, but it's actually just Kena I need to speak with. Besides, I happen to know the kitchen staff is at this very moment getting ready to go visit you in the bunks. It seems they've prepared quite the enormous basket of snacks as a sending-off gift of sorts."

Warrick held out a clawed hand to me as Hale watched us. I took it.

"I can meet you back at the bunks."

Hale sighed but turned and headed around a corner. Warrick led me toward Coalition Hall. I tried to keep my breathing steady. He cocked his head to the side, one scaled eyebrow going up as we came to the stained-glass doors I'd entered twice.

"Nothing to say?"

"About what?"

"Well, I find that most Societals are rather impressed. The gems in the door are rather magnificent, wouldn't you say?"

"Oh, yes, it is rather nice."

He shook his head, and as he let out a small sigh, I felt I'd failed a test of sorts.

"Ms. Eckhoff, I had hoped we could start the meeting by being honest with one another. Let's try again, shall we? You know, we also have a rather impressive library of holofilms and books down here." He paused, glancing at me again.

"A shame we couldn't see them all."

"Yes. A shame indeed." The edge of his lip curled upward as he bit off the last word. He waved a bangled wrist in front of his office door as we arrived, and it swung open.

"Have a seat." He gestured to a large wooden chair with an upholstered seat. Red again. The door clicked shut behind us. I sat as he placed himself behind the desk. I felt sweat beading my forehead as Warrick steepled his hands.

A light near the door flashed, and I jumped out of my seat when a beeping noise accompanied it. Warrick let out a breath and relaxed back into his chair.

"There. Now that we're away from any prying ears or eyes, I believe we can dispense with the formalities. I think I already know, but if you could kindly confirm for me just what you were after, snooping around these offices and our library."

I quickly ran over the options in my head. A flat-out lie wouldn't help us at all. And no matter what he did, the Earthers' lives were already at risk. I wasn't willing to reveal what had been on the disc I'd brought but tried to at least redirect the attention away from the others and onto myself.

"I apologize for the intrusion into your offices. It was certainly a breach of privacy."

"I'd call it a bit more than that, but I do appreciate the gesture." He waved a hand at me, and I went on.

"I was interested in gathering more information about the Societies. Who would know more than their delegates? I'm sure you've heard that while some of the Societals have been welcoming, that hasn't been the case all the way around. Each planet is also fairly secretive. There's plenty they don't know about each other but also a lot that they've figured out from a whole lifetime of living here. Given what's on the line with this Assimilation, I'd hoped to give the Earthers an advantage."

"How so?"

"We're just trying to level the playing field. Find out as much as we can. Breaking into your offices was likely the wrong way to go about it, but you know that direct questions don't always get answered here." I kept my hands clasped together in front of me, fearful that if I moved even an inch, he'd see my shaking limbs as I presented the half-truth.

"I'm aware. Even so, you had to know there was a high likelihood you'd get caught. What do you think the response would be if I revealed this little escapade to the delegates? It might cause some unpleasantness for you."

"More unpleasant than the threat of having us all killed if we can't Assimilate?"

He waved his hand, dismissing my concern.

"I meant for the rest of your planet. In addition to your lives, Earth's place in the Societies is on the line. They need it more than you might think. You will be pleased to know that I have wiped any evidence of your little excursions from our backup security files."

"I do truly appreciate it. But, why?" If he had told the truth, it helped us by limiting who had the information. I was still suspicious of his motives.

"I'm the magistrate. I am the current leader of all the Societies here. I'm also someone who pushed quite hard to reach back out to Earth. There's a lot riding on this for me, and my position here will be in grave jeopardy if it fails. Having you booted from the process before we even truly begin goes against my plans."

"What plans?"

"Those are for me to know. Suffice it to say you can move forward with the Choosing and Assimilation as planned."

"Then, why pull me in here? Why tell me at all? If you have your own agenda you don't want to share, why bother bringing me into it?"

"Because I am not the only one watching. It's important you know that. There are other players at the table here, Kena. Earth's agenda, mine, theirs ... we're all playing a very risky game. It would benefit you to consider there may be more at stake here than just Earth's reputation, or even the lives of your group. There are even more serious problems on the horizon." It was too similar to what Nien had shared. Whatever they were referencing in their frustratingly vague way, it had to be the same thing.

"Such as?"

"Have you ever bothered asking yourself why the Societies approached Earth now? Even if this is the soonest we could have found you, and it wasn't, your planet is in complete disarray. What benefit could there be to us reaching out to you? Conversely, consider Earth's history, or Lone's. There are some people who dedicate their entire lives to ensuring a catastrophe like that never happens again, and then there are others who are eager for it."

"What part are you expecting me to play in all this? Even if I do represent the others in Verkent, what could be the point of pulling in one person?"

"It's a calculated risk. A Choosing of my own, if you will. As you move forward, I would encourage you to look at the present issues. Open your mind to the possibility that what happened in the past didn't end there."

"Do you mean the Spear?"

"And what is it you think you know about that group?"

I think it's still around and you might be leading it, almost slipped out, but I managed to redirect.

"Perhaps Verkent has a little more information than you think we do. Although, before you ask, I can assure you if I had anything about settling new planets I would have handed it over. What I do know is that the Spear was a dangerous group of zealots who ruined Earth's past, and if they're still around could threaten our future."

He twisted his chair around and stood up, the motions swift and graceful.

"You're quite smart, Kena. I'm feeling very pleased with my decision to speak with you. I would encourage you not to tamp these thoughts down but continue to explore them. Now then, I believe you'd like to get back to the bunks. I'm sure you have much to consider before tomorrow. I look forward to announcing you during the Choosing." He waved his wrist toward the door, and it opened as he sat back in his chair and picked up a pen.

I rushed back to the bunks, unable to truly breathe until I sat down next to a waiting Hale.

"You look awful." He handed me a scone, and I filled him in on the conversation.

"So, he's not turning us in to the other delegates?" I shook my head.

"Then why bother with the discussion at all? And why *you*?" I glared, and he held up his hands in a mock surrender.

"I don't mean it in a bad way. But he's smart. He knows you'll just tell me and the others. So why take you, alone? It doesn't make any sense."

"You're right, and honestly I wondered the same thing. Maybe to intimidate me? If so, he did an excellent job."

I wanted to solve the riddles Nien and Warrick had left me with, but we'd run out of time. Hale made his way back to his own bunk. Hours later, I had papers laid out in front of me with jotted notes for each planet across the blankets. My indecision was high enough that I'd gone ahead and thrown all the Societies back into the ring for consideration.

I needed to be as strategic as I could, given that my very life was at stake. I was able to eliminate three Societies very quickly. I had no desire to repeat the animosity I'd experienced with the Clan. I wanted at least a fair opportunity to Assimilate, and I didn't trust that I would get one there. I eliminated the Rovers for the same reason. If they were willing to push people into sink pits on the tours, I didn't trust a real opportunity there, either. Dagan was the next to go, strictly based on the fact that I found the creatures there terrifying and didn't much care for the idea of using a reed until I grew lungs.

The last four were harder. I knew we'd been told that part of what created a successful Assimilation was an actual desire to be in the Society. That meant that, as much as I loved my friend, the Crew was out as well. I had every confidence Hale would do well, given how enthusiastic he was, but I knew my complete unease with the pirates could prevent me from succeeding.

I mulled over the final three choices. I considered each of their traits. I wanted the highest chance of survival. It wasn't just the abilities I was after; it was the culture and lifestyle. The Rift was too much of a risk. It was entirely possible there was something I hadn't learned about them that could help me, but it was equally likely I'd end up trapped in a cave with no escape. Ultimately, I decided on the Kites. At least I already had a potential friend there in Ryshal. It was also where I truly wanted to go, which Nien had suggested would help.

Decision made, I was able to sleep. I even allowed myself to dream of wings.

CHAPTER 17

All the Blanks waited together the following morning in a large room off the side of the arena. From where we stood, I heard the voices of the crowd echoing down the halls. The anxious faces and tense whispers between Earther and Societal Blanks made me think I wasn't the only one who was nervous. Cassia didn't resemble herself at all as she stood off to one side of the group, biting her lip and twisting her arms as Cassius patted her shoulders. He whispered something to her, but she shot him a tear-filled glare in response.

Dex, Pim, Silas, Digit, and Sybil were all huddled together. One benefit of my decision was staying with the older couple. Digit had Silas to help her out in the Rift. I felt a bit bad for Dex, getting stuck with the Clan alongside Derek, but he'd picked it freely. I grasped the stone Ugdol had given me inside my pocket. I still had no idea what practical use it had. I'd kept it with me as a reminder that at least some of the Societals supported us.

"Everyone in my family's been a Kite. I mean, how are they supposed to visit me underwater?" one of the Societal teens was asking his friends as I walked past. Some of the other Earthers stood together nearby. Sarah spoke in a strained voice as her friend Thea comforted her.

"We're going to get burned or bitten by a snake or thrown into the sand. And if that doesn't work, they'll just kill us anyway." Sarah predicted. At least they'd been assigned to the same place.

I jumped as I felt a hand on my arm. Hale pulled me into a hug just as the chatter around us died down. The night before, I'd tried to think of what to say to him. We had no way of knowing for sure what would happen to us after the Choosing. I hadn't been able to come up with the words to let my best friend know what he meant to me. And even if I had, knowing Hale, he would have laughed them off anyway.

"Not her again." Hale groaned, and I turned to see Iduna. She looked down her nose at everyone, grey wings so straight they could have been starched in place behind her. She stepped onto a small stage that had been erected. Beside her, Nien took the stage as well, his coarse hair combed into place.

"Does she just have an entourage follow her around to set that thing up everywhere?" Hale wrinkled his nose as she tapped on a podium with her short talons.

"Attention! Attention, everyone! We will be lining you up alphabetically for all Societal Blanks. Any *other* participants will line up at the end."

"Harpy." Silas didn't lower his voice as he spoke. Iduna pinned him with a frosty glare, and he returned one.

"I really hope I won't be seeing much of her on Kite." Cassius joined the group, his sister beside him. Her eyes were rimmed in red.

"If she tries anything, if she even *thinks* of saying something cruel to my brother, she won't like the result." Cassia's brows furrowed as she gazed up at the Kite, and her voice dripped with venom.

Nien stepped forward as Iduna smoothed her feathers and took a seat.

"Thank you, Iduna, although I would clarify that we are equally happy to be welcoming each and every one of you into a Society. Please remember to execute your salute and then move toward the group of people from your chosen planet on the arena floor. I assure you that, between the banners they hold bearing their seals and the incredible level of noise they'll be making, it will be impossible to miss. The last piece of important information to share with you is a reminder of our initial Assimilation period. Once today's festivities end, you will be sequestered with your chosen Society for the next several weeks."

"Divide and conquer. Not a bad strategy," Dex whispered out the side of his mouth.

"This gives you a chance to fully immerse yourselves in your chosen planet, and build new relationships there. While I know the event you are most anticipating is the Coalition meeting, there is another opportunity to see each other. We will hold a special event here at the arena about halfway to the meeting, at which point you can all mingle and check on each other's progress."

"Or see who's on the chopping block if they haven't started to Assimilate yet," Hale hissed into my ear. It was good news, though. That would give us another chance to check in with everyone. Maybe if there were any Earthers in jeopardy at that point, I could get word out to the task force. Up front, Nien continued.

"A month after that is when the Coalition meeting will begin. This year's will be attended by all Societal delegates, planetside rulers, and Earth's representatives. At that time, we will make final decisions on the success or failure of everyone's Assimilation, and the future relationship with Earth. The meeting takes place over several days, and you will either attend in person or watch via live holofilm."

An ear-splitting gong sounded from out in the arena.

"Ah! It's time!" Nien swept off the stage. After the line was formed, announcements began. One by one, the Societal Blanks made their way into the arena, until only a huddle of Earthers was left. A Hub worker at the entrance waved toward us.

"Well, someone has to be first." Cassia inclined her head to the Hub worker and walked through the arched entrance.

"I suppose I'll go next, then." Sybil made her way through, and Pim followed. Everyone else started to fall in behind them. I was near the back, after Digit. It felt like no time had passed before most had gone in. I tried to take slow, deep breaths. I pictured the floating greenery of Kite, and that helped.

"You're going to do great." Hale leaned in as he spoke, and I was able to take a deep breath for the first time all morning.

"You too." I turned around and gave him a hug. The Hub worker cleared their throat, but I held on for another few seconds before I dropped my arms.

As I entered the arena, the stands were lined with Societals. The Coalition's box was far above me, but a projection from a live holocorder was positioned directly on the arena floor. It looked as if Warrick were standing right in front of me in the dirt. He held a piece of paper in his hands that had my Choice written on it. I held my breath, waiting for him to announce my placement with the Kites.

"Kena Eckhoff of Earth has Chosen ... the Rift."

I started the Kite's salute and then froze as the words settled in my mind. He was wrong. It had to have been a mistake. I looked up at the flickering copy of Warrick in front of me. He smiled, tongue flicking against pointed teeth. I knew what I'd written, but I didn't feel I could challenge the magistrate in front of so many people, not with the other Earthers on the line. I'd wanted wings, but this felt like falling. Amid all the stress connected with the Choosing, even I hadn't realized how badly I wanted to be a Kite until the opportunity was taken away. And now all I could do was mourn.

I managed to execute the Riftian salute, but I couldn't muster any genuine emotion. The movement was supposed to be one of trust, and I didn't trust any of the Societals. I didn't even trust myself, not in the Rift. A memory of what I'd seen on the holofilm of my ancestors flared to life in my mind. Their glowing Riftian eyes haunted me as the image of the two brothers circled around in my brain. The mocking laughter of the Wolf rang in my thoughts, and for a moment it drowned out the noise of the arena.

I wanted to scream, but I knew any outburst would be dangerous. From the moment Choices were announced until the Coalition meeting, everything would be just a test to see whether or not the Blanks Assimilated. Throwing a fit and accusing the magistrate of being a liar seemed a less than wise move. I allowed myself one last moment of grief over the Kites, then locked a determined stare onto Warrick. I decided I would go along with the ceremony, but then I'd find a way to move to the Kites, or use being in the Rift to my advantage.

Applause from the crowd thundered in my ears as I moved to the blue Riftian banners with their blackened tree. Unlike the other Societies, they didn't yell or clap as I made my way toward them. They all inclined their heads in unison, but that was it. At least the relative quiet provided an opportunity to think. I doubted my assignment to the Rift was a mistake, given my all too coincidental conversation with the magistrate the night before. There had to be a reason he'd placed me there, assuming he was responsible. It could be as simple as him knowing what we'd seen on the film. If he'd somehow witnessed what we had in the library, maybe he knew that placing me in the Rift would throw me off emotionally. It was also possible that if he was aware of my ancestry, he was hoping I could uncover something about the brothers. If they had been the leaders, they most likely were also privy to information about settlement that the Coalition had lost.

There was also the possibility, however remote, that someone else had sabotaged me. Nien came to mind briefly, but a cryptic literary gift hardly seemed like enough motive. Unless he, too, was after something. After all, he'd mentioned the larger problems coming to the Societies. Perhaps he thought my being in the Rift would help with those, or help me. In that case, denying the Rift wouldn't do any good. I needed to fully immerse myself in the process to have any hope of finding whatever they were after. And if I did, I had no plans to share it. Across the group of Riftians, Ariadna smiled at me, arms twisted in front of her as she chewed her lip.

"Hi Kena. I, I wondered how many Earthers would decide on the Rift."

I stopped myself from making a face. After all, she had picked the planet on purpose. At least I thought she had. Was I the only one being forced to go somewhere I hadn't intended?

"Yeah, I spent a lot of time considering. I'm as surprised as everyone else with where I ended up."

"Oh. Well, I'm sure you'll be happy with it. My sister Vanya assured me we'd all really like it there."

I forced myself to stop looking up at the Coalition's box and turned back toward her.

"That's exciting. It must be nice, knowing you'll be able to see your sister so much."

"Oh yes, we get along really well. Now our whole family will be there, and I'll finally get to see the rest of the Rift."

It hit me that we'd hardly seen more of that planet than the inside of a rock. I had no idea what to expect.

"Have they said what it's like?"

"Vanya wouldn't tell me anything exact, b-but she assures me we're in for a pretty massive surprise. She told me not to let the cavern make up my mind about the rest of the place; that there's a lot more there than meets the eye."

"Do you mind if I stick with you when we first get there? I know you haven't seen it, either, but you probably know a lot more about the Rift than me."

"S-Sure. That would be nice. I'm going to go check in on a few of my friends and congratulate them. I'll meet you back here before we leave."

As she wandered off toward the mingling groups, I did the same. I didn't have time to question all the other Earthers individually, but the assigned Choosing was helpful. It made it easy to spot whether someone had ended up in the wrong place.

As I walked around the arena, everything seemed to be moving along as it should. If anything, I was surprised to find that the first several Earthers I passed were all with their assigned Society. Even Cassia and Cassius had split up, as instructed. I passed a miserable-looking Sarah with the Rover group and made my way toward her.

"Sarah, I'm honestly a bit surprised you didn't pick differently." Her eyes widened and she scanned the group around her, as if she were watching for someone.

"But ... this is what I was told. Have you seen Thea? She was supposed to be over here with me, but she never showed up."

It was a potential lead. I walked around, scanning the crowd for the other teen. Thea was two groups over, with Dagan. She was easy enough to spot. Her tawny skin and burgundy hair stood out against their oily sheens. Before I had a chance to ask her anything, Sarah had run past me and hugged her friend.

"Thank goodness! Did you come over here to say goodbye to someone before we head out? I'm not sure how I missed you at first."

Thea shifted her feet and looked at her shoes.

"I didn't come over to see anyone off. I'm not going to Rover. I'm going to Dagan."

Sarah blinked rapidly, and her cheeks reddened underneath her freckles.

"That's not possible! You're assigned to the Rovers. We're both supposed to be stuck together." I cleared my throat as people started looking over.

"Sarah, Thea, perhaps a discussion for another time?" I glanced pointedly at the group around us. Sarah stomped her foot.

"I'm going to be miserable over there. And now I'm going to be miserable *alone*? They may end up killing us all anyway, and you'd rather go become some gross swamp person than help your friend." She started to tear up.

Thea took a step back, and put a hand up to her face as though she'd been slapped.

"This is what I truly want. I knew you'd be surprised, but I thought you'd at least be happy for me. I've always loved the water. I tried to tell you to pick something else. You didn't have to go to the desert."

"Oh, what would you know about it! You didn't even tell me what you were planning. I can't even be around you right now, traitor." Sarah stormed back toward the Rovers as Thea watched her walk away. I gave her a hug.

"She'll be okay. And if she doesn't Assimilate ... we're working on something." I had no specific plans but hoped it would reassure her at least a bit.

I spotted a hand waving at me across a crowd of people. Hale made his way towards me. As soon as he got within range he grabbed my arm and pulled me to the edge of the arena.

"What happened? I thought you'd decided on the Kites. Why would you pick that depressing, damp cave?"

I made my own voice even quieter than his before responding and kept my expression neutral.

"I *did* choose the Kites. Somebody altered what I wrote. Warrick is my main suspect, but I suppose it could be anyone that had access." I filled him in on my idea to look around for anyone else who'd been swapped. We moved through the crowd together.

Pim and Sybil were on the fringe of the Kite group. I noticed her knuckles were white as they gripped Pim's hand. I was worried about what would happen if she didn't grow wings, and equally concerned about how uncomfortable it was supposed to be. Somehow it had seemed like a better idea when I'd planned to be there to support them. Still, I was glad they had ended up where they wanted. Pim leaned in.

"Glad we'll get to see you off before you leave. I must admit I was a bit surprised at your decision." I told them what I'd shared with Hale.

"Any chance one of you wrote something other than Kite?" I glanced around the group, but they all shook their heads.

"Sybil and I will find some of the others to ask and help keep an eye out for the assigned Earthers." Pim gently pulled Sybil along behind him. I looked over at Cassius with a second task on my mind.

"I know you're not super familiar, but Sybil, she's like family. She's very sweet, just a bit shy. I wonder if maybe ..."

"I could look out for her and have her back, like I do with my sister? Absolutely. I can spot kindness, and that lady has a heart of gold. I'm going to go see Cassia off, and I'll ask her about any Earthers who ended up in Canopy by accident while I'm over there."

One small worry relieved, I moved back to the problem at hand. I found Dex over with the Clan. He had his arms crossed and was glaring down at Mancio and Derek.

"No one misplaced here, although I wish these two had been. If I can get them through Assimilation without one of them inciting a violent incident, it'll be a miracle."

I sighed and started to walk with Hale back to his group. Then I spotted Digit chatting with several Crew members. She was showing them her Earth circuitry tattoo. I moved toward her, but Hale grabbed my hand.

"I see what you're thinking, but you're wrong. She wanted to go with us. I'm not that surprised, honestly. She told me hackers don't have to follow rules. Sorry, Kena, it looks like it's just you."

"Then, in addition to surviving and completing Assimilation, I'll have another thing to work on. I need to figure out who put me in the Rift and why."

"The *who* part is easy enough. It's that weaselly magistrate. And you need to watch your back with him. You remember what was on his desk. If the Spear is still around, and if he's part of it, they didn't seem too fond of Earthers."

Around us, the others slowly peeled off as the celebrations wore down and groups started gathering to leave. Cassius stopped by to report that, while Su Jin had ended up with his sister in Canopy, she'd also intentionally altered her assigned spot. Hale made a last-ditch suggestion.

"We could get Pim over here and try to sneak back to the programmer area to contact Juliard. He would know what to do. Or maybe, you can just refuse to go, just join the Kite group, and by the time they notice you'll be in the right spot, or—"

"Hale, I appreciate the offer. But I'm not going to put you or Pim at risk that way. I'll just have to go along with Assimilation for now, and try to figure it out on my own. I suspect that if I refuse to go, my life's forfeit anyway. You'd better get moving." Hale drew me into a hug. He squeezed tight before he released me.

"Don't worry, Kena. We will figure this out."

"Yeah." I grasped at something more to say as he jogged away from me, waving as he went, but nothing came to mind. I was truly on my own. I managed to follow the large group of old and new Riftians as they made their way to the Doorways. I didn't notice any turns or twists we made on our way up there. I was numb inside, my mind tingling and spinning. I'd made my way nearly up to the front of the line before I snapped back into the moment. The Doorway loomed over me. Once I stepped through, there was no guarantee I'd come back.

"Um, Kena. Sorry, but were you ready to go through? Y-you've been standing there for a bit." I turned and saw Ariadna behind me.

"Yeah, sorry. Just a big moment, you know?"

She offered me a smile.

"Absolutely. I've been jittery all day, and I've grown up expecting this. I'm sure for you it has to be really daunting, huh?"

"Yeah, just a bit." I laughed at the understatement.

Bolstered by the thought I'd have at least one friendly face with me, I took a deep breath and a step forward.

CHAPTER 18

We emerged into the Rift in the dark tunnel that led to the cavern. Lights ignited around our group. Each delegate held their arms out, and glowing bulbs floated over their palms. It was different from the torchlight during our former visit. As we waited for the remaining members of the group to enter, I examined my surroundings in a way I hadn't been able to on the previous trip. The walls were all worn smooth, like rocks at the shore of an ocean. I reached out a hand. While the air was warm, the stone was cool.

Bayard stepped out in front of the group as the last people made their way out of the Doorway. There were notably fewer new Blanks in the Rift than were joining the other Societies I'd seen in the arena.

"Welcome. The delegates and I are thrilled to have you with us." Bayard's tone was polite, but it was the same even and calm voice as before and didn't convey his supposed level of enthusiasm. If I had nurtured any hopes for a warm welcome, I would have been sorely disappointed.

"On your visits, each of you had the opportunity to view the cavern and several of the attached antechambers. At that time, I asked for your trust. Today, you will officially be introduced to the real Rift."

My mind fired pictures at me in rapid succession: a cramped, damp cave with a blanket, a small tent with the comfortable Riftian breeze next to the lake, a hammock suspended from the impenetrably dark ceiling above the lake. As our group began to move forward, Bayard continued.

"It is a Riftian tradition that we host a dinner welcoming you to our Society. Your Assimilation will officially begin tomorrow."

The cavern was just as awe-inspiring as it had been on the first trip. As I looked up at the dark ceiling, I realized I hadn't seen a Riftian sky. Did the atmosphere not allow them to venture outside?

"Kena!" The urgent whisper grabbed my attention.

"Silas?" I wanted to smack myself. In my shock from earlier, I'd forgotten the first person I should have gone to. Silas was one of the better individuals to be stuck here with—an Earther who knew what not to say, and when. He was also one of the most likely to have a good strategy.

"I'm pleasantly surprised to see you here." Silas kept his voice even, but looked pointedly at me in the dim light.

"A last-minute *occurrence*. Before we arrived, I'd been planning on getting a set of wings."

"I see."

"Before we left the arena, I was trying to find out whether anyone else had any last-minute alterations, but I think I'm the only one."

He nodded, and a frown settled over his features.

"Do you think this could have anything to do with your recent discussion?"

I suspected it had everything to do with Warrick. I was so busy trying to think of a way to verbally code a response that I bumped into the person next to me as we exited a tunnel.

"Sorry," I murmured, looking up so I could apologize face to face, "I was just thinking about ..."

We emerged from the tunnel into warm, soft light. It felt like the sun, but it was impossible to say for certain because the light was filtered through an all-encompassing view of leaves. Everywhere I looked, there were towering giants of trees before us. I couldn't have been more shocked if we had been expected to sleep next door to a crypt, which some of the Earthers had joked about. Looking up and around, I saw only signs of life. Bayard's voice drew me away from the chatter of birds that flitted through the trees.

"It is always a privilege to witness new Riftians' first reactions to their real home. You will be housed together in the Creekside oaks for this evening, and tomorrow permanent lodgings will be determined."

As he gestured toward the trees, I realized that, while they were larger than any redwood or sequoia we had, their foliage was wildly variable. There were easily dozens of varieties. Bayard continued forward, and as he did, I noted that the ground we were walking on felt somewhat plush under my shoes. Looking down, I saw soft, springy moss. The grey jumpsuit supplied by the Hub made me feel washed out in our lush surroundings. We walked into a clearing where a semicircle of massive trees faced a creek. Some of the roots dipped directly into water that flowed out of sight.

"As Riftians generally value personal space, even your temporary lodgings will be private. After you have been assigned a tree, please unpack and change. You will find suitable attire waiting for you.

The delegates will then be accompanying you to dinner. Now then. Ariadna, one. Tad, two. Zanthra, three." As he listed names, he pointed to various colored doors that all but blended into the base of each tree. It seemed keys were not required. He didn't hand out any, and as Ariadna pushed on her assigned red door, it opened, allowing her to disappear inside.

"You don't suppose that our permanent residences ...?" Silas looked back and forth between me and the foliage.

"Yes, I'm fairly certain we'll be living inside them."

"Silas, six. Kena, seven." Bayard didn't glance up as he pointed toward our assigned dwellings.

"Well, no time like the present." Silas squared his shoulders and marched forward. I followed suit. My own door was a soothing shade of ocean blue.

The interior that greeted me was cozy. There was a small eat-in kitchenette area in the entrance. There was also a bed and side table. The only interior door led to a washroom. It even held a small tub. How running water worked inside a tree I couldn't begin to guess.

I pulled a few items out of my bag. At first, I debated carrying the disc with me, but decided it was less conspicuous to leave it out of sight. I took an additional risk and jotted some notes about the Choosing. My theories had created too much chaos stuck inside my head. Warrick was still my most likely suspect. Nien was on the list as well. I added Iduna, then scratched her out. We'd had hardly any contact with her. She clearly disliked the Earthers, but I suspected she would have messed up more than one of our placements if she'd been responsible. I added Bayard's name as well. I couldn't fully discount that, instead of someone sending me from the Hub, I had been pulled in by a Riftian.

Laid out on the bed were the clothes Bayard had mentioned. After what we'd already seen, I wasn't shocked that they fit perfectly. I appreciated the chance to get rid of the repetitive grey jumpsuits.

The pair of soft cream leggings I'd been given were form-fitting. Brown boots laced over them to my upper calf. A cream top went underneath a deep green bodice that laced up the front. I was hesitant to tie the corset-like laces, but it was surprisingly comfortable. The last item was a hooded cloak. Its color hovered somewhere between grey and green. I put it on but chose to leave the hood down.

When I stepped back outside, I noticed the other Blanks were all dressed similarly. Silas's outfit featured soft black pants and boots, a red tunic with a shirt underneath, and a reddish-brown cloak the same shade as some of the trees we'd passed on the way in. Like me, he had it on, but had left the hood down off his face. His grey eyes stood out against the outfit, and it suited him far better than the jumpsuits had. Ariadna's top featured purple underneath a grey cloak the same color as the rocks that lined the creek. Bayard waited in the clearing alongside several other Riftians, one of whom stepped back after hugging Ariadna.

"If you will all please don your cloaks if you have not already done so. Hoods will remain down for the evening. Follow me." Bayard turned and walked farther into the trees.

A short distance away was another clearing. The trees were different in form but no less gargantuan in size. More of the glowing orbs were present around a dining site, floating over poles that surrounded us. The light cast a golden sheen on everything. The tables in front of us were wooden, with large matching benches.

Bayard led us all to an empty one. He then walked up toward an even larger table centered in front of the others. He took a seat next to another man, who looked so regal I could only imagine he was the planetside counterpart to Bayard's role. More Riftians joined until the whole clearing was filled with cloak-covered Societals. Their eyes glowed in the dusk.

As the regal man next to Bayard stood, everyone went quiet. He was tall, broad-shouldered, and had a deep brown beard. Lines of grey slashed through his hair, which gave him a distinguished look. The lines under his eyes and weathered features hinted at hard-won experience. His eyes were dark in color and the glow emanating from them was a black light, if such a thing were possible. While everyone else had light cloaks in shades of grey, dark green and blue that reminded me of river rocks, his was a fur of some sort. As he stood, I could also see that, unlike the other cloaks, his didn't have a hood at all.

"Welcome. As I am rarely at the Hub, I assume introductions are in order. I am Kidan, current monarch of the Rift. I, and all the Riftians here, appreciate the magnitude of this Choosing. We also recognize the additional consideration you had to make when Assimilating to our Society in particular."

I wondered if he was referencing the level of doom and gloom associated with their reputation. I looked at Silas, but he just shrugged. An all too familiar sense of foreboding swept over me, and I did my best to hold it at bay.

"As you are aware, in extreme circumstances, other Assimilated members may move Societies if necessary."

I grasped Silas's wrist under the table and squeezed. It was another piece of information that no one had shared with the Earthers. We had no hope of successful Assimilation if we were in the dark on the rules. For a brief moment, I thought about sharing my botched choice. If switches were allowed, Kite was an option. His next words ruined that plan before it had fully formed.

"This is not possible for Riftians. There are protected secrets here that cannot be risked. We do not allow anyone in or out after your initial choice. We do not take this obligation lightly. It is with sincere gratitude that we accept each new Riftian, knowing that you do not part from us until you make your journey through the Lake of Death." Kidan finished, and around the clearing, others nodded. Silas and I shot each other wide-eyed stares.

I sat stone still as waves of shock rolled through me. There was no chance my placement in the Rift had been some sort of oversight. The fact that Nien hadn't mentioned Riftians being stuck made me even more suspicious of his motives. He wasn't trustworthy. The thought hurt. I'd felt like he actually was rooting for us. There was a slim possibility he'd been ordered away from warning us, but that still meant he hadn't been willing to take a risk to help us.

It also solidified my suspicion against Warrick. It was a more diplomatic way to get rid of me. If I didn't Assimilate, I would be dead anywhere. By placing me in the Rift, he'd limited my options even further. Even if the tenuous relationship between Earth and the Coalition dissolved and the others returned home, I wouldn't be allowed to leave.

Following the off-putting speech about dying, we were invited to dig into the food that was being passed around the tables. Without really looking at what I grabbed, I scooped several items onto my plate. My head and my stomach warred with each other. The sense of impending doom that had closed in around me was definitely an appetite killer. My stomach attempted to remind me that only half a piece of toast from breakfast sustained us. My appetite won out, as I decided I could either be worried and hungry, or worried and full.

I was thankful that we were seated with the other Blanks, and I didn't feel the need to be drawn into conversation. Silas and I sat eating quietly. When everyone was finishing up, Bayard stood.

"As Kidan stated before, we welcome you to the Rift. We honor the sacrifice you have made in Choosing us. You will be learning both skill and diplomacy as part of your Assimilation, to help us maintain the respect and esteem we have been afforded at the Hub. I would have you know that while you ultimately chose to be here, you would not be drawn to this place without the qualities we seek. We consider that, as much as you have chosen us, the Rift has chosen you."

The way he worded it made it seem like the Rift's environment was a living, breathing entity. What did it mean that I hadn't chosen it at all? I worried the very planet itself planned to reject my attempts to hide out in it.

"From this point onwards, you are a Riftian. There are many decisions ahead regarding what role you will take on here. The important thing I would like you to take away from this evening is that we are thankful you are here. We in the Societies are at peace, but loyalty within the Rift is important. From now on, anyone here would lay down their life for you, because you are one of us. Where you came from before this is not important, and no one here will treat you as more or lesser because of it. We accept you. From this moment on, you will always have a place. From this moment on, you are home." It was a nice speech, but it would have meant more if I had trusted them not to kill us.

Bayard's eyes scanned the table of Blanks. It could have been my imagination, but it seemed like his searing blue eyes lingered as he looked into mine. He held up his glass, and all the Riftians at the high table did the same. As he stood, so did all the other Riftians around the clearing. Only the Blanks remained seated. Without warning, the clearing became blindingly bright. As I looked around, all the Riftians were glowing, and not just from their eyes. They'd all thrown off their cloaks. Each Riftian's body was lit by gleaming symbols of some sort, trailing up their arms, shoulders, and for some even their necks.

They were all similar and yet strikingly different in their shapes and patterns. Like snowflakes sharing beauty, but with no two exactly alike. Even more shocking than the brilliant glow was the expressions they wore. Looking around at every face, I saw sincerity. While in other Societies I had always been able to spot at least a few people looking askance at the Earther oddities, the faces staring at all of us were resolute. If anyone was unhappy to have Earthers in their family, they didn't show even a hint of it.

All those at the head table, including Bayard and Kidan, had removed their cloaks and glowed alongside the other Riftians. Kidan's gleaming black marks were a sight to behold, but Bayard was downright breathtaking. All the Riftians held their glasses up.

"Home." They said the word in unison, and then drank. The marks began to fade until they were just a soft glow. When the clearing was dim once again, they lowered their glasses and sat.

After dinner, Bayard accompanied us back to our temporary lodgings.

"I am sure you must all be exhausted after this auspicious and long day. Please rest. Tomorrow we will begin. You have seen the other Riftians that accompanied the tours. You will be more formally introduced tomorrow, as they will be working directly with you. We will also sort out housing. Until then." He turned and strode away from the grove as the Blanks headed for their various trees.

"So, that was news, huh?" Silas lingered beside me, and neither of us moved toward our doors.

I gave a dry laugh.

"It was definitely that. If they didn't share it with us, I don't suppose they bothered sharing it with Earth's task force, either. Do you see any way out of it?" If I was going to trust anyone from Verkent with a dangerous but life-saving strategy, Silas would have been at the top of the list.

"Not yet. But I'll certainly be keeping it in mind." We stood for several more seconds, silent together in the dark.

"I didn't expect it to be beautiful like this." I gestured at the foliage above us. A soft white light filtered through the trees.

"I didn't expect it to be this peaceful." I glanced over at Silas as he watched the trees.

I bid Silas goodnight and walked back to my tree. As I looked behind me, I saw his face turned toward the moonlight, eyes closed. Even with all the chaos that was unfolding, a smile lingered on his face.

CHAPTER 19

I woke the following morning to light streaming through the window. I pulled on the clothes I'd worn the night before and realized Bayard hadn't specified when we were supposed to be meeting him. As I exited my small lodgings, I saw the delegate was already outside, chatting with a group of Riftians. I recognized a couple as silent participants in our tours. I walked toward them, and Bayard gestured at the group.

"Some of your instructors have joined us for the morning. This," he said, pointing at the auburn-haired man to his left with glowing amber eyes, "is Samell, one of the arborists. And this is Hok, one of our weapons specialists." He indicated a rather enormous man on his right with tanned skin, black glossy hair, and eyes that radiated silver.

"Pleased to meet you." The larger one extended his hand. His grip was uncomfortably tight, and I could tell he hadn't had much practice at shaking hands. I pulled my hand back and tried not to wince, shaking it out once he'd turned his head.

"A pleasure." The slighter one, Samell, held his hand out as well. His handshake was much softer.

"Silas, please join us." Bayard waved my fellow Verkent member closer. I tried to reconcile the friendlier version of our host to the stoic and silent delegate that had guided us through the cavern.

"I think you and Kena in particular will enjoy working with your instructors during Assimilation." Bayard introduced him to the two men as another Riftian walked up with Ariadna. It was the same woman who had hugged her the night before. Their features were somewhat similar, their light brown skin completely flawless. Ariadna was considerably shorter. Her older sibling also had a wilder look about her, with leafy green marks illuminated along her arms. Half her head was shaved short, but the other half hung down in a combination of loose and braided pieces.

"Allow me to introduce Vanya. One of our weapons specialists, who will be working with you." Bayard indicated the woman. She nodded but didn't offer a hand. Ariadna beamed beside her.

"You'll love my sister," Ariadna whispered to me as Silas struck up a conversation with Vanya.

"I'm sure I will."

"Now that everyone is here." Bayard redirected everyone's attention back to himself as the last teens emerged into the grove. He provided a quick introduction to the other Riftians before he continued.

"You will work with each of them, and several others, during Assimilation. Use this time to learn and to consider what you may be interested in pursuing long-term. You've no doubt noticed the Rift acquired fewer Blanks than the other Societies. This is not atypical.

Even so, we will be dividing you into even smaller groups throughout Assimilation."

Silas interrupted with a question I'd had myself. It had taken a backseat to the whole "dying to leave the Rift" bit, but it had been the first thing on my mind when I woke.

"What about all the glowing marks? What are those? How do we get them?"

"Markings are something every Assimilated Riftian wears. Each possesses a different meaning. It is the job of the Reader to interpret them for you as they appear. We do not place them on you; rather, markings appear of their own accord. The rate at which they are acquired is individualized. As each of you start to gain some, we will organize a meeting with our Reader for you. She can help you interpret their meaning."

After Bayard called names to divide everyone up, I found myself in the third group alongside Silas, Ariadna, a girl named Zanthra I'd seen her chatting with before, and two other Societal Blanks named Tad and Thrax. I was thankful Bayard had placed me with the two individuals I already knew.

"First group, you'll be going with Samell to start. I'm sure it comes as no surprise that, given our environment, we remain on top of the populations and use of different trees. Second group, with Vanya and Hok. You'll begin some basic prerequisites required for weapons training. Third group, you'll be with me. It's time to find you some permanent lodgings." It seemed as if the silent tension Bayard had carried through the Hub had fallen from his shoulders. Unlike Vanya, his attire had sleeves, but I could still see the edges of glowing sapphire marks.

"Bayard, if you're here helping us Assimilate, are there currently delegates in the Hub?" I questioned.

"Yes, a few of the other delegates returned this morning. When it is time for the Coalition meeting, Kidan and I will travel there as well." As he answered, he led us into the woods.

I hated that while my natural reaction to Bayard was a feeling of respect and admiration, it was accompanied by suspicion. He seemed genuinely helpful, but that didn't mean he hadn't put me in the Rift. At what seemed to be no particularly distinctive place, Bayard halted.

"Here we are! Now then, there's really not a whole lot to this process. It's quite simple; you just pick a tree. We clear out and prepare new areas of the grove before each Choosing. That being said, just because it is simple does not make it easy. Riftians are not generally nomadic. Even if you travel to other inhabited parts of the planet, which is quite rare, your home will be left undisturbed for you. It is incredibly important that you choose wisely. The right space can leave you feeling comforted, safe, and relaxed at the end of the day. A connection with the forest is also a key step in Assimilation. For many decisions here, we will urge you to listen to your intuition. Being in tune with your own inner guidance is key to being a Riftian."

"So, we just rely on our feelings for this?" Silas's tone held the faintest trace of sarcasm. Bayard lifted one eyebrow as he responded.

"In a way. You've heard of Riftian projection, the feeling we cause in others. To successfully Assimilate, you will need to watch for the feelings caused by the environment around you. And for the feelings coming from yourself. Unless there are questions, you are welcome to begin. Our builders have taken care of the basics. Any personal touches will be left up to you."

The others had already spread out in various directions. I looked at Silas, but he just shrugged. As I chose a path to my left, I wasn't certain what I was looking for. I decided if I was going to be able to follow Bayard's advice, I needed to sit and think. Rather than looking for the tree, I started to look for a calm spot to rest.

A few minutes later, I spotted a stream. I knelt down beside it and cupped my hands, taking a drink. Afterward, I sat along the edge of the stream and closed my eyes, listening to the soft current. When I opened them, I saw a shaft of light that had broken through the trees above me. It slanted and trailed off into the woods. I did my best to do as Bayard had instructed. I cleared my mind and waited for the feeling the Riftians caused with their projections. After a few moments, I felt a pull. I followed the light.

The beam came to rest on the side of a large tree that reminded me of an elm. It had a tall and sturdy base with some upward-facing limbs, but several that randomly curved out. The leaves were jagged around the edges but smooth as I reached out to touch one. The branches off the side swept downward, their leaves creating a blanket over the ground. It almost reminded me of an enclosed porch. It was perfect.

I wandered under the branches, in no hurry to get back to the group. Bayard had certainly been correct in one thing; I felt calmer under the tree's awning than I had anywhere else since arriving at the Hub. As I circled the tree, fingertips trailing over the bark, I felt the texture change. A worn, green door stood in front of me. Pushing it open, I saw an interior very similar to my temporary lodgings. Rather than explore further inside, I sat on the ground and leaned back against the trunk, shaded by the boughs of the tree.

"A fine choice." I jumped at Bayard's voice and looked up to see his sapphire eyes peering through the leaves. As I scrambled to my feet, I realized I hadn't heard his approach at all.

"Are the others ready as well?"

"Oh yes, they finished some time ago. You've been out for a few hours." One side of his mouth tilted up in an amused expression.

"I, what?"

"It's a positive sign. You're already connecting here. Even so, the rest of the group is gathering for lunch, and afterwards you start training with Vanya and Hok. If you're ready to go?"

He held a hand out to me. As I reached for it, I felt I was agreeing to more than lunch. I was making a promise to myself that I really could be ready for whatever change Riftian Assimilation held. As we headed back to the group, I realized that the feeling of "otherness" I'd sensed from the delegate before was greatly diminished.

"Bayard? The projection from the Riftians. I felt it pretty strongly when we visited last, but I'm not feeling much of anything now."

"You're wondering if this is part of Assimilation. Yes, a near-instantaneous piece, and another sign that you'll be successful. It signifies that the Rift is accepting you, and you are accepting it."

After a quick break for lunch, our group followed Ariadna's sister as the two of them chatted. Vanya stopped us when we reached a large, dirt-filled arena with trees around its edges. As I looked left and right, I could see several smaller rings as well.

"Welcome to the arena! This is where you will be working on both weapons and hand-to-hand combat training on a daily basis. Hok and I will be your main instructors, although we'll have some guests from time to time." Vanya beamed as she swept her arms out toward the rings around her, and I sensed a level of pride.

"What sort of weapons are we talking about?" Silas asked. I wasn't surprised that he seemed especially interested in the lesson.

Vanya smiled at him and gestured for us all to follow her.

"You're welcome to take a look." She led us to yet another tree, wide at the base, with double doors. Hok pulled them open for everyone to enter.

The place was wall-to-wall weaponry, from the floor to the ceiling. There were swords of a seemingly endless variety, bows, arrows, long poles with all manner of metal shapes on the ends, crossbows, maces and quite a few items I couldn't even name. I glanced around and saw a stairwell leading even further in.

Hok pointed to it.

"Keep in mind, most things here are housed in these trees. The root system is massive for some species, including this one. It makes it the perfect place to house all the weapons."

Vanya stepped up beside Silas, proffering one of the Rift's glowing orbs.

"I can take you down, if you like." She smirked at him.

"Lead the way." Interest flickered in his gaze, and I suspected it had as much to do with Vanya as any weapon in the room.

"H-he likes my sister," Ariadna said, leaning in. I agreed.

We entered the stairwell. Weapons hung on the walls the entire way down.

We eventually hit a landing and found ourselves in yet another room within the tree, filled tip to toe with metal and wood.

"If we're in the tree's roots, shouldn't the passage get narrower the further we go?" I was a notorious plant killer back on Earth, but I knew that much.

"Bubble roots." Hok grinned as he strode past Ariadna and myself into the room. I liked Hok. He was fun despite his hulking exterior. He seemed more open than Bayard, and I hoped to learn a lot from him and Vanya.

I was excited to see the weapons for myself, but also to have the opportunity to answer a question Verkent had been curious about. What kind of weapons was Earth dealing with in regards to the Societies? What we saw inside the tree wasn't high-tech in the slightest. The walls and tables were stacked with a variety of daggers, knives, clubs, spears, swords, bows, crossbows, hammers, axes, and even a large table of darts fringed with various colors, but not a single gun or more modern weapon was visible. Given that the Societies weren't at war with each other and hadn't shared information on any outside hostilities, we hadn't been provided much knowledge of their fighting skills. Then again, they'd managed to hide a lot of important information. If they hadn't shared about their combat methods, that just made me all the more eager to learn them.

"Are we going to be fighting with all of these?" I couldn't tell if it was Tad or Thrax who had spoken. The two were within an inch or two of each other in height, and looked similar.

"No. We can provide you with basic lessons to gain familiarity with different types of weapons, but you will only specialize in one. No one can become a master of all weaponry. You will find yourself drawn to some more than the others." Vanya reached behind her and touched the fletching on one of her arrows as she spoke. She wore a quiver and had two daggers strapped to her as well.

"You will all be provided extensive training in utilizing your bodies for defense, meditation, flexibility, and focus. We believe that is equally important to any weapon you could wield." I did a double-take as Hok finished. I realized that while his sheer height and muscle were reminiscent of Dex, there were some stark differences when he spoke.

"Why not more advanced weapons? Your technology is far beyond what we have on Earth. Why not utilize massive lasers, perfected machine guns, something like that?" Silas touched on exactly what I'd been wondering as he looked to Vanya for a response.

"While it is true that we have the ability throughout the Societies to do this, generally we find it distasteful. We have an interest in skill against skill, not who can blow the largest hole in the ground. At a certain point, it stops being about targeting an enemy and starts being about decimating civilians and civilizations. There are weapons that have such capacity at the Hub, and other Societies have their own rules as to what they consider a skilled versus advanced weapon."

"No automatic weapons, then."

Vanya tilted her head at his response.

"Whatever that is, no. We put the majority of our scientific advancements toward helpful technologies such as structural safety, advanced medicine and the like."

I was tempted to ask how they'd managed all those advancements but hadn't figured out a way to settle new planets and avoid killing their own. It wouldn't have helped, though. I needed the skills the weapons instructors had, and I couldn't afford to risk offending them.

"There's at least hope for a sleeker replacement piece for this, then?" Silas pulled his pant leg up and revealed his prosthetic. I knew this was a sort of test, as I'd seen him do the same thing with people on Earth.

Vanya looked at it, and blinked a few times before she burst into laughter.

"If you're looking for a newer or more polished appendage, I'm certain we could help you out. You just won't be able to shoot anyone with it." She chuffed him on the shoulder as he covered his leg again, grinning. She'd passed. Silas would never have tolerated someone feeling sorry for him.

"Guess I'll just have to try out swordsmanship, then." Silas didn't miss a beat as he strode over to one of the tables. He hefted a broadsword off the nearest stand with relative ease.

After we'd looked our fill, Vanya and Hok led us back to the surface. We stepped out of the weapons shed, and I saw Bayard awaiting us in the dirt arena. He stood next to several other Rifitans, who were placing the last few weapons onto tables and racks in the center.

"As I'm sure you've noticed by now, the Choosing is only the first of many decisions you make. Some things happen without your conscious control, but we are always continually making choices that lead us down one path or another. Once again, I will encourage you to listen within, and let that guide you. In this way you will pick the weapon you will work to master."

He was right. Getting sent to the Rift had been outside my control, but once there, I had my own decision to make. If I were truly honest with myself, the childhood dream of carefree flights through the skies had died once we'd arrived at the Hub. Even if I'd gone to Kite, I would have been worried about Assimilating. I also had the other Earthers to think about. If I rejected the Rift, I risked not just myself, but the relationship of all the Earthers with the Societals. I needed to embrace the situation I'd found myself in.

"W-we're doing this now?" Ariadna's voice squeaked as she cast a wide-eyed glance at her sister.

Bayard nodded, as usual managing to make the motion look dignified. Thrax was instructed to approach the table, and he walked the length of it just once before hovering over the center for a moment. He picked up a pair of sai, their three points shining, before Hok walked him to the side of the arena.

Ariadna was called up next. She glanced at her sister. Vanya's daggers glinted in the light. Perhaps, working with weapons, she was an exception to the "best at one" rule. Her face gave nothing away as her younger sister stood in front of a set of small daggers similar to hers. Ariadna reached toward them but her hand stopped, hovering in the air as she continued to scan the remaining items. She took a deep breath and looked at her sister once more before pulling her hand back from the daggers. She strode to the end of the table and grabbed a flail that ended in a spiked mace, off one of the racks.

The weapon wasn't at all what I would have anticipated someone of her size and timidity to pick, but Vanya grinned as her sister walked toward her. Ariadna was beaming.

"Kena." Bayard's smooth voice startled me, and I jumped before moving toward the table.

I started walking slowly down the line. I passed a sword but dismissed it before even registering what style it was. I also walked right by the bow sitting on the table. Vanya carried it easily, but I couldn't picture myself using the weapon with any level of grace. The next few items were the same, just not meant for me. I paused briefly at a falx, the curved blade holding my attention, but continued on. As I came to the end, nothing really felt right. I looked at Bayard.

"We have to choose something from this table or the racks?" The glow in his eyes increased an infinitesimal amount.

"You are welcome to pick anything that is currently in the arena, unless someone else already wields it."

It seemed like a test, and I intended to pass. Taking a deep breath, I tried to clear my mind the way I had when looking for a tree. I was pleasantly surprised when I felt a pull. The process reminded me of when an item was lost and I had to mentally retrace my steps to find it. I was visualizing a path to an object I'd never seen. I walked toward the far side of the arena. On its edge were a small group of trees, their shade obscuring another weapons rack that seemed to be supplying some other Riftians training in one of the smaller rings. Beside the rack, resting against a tree, lay a double-sided ax. I knelt to pick it up and found it lighter than I'd expected. I likely should have waited for instructions, but my instinct was to swing it, so I did. It felt like a natural extension of my arm. Before we'd left Earth, if someone had told me I'd be swinging a massive ax around, I would have been afraid I'd let the thing slip and slice into my own leg. But the weapon in my hand felt perfectly balanced.

"Interesting choice." Hok stepped up from behind me. It was hard to adjust to the silent movement of the Riftians. I lowered the ax and turned to see Bayard had joined him by my side.

"Does this count?" I held up the weapon, worried that its location would exclude it.

"It must. The ax is meant for you." With no further explanation, Bayard returned to the table, where Zanthra was perusing the weapons.

"With the specialists, we always hope to have a well-rounded group. People who are good with a variety of weapons. We'll definitely be able to instruct you on how to use that, but if it comes as naturally to you as first picking it up, you may surpass us quickly. None of us has ever really felt a connection to that piece." Hok pointed at the weapon in my hands.

"We all pick one, but you and Vanya seem to be different." She had the bow and daggers; Hok had a pair of sickle swords strapped to his back and held a staff I doubted very much was a walking stick. He smirked.

"You have a keen sense of observation. She and I are dual masters. It's very rare. You have to become incredibly good with a weapon to be rated as a master. Until you can use it as easily as you would a limb on your body, it's a rating you won't receive. To become a dual master, you're training with the second weapon that you weren't initially called to. You have to find a master who is willing to teach you. It takes years of effort, not only on your part but also theirs."

"How did you come to be dual masters, then?"

"My father taught me once I'd Assimilated. I was initially drawn to the staff, and I'm very effective. Still, he felt I would need something a bit sharper. He passed on the skill with the swords."

"And Vanya?"

"She found a different teacher." His statement was cryptic, but I didn't push. I was thrilled he'd shared anything at all. It was a sign that I was truly being accepted as Riftian, and not seen as an outsider. We made our way back to the other end of the arena.

Silas was last to go, and he walked up to the table with the sword he'd picked up inside still held in his hand. He lifted it up onto his shoulder.

"All set."

"Another interesting choice. It seems today is full of surprises." Bayard had the smallest hint of a smile. Once again, I felt the urge to trust him. I remembered what he'd said about projection not affecting Riftians, but I wasn't going to take his word for it. Maybe some of the others were trustworthy. Truthfully, I'd have to open up to some of them if I wanted a support network and the best chance of survival. As a delegate, he was just too close to the Hub for my liking.

"Training with these weapons will become a part of your daily routine. This will continue through the Coalition Meeting. By that time, if you wish to pursue other interests you will have the option of limiting your time in the arena. Trust and listen to your instructors. Our specialists are vastly knowledgeable, even if your weapon of choice isn't something they personally work with."

I found myself vowing that I would master the ax I held. If the worst happened and I didn't Assimilate, I wasn't going down without a fight. Not even two days in the Rift, and the girl who had been afraid to hold a pick-ax to defend her friend in the Clan seemed far away.

CHAPTER 20

The next morning, our group was headed off with Samell for a lesson in arboriculture. Ariadna skipped beside me.

"I'm really excited for this training, aren't you? Not only does the Rift have this amazing forest, but we get to learn all about it!"

While curious, I couldn't match her level of enthusiasm. Still, Ariadna was so sweet that I faked some excitement. Secretly I longed for the next training with Vanya and Hok. Samell stopped us in a clearing where tables and planters of all kinds were set up. I supposed there was no need for a greenhouse in an environment like the Rift. He moved among the different plants, his movements jumpy and his marks flickering. I'd noticed some Riftians seemed to maintain a very even glow, like Bayard. Others seemed to have marks that changed frequently in intensity.

"These are samples of the most common plants you will encounter in the Rift. Arborists are responsible for cataloging them. We track their uses, locations, and populations. We have a very important role here in making sure we do not overuse any of the resources. Almost everything here can be traced back to a plant. Our homes, our clothes, our banquet tables, and much of our food. If you choose to spend a lot of your time training in arboriculture, we will also move on to more advanced uses. Many of the plants are medicinal or, adversely, harmful. We have workers who specialize in mender-related uses for plants, as well as poisons and antidotes."

Beside me, Ariadna leaned forward on tiptoes. Samell passed several clippings around our small group. With each one, he explained their uses and basic care. Then he called us up individually to discuss the trees we'd picked out to live in. He said he wanted us to have an appreciation of the individual nature of each of our dwellings.

He smiled when he got to Ariadna's home.

"A gleaming willow. Excellent choice. I live in one myself. Coincidentally, a fairly popular pick among future arborists. The willow sprays are quite useful for medicinal purposes." Ariadna smiled under the praise. She clutched at my arm as her turn ended.

"Did you hear all that, Kena? H-how fascinating! Who knew I could do so much with just the tree I live in? Also, what he said about the arborists. Do you think that would be a possibility for me?"

"I bet you'd be very good at it, if that's what you'd like to specialize in." I felt protective of her. She and Vanya seemed so close; I couldn't imagine the weapons trainer accepting it if Ariadna didn't Assimilate. I didn't think I could have, either. She reminded me a lot of Sybil, so timidly optimistic. I thought of the other Earthers and hoped they were doing okay.

Up front, Silas described his tree, an enormous aspen with leaves not even starting until the branches were several stories above his head. Samell declared it a strong choice, which hadn't surprised me in the least. He also informed us that Silas's home retained amber leaves most of the year, shedding them in what he called a jeweled cascade of foliage. When I described my own tree, Samell seemed far more intrigued by its solitary location than its type.

"Aha, so we did have someone decide on one of the outskirts dwellings. How wonderful! Before each Choosing, we prepare a cluster of homes in specific groves, but we always have some more isolated options throughout the forest. They're not often picked, although some of our more interesting residents often come from them. I'll be very curious to follow the journey of your Assimilation." I was proud to have chosen something unique.

The rest of the lesson was engaging enough, but I wasn't particularly drawn to arboriculture. I certainly didn't have the same level of enthusiasm as Samell and Ariadna, their expressions rapturous as they examined each twig and leaf.

The first few days at the Rift followed much the same pattern. The trees all seemed to have similar sparse interiors, but mine felt homey regardless. I relished the feeling of calm that swept over me when I entered it after a day of activity. Before my arrival I'd thought of Assimilation as primarily physical alterations, but the changes I experienced first were internal. I felt a sense of belonging I'd never experienced before, even with Verkent. It made me feel guilty. After all, I'd been sent here by someone else. If I belonged in the Rift, it was more difficult to remain angry at whoever had sent me.

Even with the lessons, we had ample free time, and I spent much of it wandering around the forest. It was the kind of beauty I didn't think I could ever get tired of. I often sat with Silas. Occasionally we pulled out Nien's book and stared at the mysterious symbols. We alternated between discussing the others and trying to figure out what had happened with my Choosing. Our best guess was still the magistrate.

"From everything you told me, he seems the most likely culprit. He has power, he's clearly got a strategy in mind; he's just keeping it close to the chest. Make no mistake, though, you being here benefits him in some way. And I still think he saw what was on that film."

"What do you think he's after?" I asked. He ran a hand over the stubble that had grown on his chin.

"Best guess, the Spear is still active. If their leader was from here originally, it makes sense; they had a strong hold in this Society. It's possible he just sent you here to dispose of you, believing either you wouldn't Assimilate or you'd be trapped here when things go poorly with the task force and the Coalition. Or the opposite. The head Earther was from here, too, and he seemed like a well-respected leader. Maybe you being here is meant to bolster you in a similar way, as leader of Verkent. It seems unlikely, but it's possible he was trying to help you somehow."

"He might be trying to assist me, even if he is doing this for himself. That would put us on the same side. If that's the case, he has a funny way of showing it," I grumped.

Still, it was impossible to deny how well I'd already begun to fit in with the Riftians.

"Again!" Bayard instructed from the side of the training arena. It was only our fourth weapons training, but he'd come back around to see how things were progressing.

Breathing heavily, I swung at Hok and his staff. He sidestepped easily, and I missed by a wide margin. Bayard sighed and gripped the bridge of his nose. I might have been insulted if he hadn't had the same reaction to every new Riftian at training. It appeared he was difficult to please.

"You are wasting energy. Energy is valuable. At any given moment, you have a finite amount. Do not frivolously spend it on punches you have no intention of landing. You are lashing out in frustration, and desperation. Your moves need to be calculated and well thought-out."

"I don't have any time to think them out! If I had, he would have anticipated and hit me before I even got close." My temper had snuck out, but I didn't regret it. I had potentially limited time. I had no intention of wasting it on timidity.

"And yet, you didn't get close regardless. That is part of what training is for. Plenty of individuals want the ability to be an amazing fighter, or linguist, or leader. All of those things require practice and skill. You practice over and over and over until the thinking becomes second nature, habitual. Many are very disappointed when they realize much of the magic and abilities they think they are Assimilating into also require hard and consistent work."

I was sweaty, I was out of breath, and I was ready to take a nap. But I also respected what he said. I had begun to realize that the Riftians' values often lined up with my own, even when they were frustrating. My dad had also believed in always being willing to back up anything with hard work.

"If you want to be excellent at it, first you have to be willing to be terrible at it repeatedly," I muttered one of my father's mantras to myself under my breath.

Bayard took his fingers off the bridge of his nose.

"Exactly!" He nodded with enthusiasm.

I smiled, glad to have said or done something right.

"Consider the other Societies," he said, his voice growing louder so that the other training pairs stopped to listen. "Kites may grow wings, and they may fly, but to be truly great at soaring through small crevices or avoiding loose rocks from their planet's atmosphere, they must train. Dagan can all swim, but knowing the movement patterns of their various creatures and how to avoid them requires hours of study if they want to venture outside their domes. Similarly, the Crew may seem reckless, and many are, to an extent. Still, to work their way up the ranks of their ships and command full groups requires years of effort. They don't take the safety of those under their command lightly." Everyone watched him as he wrapped up the point he was making. I was glad to hear what he said about the Crew. Hale was my biggest worry, outside of my own predicament.

"With many Societies, the skills they are learning are useful every day on their planet. It is my hope you will discover how the skills you are learning translate into other daily activities you will use in the Rift. Even so, fighting in and of itself may seem either a waste of time in peaceful planets, or a skill you wish was instantaneous. Neither is the case. We hope you do not need to utilize this direct skill frequently but recognize the importance of it. Therefore, you will continue to put in hours, days, and years of hard and consistent work if you wish to master at least one weapon. Now." He turned his attention back to our ring, where Hok paced across from me. "Try again."

Even after limited time in the Rift, it was clear to me the other Societies misjudged them. In the Hub it had appeared they were always calm and controlled. Perhaps that is why the others thought of them as being so somber and organized. In reality, the Riftians were more like the snakes that the Rovers valued so highly. Poised and ready to strike. They were calculating and didn't believe in wasting energy or emotion where it wasn't justified. I imagined them being quite formidable if they ever felt the need to reveal their skillsets. I respected the control it took, not only to have the abilities they possessed but also to humble and temper themselves. In addition to bolstering my own skills, it would benefit me to win some of them over to Earth's side.

After several days of training, I had fallen into a comfortable pattern. I'd also come to a decision. Vanya and Hok were good people. I watched Ariadna's interactions with her sister closely and became more and more convinced she'd never allow her sister to come to harm. They could help us if they chose to.

"Today, bracers." Hok walked around, fastening the items around each of our arms as Vanya explained them.

"Useful in archery, but we also utilize them to block attacks. These are made of a unique Riftian material called ocala. It has a similar quality to the other textiles here. It is both lightweight and extremely durable. Ocala also helps to absorb and distribute force."

Hok had reached me and attached the first bracer to my right forearm. I held it up, marveling at the lightweight material. Its appearance reminded me of leather, but it had a softer, smoother quality to it. Like everything else we'd been provided, they fit perfectly. I was a bit surprised to find my bracers a solid black instead of the more common Riftian neutral tones.

"Where does ocala come from?" I shot a glance at Hok as he finished helping me with the second one.

"Trees. The answer here is nearly always that things come from a plant. Ocala is a very rare variety around here. They only harvest limited amounts, and our arborists keep a particularly close eye on their population, given how tricky they can be to grow. They won't allow us to ever harvest an amount that puts it in a negative growth pattern, so, while it's durable, you have to care for it well. They don't lightly hand out second sets, so try to go easy on me in training." He winked before moving on to help Thrax.

The response made me laugh. I stood more chance of damaging the things by failing to defend myself from his blows than anything else. After we'd all been equipped, Vanya and Hok stood in the center of the circle as we gathered around. They struck out at us, Hok with his staff and Vanya with wooden counterparts of her daggers, as we attempted to block their blows. The bracers had an almost numbing effect; I felt the soft thud of impact with each blow rather than a stinging slice through my arm. I suspected bruises were forming underneath, but I was just proud that I had picked up the motions and blocked the majority of strikes.

Hok managed to nick me just above the bracer when I moved my arm too slowly. I'd allowed myself to get distracted by their movements. He and Vanya weaved around each other and the circle with grace I'd only ever seen in a ballet. It was mesmerizing. I hissed in pain as I withdrew my wounded arm and shook it. He'd been using very light blows, but it still stung. Next to me, Silas grunted as the same thing happened to him.

"Your problem is a lack of ease." Bayard's voice drifted over the group as he materialized from the sidelines, appearing unannounced and undetected, as he often seemed to.

"You're progressing quickly, and I commend you for that. However, do not become complacent, merely getting body parts into the right spot at the right time. The secret is to move with the fluidity of water. To appear effortless. Right now, your movements are forceful, disjointed. For all of you, your motions are the loud banging of a drum. It's eating away your energy slowly, which is how Hok and Vanya have managed to get the best of you. What you need to do is think of it more like a flowing melody. Continuous, graceful movements."

Bayard gave a slight nod to Hok, and they walked silently to the center of our arena. Our group backed away. Hok tossed down the staff we'd been training with and grabbed his sickle-swords from the straps on his back. Bayard gave the slightest inclination of his hand and they were both a flash of movement.

There was no denying they both moved with a grace I had never possessed. Bayard had said *fluidity,* and that description certainly fit their motions. While I had never seen myself train, I could tell the difference instantly. When I blocked, I could feel the effort, the sharpness of my motions as they collided with my opponent's. Bayard looked more like he was doing some form of martial arts or professional dance. Each time I swatted away an attack, I felt the impact. Bayard swept the blades along with him without ever being touched.

Hok's movements were equally impressive, although there was a clear ferocity behind them. It was more evident than ever that he and Vanya had absolutely held back to an extreme degree to be able to train us. I imagined that was tricky, given his sheer size. He had to be at least six foot four, with broad shoulders and massive arm and chest muscles. Bayard was also tall, but Hok's sheer mass made it look like he towered over the head delegate. Bayard moved like a swooping bird in flight, parrying some blows with ease using nothing but his bracers, and sidestepping others. Hok had a similar level of control, but he looked too predatory for the movements to come off with the same elegance. With no prior indication that the end was nearing, Bayard twisted his way into having an arm around one of the swords. He moved inside Hok's other arm, and in the blink of an eye had hold of one of Hok's swords. Bayard pressed it lightly against Hok's neck. Somehow, he'd also managed to use his other arm to grab ahold of Hok's wrist holding the remaining sword, pinching in such a way that Hok's grasp on the weapon was awkward and loose.

"Balance, level-headedness, fluidity. These will all help you as much as mastering moves with a weapon or your own body." Bayard twisted and released Hok as he spoke. Hok had a sheen of sweat on his arms and forehead as he went to put away the swords. Bayard didn't even have redness in his cheeks.

The delegate strode away as our group went back to practicing, and my awareness of my own bodily limitations was at an all-time high.

CHAPTER 21

We were scheduled to report again to the arena the following morning. I woke up to warm sunshine coming into my tree and a bracing cup of Societal coffee. I'd adjusted to the routine quickly. The days of training amid the surrounding trees felt more *right* than any time I'd spent on tasks back on Earth. When I entered the arena, the other new Riftians stood in front of Hok, Vanya, and Bayard, inside one of the training rings. My eyes were drawn to another figure emerging from the tree line, whose features were obscured by the shadows.

A hand wrapped around my wrist, and I turned to see Silas staring down at me.

"What are you doing?" he asked as he released my arm.

"What do you m—" I looked down at my feet and realized I was halfway out of the arena, headed toward the stranger. I gave my head a shake to clear it. Riftian projection was no joke, and I'd never felt a sensation so strong. Even the impression Bayard had given off before the Choosing hadn't come close to the draw I felt toward this newcomer.

Vanya clasped arms with the stranger before turning back to our group.

"Today, we will be working on something different. While much of our training has been focused on weaponry, you all had the opportunity yesterday to observe the importance of being able to move well with no weapon at all. That in itself can be utilized offensively or defensively. Fell is an expert in this skill."

The figure stepped forward and removed his hood as he took his place next to the other instructors. Under the trees, it had appeared he was covered by their shadow. Standing in the light of the arena, even with pale skin, he managed to blend into them. His cloak was nearly but not quite pitch-black, a perfect match for his hair where it swept his shoulders.

His eyes lived somewhere between blue and purple, a deep but vibrant shade that I found myself unable to name because it simply didn't exist on Earth. The soft glow emanating from them smoldered like coals at the end of a campfire.

"I will be instructing you on the art of forest walking. Before you successfully use your movement to fight, you need to understand the concept of controlling your own motions."

His rich voice only added to the pull I felt, and I had to physically will myself not to step closer to him. He might have been assigned to work with us on forest walking, but his projection was stronger than that of any Riftian I'd come across. I didn't like feeling so out of control.

I distracted myself from the ludicrous urge to run to the stranger and embrace him by cataloging the rest of his features. Not at all shocking was the fact that he was tall. It was far rarer for Riftians to be shorter, like Ariadna. His build was somewhere between Bayard's lithe but clearly athletic form and Hok's undeniable mass of muscle. He glanced in my direction as he finished his introduction, the twilight-colored eyes searing into me. The effort of staying away from him made me lightheaded.

"... of course, just because they're beautiful and the groves that are occupied are relatively tame certainly doesn't mean we don't have our fair share of predatory creatures as well. Mangots, ixtors, and pentalls, just to name a few."

"Pentalls aren't dangerous! I've seen one at the Hub. One of the computer technicians who works alongside my brother keeps it as a pet. He's just a harmless, puffy little avian that sits on the desk and eats nuts and seeds." Our instructor raised a brow at Thrax's interruption.

"That pentall is a special case. Ketar, his owner, went through the Choosing the same year as me. We learned forest walking at the same time. His pentall was very young and had been separated from its swarm and injured when he found it. It took months of rehabbing, and since it couldn't be released back to the wild, he kept it. Typically, though, pentall travel in groups. They operate with a mob mentality. They may look like small puffy clouds flying about, but if you wander too close when they're nearing a frenzy, they'll swarm you and strip you to your bones. Those beaks are hiding rows and rows of small, needle-like teeth. While unlikely, given it's now their nesting season, it's always possible we could see some today. Everyone will need to remain alert and aware of their surroundings during these lessons."

A vivid and violent image filled my mind. I wouldn't have been as calm as our instructor if I'd come across a horde of carnivorous birds.

"None of the creatures is inherently good or bad. It's simply a matter of learning their behavior and respecting it. Today, we'll be walking to a clearing a couple hours away to gather petals for our Reader, Ama. You will all meet her as you attain your markings. The first principle of forest walking is silence. To start, we'll need to get an idea of your current skills. Please observe me as we make our way into the forest, and do your best to mirror my steps."

"Has your sister mentioned anything about Ama?" I kept my voice low as I whispered to Ariadna.

"Not until after the Choosing. She says Ama can see into your mind and soul just from reading your marks."

That wasn't good news for me. If I managed to get any, what incriminating things would she see? I was very likely descended from Riftian traitors. If the Societals as a whole were still hung up on that, I was willing to bet the Riftians took it more personally. Then there was the rather large matter of my complete lack of choice in being in the Reader's Society in the first place. Given the sanctity of the whole process, I rather doubted she'd appreciate my deceit in remaining there.

By an hour into the hike, it was apparent to me that forest walking was not going to be something I held a natural talent for. Our group moved high above the ground on a series of moss-covered logs that formed a natural spiraling stairway around a waterfall. At the base of the falls was a series of separated, multicolored pools that sparkled like gems.

"Kena! I can hear each of your steps, even though we are on soft moss. You do not need to press your feet down so hard to maintain balance." Fell's voice carried on the soft breeze from the front of the group to where I walked at the back with Ariadna. My earlier sense of enchantment with him dwindled. The frequency of his reminders had done nothing to stimulate improvement. I had all the grace of a swan wearing clogs.

"W-w-where do you think the colors come from?" Ariadna stared down at the multihued pools.

"Good question." Silas beat me to a response, casting a glance up toward Vanya as he spoke. In spite of his leg, forest walking seemed to come easily for him. While it was possible that he was already Assimilating the Riftian's increased balance, I was certain his natural athleticism had to be helpful.

"Crystals line each of the pools. The pools' inhabitants vary as much as their color. Some contain lovely water florals; some contain schools of ataran, which will clear you off just as easily as a pentall swarm in the air." Vanya smiled at Silas as she spoke of the dangerous fish, and I had a hunch she'd come more to see him than to help instruct.

"Space piranhas." Silas chuckled to himself.

No sooner had the words left his mouth than a loud rustle filled the trees around us. The sound rose to a thunderous roar in a matter of seconds.

"Pentall!" Fell yelled the warning to the group.

"Fell, the hollow!" Vanya shouted as she waved an arm toward a tree with a massive hole in its center.

"Follow our steps!" Her voice was drowned out as the pentall burst through the trees.

As I stared at the swarm of approaching birds, my first thought was that they were quite cute. Puffy, cerulean, and about the size of our heads, with beaks like a shortened toucan. Then the group pulled their beaks back, revealing rows of tiny, needle-like teeth. They started screeching in unison. The sound hummed through the trees unpleasantly, so loud it shook the very logs we stood on.

With Ariadna in front of me, we scrambled after the rest of the group. We were nearly to the tree where Vanya and Fell reached their hands out toward us when Ariadna screamed. The diving birds buffeted her as she frantically tried to wave them away. Everything seemed to slow as I watched her lose her balance, her hands wheeling through the air. Her mouth was open in surprise as she fell backwards over the edge.

"No!" Vanya and I screamed at the same time.

I threw myself after Ariadna. The air was knocked out of me as I landed stomach-first on a log with my arm hanging over the edge. A scream escaped me as something pulled painfully on my arm. I looked down to see Ariadna dangling from my hand.

"H-help m-m-me!" she squealed, her legs kicking as she tried to heave herself up.

I sensed footsteps above me and turned to see Fell. He was balanced on his toes at an impossible angle, and I couldn't imagine how he didn't fall as he reached down to haul Ariadna up. Vanya stood beside him, rapidly firing arrow after arrow at the swooping creatures. Birds dropped out of the air as the arrows met their marks.

"They're circling but they're not in swarm mode. They could have torn the skin off her," she yelled over the screeching birds.

Fell cocked his head to the side.

"If they're not swarming, then what are they running fr—"

"Ixtor!" Vanya yelled as a mammoth-sized feline burst through the leaves. It resembled a shaggy, cream-colored sabretooth, with a sparse smattering of light grey whirls on its coat. Vanya spun around and covered her sister as the massive cat sailed over them.

I didn't have any time to react as the ixtor collided with me in its pursuit of the birds, smashing painfully into my ribs. Screams resumed above me as we plummeted off the edge of the log. As the ground loomed closer, I felt arms wrap around me, pushing just hard enough to shift our trajectory toward the water. I hit the surface hard, and swallowed water into my lungs as I flailed. Through wet sleeves, I felt hands hook under my shoulders. I was hauled up to the surface of the pink pool. The pain in my side was agonizing as I coughed and sucked in air.

"I'll pull us out." I looked up to see Fell, wet hair falling over his face as he tugged on my arms. He cursed as we reached the shore, and I followed his gaze down to my torso, where an ugly red stain was spreading. That couldn't be good.

Without another word, he scooped me into his arms and started to run. The forest around us was a blur, and I chose to believe this was because of his speed and not my flickering consciousness. I wanted to ask him about it, but it hurt just to breathe, let alone speak. As he ran, we moved through a grove that was familiar.

"We'll get you back to the arena and have someone call for a mender."

"No. This grove. My home." Each word hurt, but he got the gist. I lifted a hand to point him in the right direction, and he found my house easily enough. I cringed as he kicked the door in, but I preferred that over being dropped. After setting me on the bed, without a word, he turned and left. I sucked in one painful breath after another, working to stay conscious. I was fairly certain falling asleep was a bad thing. Or maybe that was for frostbite? The door swung wide again as Fell returned, Bayard and an unfamiliar woman in his wake.

She carried a bag to my bedside and pulled out a bottle of pills. She popped one in my mouth, and I took it without objection, happy for anything that might dull the pain in my side. Fell moved toward the bed as the woman I assumed was a mender lifted my shirt and swiped something over my wound. I let out a sigh of relief at the instant numbing sensation.

"You'll be okay." Fell's eyes locked on mine. I sucked in a breath, determined to thank him, when a shock went through my arms.

I jumped, the motion jostling my injuries. I sucked in a breath again at the pain, then looked up at Bayard as he made an identical noise. His gaze was locked on my arms. My water-logged sleeves had become transparent, and I saw what had drawn his attention. Both my forearms were glowing.

CHAPTER 22

A warm, opalescent light emanated from beneath my sleeves. As I pulled them up to reveal my arms, I saw whirling symbols from my wrists to my elbows. I stared, fixated, as they radiated like sunlight filtering through my skin.

"Your first marks, congratulations!" A voice I didn't recognize rang out. I looked up to see the pleasant-faced mender with dark hair who stood next to me. Her pale lavender eyes crinkled as she smiled, then leaned down to wrap my ribs. I heard shuffling as someone else entered.

"See I told you sh—"

I looked up to see Vanya and Silas join Fell and Bayard at my bedside. I felt tension mounting in the room, as they all stared at my marks. It broke as Ariadna ran past Bayard and Silas with an excited squeal and launched herself onto the edge of the bed. She threw her arms around me, and I let out a pained grunt.

"You're all right! Th-thank goodness! I was so worried! After you pulled me up, and then the ixtor ... can you even believe? And on our first forest walk. Vanya says that's never happened to a group before. I-I'm so thankful for what you did." Vanya's hand gently grabbed Ariadna's shoulder, and she pulled back a bit. The air rushed back into my aching lungs as she let go.

"Right, sorry!"

"It's all right. Just a bit sore." Which was odd, because I distinctly remembered being in utter agony, convinced when Fell first set me on the bed that I'd broken some ribs.

"How long has it been since you carried me back here?" I leveled the question at Fell, but it was the lavender-eyed mender who responded.

"Fell reached us about an hour ago. I got my pack ready as quickly as I could."

"In that case, I don't suppose some sort of expedited healing is an Assimilated quality I should have been looking forward to?"

Bayard's eyes had been glued to my arms as I asked, his expression uncomfortable, but he schooled his face into a look of nonchalance as he answered.

"While it is true that most Riftians possess a faster general healing timeline than other Societies, mere hours would be remarkable. Perhaps Tasya's newest medication is even more potent than we realized. She is one of our most gifted menders."

Tasya blushed at the compliment.

"Although, given what Fell indicated the extent of your injuries to be, I am admittedly surprised ..."

Fell raised his eyebrow but kept his mouth shut.

I stretched and twisted my arms, testing them to see if anything hurt.

"Now that we can be assured you are all right, we will leave you to—" Fell hissed in a breath as the back of my arm came into view. Bayard's jaw worked as he looked towards me. I glanced at Silas and saw him monitoring Bayard's reaction.

"You should refrain from motions like that. Just for the next few days. You wouldn't want to exacerbate the injury to your ribs." Tasya's voice cut across the awkward silence, too loud for the space.

Looking back up, I saw Bayard's eyes still lingering and Fell doing something even more odd. He had pulled the neckline of his tunic to the side and was staring intently at his own chest underneath. Bayard spoke again.

"Well, as I was saying, it's good to see you're not as injured as we'd feared. Please take the next two days to recuperate." He looked at Tasya, who nodded, approving the timeframe.

As everyone shuffled out the door, Bayard turned once more.

"You will begin training with Fell. Forest walks, movement, whatever he deems appropriate. Check in with him when you return to weapons training."

"I really don't think it's necessary, Bayard," Fell protested. "She's certainly not the most graceful, but she's also far from the most ungainly Riftian we've ever worked with. It was simply the ixtor that threw her off-balance. Surely the number of lessons she'll have with the rest of the group would be more than adequate."

"Private lessons. Forest walks. Every day. Starting in two days."

Bayard turned and strode out before Fell could raise any further arguments. The forest walker followed him out. Silas lingered behind the others.

"Something about your injuries, your markings, or both has them on edge. They had a pretty strong reaction to that partial one on the back of your arm."

"Partial?" I twisted my arm back and saw what he referred to. The mark did look less complete than the others, somehow. While those from my wrists to forearms seemed matched on both sides, the one above my elbow appeared only on my left arm.

"Maybe they're just different from how marks normally look? Not that we'd really be able to tell," he guessed. I was glad I wasn't the only one who'd sensed the tension.

"Fell didn't seem happy to be stuck with me." I was more hurt by this than I should have been. I didn't even know him, but it bothered me that he'd seemed so averse to having me around. Especially when I still felt such a strong pull towards him.

"He'll come around. You've got that same ability to win others over that your father had. And you're very personable. You're very persistent, but in a compassionate way. You know, it wasn't until after your visits in the hospital that I agreed to actually start treatment."

"Really? All I did was bug you with board games and talk."

"Yeah. And that's what I needed. Not the people reassuring me everything would be fine, or praising me for being tough, or pressuring me to relive the whole experience. Just someone who treated me like myself. You'll find a way to do the same thing with the forest walker."

His words meant a lot. We hadn't talked about his hospital stay in a long time, and I'd never really known if my visits had been that helpful. He turned to leave, then glanced back at me.

"They look ... nice on you. I'm not sure how to describe it, but even without knowing what they say, I feel like they're meant to be there." He rubbed a hand across the back of his head, looking at his feet.

"Into tattoos?" I teased him, in a way I only could have with a fellow Verkent member. He looked back up, a smile lighting his face as his hand fell back to his side.

"I guess I'd better be. I'll be wearing them soon enough."

Of that, I had no doubt. I couldn't imagine someone like Silas not managing to Assimilate. He'd never backed down from a challenge. After he left, I found myself out of bed and staring in my mirror. I twisted around, trying to get a good look at all the markings. My arms were all that had changed. Even my eyes remained steadfastly green; no glow emanated from them. I was relieved that they were probably providing some safety, since marks were solid proof of Assimilation. But beyond that, I found myself wanting more.

In the past I'd done my best to fit in on Earth while being in a hidden group, then to fit in at Verkent without my father. At the end of the day, I didn't know if I could trust Juliard, or the magistrate, or Earth's task force. I could trust myself, though. I could choose myself. My hands became fists at my side, and the marks on my forearms brightened as if they agreed with my internal decision. I was still determined to find out how I'd ended up in the Rift, but I wanted to take full advantage of the situation. I was going to gain every skill I could, and if the others did end up in jeopardy, I'd help. If anyone tried to hurt the Earthers, I'd be able to make them regret it.

The next morning, I rose from my bed to find Vanya seated and staring at me. The leafy green that emanated from her marks and eyes lit up the small space. I jumped back.

"How long have you been sitting there?"

"About an hour. I wanted to come to thank you, but waking you up seemed a poor way to go about it."

"That's considerate, I guess."

A bag hung off the chair she sat in. She put her hand in and pulled out two leg sheaths, each holding an identical dagger.

"These are for you." She held them out to me. Their handles were black with gold markings, and as I pulled one out, I saw the blade was a dark, shadowed shade as well.

"You already know I've mastered two weapons. I debated whether to get you a bow, but, given your natural skill with the ax, another hand-held weapon might be easier to pick up."

"Thank you, Vanya. I will treat them with respect. But why give them to me?"

"You hardly know my sister. Sacrificing yourself for another is a Riftian ideal. That's not your background, though. You could have easily just watched her fall, and no one would have questioned it. We would have assumed you were scared, or simply didn't have the ability to save her. Ariadna's the most important person to me. We have our mother, but she lives in the Mists and ... anyway." She cleared her throat and continued before I had a chance to ask what the Mists were.

"I'll teach you how to use the daggers. Not just basic training, but every skill I've picked up. Even if it's not your intent to become a weapons specialist, I'll help you become a dual master." The full weight of her statement hit me. Not even a full day after my decision to embrace my Assimilation, and she'd offered to help me gain a skill few Riftians possessed.

"I'll take the training seriously. I won't let you down."

"We'll fit the lessons in with your other training, so you won't get overwhelmed on top of your schedule with Fell. You'll alternate days between Hok and myself. We can start when you come back."

She stood to leave but lingered at the door. I could tell something bothered her and took a guess.

"You know, you're her hero. Ariadna thinks the world of you. She knows you would do anything for her."

"Thank you." She swept out, but not before I saw a tear threatening to spill.

With no training to attend that day, I chose to take an afternoon walk through the trees. I watched dots of dust dance in the sunlight. Above me in the trees I saw aqua birds flitting through the branches. I shuddered a little until I realized they were lighter and smaller than the pentall as they hopped through the branches, their eyes a pleasant amber the pentalls didn't possess.

Something was wrong. From my spot on the ground, all I should have been able to see was a small, aqua blob. I looked at the surrounding trees. Had the mossy grass in the Rift always held that many varying shades of green and brown? Needing confirmation of my suspicions, I made my way to a creek and knelt in front of it. When I looked into the water, what I saw had me scrambling back a few steps.

I saw several different shades of clear liquid running over the rocks beneath. Colors that I knew very well didn't exist. It was overwhelming. Then my focus centered on my own reflection. Staring back at me was the same woman I'd seen in the mirror every day. The same blond hair, the same fair skin that never held a tan, the same green eyes, but with one very important exception. They were glowing with an opalescent light that matched my marks. A soft cream light that fractured with shafts of greens, purples and sunset pinks breaking through.

As I continued to stare in shock, the marks on my arms grew brighter. They'd done the same thing the night before, as I stood in front of my mirror. Testing a theory, I forced my thoughts to the uncomfortable topic of my uncle. I loosed my pent-up anger at him. He'd either lied about what awaited us in the Societies, or he'd allowed himself to be fooled. Either way, he'd put all of us in danger. As my frustration grew, the light on my arms flared. My suspicion seemingly confirmed, I took several deep breaths to calm back down. It seemed that intense emotions affected the light. Before I went home, I allowed myself another look at my face.

My new appearance was both odd and beautiful. I was normally self-conscious about my own looks. But as I stared at my reflection I felt like I truly saw ... *me*. The person in the water somehow embodied the way I felt inside, more than the person who had stared back at me in the mirror for years.

I had also quickly grown to like the Rift, even if I hadn't meant to choose it. The marks faded with the sting of that thought. I was a fraud, and I was supposed to be figuring out why I'd ended up in the Rift, and how to get out. I rubbed my hand across a glowing forearm, then leveled a gaze at myself in the water. Maybe the first time, when Warrick had announced it, it was a mistake, but the way I felt staring at myself wasn't.

"I, Kena Eckhoff, choose the Rift."

With no one around but my own reflection, I gave the Riftian salute to the water. I still wanted to find the person responsible. And I was still worried about Warrick. But I wasn't upset about being in the Rift. Even if the opportunity presented itself now, I wouldn't be willing to give up my new home.

CHAPTER 23

The evening before I rejoined training brought another surprise. I was already in bed when someone began pounding on my door.

"Kena! Open up, I need you to see something!" Silas's voice sounded uncharacteristically frantic. I opened the door and he spilled in, shirtless and glowing.

"Silas, what—?"

"I got home from the arena. I've been staying there late for extra training. And they just appeared! Also, my eyes. I can see ... *everything*. Kena, what is happening?" He pulled at his hair, muscled arms on full display. I reached out and guided him to a chair. He didn't resist as I sat him down in it and handed him a glass of water.

"Breathe, Silas. It's all right."

When I considered the changes Silas's body had already gone through with his leg, it made sense the marks had unsettled him. I was relieved, though. If he was Assimilating, that meant he was safe. Silas's eyes flared with a red light. On the left side of his chest was a large circular border with more marks inside. Sprawling from outside the circle, they ran across his left shoulder and covered his arm all the way to his wrist.

The glow shining from them cast light on another of Silas's features, his scars. I knew better than to ask. He'd never mentioned them when I'd visited him in the hospital, although I'd caught him glaring at them from time to time. I wondered if the marks would eventually swallow them up.

"It's jarring but completely normal for Riftians. We have to remember that." I hesitated, trying to decide whether or not he'd want a hug. He downed the water before he answered.

"Right. I just … panicked for a moment. It's just … the last time I saw my body suddenly covered in anything remotely close to this color …"

I followed his gaze down to his prosthetic. Whatever had caused it had to have been horrific for him. No wonder the marks had provoked such a reaction.

"Completely understandable. It's okay, though. You're not hurt. You're in the Rift, and it's completely expected for these markings and senses to appear. Tomorrow, when we go to the arena, you can ask Hok and Vanya about them. They'll get you set up with the Reader, and she can help you understand them. They're just information to be interpreted." Given my own fear at meeting the Reader, it was a hypocritical thing to say, but Silas gave me a shaky smile.

"Yes. That's a good plan. I prefer having a plan to stick to."

He stayed for maybe an hour as we spoke about Verkent and the others. Anything to take his mind off the marks. Truthfully, they were quite handsome.

"I keep thinking of them all, especially Hale, Sybil, and Pim. Are they Assimilating? I'm concerned for the others. Juliard mentioned trying to get everyone out at the Coalition meeting, but I have no idea whether he'll be able to come up with any real plan."

"He will. Your uncle's a very determined man." He scowled as he said it. He and Hale were the only ones who knew much about Juliard forcing me out.

"That's true. I'm also a little worried that if things don't go well, we'll be forced to leave. And even if they could remove us from the Rift, I'm not sure I want to go. That's a lie. I *know* I don't want to leave." I held my breath and waited for Silas's judgment on the matter.

"I know what you mean. Other than these,"—he waved a glowing arm—"I'm feeling a lot more at peace here. It's ironic, given the deadly consequences for failure in this whole process. That and the fact that I spend a lot of my time fighting. Still, it's a much better fit than an office ever was." As his agitation decreased, the red faded until his eyes hummed with just a soft light.

"As long as we're being honest, I have concerns about the others. Verkent, because I love and care deeply for each of them. The rest of the Earthers, because if this whole thing is unsuccessful, I'll feel a bit like it's our fault as well. We were the ones with the information on the Societals. They trusted us, and we let them get blindsided." It was a worry I'd been afraid to admit even to myself. It didn't matter that we hadn't known. It seemed like we should have.

"There's nothing that could have prevented that, but I understand what you mean. I feel a level of responsibility for them. That's why, if we do have to leave, I'll be doing everything I can to get them all out safely."

"They also may be less likely to Assimilate, if what we were told about needing to pick your Society really is helpful."

He ran a hand through his hair.

"Truthfully, I worried about that same issue with you when we first got here. I was relieved when you got those opal marks. They made you safe. You and Verkent mean a lot to me. And this place is beginning to mean a lot to me as well." Silas didn't often share, and I tried to break the tension with humor.

"And perhaps certain people in the place are beginning to mean a lot to you?"

"Yeah, maybe."

When we arrived at the arena the next morning, the first thing Silas did was pull Hok and Vanya to the side. Vanya left with him and came back quickly. She informed me that she'd had Bayard take him to the Reader. The hope was that understanding the marks might help him to accept them a bit more. I was thankful she already seemed to care for him so much.

We began work with the daggers. I doubted that I would ever match Vanya's skills, but she had been right. I was much more comfortable with them than I would have been with the bow. After training, I waited at the edge of the ring, panting and sweating. I stood under the shade of one of the trees that lined the arena. As I looked at my dirt-covered arms, I willed the marks to glow on my glistening flesh. If my theory that they were triggered by emotions was correct, it was something I wanted to gain control of sooner rather than later. Nothing happened as I focused on them; the swirling opal stubbornly remained only a soft illumination against my skin.

While I looked at them, a dark figure stepped in front of me. I jumped, and the marks flared to life on my arms. Fell cast a glance down at them but said nothing. We stood for a few moments in silence before he turned back toward the trees.

"This will be similar to our walk with the group, although we won't be going back to the falls today. Try to copy my steps as exactly as possible. We'll stop for feedback once I've had some time to observe."

I followed him back into the forest, and after several minutes of making what I was certain were poor attempts to mimic his movements, I chose to interrupt the quiet between us.

"Thank you. For saving me. Vanya mentioned each of those pools were different. Out of curiosity, what would happened if we'd landed in the ones on either side?"

He grimaced before responding.

"Nothing you would have liked. Ataran are more dangerous than pentall in groups. They are always ready to feed."

I shuddered, thankful when he changed the subject.

"We'll be focusing on stealth today. I can see you trying to copy my general path, but you're missing my footfalls. Try to step just where I step. The key is silent movements."

I focused for maybe a half mile, and then found myself unable to contain another question.

"How did you do it? It couldn't have been easy to aim and intercept me while I fell."

"I'm very versed in that area of the forest. And I'm the best forest walker in the Rift. I was able to leap between the branches and push off them to get to you." From most people, it would have sounded conceited. Following Fell's silent steps through the woods, it came off as an indisputable truth.

"I appreciate it. Still, how could your speed match that of a freefall?"

"I can be quite fast when I need to be."

"More than other Riftians?"

"Yes. Not to an extreme, but enough to have an edge."

I was enjoying the conversation but turned my focus back to my steps. If anything like the ixtor happened again, I wanted his same ability to move through the trees. I needed to be able to save myself. As we continued, I thought about how Earthers considered themselves the apex of evolution. Verkent may have believed we were merely the jumping-off point of something much larger, but not most people. Even our group had barely scratched the surface of information on the Societies. It was truly incredible, the abilities achieved by Societals in a single lifetime.

I made my way home later in the evening, having thoroughly enjoyed the lesson. When he spoke, Fell's voice had a calming cadence, smooth like his steps. Even when he was silent, I felt a companionable ease in his presence. I craved more of it. The next day I arrived with my questions ready.

"What does everyone in the Rift do?" We walked through willows of some sort, their branches dangling ribbons of intertwined leaves and small flowers of white, champagne, and gold.

"What they feel drawn to do."

I ducked under a ribbon of leaves and golden flowers as he held it above my head.

"Yes, but for jobs, what does everyone do? How do the different Societies balance each other out, and contribute to the group as a whole?"

He tilted his head.

"The planets are each capable of being self-sufficient. One of the main points of the Societies is not to deplete resources."

"Then why bother with them at all? Why not just do a more purposeful version of what was done with Earth? Plant a group, get them set up, and then leave again?"

"Partially for the same reason. Our balance as a unit is part of what makes the system work. By utilizing the Hub and delegates from everywhere, we maintain an open dialogue with many perspectives. Each Society is run a particular way, but the differences are meant to benefit us all. The idea is to keep each Society from going too far down the path of its own flaws, which all of them have."

"Then what about just on the Rift? How are jobs determined?"

He stopped our walk and beckoned me to sit down on a flat stone underneath one of the willows.

"I don't think our idea of work is the same as Earth's. We mainly choose how to spend our time and utilize our skills based on preference and aptitude. If there are any tasks that need to be done and there aren't enough people to do it, we rotate until someone steps in more permanently. We have weapon instructors like Hok and Vanya, and myself even, if my training is different from theirs. We have menders who heal both physical and emotional wounds. Arborists who help monitor the health of our plants as well as partnering with other scientists to help us benefit from the use of them. There are the delegates, including Bayard at their head, who act as our main representation at the Hub, and Kidan, along with a planetside council, who govern here. There's also Ama, our only Reader. You'll be meeting her about your markings soon enough."

She was a Riftian I wanted more information about. I checked in with Silas when I got back that night.

"Glad to see you looking more like yourself. Was the Reader helpful?"

"She was ... not what I expected her to be. Very brash. Kind of cooky. Short."

"That's your description?" I laughed.

"She was able to read the marks. Mine apparently relay some of my previous struggle." I waited to see if he would add more.

"She saw some details I didn't really care to revisit, but she didn't make us linger on them. I appreciated that. By the time I left, she had me actually looking forward to seeing what comes next. Weird, huh? I'm hoping the marks that show up after these are maybe a bit more predictive, rather than reflective on something that's already past." I tried to make sense of his statement. The Reader sounded a bit like a psychic to me.

"I'm glad she was helpful. I wonder what she'll have to say to me."

"No idea. But she did mention she looked forward to meeting you soon. It was interesting, because I actually hadn't mentioned you."

Fell brought it up the very next day.

"It's time you met Ama."

"When?" I knew it was inevitable, but I wasn't prepared.

"Tomorrow. We will walk there instead of training. For today, let's focus on letting your Assimilated senses take over as we walk. It's trickier than most think it will be. People spend all their time exerting mental and physical effort to hone their skill. That's a worthy endeavor, and there are moments when you do have to carefully consider your options when forest walking. Most often, though, things need to be instinctual and natural. If you spend too much time staring at your feet and thinking about how to place them, you lose your fluidity."

"But I thought you wanted me to watch where to place my feet." My marks flared slightly as my frustration grew. I'd only just gotten the hang of monitoring my steps.

"That was to give you an idea of where I chose to place my feet and why. Now that you have a better idea of what makes a quiet or a solid step, you can start working toward doing it instinctively. Trust your senses; they're developing rapidly."

He wasn't wrong. I'd actually progressed quicker than any of the Societal Blanks. I'd become significantly quicker, with increased endurance. My eyesight had improved as soon as my eyes started glowing, but my hearing had gotten sharper as well. It made each misstep much louder, and I understood why Fell had harped so much on the importance of silence.

I also appreciated the emotional benefits of our walks. In the forest I was able to let go of my concerns for a short time. I told myself it was because my skills improved each day, which meant I was safer and better equipped to help the others. That wasn't all of it, though. I genuinely enjoyed the conversations with Fell.

At one point we got into a discussion about the various abilities of the Societies. Whether they were truly some high-speed versions of evolution, or magic, or something else entirely. The best part of the conversation was that Fell had been the one to initiate it.

"It is strange that Earth lost the magic of Assimilation, if that's the wording you'd prefer. The very thought of it makes me feel ..."

"Sad? Angry? Horrified that Earthers could have gone this long without Assimilating at all?" I rattled off several options.

"... Adrift. Our connections to our planets grant any ability we have. And our connection to each other helps widen our minds and our hearts. Earthers have no true connection to their planet, or others. Everything there has happened on a smaller scale. Their relationship with nature, with each other, with their attempts to reach out beyond their world. Earthers have been alone." He came to a halt and looked at me with an expression that resembled pity.

"I had connections. Just because things on Earth weren't done the same way as the Societies, doesn't mean they were wrong." I tried and failed to not feel defensive.

"Yes. You had family and friends. But think of relationships like the ripples in a pool of water that has been struck by a stone. The ripples someone creates on Earth stay at your feet. Pretty to look at, but going nowhere. The ripples created by the Societies are like tidal waves. They spread through whole planets and beyond. Related but hardly comparable."

I tried to think of all the ways he was wrong. It was so difficult to explain how Earth operated to Societals.

"A lot of Societals formed opinions without all the information. I agree we've shattered many of our connections. We have legends of magical creatures and massive events. I wonder if some have bits of truth embedded within. If Earth ever had the opportunity for Assimilated abilities, we might have wiped it out for good. The Societies all seem to see the Choosing as the moment someone becomes unique, or really starts becoming themselves. I think many Earthers would see it as the moment the self dies. Societals see the Blank faces of Earthers as unrealized potential. Earthers see themselves as varied already. In order for this to work, I think Earth will have to be allowed to exist in its own way, but they'd also have to be willing to make some compromises. It's not something they're good at."

I looked up at Fell as I finished; his glowing gaze was locked on my face. His eyes seemed a bit brighter than before as he held my stare. He never scoffed at me for being too new to the Rift to have an opinion.

"I cannot predict what will happen between Earth and the Societies. Regardless, do not doubt you belong here, with us. We would not let them separate you from your home." His eyes locked onto mine as he leaned closer. I sucked in a breath, unable to look away.

"And Kena?"

"Yes?"

"Thank you for sharing your perspective. You, and your thoughts, mean a lot to me." He pulled back and led us towards the arena.

I felt off-balance as we moved, thoughts on how close Fell's lips had been to mine distracting my steps. By the time I reached home I was able to focus on an even more important point. I liked Fell, and I respected him. I'd grown used to the intensity of the pull I felt towards him, and I decided to trust it. If the others needed to get out of the Societies, having someone with his skill at sneaking around unheard was a benefit. I decided to go see the Reader and then tell him my plans.

CHAPTER 24

The following afternoon, we arrived at a tree that was rounded at the bottom, with roots that stretched in every direction. They emerged from the ground in various spots, twisting around the perimeter of the clearing. The base of the Reader's home was wide, with low-hanging branches that reminded me of my own home. The bark had markings in the same style the Riftians wore, and they glowed in a variety of shades.

From the branches dangled all manner of wind chimes, some decorated with birds at the top, others with long metal pieces that spiraled down. As a soft breeze stirred some of them, a trilling melody filled the air. Beautiful as the sound was, the sudden notes startled me, and I took a step back, bumping into the black ocala tunic Fell was wearing. It bore a mark of its own in the center, which I'd been tempted on our walks to ask him about. Aside from his eyes, it was the only visible mark on him. He kept everything else covered.

"They play actual songs?"

"They play emotions. It depends on the wind. Right now, we're hearing a soft western breeze of expectancy."

He closed his eyes, his head moving back and forth with the melody for a few moments.

"Are you coming in with me?" I was anxious to know what the markings said, but wanted to hear it alone. At least initially. He might have been able to get the gist of them already, but it was said that only Ama could truly interpret the marks fully.

"No. Only the bearer of the marks and those they approve may enter. It's a very private event." I tried not to look too relieved; I didn't want him to feel he was unwanted.

The door swept open to reveal a short, striking woman. Her markings were a warm sunset-orange that bathed her in light. So many illuminated symbols covered her that the glow engulfed her whole form. She spoke in a low, commanding tone.

"Welcome, new Riftian, to the dwelling of Ama, decipherer of symbols, and Reader of the markings of essence. Interpreter of what lies beyond, what lies ahead, and what lies within. In these woods you will—"

Her gaze landed on Fell, and her expression changed from one of stoicism to a wide grin.

"I didn't realize you'd be the one escorting our new Assimilators. How is my favorite Riftian? Not that I'm supposed to have a favorite, mind, so no telling the others about that. Are you hungry? Baked some delicious scones this morning." She grabbed his arm and started examining him, lifting and prodding as she circled him.

"You look like you need to eat. All this wandering around in the woods requires sustenance, you know."

"Tank you, buh I'm goot, Ama," Fell said as Ama squeezed his cheeks and stared up at him.

I tried unsuccessfully to stifle a laugh. She glanced over at me.

"This one has quite the story of his markings. Deep meanings of—"

"Ama, this is Kena. She is one of the Earther Blanks. *Was.* She is now Riftian and here to have you interpret her markings for her." Fell took the opportunity while Ama sized me up to step back and away from her exploratory grabbing.

"I will leave her in your charge and come back to collect her at sunset." He backed further away from the door, his formal composure regained.

"You will come back for dinner. I am insistent upon it. No dinner, no Assimilator. That's the deal. Kena will stay as well, and I will release neither of you until I'm sure you've been properly fed." She stomped a foot and shot him a look that I took to mean she wouldn't entertain any arguments.

Fell's face broke into an indulgent smile as he relented. I loved seeing that expression on him, and he wore it so rarely.

"Of course, Ama. I would never deny your requests. I look forward to seeing you this evening."

"I love that boy. Kindest heart under all that serious pomp." She smiled at him as he walked away, her expression wistful.

"Now then, on to the reading!" She grabbed my wrist and pulled me into her home.

Inside, it gave off the same warm feeling as the rest of the grove. It had a lived-in and somewhat cluttered look to it, but I had a feeling that there was a method to the madness of stacked books, jumbled furniture, and the various baskets, plants and other items hanging from the ceiling.

"Clear off any chair you like and have a seat over at the table next to the window." she directed, with her back to me as she waved a hand. Ama bustled around a countertop, picking up and putting down items.

I checked the area for a clear chair. Seeing none, I just chose the one nearest the table and lifted the stack of books and papers off it, setting them carefully on the floor.

"I'll be just one moment, dear!" She continued perusing vials and containers. I wondered if reading involved some sort of potion or elixir. I hoped not. Things were different in the Societies, but at least on Earth stories of potions tended to involve unsavory ingredients.

"Got it!" she exclaimed as I heard a cork pop loose from a container. I heard the clink of glass on glass as she poured something into a cup for herself. She started to turn toward me; then, with a considering look, turned back around and poured a second glass. When she walked over, she set it in front of me. An amber liquid swirled in a perfect circle within the glass.

"Whirlpool whiskey. Spicy, warming, and ironically helps calm any turmoil inside." She downed her glass.

"Go on, drink. Drink. I always have one before Interpretations, to settle my thoughts so I can focus on the person I'm reading."

She leaned forward, her chin propped up on her hands. From our interaction outside the tree, I got the idea that she was someone who was very caring and doting if she liked you, and terrifying if you crossed her. I picked up the whiskey and drank it. As I set the glass down, a smile spread across her face.

"Now we get down to the matter at hand." She held out her palms. The moment I placed my hands on hers, light flowed from my wrists up to my elbows as my marks grew brighter.

We sat in silence for a few moments while she examined the markings. Her grip was firm but gentle as she tilted my arms. I sensed it was important that I not interrupt her, even though I was dying to know what they said. If they gave away the fact that I hadn't chosen the Rift, would she kick me out? After what seemed like an eternity, she set my hands back on the table and drew away. My marks continued their warm glow.

"I will first give you the overt meaning. What everyone else here can see, if they've bothered to study such things. Then I will help you delve deeper into the *why* behind the markings. In our lives we have many experiences, desires, and different traits that make up our personalities. Yet, not everything ends up in our markings. They are a reflection of your very soul. They represent who you are, and who you are *becoming*. What you have done, and at times what you are destined to do."

"They can tell the future?" I worried the interruption would annoy her, but she continued unfazed.

"Our marks tell us about ourselves. They are a declaration of who we are—and sometimes a sign of other things. Occasionally we see what someone may do. Markings have predicted great acts of bravery, harrowing challenges we are destined to face, or even people we are destined to love. Sometimes events or people can trigger a marking to appear. There was a Riftian once who touched a tree in an area of the forest that would face a massive fire years later. A prediction of the very event sprawled from his elbow over his shoulder. He spent the next several years perfecting an irrigation system that allowed him to save the grove from burning down. There have been couples who trigger markings in each other. They may acquire them when they first see or touch one another. Some receive markings indicating they will become Whispers, who assist with the journey of souls at the Lake. There are many possibilities."

She stood up from the table and came back with the bottle of whirlpool whiskey, then poured us each another serving. She downed hers again and continued.

"Now then, your interpretation. While you may become more knowledgeable about the meanings of the markings, it is still important to visit me when new ones appear. So many symbols seem obvious to people, but some can be quite hard to read. Riftians always get markings somewhere on their arms. They have a continuous flow. There are none, like your Earther tattoos, that just sit on our bodies, disconnected from the symbols around them. Their presence joins us to other Riftians. Each set is unique. You may end up with markings down your fingertips, or none on your hands at all. Some individuals have them winding around their arms and down their side or back. Others have markings on their heads, necks, or around the sides of their face. The overall amount is not as important as what they say. You may end up with nothing more than your arms, or you could have vines of markings weaving their way across every limb and surface. I cannot make, with utter certainty, predictions about the future. That being said, I would hazard a guess that we have more to see from you."

"I am happy to hear any information you can give me, Ama." I was impatient but appreciated the explanation.

"Your markings on each arm mirror one another, as first markings often do. At times this can indicate a balancing or a contradiction. In your case, it is both. The symbols show that you have intelligence, specifically good intuition. I would hazard a guess that you can quickly discern a lot of information from a situation or a person, but that your ultimate decision-making is based on your feelings rather than what your senses have taken in."

She was extremely accurate. I knew that many Riftians picked up on very small details, and they were renowned for their intelligence. It made me feel more at home among them.

"There is also indecision. You will notice, down here on your wrists, are near-identical symbols. Near, but not quite. I see above them a fierce protectiveness, a loyalty. But there on the edge I see on one side a symbol representing what was, and the other representing what is. This tells us that you are facing a choice. Perhaps a decision between your loyalty to the Earthers or what you have found here in the Societies. Or maybe you will need to pick between two versions of who you could be."

"I don't like the idea of abandoning my loyalty for anyone." I had a duty to the Earthers, but I didn't want to accept the life-ending consequences of betraying the Rift. That, and I genuinely wanted to stay.

"Such tension. You balance your words so carefully. It will exhaust you. You have no reason to hide from me. Despite my earlier teasing for Fell's benefit, I can assure you that all interpretations are a private matter between myself and the bearer. Others who look would see the basic traits we mentioned. They will not be able to read what it is for. You'd be surprised how many Riftians avoid the study of markings. Many are only interested in their own."

"But you can see *everything*?" I prodded. She tsked, and pushed my glass closer to me.

"You're not listening. You do not need to dance around me. I can tell that you didn't intend to come here, but no one else would be able to see that, if you're worried. I'm the only Reader the Rift has, and I'm not planning to share that information. Although you might consider trusting a few people enough to tell them. There are those here who have similar aims to your own. A certain handsome forest walker, maybe?" It could have been a trap, but I got the idea that Ama said what she meant.

"If you know I didn't try to come here, is there any way to see who caused it?"

"If your marks revealed that, but they don't. You'll need to figure that out on your own if it's a priority. Although that may not be your most important obstacle. Now, why don't we have some tea and chat, while we wait on my other dinner guest?"

"Wait, Ama, one more question if I may." She inclined her head.

"What about this marking on the back of my arm? The one that's further up than the others?" Bayard and Fell had seemed so focused on it when it had appeared.

"Ah, yes. That, my dear, is an Incomplete marking. They're rare, but not unheard of. They're read only a time or two in a generation. Although you're not the only one walking around wearing one currently. I will need to wait for the rest of it to come in before I can accurately interpret it for you."

"But could you guess?"

"Yes. I could." I waited for a few moments to see what she would say.

"But I won't." I sighed with disappointment.

"I pride myself on accuracy, and I'm afraid there just isn't enough there to provide you with an explanation without the risk of being disastrously misleading. You'll simply have to wait." She went back to the counter to make some tea, and I risked one more question.

"My marks seem to glow more intensely when I'm feeling strong emotions. Is that something that happens to all Riftians?"

"Initially. Most Riftians don't like being so easy to figure out, so they work hard to temper their emotions and their reactions. It takes concentration and willpower," she answered, without turning back to me.

We fell into conversation about Earth, and after a short time we heard a soft knock on the door, followed by Fell entering the tree. Ama and I were both doubled over with laughter from a story I'd been telling about my one snowboarding attempt.

"And it landed in a tree? How did you manage to get it down?"

"Oh, it did that itself. It fell on my helmet!"

Fell cleared his throat.

"Ama?"

"Goodness yes, hello dear! We've just been chatting. Kena has some fascinating Earther stories. You should ask her to tell them sometime." Ama got up to bustle around the kitchen, patting him on the arm as she walked past. It was warm, but he wore the same bracers and sleeves under his ocala tunic as always. After my own interpretation, I was even more curious what marks he had.

"It would be good for you to really converse with someone. You get so broody sometimes, dear."

"Kena has been trailing my forest walks for over a week. We've talked quite a bit."

"Oh, that's excellent to hear, Fell. What have you learned about her, then?" She stared at him.

"Well. That is to say, we mostly talk about the Rift, actually. Not Earth. Or rather, we discuss Earth generally, but not specifics."

"Oh dear. That's too bad. So many interesting things to learn about an entirely separate planet. I would have thought you'd be vastly interested, considering how studious you've always been. Then again, who am I to pry into things?"

He shifted his feet. He typically seemed much more at ease and self-assured. It was a bit comical. Still, I felt protective of him.

"In fairness, Ama, I've been very pushy asking about the Rift. I've probably annoyed him with all my questions. He's been really helpful getting me acclimated. I appreciate it." I directed the last bit at Fell.

The shuffling stopped.

"It is an honor, Kena." I saw light out of the corner of my eyes as my marks grew brighter.

"So formal always. Well, I'm glad you've been helping her. It's the least someone can do, considering how little information the Earthers were given before all this. A serious disadvantage, if anyone had asked me, which I note they didn't. We prepare our youth their entire lives for this decision, and yet there are those who would give the Earthers a hard time when they've voluntarily put themselves in a position to make that decision after a matter of weeks! Positively shameful, really, is what it is!" She continued to mutter as she moved among the pots and pans.

I appreciated the support. It was nice to have someone acknowledge it. She shuffled back over to the table and handed me a plate, then gestured at Fell.

"Sit! Sit! Don't just stand in a corner the whole time. I'll think you're not excited for my cooking."

He took a seat next to me and leaned over.

"Her cooking is actually phenomenal, but don't tell her, or she'll get a big head about it."

I snorted at the whispered information. It was out of character for him, and I liked the side Ama brought out in Fell. We dug into the food. Some sort of fish from the creeks and greens alongside. There was definitely an abundance of fresh produce in the woods. We chatted pleasantly throughout dinner, and I helped Ama clear away the plates. Fell stood up behind us.

"It's been lovely to see you. I'll walk Kena home, and—"

"You're not leaving without dessert, surely? And a small after-dinner drink?"

"It's already dark, Ama, you know ho—" She ignored him completely and placed large cake slices on the table.

He planted himself back in his seat, and I chortled into my arm. She sat as well and looked at the forest walker.

"If you'll please grab the brandy cups. You know the ones I like."

He busied himself in the kitchen.

"So Kena, while Fell's preparing our drinks, why don't you regale us with another Earth story? We can begin his education on the subject here and now." I already knew better than to argue with Ama, but all I'd shared with her before was humorous moments from my own life. None of it had been overly personal, although she'd probably gleaned plenty of information from it.

"What would you like to learn about?" I asked.

Ama looked at Fell instead of responding. It took him a moment to notice as he turned from one of the cupboards balancing three ornate and absurdly colorful pieces of glassware that I assumed must be brandy snifters. His eyes widened and glowed just a bit brighter as he realized he'd been put on the spot.

"What? Oh. Well, I ... I'd like to learn about books."

I didn't know what I'd expected, but that wasn't it.

"I mean, of course, we have them. But as you've seen, we keep a lot of records digitally or with holocorders. And a lot of our texts made in recent generations are purely informational. Most books for entertainment purposes are much older. And I've heard on Earth they have a much wider variety, so ..."

"Absolutely I can share about books. It's one of my favorite topics, actually." He carried the brandy snifters to the table. We enjoyed the cake while I shared about literature back on Earth. The variety, the availability, the options of both paper and digital readers.

"A few of my favorite places were bookstores, growing up. There was one, a used-book store that had shelves stacked floor to ceiling. They wound around in an almost maze-like way. It was organized by genres determined by the proprietor. So instead of history and romance, you might see things like 'medieval thrillers' or 'paranormal with a touch of sass.' You could always find a quiet corner there. My father and I used to go all the time. They'd decorate the stacks for the holidays. It cluttered the place even more, but it was beautiful. Our birthdays were a week apart, and we'd always go and pick out a book for each other. It was one of our traditions. Then we'd go home and have a warm drink and read together." I'd wandered into personal territory.

"It sounds wonderful. You miss your father?" Fell nudged his chair closer as he spoke. I fought the urge to lean into him.

"Terribly."

"He's back on Earth, then? That has to be difficult, with no transport to be able to see him during this process."

"I'd give up almost anything if that were the only distance between us. He passed away. My Uncle Juliard is the only family I have. Well, that's not entirely true. Verkent is my family."

"I apologize, Kena, I didn't realize."

"There's no way you could have known. Truthfully, not having anyone to go back to made the decision to come here easier. It had to be difficult for the Earthers with lots of connections, and those closest to me are in the Societies now as well. Actually, I brought a collection of books along with me. If you come by, you're welcome to browse and borrow whatever you'd like."

"That would be nice, thank you."

Once we'd helped clear everything away and Ama seemed satisfied that everyone was past full to the point of mildly uncomfortable, we made our way back toward the grove where I lived.

We started the walk in silence. I thought through everything Ama had told me. No one was above suspicion, but I trusted Fell, and I trusted her. I had just decided to open up to him about how I'd ended up in the Rift when he turned to me.

"You mentioned that coming to the Societies was easy because you had nothing to go back to. Do you not? Have anything to go back to? Or anyone?"

It was by far the most personal question he'd asked me, but I didn't mind.

"Yes and no, honestly. I have friends, but my closest friend is here. Well, not exactly here. He's with the Crew. My Uncle Juliard, he was the head of Verkent, but our relationship is complicated. And as for other Earthers, no one thought you were real. No one but Verkent knew about the Societies. To others, you would have been a fairytale at best, and a dangerous conspiracy theory at worst."

"They would have thought ill of you for believing in something they didn't realize was out here?"

"Yes. I couldn't really tell others anything about my life if I wanted to be taken seriously. So while I made friends, I was never able to share a large part of myself with them. And honestly, I'm not sure I fit in all that well, anyway." I took a deep breath and shared the more important piece of information.

"I'm not sure I fit here, either. I haven't been completely honest since arriving here. The truth is, I didn't choose the Rift. I wrote down Kite. Someone else put me here."

Light flared from his twilight eyes, and while his arms remained covered, I saw a shine creep out the edges of the fabric. He glared, and the intensity of his reaction scared me. He'd always been calm and collected.

"This is an outrage! The sacredness of the Choosing is supposed to be absolute." I held my arms up as he stepped towards me.

"I wasn't trying to disrespect the process. I was going to try and figure out who had done it, and then change Societies if needed. Then I got here, and we got told you can't leave the Rift. I didn't have any options left but to try and Assimilate here."

He stopped in front of me, the light fading from his eyes. He reached out as if he were going to take my hands, but then pulled back. He sighed.

"I wasn't angry at you. Whoever did this to you, it's despicable. You'll have to give me some time, but we'll figure this out. I don't recommend telling everyone, but the other trainers would be safe, if you're comfortable. Hok and Vanya would keep this to themselves. Has this happened to anyone else?"

"Just me, as far as I know. But what do you mean by 'figure it out'?"

He blinked down at me.

"I mean we can try to get you moved. We're not going to force you to stay somewhere you didn't want to be. We'll find a way to get you wings." I was torn between thankfulness that he wanted to help, and disappointment.

"You're misunderstanding. That *is* what I wanted, but it's not anymore. I belong here. At least, I feel like I do. I want to stay. Unless you all don't want me here." In two long strides, he moved in front of me and his arms wrapped around my tunic as he pulled me into a hug. Though I was startled, my body relaxed into his. My head pressed into his chest, and he spoke above me.

"Riftians do not betray their own. If you want to stay, you'll stay. You're very intelligent, Kena, and you pick up skills quickly. A natural Riftian. I know you took to the ax with speed, and honestly your forest walking is coming along much faster than it would for most people."

"But you've given me such a hard time about it!" I protested. He looked sheepish as he pulled away.

"Yes, well, I'm used to walking alone. I know I'm a bit of a gruff teacher, but I enjoy your company. I would have been sad if you'd left, but I would have supported you. I still think you should consider telling the others, and that we should look into how this happened."

"That means a lot to me. I'll consider it."

Back home, I shut the door and slid down with my back to it. I'd told him, and he hadn't rejected me. He'd been determined to protect me. It had gone far better than I could have hoped. If anything, I was disappointed with how easily he'd been willing to give me up. I didn't think I could have done the same with him. It had been just a short time, but imagining my days without Fell in them was becoming increasingly difficult.

One thing he'd mentioned stuck in my mind. He'd said "Riftians do not betray their own," but I knew of at least one case where that exact thing had happened. My thoughts went back to the brothers from my holofilm. Surely at some point they must have trusted each other, and the results had been disastrous. I'd already opened up to Fell and Ama. I wasn't able to accomplish everything myself. I decided Fell was right. I needed to tell at least Hok and Vanya what was going on with the Earthers. I only hoped that history wouldn't repeat itself, and that the Riftians were as honorable as I believed them to be.

CHAPTER 25

Silas agreed with my plan, but it had to wait. We'd reached the day of our Hub visit. I was eager to see the others, especially Hale. I needed to know who was Assimilating and who was in danger. If the opportunity presented itself, I also wanted to reach out to Juliard.

"How do you feel about seeing everyone?" I posed the question to Silas as we waited in the cavern for everyone to arrive.

"Conflicted. It's not at all what we thought, is it? It turned out to be something else. Something, more." He stared back toward the entrance to the grove.

"I feel the same. Almost like I'm waiting to see the others and whether their experiences line up. If they've been having a rough time of it, I'll feel awful. If anyone is getting targeted in some way because of our Earther status, I won't tolerate that."

I fidgeted, kicking my feet at the dirt as I thought about how to word the next bit.

"It will also be difficult having to hide ourselves from the others. I'm proud of these marks, but I know we're supposed to keep them covered. I am content with our new home, though. And if everyone else feels that way, then maybe ..."

"It would be like getting permission to enjoy it here without guilt. It's all right, Kena, I feel the same way."

Some of the others had entered the cavern, including Bayard and our instructors. Fell made his way over to me.

"Did you think more about what I said?"

"Yes, and I think you're right. When we get back, I'd like us all to meet, Silas included." He nodded.

"Good. But before that, I'd like to see you once you return. Just us." Excitement and nervousness warred in me as I agreed. He turned back toward the trees.

"You're not coming with us?"

"There's something I need to take care of while you're gone. Hok and Vanya will be there, though. You can trust them if you need anything."

I'd waited weeks to see the others. I missed the other members of Verkent, and I especially wanted to see Hale. Still, part of me wanted to run after Fell into the forest.

After exiting the Doorway, we made our way to the arena where the Choosing had taken place. Several of the other Societies had already arrived, and the entire event looked like a giant celebration. Hub workers, Assimilators and trainers alike were strewn about the space, chatting in loud voices while holding food and drinks. I scanned the mass of people for Hale, but it seemed the Crew was running late. Instead, my attention was drawn to the Kites. I was relieved when I spotted Pim and Sybil, wings sprouting from their backs. Pim was engaged in a lively discussion with Dex, who had short horns protruding from his head.

"I've figured out how we manage to stay with our feet on the ground when we aren't flying even in such low gravity. We grow an extra organ inside! Think of how fish use a bladder to avoid sinking, and then sort of halfway reverse that concept." Pim's wings flexed behind him as he explained.

"He says that as if it's the most impressive feature we've acquired." Cassius joined the group, grinning as he spread a set of wings out behind him. They were a soft eggshell shade, but they shimmered when he moved. Flecks of gold showered each feather. The effect was angelic.

"Are any of the Earthers missing wings?" I wasted no time with introductions as I joined the discussion.

"No, thank goodness. We're all Assimilating. And I have to say, I much prefer getting around Kite with these instead of those gliders they gave us on the tours." Pim smiled. He wrapped his arm around Sybil's shoulders, careful to avoid her own wings. They were gorgeous, filled with rich iridescent blue and green shades. They were shaped like pointed butterfly wings, with a long train at the end of each one that swept as she moved.

"Stunning, isn't she?" Pim kissed her cheek.

His own wings were more low-key. A soft, smokey grey. The tips were darker, with the color fading toward the top, like smoke from a campfire as it rises toward the sky.

"I can't wait to show mine to my sister once she gets here!" Cassius scanned the crowd, and I did the same, eager to see Hale.

"The opalescent color is gorgeous on you, dear." Sybil placed a hand on my sleeve as I looked through the crowd. In my anxiousness to make sure they'd all Assimilated, I'd nearly forgotten my eyes.

Most of the Earthers had found their way over by that point. I was relieved to see that almost all of them had some Assimilated features.

The Crew remained absent as we spoke, and I grew more frantic. As I swept my gaze over the crowd for the seventh time, I saw Bayard in a discussion with Kidan. I'd barely seen the Riftian ruler since our initial welcome dinner. It had been my understanding they weren't venturing back to the Hub until the Coalition meeting. Their expressions were neutral, but Bayard's shoulders seemed tense.

I suspected he wasn't in a good mood. When Keldrin, the Kite delegate, walked up to the pair, Bayard's posture shifted into a more relaxed pose. He turned away from Kidan and spoke with his fellow delegate. My curiosity in them was broken as Digit walked up. Etched into her left cheek was a gruesome, slanted scar, and under that was an inky black tattoo of a cutlass. I pulled on her arm, tugging her away from prying ears.

"Who did this to you? Did they target you because you're an Earther? I can try to contact Juliard. We'll find a way to get you out." Digit started laughing and I looked at her as if she'd gone mad. She just patted my arm, giggling so hard she had to wipe a tear away.

"I'm sorry, you are sweet to offer that. But it's just so ludicrous. I'm completely fine."

"It doesn't look fine. Have you seen your face?" I winced at Dex's loud voice but realized I'd been no better. Digit offered the group a wolfish grin.

"I can see I'm going to need to explain myself. Our crew—big C for the Society as a whole, small c for the different groups on the ships—had been chasing down a breed of sea monster called the ahgika."

As she went on to describe it, I got the mental picture of a massive, spiked, serpentine creature. It had the ability to eat away at materials with venom it could spray at its enemies. It also grew algae on its scales that could be ground up and, with a few other key ingredients, sprinkled over food to preserve it indefinitely. Risky to retrieve, but very valuable.

"As the ahgika lifted its head from the water, it sprayed venom on the sails. People were scrambling to get out of its way. Laramie and I leapt onto its back, clinging to the algae-covered scales to avoid getting thrown into the surf. It flung us off, and as we plummeted toward the churning waters, I managed to sink my cutlass into its side and lock onto Laramie's arm. The ahgika flicked its barbed tail at us and got me on my cheek, but I managed to hold on until the others could subdue it and pull us back in. I bled all over the deck, but it earned me my first tattoo." Digit was all smiles as she finished the story, but a few of the Earthers grimaced as she pointed to her cheek.

After the others congratulated her, I pulled her to the side.

"Do you have any idea where Hale is?" I craned my head as I asked, half expecting him to waltz up on cue.

"He's not coming. His crew got pulled out into open water further than anticipated during a recent storm. They were out tracking an arga and his captain, Karo, wasn't willing to lose it just to come back."

"Is he all right?" Worry flooded me.

"If you mean with his ship, argas are dangerous, but they'll be fine. If you're talking about Assimilation, I'm not sure. Our crews met on the same island about a week in, but that's the last I've seen him. At that point he didn't have any tattoos, and he wasn't shadowing yet."

That settled it. I had to get in touch with Juliard. With my friend in jeopardy, I needed to know whether my uncle had any real plan in place to get the Earthers out if the worst happened. I found Silas in the crowd and shared my concern.

"I think we need to try. So far, quite a few of the Earthers are doing okay, but several aren't showing any Assimilated features yet.

Dex already has horns and hooves, but he said Derek and Mancio aren't showing any signs of being able to stay in the Clan. The Verkent members are doing all right, but not everyone." He led me over to Sarah and Thea. I was shocked to see that while Sarah sported leathery skin and had a snake weaving through her hair, Thea still appeared completely human.

"You still have time, Thea. It will be okay." Sarah's gleaming emerald-and-black scaled snake weaved through her hair. I hated to see the tears forming in Thea's eyes but was glad that the two seemed friends again. Silas and I joined the girls.

"Don't worry. I'm going to reach out to the task force. If for some reason you don't Assimilate, we'll find a way to get you out of here," I reassured her.

"You have a plan?" Thea wiped away a tear, and the pressure of the situation hit me as she looked at us.

"Sort of. But Juliard should know more." Silas grabbed my arm and pulled me back off to the side.

"We need to reach back out if this has any shot of working. I can go to Vanya and Hok and ask them to help us. It'd be a quick way to find out how supportive they are. Unless you have another plan?"

Another option had occurred to me. I didn't like it but it seemed safer, for the others at least. It risked only myself. If the Riftians helped and got caught, they'd be in jeopardy as well.

"I do. I'm going to ask Warrick directly. Or rather, I'm going to negotiate with him."

"With what? He kind of has the upper hand here, Kena. We're already up here without help. He's the leader of a more advanced group of people. We don't have anything he needs."

"Maybe not, but he thinks we might." I reminded Silas that the magistrate had hoped to find the key to settling new Societies on Earth. I had never seen it, and I had no idea whether Juliard had, either. I believed that if I convinced the magistrate that Juliard was able to locate it, he'd let me reach out. We began to search the crowd.

"And have you seen Su Jin's teeth?" I overheard one of the Earthers say as we passed through the Canopy's group. Su Jin gave a timid smile, her teeth sharp and pointed. Her eyes had taken on a yellowed, feline quality around the pupils.

"It looks like you two are on a mission. Need any help?" Cassia stepped in front of us, his sister at his side.

"Nice eyes, Kena." Cassia smiled as she spoke, elongated canines showing. Her own had gone from deep brown to a metallic, steely shade. A tail flicked out from behind her.

"We're looking for the magistrate. I need to convince him to let me reach back out to Juliard."

"Say no more." Cassia tilted her head, her eyes narrowed. We only had to wait a few seconds.

"He's over at the north end of the arena. This way."

"Assimilated hearing?" I guessed. She smirked.

When I reached Warrick, he was deep in conversation with Kidan. Glancing around the arena, it appeared he was the only planetside ruler who had chosen to attend. He didn't look any happier speaking to the magistrate than he had during his conversation with Bayard. When I joined them, he broke into a smile. The odd black glow from his eyes never wavered.

"Ah, and here's one of our successful Earth Assimilators now. I'm sure you're already familiar with the Verkent leader? I've been keeping personally advised of her progress, and I can assure you she's doing quite well." I wasn't sure what to make of that. It came off as a brag, but I'd never spoken directly to him before. I thanked the Riftian before turning to Warrick. There was no point mincing words.

"I need to talk to you."

"As stimulating as our conversations are, I'm afraid I really don't have the time tod—"

"You indicated there was some information you wanted, last time we spoke. My uncle can help you with that."

"Would you excuse us, please." Warrick wrapped his hand over my bracer and hauled me away from Kidan. He squeezed hard enough that it hurt, and I shook him off as soon as we were apart from the Riftian. I felt my marks flare with anger at the rough treatment.

"I need to talk to Juliard. We both know that's not going to happen without your help. That information you want about settlement is on Earth. Juliard will have it." I didn't know if this was true, but there was always the possibility. I couldn't think of a reason he or my father would have kept it to themselves, but I wouldn't put it past Juliard.

He looked me up and down, gaze calculating.

"Why reveal this information now? You could have used it to bargain at any time, if you really had it."

"The stakes weren't as high then."

He actually laughed, and I corrected myself.

"Okay, they were high, but there was a chance we wouldn't need it. Now that we're only a few weeks away from the Coalition meeting and I've seen for myself that not all the Earthers are Assimilating, I'm willing to bargain."

He looked unconvinced.

"Juliard and I are directly descended from the original Earth settlers. Not just that, but we are the last remaining family of their leader. We're your best and only shot at obtaining the information you need."

After a moment, he nodded.

"All right. I'll take you to contact him. You'll tell him to bring the information. Whatever holofilms, notes, books that Verkent has which could help. After I've seen them, I'll make the necessary announcement at the Coalition meeting to save your friends." I didn't bother to argue with him, although I had no intention of relying on his word.

As we exited the arena, I scanned the crowd and noted Silas watching us. I needed a way to separate myself from the magistrate once I had reached Juliard, but had no way to tell him. I did the only thing I could think of and let my emotions go. As panic for the other Earthers washed over me, my eyes flashed with light behind Warrick's back. I knew Silas had seen it. I was led to the communication room Digit and I had used before. The magistrate activated a series of switches and buttons.

"All right, whenever you're ready."

I stared at him.

"You're not going to give me some privacy for this call? This is my uncle, and I haven't spoken to him in some time."

"And this is my Hub. I remain here." It had been a longshot request anyway. I steadied my breath as Juliard's face flickered to life in front of us.

"Niece! Is everyone doing all right? I hadn't expected t—" His eyes went wide and he pulled back from the screen.

"Your eyes. They're ... you went to the Rift."

"Well, yes I am *in* the Rift. Although I wouldn't say I went to it of my own choice." It seemed as good a time as any to get things out in the open with Warrick.

"What!" The magistrate's voice echoed in the small communications room, and Juliard's eyes flicked toward him. Warrick sounded shocked, which meant he was either a very good actor or not the person who'd placed me with the Riftians. My uncle's face fell into a completely neutral expression, although even on the film I swore his eyes had the stormy gaze that had terrified me as a child.

"I see you have prestigious company with you, niece. What exactly is it I can do for you, Magistrate?"

I answered for him, determined to take control of the conversation and hint to Juliard my true purpose if I could.

"Juliard, the magistrate is quite interested in some of our texts that were saved from when Earth was cut off originally. Particularly anything that provided information on settlement of new Societies. In exchange for whatever you have, Warrick has graciously agreed to help protect any Earthers who don't Assimilate."

"Provided what you have is of value to us," Warrick spoke over me, and my uncle scowled. A knock sounded at the door and a horned Hub worker entered. The magistrate bared pointed teeth toward him.

"This is a private meeting. I am not to be interr—"

"I'm sorry, Magistrate, but you'd better come quick. There's a bit of an emergency th—"

"What could be so important you'd come and bother me? Can't the delegates handle it?"

"Sir, your offices are on fire."

Warrick ran out of the room with the Clan member. I didn't question my luck but turned back to Juliard before we got cut off.

"Whether you have those films he's after or not, I don't trust him. We need a better plan to get some of the Earthers out of here ... and any Societal Blanks that didn't Assimilate as well." The other teens were an afterthought. I wasn't sure whether they'd agree to go, but leaving them seemed wrong.

"Consider it done. That meeting of theirs is set to last several days, and the task force is invited to attend in person. Since you last spoke to me, we've been working on a way to smuggle out those who need it. We can't do it day one, though; they'll be on the highest level of alert when everyone is first thrown in together like that. Some of you will be asked back to the Hub for it, but we were told most others watch planetside. It would be best for my plans if you could get the Earthers not invited to the Hub together in one spot."

"I'll figure something out. Juliard, what I said about the Rift ..."

He waved me down.

"Before he's back. Kena, there's something you need to know. I'd hoped it wouldn't matter, but before we get up there I want you to be aware that—"

His face disappeared as the communication suddenly shut off. I expected to see Warrick, but it was Digit who poked her head through the door.

"Time to go!" Her voice was cheerful, but she scanned the hall outside several times as she beckoned me out. I ran after her.

"Digit, you didn't set fire to the Coalition Hall, did you?" I imagined Warrick's response would be harsh. She shook her head.

"No, just hacked into the system and tricked their sensors into *thinking* it was on fire. That, and got a few willing actors to scream about smoke and such. People tend to listen when respected Societals go around yelling, 'Fire!'"

"Who?"

We rounded a corner and nearly ran into Silas as we entered the room with all the Doorways. Vanya and Hok stood next to him, arms around each other's shoulders and near-identical grins on their faces.

"Silas told us you needed some help. I didn't realize it would be so much fun. Bring this chaotic one around more often." Hok pointed to Digit, who smirked before joining the Crew at their Doorway.

"I told them, Kena. About our plans with the Earthers. We needed allies, and I think they're a solid choice."

Vanya rolled her eyes as she wrapped an arm around me.

"He really sells us, doesn't he? We are the *best* choice. And, we have something to share with you all too, although it'd perhaps be best to do it back home, when the whole group can be there."

She and Hok went down the tunnel that led to our Doorway. I was bewildered. Our situation had changed so quickly. In the span of a day, we'd gone from working on our own, with little chance of helping the Earthers, to being aligned with powerful Riftians. I'd never have guessed they'd be willing to deceive the magistrate or delegates. Both of them came off as so much more controlled in training.

"Was Juliard helpful?" Silas asked after we'd made it back to the Rift. We moved through the cavern and toward the trees.

"He thinks we should gather any Earthers together who aren't going to the Hub for the Coalition meeting."

"We could ask them to the Rift. I bet Vanya and Hok would help us."

"Host them in the cavern, you mean? You know we can't show them anything beyond that."

"I know, but those antechambers are plenty large enough. I'll reach out and see what they say. After today, though, I'd be surprised if they couldn't help us."

"Juliard had something he wanted to tell me, before Digit showed up."

"Any idea what it was?"

"Several possibilities come to mind. He's interacted with the delegates; maybe he had some idea of who would have sent me to the Rift. He seemed bothered by it when he realized where I'd gone. That could just be me reading into it, though; he knew I'd always dreamed of the Kites. Still, if you could have seen his face! I'm also a bit worried about the task force, and particularly Kaiser. You remember how against this whole thing he was? How will they respond if we do end up needing to execute an escape plan? Will they try to engage the Societies in some kind of hostilities? If not that, maybe they'll treat the returning Earthers or Societal Blanks we bring like science experiments. We need to try and ensure their safety once they're back as well."

"Hmm, so just a few possibilities, then?" He laughed at his own joke, and I smiled as I let some of my tension fall away.

"Just a few. We have a lot to do."

"We'd better get started, then. But first, didn't you promise the forest walker a meeting?"

CHAPTER 26

As Silas and I walked up, I saw Fell standing outside my house. He gave me one of his rare smiles as we approached.

"You must have made quite an impression. Ama's asked you back. She wants to train you."

I froze, certain I'd misunderstood him.

"As a Reader? But ... isn't there just one in all of the Rift?"

"Exactly. She's been stubbornly refusing to take on anyone interested in the role for years. Some Riftians would kill for this kind of honor." He may have meant it metaphorically, but I wouldn't have put it past some of the Societals.

"You could of course attempt to turn her down, but I should warn you, Ama can be relentless when she's made up her mind." I imagined he was right, but it didn't matter. I readily accepted. I did have another question.

"How did she refuse the others, the ones she wouldn't train?"

"Most were simple conversations where Ama declined, and that response was accepted. It's the only smart way to treat the Reader, with respect. There was one girl, maybe thirty years ago or so, that didn't want to take no for an answer. Ama shut herself in her tree for a month and refused to interpret marks for anyone until she went away. That woman is an arborist now, specializing in uses for poisonous sap."

"Delightful." I made a face.

"Anything but. Even the Riftians have their fair share of troublemakers. Hella's been on her best behavior since, but Ama insists on being present when leaves for her tea are collected. I doubt she trusts Hella not to poison it." It was a healthy reminder of the danger some Societals posed.

"Fell, did you ever ask Ama to teach you?" I asked the question as soon as it came to mind. He stopped walking, and waited several seconds before he responded.

"Yes, I did. Just once. She told me it wasn't my role."

"And you accepted that?"

"Not gracefully, I'm ashamed to admit. I was young. I'd spent a few years here and had already grown close to Ama. I knew she favored me. I'd arrogantly assumed she'd say yes. When she didn't, I handled it poorly. I told her I'd respect her decision, but I sulked about it. Instead of facing her, I removed myself. Packed all my stuff and moved myself to the Twilight Grove without so much as a goodbye."

"Where?"

"You'll actually be visiting it soon. It serves a key part in Assimilation. It's one of the rare Riftian outpost settlements. We've got the main grove, of course, where almost all of us reside. The

Twilight Grove is different, though. I won't spoil it, but suffice to say it stands out even by Riftian standards. I spent a few years there, alongside the makers, but I used the time to perfect my forest walking. It's much quieter there, so you have to be especially skilled to go undetected."

"*Makers*. What exactly do they do?"

"You'll see."

"If you don't want to reveal much about the grove, will you share what made you come back here?" His smile dropped, and I regretted asking the question, even though I wanted to know more about him.

"My sister, Evienne. I got word there'd been an accident. She lived in the Canopy. Still, we'd been very close growing up and had visited each other often. I used to go stay with her and her partner, Alsey, for weeks at a time. When I'd gone to the Twilight Grove, I spent all my time obsessively working on forest walking. I barely visited the main grove, let alone the Hub. I hadn't seen her in over a year. I didn't mean for so much time to pass. I just got distracted. I left as soon as word reached me, but it was too late. Her last letter to me had encouraged me to move on from the Reader rejection and use my skills to benefit someone other than myself. It seemed the right thing to do to come back and help train the Blanks. That, and after she was gone the silence didn't feel as comforting anymore. It left too much room for grief."

"I'm so sorry, Fell." I reached out a hand and placed it on his arm where his cloak covered it.

"I'm sure she'd be proud to know you took her advice. What was she like?" A small smile formed as he answered.

"Headstrong. Talented. She was a forager. She spent a lot of her time on multi-day hikes to gather food. We were alike in that way, with our love for spending time in nature. She wasn't a mender, but she often picked up specific items requested by them. There had been an outbreak of a horrible disease. It showed up after a herd of elderbeasts ran through one of their larger settlements near the Doorway. That species normally resides on the far side of the planet. By the time they realized the connection between the migration and the illness, they had dozens of dead. The menders and their scientists figured out a cure by looking at the animals themselves and what those who recovered had recently eaten. The Canopy had shut their Doorway down and sent the foragers out to gather what they thought they'd need to formulate a cure. A thorned flower growing only on steep, well-watered cliffsides."

His breath shook a bit, and I squeezed his wrist over his bracer. He looked at me with his eyes flaring brighter before he continued.

"After days of searching, she and Alsey located some at the precipice of a falls. They'd made it there just as a fierce rainstorm was starting, and they realized they'd have to scale the rocks to get to it. Alsey urged her to wait, to go back and get equipment and a team. Evienne knew time was a factor, though. If they'd done that, it would have been enough time for dozens more to succumb to the disease. So, she scaled the falls. She'd made it all the way to the flowers and was preparing to come back down when a dam broke further upstream. All the water and debris rushed over the edge and swept her with it." I hung on every word.

"Alsey found her washed up on shore further down, still clinging to the flowers. She said Evienne had saved innumerable people. Their menders were able to work up a cure, and the Doorway was reopened. Alsey never recovered, though. She didn't want to be anywhere near the Canopy. She was so aggrieved she re-Assimilated. She's a Kite now, though she has to get by without true wings." I tried to imagine that kind of feeling. To love someone so much that you literally had to leave your world behind if they weren't in it. I supposed I'd been given a similar opportunity, leaving the planet that no longer held my father.

"So Alsey left the Canopy and you left the Twilight Grove."

"Yes. You already know we can't leave the Rift, but I would have chosen to stay regardless. I just needed to alter how I was spending my time and use it to give back a bit. When I'm not training, I often fetch things on my walks for menders or Ama. It's my way of honoring Evienne's memory."

"I'm sure she would have liked that. I'm glad you and Ama are close again."

"You know, I expected a severe tongue-lashing from her when I returned. She never said a thing, though. I saw her for the first time since I'd left at Evienne's funeral. We were able to bring her to the Lake. Without a word, Ama came up and held my hand as Evienne drifted away. Then she walked me back to her home, where she had a warm drink and spare bed ready. She said hardly anything, but she stayed up with me the whole night. After that, things between us went back to how they'd been before I left. She never brought up my years of absence." It seemed Ama could read what people needed as well as she read markings.

We'd circled back and had come to the grove where I lived. I wasn't ready to go in, even though I knew we were only a few hours from the light of day breaking through the trees. I stood next to Fell in silence for several minutes. It meant a lot that he'd been willing to share something so personal. A bird sang in the trees, and it spurred me into motion. Fell reached out an arm as I moved away from him, and grabbed at the edge of my sleeve. When I turned toward him, he bit his lip, his eyes flickering.

"The first day we met, with the ixtor. When you went over the falls. It was like I was being given the opportunity to do what I couldn't before. To save you in the way I wasn't able to save her. Once she was gone, I vowed never to let someone I cared about come to harm if I could prevent it."

"But you didn't even know me."

"No. I'd heard of you, though. Riftians and delegates aren't above gossip. And I *do* know you now, or at least I'm getting to. I would make that same choice again, any time it was needed."

"Are you saying that you would put yourself in harm's way to save m—" Fell grabbed my sleeve and pulled me behind him, just before I heard footsteps approaching.

"Kena! You couldn't sleep either, huh? I was thinking that ... oh, sorry, I didn't realize you had anyone with you. I saw your marks glowing from the grove." Silas frowned, his head tilted, as he looked past Fell toward me.

"I'll come back in the morning to fetch you for our forest walking lesson. For now, I will leave you with your friend." Fell leaned in, and I could feel his breath on my neck as he spoke. He was gone before I could turn around. Just the sensation of having him so near had woken me up again. I knew I wouldn't be able to rest anyway and invited Silas in instead.

"Kena, I've been thinking. The book Nien gave you before we left. The symbols could be marks, right? What if *he* put you here, or knew you'd be coming here, and that's why he gave it to you?"

It wasn't any of the things I'd expected him to bring up, but I couldn't ignore it, either. I walked over to my bed, rummaging beneath it. I had the book stuffed under the clothes I'd come to the Hub with. I held it out to Silas, and without a word he pulled his shirt off and slung it over the back of the chair. We both stared silently for a few moments, comparing the cover of the book with the marking over his chest. There was no denying the resemblance.

"But how would he have known about the markings in the first place? Aren't they incredibly private? And even if he did plan for me to come here, why would it be necessary for me to have the book? Any Riftian can figure out how to—"

"Figure out *what,* Kena? You just kind of stopped."

"Wait, no. That's not right. Ama said Riftians *could* figure out the gist of markings, but most don't bother. And even then, it takes a Reader to accurately interpret them with detail. If he had a way of knowing that I'd be trained by her, then he could have given it to me in the hopes that I'd interpret it for him."

"Possibly. Or, maybe he didn't think you'd be able to read it, and it's a taunt? You said she's refused to train anyone for years. The chances were slim she'd choose to pass her knowledge to an Earther."

"I guess, but if that's the case he's basically outed himself, just to frustrate me. If he'd already put me in the Rift it seems like wasted effort. He'd already done something more damaging, or at least that's what he would have thought."

"Okay, then we go with the theory that he knew Ama would help you. Assuming he's the one responsible."

"That seems more likely. Although surely, he would have to know I'd figure that out, and why would I share the information with him? The most likely scenario would be that Ama was in on it, which I hate to think." I'd only met the Reader once, but I'd liked her immediately.

"You're right. If he gave it to you, and you figured out he'd altered your Choice, he had to know you wouldn't trust him. But if he gave it to you hoping to get it interpreted without knowing your Choice ..."

"Either he was making a very risky bet this is where I'd end up, or he had some knowledge I'd be placed here anyway, by someone other than himself. Also, if Ama knew, she could have just interpreted it for him herself. There's something we're missing."

"It's no good. We need more information."

A knock sounded outside.

"Kena, ready to go?" Fell's voice rang out.

"Just a moment!" I shoved the book back under the bed while Silas threw his shirt back on. I couldn't believe we'd managed to spend hours on the discussion. I hadn't gotten any sleep.

When we walked out, Fell's eyebrow raised infinitesimally. I felt my face heating as I looked behind me and saw Silas adjusting his shirt. I could only imagine what Fell thought. Silas, for his part, was either oblivious or had a very good poker face.

"Kena, I'll be at the arena with Hok today, if you want to talk after you meet with Ama." He gave a small wave as he walked off.

Fell cleared his throat behind me. My mutinous marks chose that moment to ignite as I watched Silas walk away.

"So, you and he came to the Rift *together?*"

I felt the marks glow brighter still. I trusted Fell, I felt calm in his presence, and I was unable to deny an increasing attraction to him. It was the last thing I wanted him to think.

"Silas was in Verkent as well. But no, nothing romantic has ever gone on between us, if that's what you're asking."

He gave a slight nod, but I felt the need to explain.

"It's not that I don't think Silas is handsome; he is. It's just, I don't think of that. He's part of our family. And also, he's really not even in my age bracket. I mean, he's two decades older than me. I trust him implicitly, but I couldn't date him."

"So, he's attractive to you, but too old. I see."

"That's what you took from that? It's not that he's *old.* It's that he's basically family. It's certainly not unheard of for Earther relationships to have larger age gaps. I just don't—"

"Kena. It's okay. I'm just teasing. You can relax." He smiled, but I bristled. He wasn't the teasing kind, and I'd been completely unprepared.

"First of all, that's not funny. I was really embarrassed! Second of all, I had no idea you had a sense of humor." I slapped my hand over my mouth, worried he'd take offense. Instead he started laughing.

"True, I can be rather serious. A fact Ama has pointed out to me multiple times. She thought having you around would be good for me. It appears she was right, which she typically is."

We continued the walk for quite a distance before another question popped into my mind, based on what he'd said earlier.

"Fell, how old are you, anyway?"

"Positively ancient." The statement was accompanied by a rakish grin that had my marks flaring as he led on.

CHAPTER 27

Fell dropped me off at Ama's front door with a promise to return in the afternoon. As I watched him recede into the distance, I felt the familiar pull. At some point I needed to ask how he'd managed such strong projection skills. His quiet presence steadied me. I'd always kept a fairly small circle of friends, both out of necessity with Verkent, and general personality. It was an oddity that I'd always been so attached to Hale, with his loud humor. It had seemed to be a perfect balance. Spending time with Fell was a completely different experience. I was by far the more talkative one, and yet it felt just as balanced but in a different way.

There was a faint breeze from the southwest as I approached Ama's door. A low, haunting tune was picked up by the chimes. I couldn't help closing my eyes to listen, as I thought of Earth, and my dad. My mind went to a time where he and Hale's mom had taken us to an animal sanctuary. As we stared out at the giraffes, I mentioned to my dad how sad it was, the way some of the animals had ended up in such a place. He responded that it was also a testament to people's capacity for compassion. Hale speculated whether the large cats ever tried to eat the other animals. Dad laughed.

The sound of a throat being cleared pulled me back to the present. Orange light surrounded her as Ama stared at me.

"Memory. That's the song you're hearing."

"It reminded me of my dad." I wiped a tear from my cheek, along with the admission.

"That's good. It's nice to remember loved ones, but even happy memories can hurt." I noticed her eyes were watery as well.

"Who do you remember when you hear it?"

"I remember everyone." Her voice was weary as she entered her home. The mess was the same as before, except Ama had cleared off two chairs, and the table was bare save for some books and two cups with steam drifting off the tops.

"Tea?"

"Coffee and liqueur."

"Isn't it a bit early in the day for that?" I picked up my cup and took a sip in spite of my question. It tasted heavenly. A creamy chestnut flavor.

"Perhaps, but at my age I don't really keep track of such things. Let's get right to it. As you're aware, I'm presently the only Reader in the Rift. To be successful in this position, you need to see the literal meaning of the symbols, but also their context. The same mark on two different people could mean different things. It can also vary depending on what symbols surround each other. Learning to interpret takes dedication but also a natural proclivity for such things. I am of the belief that you possess just such an ability."

"What makes you think that?"

"I believe it. Based on what I saw in your marks and my intuition when I met you. I put a great deal of stock in my own opinions."

I was flattered. The ability to read the others also had the potential to be very helpful. If only the magistrate had been Riftian. That would have made things a lot simpler the next time we met. Ama spread some books out across the table. The spines creaked as she opened them, and the pages were stained with age. Each held different marks, with handwritten notes to the side.

"Now, then. When the Riftians first settled here and began showing markings, they had to do this process in reverse. They started cataloging each and every mark that appeared on people. Slowly they were able to build up meaning, based on what they witnessed."

I focused intently on every word. By the time Fell showed up to escort me home, I'd been given an overview of some of the marks that showed up most frequently. My arms held three heavy books that I was supposed to study.

Once we'd reached my home, I was exhausted, but I took the top book and walked over to Silas's anyway. We were poring over the marks when Vanya showed up and announced that it was time for a dagger lesson with her.

"If you're determined to anger the Coalition and save the non-Assimilators, you'll need all the help you can get." By the time we finished, I was sweaty and more tired than I remembered ever being. She had been right, though; I knew I needed the help.

"Go get some sleep. You look like you need it. Tomorrow, though, Fell set up a small meeting. The Coalition meeting is getting closer. You and Silas deserve to have all the information we have, and I know we'd like some of our own."

The next morning, Fell walked with me to Ama's, but when we arrived there was already a group there. Silas, Vanya, Hok, and

Ariadna stood under the chimes. The music they played seemed to fit the moment, and I felt that we stood at the precipice of something important.

"Anticipation." Fell whispered the name of the song into my ear. I sucked in a breath when I realized how close he stood to me.

Ama appeared, but instead of ushering us inside, she led us around the back of her home. There was a shaded area hidden beneath the branches. After everyone took a seat, she swept her gaze around the group.

"I think it's high time we got some things out in the open. This whole process is going to go much smoother if everyone is on the same page. Now, I fully anticipate we're going to have a lot of questions on both sides. That being the case, I'm asking that we let each group have a chance to speak before commentary starts going back and forth. Fell, if you would proceed, please." She grabbed a tray and passed out whirlpool whiskey to the group while he started, pacing in front of the rest of us as he spoke.

"No character trait found in the Societies is all-encompassing. Just as each Society is unique, so is each individual within them. That being said, there are value systems that tend to draw in Blanks with similar beliefs. The members of the Crew are often daring to the point of recklessness, but you can count on them to say what they mean. The Kites tend to be personable and helpful. They are more open to sharing their discoveries than many other Societies. The Canopy has elegance. They are proud and powerful. Rovers are tough, tenacious, and enduring. Dagan are resourceful and can be quite innovative. The Clan are sometimes seen as wild, but they are also industrious. They're also typically very fierce in guarding their Society's secrets."

"Oh, they're fierce all right," I grumped. I still hadn't forgiven Toth for his treatment of Sybil, and with my improving weapons skill I would have relished a rematch.

"What do you mean?" He stopped pacing. I wanted to know what he'd been leading to, but if the point of the meeting was honesty, it seemed pertinent to fill them in.

"There were quite a few Societals who didn't approve of Earth being included in all this. They kept calling us Deserters, or outsiders, and caused trouble on the tours. We had a few problems, like a girl getting pushed into the sinking sands on Rover."

"Then there was an incident when Sybil and Kena visited the Clan." Silas added.

"What incident?" Fell resumed his pacing. I relayed the confrontation between Sybil and the miner, and my response with the pick-ax. Vanya and Hok laughed as I described my sad attempts to lift it, but the forest walker glared.

"He *threatened* you?"

"Well, it was more like he threatened Sybil and then I got in the w—". I snapped my mouth shut as he moved close to me. His fists were clenched at his sides, and his eyes flickered with vibrant light. When my uncle or father had been upset, their eyes had reminded me of a lightning storm. Fell's looked like shooting stars raining down amid the regular twilight glow. They were captivating, but his voice was clipped.

"What is this coward's name?"

"Toth, I think. But it's already been handled." I filled him in on Ugdol's response and his gift to me. When I described the stone, Vanya hissed in a breath.

"Do you have any idea, the worth of that stone? Tell me you're keeping it safe."

"It's in my home. But what's so important about it?"

"They call it moon quartz. It's near-indestructible when their makers create things with it. They're very greedy about it as well. It's hardly ever given or even sold to other Societals. He must have been very impressed with you."

"I do want to hear anything else you know about it. But we've gotten off-topic. Fell, there was only one Society left, right?" We needed to get everything else out in the open before I was willing to be side-tracked.

"Yes. Ours. I would agree with the stereotype that Riftians are often intelligent and controlled. I think it's partially because we are able to temper ourselves that we command respect from other Societies. We're able to put our duties over our desires. Authenticity is important to us. While we are private with others, we place great value on both knowing and bettering ourselves. Because of that, we tend to grow quite skilled at whatever we pursue. While the other Societies might disagree, I feel we have the potential to be both dangerous and relentless if the situation called for it, and that is exactly the point of our group here."

"You're ... warriors of some sort?" Silas guessed.

"Yes and no. Riftians are naturally peacekeepers. It's one of the main roles our delegates serve with the Coalition. Given how carefully we weigh our choices, we would only ever fight for that which we could not afford to lose." Vanya turned toward him as she answered, and her green eyes and marks lit up the area.

"We're trying to save the Earthers, and any non-Assimilators," I volunteered. "What is it you all are worried about losing?"

"The Societies. Tell me, have you ever heard of the Spear?" Ama's voice came from behind me.

I shared with the group what we'd seen on my holofilm. I'd thought we had the only knowledge about them, but according to the Reader, at least some of the Societals had been aware for some time. In the generations after Earth was cut off, there had been skirmishes between family members and friends of those who had been lost on both sides, although the Spear had managed to keep their name out of things. According to Ama, once the Societies started to reach capacity, with no progress on being able to settle new planets, tensions rose. The decision to start killing those who didn't Assimilate had been introduced slowly.

"At first, it wasn't as out in the open as all that. Those who hadn't been Assimilating started to have accidents, and some of the trainers and delegates began putting out the opinion that certain individuals simply weren't capable of joining a Society. Over time, people shifted from viewing the deaths as tragic accidents and looked at them as the fault of the Blanks who weren't able to make it on their chosen planet. After years of this, there was an official statement by the Coalition where they preyed on the fear of depleted space and resources, coupled with commentary that placed blame on the non-Assimilators. They tried to make it seem like getting rid of them was a reasonable alternative. The Spear was never officially involved, but it's a symbol and name that I started picking up on, along with some older Societals I'm in touch with across the various planets. I used to be much more active at the Hub. I began to see a connection between those controlling the population and the Spear. So I put myself behind the scenes, and formed this group as a resistance." Ama swept an arm to indicate the rest of the group.

According to her, there were members of the resistance in all the Societies, though the Rift had by far the most. They'd monitored the situation for years, looking for solutions and watching for any signs the Spear was going to come back out in the open.

"We think it was the Spear who pushed for Earth to be pulled back into the Choosing. We haven't been able to figure out their motivation, though. Oddly enough, once you were here, it was a lot of their members who were vocally against your participation. They're presenting two faces, but without openly naming themselves. It's been making us uneasy. We're hoping they'll tip their hand during the Coalition meeting, when the Earth representatives are here in person," Fell finished.

It was a lot of information to process. The upside was that we had allies against the Spear, and they were willing to help protect the others. The obvious negative was the increased risk. I had seen what the Spear had done to Earth generations ago.

Silas and I shared our own side of things. I informed them that the other Earthers had been preassigned, told them about my own sabotaged Choosing, and shared the rest of the hostilities the Earthers had faced during their tours. I also told them about the holofilms we had seen, both the one from Lone and the one showing how Earth had been cut off. The only piece I kept to myself was the resemblance of the brothers to my uncle and father. It wasn't relevant. Silas let them know about the potential complication of having some Earthers on the task force, like Kaiser, who had been very anti-Society from the beginning.

"I'd be surprised if at least some of the task force didn't have their own agenda prepared for this meeting," Silas stated.

We all agreed that protecting the non-Assimilators, Earthers included, was the top priority. The other important piece was monitoring the Coalition meeting participants to try to figure out the Spear's level of involvement and their motive. Vanya and Ariadna volunteered to organize an event in the caverns to host the Earthers and other Blanks.

"We can screen the entire meeting from there, and I'm willing to bet people will come. The Rift so rarely hosts anything."

As the meeting dissolved, Fell drew me aside.

"Would you walk with me for a bit, before we go back?" I nodded, and he led me away from Ama's and deeper into the woods.

"There's something I wanted to say, regarding what happened to you with the Choosing. I know you said you're okay with how it turned out, but it bothers me. Assimilating is an incredibly personal experience. It's not something anyone else should decide for you. It is not just about what physical attributes or abilities the different

Societies have, what rules you follow, or what climate you live in. At its heart, the process is supposed to be about looking deep inside and asking yourself who you really are, where you feel drawn to, what you truly value. Really, you aren't picking a planet, you are Choosing yourself."

"I've never heard it explained that way before." What he described was everything I'd felt robbed of when I'd been put in the Rift, but I'd managed to find it regardless.

"After what you and Silas shared, I understand the pressure you were under. The danger you're in. So, even though you say this place will work, I wanted to extend my offer again. If you end up needing to go somewhere else, I will find a way to make it happen."

"It means so much that you would offer, but really, it's unnecessary. My being here initially may have been unintentional, but I'm making the decision to stay. When I first arrived, I felt a bit lost. Not just in the Rift, but the Societies in general. I'd spent my whole life hoping to see them someday, and then when I got there, they weren't what I thought. To be honest, I wasn't exactly who I thought. I grew up in the shadow of my father and my uncle, and I wanted nothing more than to lead Verkent like they had. Now, I still want to protect the Earthers, but I'm discovering all these other aspects of myself that are just for me. And when I look in the mirror and see these marks, I see me. It's the other person, from before, that I don't recognize."

"I'm glad." He reached out and wrapped his arms around me, so I was enveloped under his cloak. My head rested against the ocala tunic he always wore, the symbol stamped on it one I still hadn't learned. I put my arms around him as well, torn between two feelings. He was so close, and yet I wanted more. To see his markings, to truly understand him. Too soon, he stepped back. There was one thing I wanted him to know about his home, given all my commentary about not picking it for myself.

"One thing I appreciated about the Rift from the first visit was that you were all uniformly polite and respectful. Honestly, a lot of the Earthers found the caverns off-putting, but we all appreciated that you didn't treat us as unwanted, like other Societals did."

"And now?"

"What do you mean?"

"Can you tell that you are wanted?"

His words lingered in my head that night as I dreamed. I hadn't been able to answer, but I knew what I wanted the answer to be.

Vanya started to work with me even more on using the daggers. As my lessons with Ama continued, I had plenty of opportunities to practice interpreting as well. Silas acquired marks at a rapid pace. He still went to Ama, but he liked to let me try first.

"It looks like the ones running down this forearm are referencing physical strength." I pointed to his right arm. "But the ones over here are about mental fortitude." I pointed to the left.

"So, I am both smart and fit." He smiled.

"Something like that. She'll probably have a much more detailed explanation. I still can't tell if it's supposed to just be describing you now, or predicting some later quality or achievement."

"You've been doing really well. The last three marks, you've gotten the general idea of what she said."

"Thanks. Ama's been trying to help me hone in on details I've missed. It's nice of you to let me use you for practice. She says it's a lot more valuable to study the actual people than the books."

"You could ask some of the others to help as well; I'm sure they wouldn't mind."

"I don't know. Some of them are rather private." My mind immediately went to Fell. Silas seemed to guess what I was thinking.

"It doesn't have to be him. Come to think of it, I've only ever seen his eyes glowing. I wonder what marks he even has under that cloak. But Vanya or Hok wouldn't care. They train with their arms or legs showing all the time."

"I'll ask them, see if Vanya's willing to lend me a leg. I think I've got a good idea of what her calf says. Let me see if I can interpret yours as a whole."

Silas sat obligingly in shorts while I walked around him, taking notes. He had the original emblem and background on his left shoulder and upper arm and the lines of symbols down each forearm. The rest of his left arm and side of his ribs had filled in as well. Marks ringed his neck. He also had a decent amount across his left thigh, down to where his leg ended.

"Okay, so altogether, your marks talk about a great warrior. Don't let this go to your head. Your chest and arm do reference your past." I chose to gloss over the details I was able to read thanks to Ama, even though I was deeply curious. One of the markings indicated children. If he ever wanted to share, I would listen, but I wasn't going to dredge up a painful memory just to check my own accuracy as a Reader.

"Your neck signifies leadership. I think you're naturally inclined toward it, but these specifically reference something that will occur later. Your ribs are tougher. Those, I believe, are speaking to actual events, but I'm guessing they're predictive? Ama was hopefully more helpful. 'Battle' is included somewhere, but again, given your former occupation, I'm having trouble deciding where in a timeline they would fit. Your leg balances the whole thing out. At that point, the markings transition to character qualities like loyalty, determination, dedication, that sort of thing." I looked up to get his reaction.

"I'm impressed. You saw quite a bit."

"Not nearly as much as Ama, I'm sure."

"No, but who knows how long she's held her position as Reader? Maybe by the time you read them with the detail she does, I'll be ready to share those details with someone."

"Whenever that day comes, I'll be more than happy to listen."

Together we walked to the arena for another round of training.

"What have you been spending the rest of your afternoons with while I'm off forest walking?" I realized I wasn't sure what he did, other than hang out in the arena, when I went off with Fell.

"Mostly I help out Vanya and Hok. Hok's been giving me some extra lessons with the sword. Vanya's been working with both of us on some of our movements. Getting large frames to move gracefully is a bit of a trick. They're also letting me stay and help run scenarios with some of the other Riftians in the afternoons. Apparently, my work experience has provided me with some unique scenarios to present as training exercises. It's definitely challenging to combine a special-ops training scenario with the use of swords or darts."

"And you're enjoying it?"

"Immensely."

"Any *other* reason you might be spending most of your time around the arena?" He caught my pointed question and shot me a smile.

"There might be. Any other reason you're spending your afternoons on such long forest walks, aside from the scenery?"

"Unlike the rest of you, I was assigned. You're right, though, who you're spending your time with is completely up to you. And I like Vanya." I realized I had been hinting, and I'd always hated when people did that with Hale and me. Growing up with him as a best friend, we'd heard remarks for years, and both of us had resented each and every comment that insisted we couldn't be just friends. It was as if people found the mere idea of deep and meaningful friendship offensive if it didn't include a romantic relationship between us.

"I *am* interested in her," Silas admitted, "I just wanted to give you a hard time. You and Fell, though ...?"

I was saved from having to answer as I saw what awaited us in the arena.

CHAPTER 28

All the Blanks, not just the ones from our group, lined the edges of the arena. Bayard stood in the center with Vanya, Hok, Samell, and Fell. Next to them, short enough that she'd have been hard to catch if it weren't for her sheer blinding brightness, was Ama. She held onto Fell's arm.

"Clearly, we will be doing something different today. Many of your trainers are here to accompany us as we embark on an overnight forest walk. We will be going to the Twilight Grove, one of our few other permanent settlements in the Rift. It is also the area where your ocala bracers come from. While you have been Assimilating, we have relayed messages to the makers in Twilight Grove. Your interests, skills, and habits. We are going to retrieve what they have created for each of you. This is a symbolic step, which signifies your official, and successful, completion of Assimilation into the Rift." Bayard's voice rang out across the clearing.

As his words sank in, so did a feeling of relief. There were so many problems to sort out with the Earthers and Societals. Having my own Assimilation officially recognized saved me from having to fight for myself and freed up all my energy to help the others. Ama stepped to the front.

"Unlike many exercises here, this one is not about personal choice. While the makers have created items for each of you, I have designed personalized markings to be imprinted on each one. These will be stamped directly into the ocala during a ceremony, where I will share the reason behind each design." That was interesting news.

Even at Riftian speeds and with increased Assimilated balance, it was a rough hike across varying terrain that took us the entire day. My endurance was waning when we neared a wall of particularly close-growing trees. They were oddly uniform in shape and height. Bayard led us through a gap barely large enough for an adult to fit through. As we squeezed between branches and through to the other side, there was a collective gasp.

They'd named the grove literally. We stood in a dark forest, bathed in the deep purples and blues of a sky on the verge of night. I wasn't the only one who scrambled back through the gap. On the other side, the sunlight still filtered through the trees. It was only in the grove that the sky was changed. As I stepped back through, Fell walked up beside me.

"So, what do you think?" He gestured towards the sky.

"It's magnificent. I can see why you waited to let me see for myself. Descriptions wouldn't have done it justice. Are those ... stars?"

"Yes. One of the few places in all of the Rift you can see them. We're in what they call an atmospheric tunnel. It changes the whole environment within the grove. Think of us like a large greenhouse. There's actually a fog layer surrounding most of the Rift. Our sun can get through, but not much else, except in these tunnels. You'll notice it's colder as well."

I held my arm out in front of me, watching for goosebumps, but noticed something else instead.

"Everyone glows brighter here." Fell answered my unspoken question. His own marks were covered as usual, but all around us the others lit up in the dim surroundings.

"I can see why you liked it here. It suits you. Your eyes are a perfect match for this place. It's like you were made for it." He seemed very at ease in the grove. I continued to stare up at him, marveling over how perfectly his eyes blended with the gorgeous twilight sky. He took a step closer, and his eyes locked onto mine as he lifted a hand towards me. His fingers were an inch away from grazing my cheek when we were interrupted.

"All this long walk, and no one's going to offer to help carry my pack for this last bit? I'm an old and frail woman, after all. But no mind, no mind. I'm not one to complain. I can certainly handle it myself. If I dislocate something, there's no need to carry me back. I'll just walk alone once I've recovered." Ama sighed dramatically as she walked past us.

"Don't fall for it. I carried that pack the entire way here," Fell whispered.

"You realize you were the only one allowed luggage on this trek to begin with?" His voice grew louder as he addressed the Reader.

"Yes, being elderly should have some advantages. Besides, my *luggage* happens to be a vital part of this whole event." I stifled a laugh. While Ama could believably be a grandmother, she definitely didn't fit my vision of a frail, elderly woman.

"If Fell has your bag, please allow me the privilege of escorting you in, Ama." Bayard materialized, his arm extended. She beamed.

"Such a gentleman." He led her forward, his size dwarfing her. We made our way to a singular tree in the center of the grove. It was larger than anything I'd seen since entering the Rift. It had blackened bark, identical to the smaller versions that surrounded the perimeter.

"It's pretty, right?" Ariadna took the spot at my side.

In front of the tree was a large campfire, surrounded by smooth stone seats. Several Riftians stood near the flames in dark cloaks the same shade as Fell's. I guessed they were residents of the grove. Each held a parcel in their arms.

After we'd seated ourselves, one of the cloaked figures made his way over to us. He removed his hood to reveal glowing emerald eyes and marks that framed his hairline. Chestnut ringlets spiraled out from behind them.

"Good to see you, Fell."

"You as well, Marx. Any chance you'd like to let us in on what you've been making for this?"

Marx gave him a sly grin.

"Not a chance! I'll tell you it's good, though. A very interesting year." Marx walked toward the campfire. Fell leaned toward me.

"He has also been helping us with the Spear. Twilight Grove does a lot of trade with the Clan. Of course, we have to tell them the materials come from the caverns, but it's an easy enough lie."

In the center of the circle, Bayard held out a hand, silencing the group. Marx stepped forward and began to speak.

"Welcome. We are honored to host you for tonight's ceremony. The Twilight Grove is made up entirely of ocala trees, and we are the only grove of such a variety. Since your arrival to the Rift, we have been kept informed of your training and interests. You will have all been told of the rare nature of ocala. Tonight's gifts are unique to each individual, and therefore even more precious. Treat them as irreplaceable. We can mend various items, but they can only be made once." As he moved back, Ama stepped forward. Her orange glow seemed to pull from the fire in front of her, expanding as she spoke.

"While it may not seem like it, you have a large part in determining what markings end up on you. This is the one time you will receive one from an outside source. While not stamped permanently on your skin, please treat it with the same reverence as though it were. Let us begin. Tad." Ama motioned the teen to the center. One of the cloaked Riftians stepped forward and unrolled the parcel in his hands, revealing a pair of boots. Another reached into the fire and pulled out a metal brand. I knew from my lessons that the mark had something to do with dignity or being official. As Ama explained it to the group, the maker branded the boots.

Ariadna was next, her violet marks flaring when her name was called. Her parcel contained ocala chain links, and a belt attached to something akin to riding chaps.

"For her flails," Fell whispered.

"But ... she's just training with those because we all have to. She wants to be an arborist!"

"They must have something else in mind."

In the center of the ring, Ama held up another symbol. This one appeared to be two marks woven around each other at the edges. I couldn't remember them. Ama interpreted her own design to mean *defender*. After they'd branded the chaps with a large mark, and even the chains with a minuscule version, Ariadna stepped back. She looked utterly confused and took the items to her sister. They whispered to each other as the next several Riftians were called forward.

"Silas." He walked to the center of the circle and looked unsurprised as they unveiled a sheath and shield. Ama held up his mark and had the items branded with *wisdom*.

"Kena." I was the last to go. As I joined Ama, two Riftians moved toward the center, each carrying a bulky parcel. First, they unveiled a pair of black knee-high boots. Next was a full black bodysuit, sleeveless and held in place at the neck. I couldn't fathom the purpose for it, when Riftians always kept their marks covered. They pulled out a full hooded cloak as well, the same color as the makers wore. The last item was a pair of black bracers already bordered with an intricate design. I was more bewildered by them than the bodysuit. I already had bracers, and we'd been reminded repeatedly how irreplaceable they were.

"I put in a special request." Ama winked as she stepped up beside me. One of the makers started to brand the items. I was shocked to see him holding up a mark I knew incredibly well, because it already resided on my body.

"An incomplete mark. This represents a journey. One that is still being experienced. It will be up to the mark's bearer how it is completed." As Ama finished her explanation, the maker started the arduous task of stamping all the items. When they were done, I realized I'd never be able to hold it all, and I was exceedingly grateful when Fell stepped up to take the cloak and bracers back to our seats. I felt conflicted. It wasn't as if the mark being announced hurt me in any way. My arms were often bare during training. Still, I wasn't sure I liked her drawing attention to their unfinished nature.

Presentation completed, Bayard stepped up one final time to thank our hosts and let us know where we'd be resting for the night. The Twilight Grove residents didn't reside in the rare ocala trees. They slept in structures assembled from other wood, which featured transparent roofs that allowed viewing of the stars. Fell followed me to the lodging I was set to share with Vanya and Ariadna. He dropped off my new items, and I followed him back outside as the sisters chatted.

"You look ... distracted." For once, it was him drawing me into conversation instead of the other way around.

"I'm just surprised. By the sheer volume of things Ama had made for me, but also the brand. As far as I know, she didn't use anyone else's personal markings on items that are going to be easily seen by others. Even people at the Hub will be able to read this. Well, maybe not *read* it, but still."

"Does it bother you?"

"I'm not sure. Honestly, if it weren't a tradition, I don't think I'd mind other Societals seeing my markings. I'm not sure I'd want them to be able to interpret them all, but I like how they look. This particular one, though, even Ama doesn't know what it means. For some reason, that just makes it seem more personal. Does that make sense?"

"Yes. You've no doubt noticed I keep my own marks covered."

"Ama did mention I'm not the only one here with an incomplete mark. Maybe if I could talk to the other resident who has one, or who had one if it's been completed, that would help. I know you're not a Reader, but you've spent a lot of time with Ama. What are your thoughts on it?" I'd begun to suspect he might be the one she'd referenced, but it seemed rude to ask directly if he had no desire to share. I held my arm out toward him, twisting it so he could view my mark. He reached out a hand, but at the last second drew it back.

"Kena, I—"

"S-sorry for keeping you outside! Vanya was talking me through my items," Ariadna said. "I'll admit, getting something for weapons was a bit of a surprise. Samell has arborist gloves. I was hoping for something like that, you know? I'm feeling better now, though. My sister assures me it will all make sense in time. Anyway, we're ready for bed if you want to come inside."

"Yeah, just a minute." I turned back to finish my conversation with Fell, but he was already walking across the grove.

The following morning, we were each given packs to hold our new possessions. We left uncomfortably early, and I was surprised to find the grove maintained its nighttime coloring even though the rest of the forest, when we stepped out, was experiencing the sunrise. I shot a questioning glance at Fell.

"You said the atmospheric tunnels let the stars in. How is it that they maintain the same sky while all the area around changes?"

Marx, who had chosen to accompany us back to make deliveries to the main grove, answered.

"That, dear, is one of the mysteries of the grove. Best not to spoil it." He winked at me with a smirk.

"Societals and their secrets!" I muttered as I walked to where Ariadna and her sister were.

"I'll help you get the flails attached, and we'll figure out something for the chaps. They're very beautiful, Ariadna. I bet they'll look great on you." Ariadna beamed under her sister's praise. I spent most of the walk in silence. Ama didn't make mistakes, or at least that's what she insisted. Had she commissioned all those items out of affection, or was I expected to need all of them?

CHAPTER 29

"Vanya wanted me to tell you that you're supposed to go to the cavern today, not the arena. Also, wear your cloak." Silas's news surprised me. We had less than a week until the meeting, and I'd planned on another day packed with training.

"Do you have any idea why?"

"Yes, but I'm not going to tell you. See you later!"

When I entered the cavern, Fell stood by the lake. I paused as hope built in my chest. I'd been doing much better with my marks, but I could feel them flaring underneath my cloak. I watched him at the edge of the water, his tall form a shadow against the soft waves. He turned toward me, and I felt anticipation rising as he moved closer. Each time we'd come close to a deep discussion, we'd been cut off. It seemed the perfect opportunity to get things out in the open. His voice echoed as he spoke.

"You have a visitor."

Another figure emerged from the Doorway tunnel, and as they came into the light I saw Hale walking toward me. My elation at seeing him warred with disappointment. The fact that I could feel anything other than joy over my best friend's arrival added guilt to everything else. When Hale squashed me into a hug, though, a lot of the tension seemed to evaporate. I was back on Earth, spending time with him like I always had. Over his shoulder I swore I saw a scowl on Fell's face, but when I checked again it was gone. As Hale released me, I gave him a playful slap on his shoulder.

"You missed our meeting! Do you have any idea how worried I was? Digit couldn't even tell me whether or not you were Assimila—" I stepped back and looked him up and down. My eyes landed on his arms, and I gasped.

"You've got a tattoo! And you're shadowing!" It was hard to tell, with the dim light in the cavern, but his form flicked just a bit. Relief washed over me. Both were such key pieces of Crew Assimilation it had to mean he was safe, even if our plan failed.

"I was wondering how long it would take you to notice that! And look at you, glowing eyes and all!"

"Well, out with it! How did you get the thing?"

"An excellent question. In the Crew, they use a much simpler-looking device than our tattoo guns back home. More traditional and hands-on. Whatever they use for ink, though, it comes from some squid creature, and it's far more durable than ours. Between my Shadowing and the ink, it will never fade or blur. But what I did to earn it ... can I help you?"

I turned to see that Fell had moved and was standing mere inches behind me. He leaned down and spoke to me instead of Hale.

"You're going with him to visit the Crew. I thought seeing your friend settled would help ease some of your worry."

"You did this?"

"I know his captain. He plans to stay close to the main port until the meeting is over with, so he agreed to stop by the harbor and have you on."

"Fell. This is ... more than I would have known to ask for. Thank you, really." He just nodded, his eyes focused over my shoulder. As he walked away, I looked to see Hale watching him with a small frown.

"Who's that? Your Doorway's guard or something?"

"One of our trainers. He's been working with me on—." I realized I wasn't supposed to mention the woods. "He's my .... Well, not my anything, really, but I ..."

"You like him. Hmm, a bit dreary for you, don't you think?" I couldn't tell if he was kidding or not. I shared everything with Hale, but I didn't know what there was, really, between Fell and me. Or rather, I knew there were growing feelings on my end and had no idea what was happening on his. I changed the subject as we moved toward the Doorway.

"So, you were telling me what you did to earn that tattoo?" It was the right question. Hale grinned and swept his arm out as he set the scene.

"It was dark and stormy, which is saying something, since it was the middle of the day. The wind whipped water across the deck. The thunder was so loud we could barely hear each other over the din. Our oceans have some massively wide trenches, and in some there are underground volcanoes that, when active, can really impact the waters. We'd been swept right over one as it blew hot steam towards the surface. Suffice to say, conditions were rotten. Those trenches also house all manner of sea life when they're not busy boiling everything. When things are erupting, those animals come out into the open water in droves until things cool down again. It was the perfect storm, if you'll pardon the pun."

I rolled my eyes, but I could tell he was enjoying himself. We'd entered the Hub but moved swiftly across the Doorway lobby towards the Crew's entrance. I quickened my steps, in no hurry to see the magistrate after our last encounter. Hale continued after we exited on the Crew's side.

"We saw claws start snapping up out of the water. The trench is home to a crablike monstrosity. They're the size of a car, with pincers to match. We're observing them when a massive wave hits the side of the ship. It must have been strong enough to throw the crabs, because someone noticed one scuttling up the side. A few of the crew went to get the hookspears we have to pry it off, and while they were gone the creature managed to make it up on the deck. Next thing I know, I heard this scream pierce the thunder, and there's one of the other Blanks—skinny, dark-haired girl. She's shaking up against the wall on the deck, with this massive crab closing in and another one climbing up to join it over the side. Well, I look around for anything I can find, and all that's there is a bucket and a mop. Can you believe that? Middle of a storm, and apparently someone still felt the need to clean the deck."

I couldn't help but giggle at that part. He went on.

"I did the only thing I could do. I held that stupid bucket up like a shield while wielding the mop and charged the thing. The crab clamped the edge of that mop and snapped it like a twig. While it was swiping at my face, I ducked and rammed it from under its side. I managed to push it off balance and tipped it over. While it was scrambling, I threw the bucket in front of me and charged a second one that had climbed on deck with the remaining half of my mop handle. With all our shoving and pulling, we ended up at the railing. I let go of the mop, and it went flying off the side of its own momentum. By that point, the girl was crying on the deck and people had come back up with the hookspears. Anyway, she was fine, and the crew ended up catching a different crab for dinner."

"Hale, that's amazing! She must have been so thankful."

"Honestly, I think she was more embarrassed than anything. They're pretty keen on bravery in the Crew. She's started shadowing since then, though. Anyway, afterward Captain Karo himself drew up the crab for me and had our Inker put it on. So now I've got one of those enormous crabs permanently etched on my arm. Now, allow me to show you my ship. This is the Diamondtooth." He waved his tattooed arm at the wooden behemoth that towered above us.

I had to admit that once we were on the deck, with the sea breeze in our faces, I started to see the appeal. It became even more apparent when a petite woman walked up to us and Hale's face lit up. I remembered her from our tour.

"Hi, Nix!" He waved his arm so fast I worried it might fall off.

She sauntered over to us. She looked Hale up and down, then turned her face to me. I felt like I was being sized up and she hadn't quite decided what to make of me. Her amethyst eyes continued to scrutinize me as I held out my hand.

"You must be Kena. Hale's told me a lot about you."

I was about to remind her we'd met once before when she grabbed my wrist, pulling at the cloak. I yanked my hand back, and put the cloak back in place over my bracers.

"What are you doing?"

"Was hoping you'd have bare arms under there. I wanted to see if those rumors I've heard about Riftian tattoos were real, or just a myth. No harm in trying, right? Nice bracers, by the way. Sturdy?"

"Very." I had no idea how popular rumors of our markings were, or if she had any idea how rude she'd just been. It was frustrating, but I could have pictured Hale trying the same thing if he were curious. He had a giant smile on his face as he looked at us, and I decided to try extending an olive branch. I had enough to worry about without alienating someone he potentially cared about.

"So, what sort of weapons training do you all have in the Crew?"

It was the right question. Nix launched into a speech about all her experience and ended with an offer to provide a demonstration.

"I'd be happy to spar with you, if you'd like to see our style. Of course, I understand if you're not up for it. Riftians aren't known for their fighting abilities, after all. And we're certainly fans of a more offensive, aggressive approach here." I was on the verge of acceptance when Hale stepped in.

"Can't today, Nix, sorry. We're docking at the island soon, and I'd like to show her around." I suspected he was trying to protect me. In fairness, he had no idea I was completely capable of defending myself, but it still annoyed me.

"Shame, I would've liked to see a Riftian in a fight. Nice to meet you, Kena. See you around, Hale." She blew him a kiss before she walked across the deck, hips swaying.

"Is she always like that?" I gestured at her retreating form.

"Spunky? Yeah. It's one of the things I like about her, you know? I'm not saying she doesn't come on strong to start, but she's really just curious. She likes to learn about everyone. You're a bit of a puzzle to her, being both an Earther and Riftian. You know they're the most private Society."

"So, she's nosy?" I huffed.

"Be fair, Kena. You like to analyze people, too, and don't deny it. She's just not as subtle about it. It's one of the best things about people here. They may joke around, but you always know where you stand. It's simple."

"Just so you know, I actually could have knocked her into the dirt."

He gripped his side as he laughed, and I got offended all over again.

"We both know you are ruthless when truly angry, but I don't think I believe that. Still, I like the confidence. You must be learning something good with the Cloaks."

"The what?"

"One of the terms for Riftians. Basically, their most defining feature."

Soon after, we stood on the shore of one of the planet's islands. The sand glistened. I was struck by the contrast of the beach and the people. The Crew were rough, tough, coarse, and loud. Their sunsets and beaches were shimmering, eye-catching marvels.

Hale led us across soft sands that reflected cream and pink hues before we made our way through some dense trees. Just when I started to get sweaty and uncomfortable, shoving our way through tall brush, we emerged at a rock formation that overlooked a pool of water. It was completely hidden by the surrounding flora.

"Fresh water! It's a perfect swimming hole! Come on!" He pulled his boots and shirt off, then dove in.

"Is anyone else likely to see us here?"

"Nope! It's completely covered by the surrounding trees and plants. Just us."

I only hesitated for a minute before I took my cloak off and folded it next to his boots. I stood at the edge of the water in my leggings and a sleeveless tunic. I had decided against telling him about the forest, but the marks were mine to share. They grew brighter as Hale stared, but for once he held in his words. I dove into the water but came to the surface quickly, arms flailing.

"You didn't tell me it was going to be a frozen swim!" I shivered.

"Oh, come on you big, glowing, baby! It's not cold, it's bracing!" He splashed water across the surface toward me. Teeth chattering, I forced myself to take slow breaths as Hale rolled his eyes at me. For a few seconds, all my nerve endings screamed at me that it was too cold to continue. Within a minute, they'd calmed as I got used to the water.

"Hale, a thought occurs to me. I hate to imply you would do something this sneaky, but is there any chance that your Assimilation makes you a bit more immune to things like frigid water temperatures than the average Societal?"

"It does *exactly* that, actually! It's like having a permanent wetsuit for my skin. You should have seen your face when you first got in!" He grinned as I slapped water at him.

"You could have mentioned that you knew! I wondered how you all managed to walk around bare-armed on that ship with the chill of sea spray on deck all the time."

Hale turned the conversation to the Rift. As we swam, I told him about the ixtor and how first markings appeared. I had to change several key details, but given the Rift had a famous lake, it was believable there were waterfalls and animals hidden in the cavern somewhere.

"That sounds exhilarating! I'm kind of jealous, honestly! I know I poked fun, but really they are beautiful, and I appreciate you showing them to me."

A branch snapped in the trees. I tensed as my marks illuminated the water around us. Another crunching sound reached our ears. Clearly, someone had never heard of forest walking.

"Deserters." A crooning voice came from the trees near the pool.

"I know we saw you headed this way before we docked. Why don't you come out so we can finish what we started?" A second voice joined the first.

Hale cursed under his breath.

"Friends of yours?" I whispered.

"That's Yerius. He's from one of the steel ships. A complete jerk, if you couldn't tell."

"And why is he looking for you?" I edged closer to where my cloak and boots sat on the shore.

"It will be no shock to you that the Earther Assimilators here didn't get a warm welcome from everyone. Some ships refused to even take us. There was a huge meeting of the captains about it. They finally had to compromise by pushing quite a few of the anti-Earthers together on some of the ships. Good, since it left so many ships open to us, but also bad since it put all those bigots together in limited spaces. Conflict was bound to happen at some point. We were landside at one of the pubs when a bunch of the anti-Earthers came in. They said some insulting things, and we got into a fight."

"Well, he came looking for you, so it would seem he's holding a grudge."

"That might be because I broke his nose." I frowned, but I didn't chastise him for it.

"You're really dragging Riftian tail around here? That's what you're going for these days? What's the matter, did Nix finally tell you she's sick of you following her around? Or is this one of your little Deserter friends, playing at Societies?" The new voice was female. I'd planned to grab my cloak and leave, but her words changed my mind.

"I'm going to go out there and give her a piece of my mind. Riftian tail? Who does she think she is?"

"Nix's ex. They were on the same ship together until the whole Earther debate sprang up. Nix left for a pro-Earther ship and Zalia didn't. It was not an amicable breakup. Nix was one of the people in that pub tussle, and I'm pretty sure Zalia took it personally."

That endeared Nix to me a bit more. We finished dressing and had retreated into the brush when the Crew members entered the clearing.

"Knew there was a swimming hole around here somewhere. Now then, where are they?"

"I swear I saw them walking this way when we were docking. Maybe they're at another one of the swimming holes."

They headed off the direction we'd originally come from as we veered around the side. After they disappeared, I turned to my friend.

"Wait a minute. You would've wanted to fight them, but you led us away instead. Did you stay hidden because of me?"

"It's like Nix said, you Riftians aren't known for your toughness. I don't mind getting knocked about some, but I'd never put you at risk."

"Hale Ochter, I'm not useless! I told you, I can fight! Now why don't we go after those closed-minded jerks and I'll show you just how well I can stick up for myself."

He grabbed my arm, hauling me back towards him.

"Hold it! You don't have to prove anything to me. If you say you could take them on, I believe you. No need to go looking for a fight, though. That's one thing I'm learning here. There's plenty of them that find you eventually. You don't have to seek more out."

"Sorry, you're right. It's not just them. It's seeing you and knowing that while I'm finding myself out here, so are you. We're both changing, and you're not around for me to share it with. It's odd realizing there's been so much going on in your life that I didn't know about."

"Yeah, I know what you mean. Speaking of, now that we're away from the gang of idiots, mind if I see those marks again?"

I felt much better by the time we'd reached the ship. I'd also filled him in on our plans to help the non-Assimilators. For his part, Hale agreed to try to get the word out to the Earther-friendly ships that the Rift had offered to host them during the Coalition meeting. As we walked back, I did my best to hide my sopping leggings under my cloak and put on a Riftian air of gracefulness. It was likely diminished by my damp hair that dripped water down the back of my hood. We passed Nix as we made our way on board.

"Pushed her into the sea, did you?" Nix's laughter was softer than I would have guessed.

"He tricked me into taking a bit of a polar bear plunge." I grinned, trying to break through her forceful exterior with humor.

"Yeah, it's pretty cold out there. Though I'll bet he forgot to mention his reaction when he first plunged into one. I'd never seen anyone jump quite that high. We take all the new Crew out to the swimming holes. It's a bit of a tradition." She wiped a tear away as she giggled.

"In my defense, it was—" The rest of Hale's explanation was drowned out by our laughter.

Nix slapped me on the back.

"I like this Riftian. You can bring her around more often."

Hale filled her in on what had happened to us on the island, and her expression turned to a scowl.

"Yerius has always been a jerk, but I can't believe my judgment was so far off with Zalia. It's not right. Everyone here chose this. Every Crew member has worked to earn each tattoo, and their spot here. It's not up to them to decide."

The day ended too quickly. As I returned to the Doorways that evening, I was glad that we had at least some allies among the Crew. The anti-Earther ships had me even more concerned than before. Even if the Coalition meeting ended with Earthers officially being accepted, and with no appearance by the Spear, would that be enough for some of the Societals?

CHAPTER 30

With only a few days until the meeting, I recognized I had improved in almost every area.

With Vanya and Hok's teachings, I felt like a force to be reckoned with. I'd managed to knock them both into the dirt once, when they'd come at me with daggers and a staff, Hok had looked at me with shining silver eyes the size of saucers as I'd toppled his six-and-a-half-foot frame. Instead of being upset, he just slapped me on the back and told me how impressed he was. I knew I'd grown quieter as I moved through the woods with Fell.

One thing that bothered me was my lack of any new markings. During training, Riftians dressed more sparsely, and each time I looked around it was clear I had the least of any who had chosen my new home. Ama said marks showed up when they were meant to, and not a moment before. Still, it was difficult watching the others gain them while I remained in limbo. I knew it was a small issue compared with everything going on, but something about it gnawed at me.

Reading the others, however, had been going well. Quite a few of them had volunteered for me. Ariadna's violet marks covered both her hands, ran in a spiral up her right arm, and then in a solid and thick line of markings down her left. I'd been thrilled when she convinced her fellow Societal Blanks to lend themselves as well. Tad had an erratic zigzag pattern on both arms; Thrax was covered in markings down the length of his spine. Even Zanthra, the least marked Riftian aside from myself, had her whole right leg covered. Each time I practiced reading for one of them, I was both thankful for their help and envious.

My fellow former Blanks weren't the only ones who had opened their markings up for the cause. Vanya and Hok had been eager to hear an Earther perspective on theirs. Silas walked with me to the arena two days before the Coalition's meeting for just such a reading attempt. He planned on sparring with Vanya while I tried to read for Hok. I didn't bother pointing out to him that they spent just as much time flirting as they did training.

At the edge of the arena, Silas broke off toward Vanya. She'd secured the cavern for the other Earthers and non-Assimilators, and we awaited their responses to our invitation. She shot arrows repeatedly at Silas, which he deflected using his bracers and sword. He'd begun to move with a grace that was surpassed only by Bayard's own dance-like motions. He'd told only Vanya, Hok, and me that he'd been given a new prosthetic. Ama had it made for him in the Twilight Grove but had bestowed it on him after the official ceremony.

Hok sat cross-legged in front of me in an adjoining ring. He seemed at ease dressed in what was basically just a pair of briefs, on full display for anyone who showed up at the arena. I got started with his legs.

"Okay, so what I think the left one says is something about contemplation and preparation. Basically, you think very carefully about things before acting. Now, this small one here"—I pointed to the side of his leg—"seems to indicate present tense, or an action about to occur. Which means there is something you've planned carefully which is close at hand."

"That is my newest addition. Didn't get it until you Earthers arrived."

"I wonder if it has anything to do with your resistance, or our plans to save the oth—"

He spoke over me in a loud voice, pulling away from me with an affronted expression.

"Yes, I *know* the markings add to my good looks, Kena. I appreciate the compliments, but really, if you could focus a bit more on reading them and a bit less on my handsome physique, the process might go quicker."

Shocked by his sudden and confusing words, I looked around and saw Fell walking toward us from the trees. Hok started to laugh, and I slapped the weapons trainer on the arm. Fell grimaced.

"I didn't! I wasn't! This is strictly academic!" The explanations spilled out of my mouth as Silas's laughter added to Hok's.

He and Vanya joined us in the ring as Hok stood up and started flexing his muscles. He even leaned over to kiss his own bicep.

"It's not our business if you want to spend your time staring at him, but you might want to find yourself someone who isn't so into their own looks," Silas teased.

"But I was just trying to re—"

"I am not certain this is what Ama had in mind when she recommended you practice on the others." Fell's smile as he joined in shocked me into silence. I appreciated many things about Fell, but the burgeoning sense of humor still caught me off-guard.

With a sigh, I ran my hand down my face as the four of them walked away to put some items in the weapons shed. Hok poked fun at everyone. I'd decided it was how he showed affection. They were all laughing, even Fell. At least he knew it wasn't serious. Anything was possible after the Coalition meeting, which meant our time together was possibly limited. I'd gone back and forth on whether to express my growing feelings toward him, but a good moment hadn't presented itself. I swapped out weapons and joined Vanya back in the ring. She blocked me as I sliced downward with one of the daggers she'd gifted me, and grinned up at me from beneath the blade.

"Close, but still a miss." I believed her taunts were meant to be motivating.

"I'll never be as good as you with these things."

Her smile grew wider.

"Of course not, but that's no reason not to practice." She flipped both daggers in the air, caught them, and sheathed them in a fluid motion.

"You could at least pretend there was a chance I might outpace you," I groused. In truth, I knew I had gained skill rapidly. She'd told me before that she was impressed. Still, the more I trained, the better I desired to be. It was as if each new move, offensive or defensive, pulled me a step further from the Earther girl who had longed to defend her friends but had not known how.

"No one is a master of everything. Hok and I are very good at handling weapons. I never could have muddled through my markings without Ama, whether I had her books or not. Hok is useless as an arborist, and if it were left to him, we'd probably kill off a few species within the next year." Vanya lectured as we continued to spar, and Hok nodded his assent from the sidelines of the ring.

"It's why we specialize. Having options is good. Making it your goal to be the best at all of them isn't. Besides, the way you're picking things up with the ax, you've already surpassed our skill with it."

"But you still beat me; you just used a different weapon. So even if I'm better with the ax, you're better overall," I reasoned.

"That may be so, and if I were your real opponent, you would have lost. That doesn't mean you stop learning. We've trained for years and years, with no real threat forthcoming. Now we've learned of the Spear, and there could be true danger. We can only seek to do our personal best, and if we are still out-fought, at least it was honestly."

"Maybe, but what if it's still not good enough?" My mind moved from weaponry to my marks, and I looked down at my arms, with the familiar opal shine that ended at my elbows. Hok stepped forward and put a hand on my shoulder as he looked down at the glowing symbols.

"Those, too, will come in time. I know something that'll cheer you up! Let's take a break and watch Ariadna kick her older sister into the dirt."

"I can hear you, Hok!" Vanya deflected the next shot in his direction, and a dagger whizzed past his cheek. He just laughed.

That afternoon, the windchimes outside Ama's house greeted me. The breeze was out of the north, which meant I heard an upbeat melody of staccato notes. The tree itself was as vibrant as ever, with the markings on its bark cycling between white, blue, and green for the day. Ama opened the door as I raised my hand to knock. She was ushering me over to the usual spot at her dining table when I noticed the disarray that typically surrounded it had been tidied.

"Ama. Did you ... clean?" I gawked at all the glistening surfaces.

"As a matter of fact, yes. Don't sound so surprised about it! My house isn't ever dirty, anyway, it just has personality. But I'll be going away for a while, and I wanted to leave it a bit of a blank slate for when I return."

"Will you be going to the Hub with Kidan and Bayard, then?" Our group had debated back and forth whether it would serve us better to be available to the non-Assimilators and Earthers, or to have some individuals in the Hub. The decision had been to split up.

"I'll be taking a bit of a solo journey, actually. You already know how important the idea of balance is to each of the Societies. We only permanently occupy relatively small areas of the planets we reside on. The Rift is unique in that we have the fewest permanent settlements, and a lack of frequent travel. Of course, we have some loners wandering the woods, but they're few and far between. Every once in a while, it's a good idea to go on a bit of an exploratory and self-discovery type trip, and this is the time for me."

I tried to digest what she'd said. It didn't make any sense that she'd leave on the precipice of everything else. She smiled at me, and while I normally found this comforting, I felt frustration building. Ama was quirky, but I hadn't thought she was careless. I tried not to snap at the Reader as I responded.

"But why now? The Rift, the non-Assimilators, the other Earthers ... they all need you. Don't you care about what happens at the meeting? About what could happen to them and to us for defending the others?"

"Of course I care! I have an inkling of what's coming, but there are details that must be figured out."

"And you're going to do that by running away? Aren't you even going to try and help?" In fairness, I didn't actually know whether Ama possessed any physical abilities. For a moment, I wondered whether she'd be just one more person to defend; then she leveled a glowing glare at me.

"I have *always* helped the Rift. Helped the Societies. Helped look after everyone else. I care a great deal for you, girl, and for the others. Do not question me in that. Everything I do here has a purpose. I'm asking for your trust, and given all I've shared with you, quite frankly I'd say it's owed." She wasn't wrong, but it didn't stop the rest of my questions.

"But what do you mean you just got it in your mind to go? Do Kidan and Bayard know you're going? Does Fell?" Ama puffed up a bit, her face indignant.

"Kidan and Bayard, pah! Whether they're the monarch and head delegate or not, no one tells me what to do. I am an old woman with a mind of my own, thank you very much. I did mention it to Fell. He was less than pleased—worried, actually." She frowned.

"Ama, is this trip dangerous? Should you take someone with you?" I didn't like the idea of another from our group leaving on the verge of the meeting, but it was preferable to her getting hurt.

She walked up and stood on her tiptoes, grasping my chin in her hands as she looked into my green and opal eyes with her sunset orange ones.

"Every journey has the potential to be dangerous, but I've got things I need to do. Now then, how about some pie?"

I allowed myself to be talked into dessert. When we finished, she walked me out under her tree, where a melody I recognized as longing was in the wind for the night. She hugged me tightly before I left, and as I started to pull away, she held on.

"You're going to get answers to a lot of your questions very soon, I think. Trust what they tell you. If you need help, go to the Mists."

She let go and shut the door behind her. By the following morning, I'd talked myself into going back. I wanted to convince her to stay, or put off her journey until Fell or I could accompany her. The tree was empty, with only the music of foreboding in the winds. I returned to the cavern to help set up for the visiting Societals and found it transformed. Lights were hung from the ceiling. There were potted plants decorating each table and the perimeter of the room. Ariadna came up beside me.

"W-w-what do you think? Samell coordinated it, and those of us interested in becoming arborists helped him pull it off. If anyone asks, the plants were shipped in, of course. Still, it's nice to think the Earthers will have a chance to experience a bit of the real Rift, even if they don't know it."

"It was a brilliant idea. I'm happy the Earthers will get to see a bit of my new home while they visit." She shot me a smile that reached all the up to her glowing eyes.

"I thought you'd like it. And I wanted to be with you when you saw it, before I head out. Bayard wanted some of the new Riftians to accompany the others to the Hub."

"What does Vanya think? Is that the safest plan?"

"She supported it. I clearly Assimilated, so I should be okay. If anything, she thought I'd be in more danger here, with all the non-Assimilators and lots of the Earthers in one spot." She shuffled her feet.

"She's likely right." It didn't help any of us to worry about the Spear, or the meeting, until we knew the results. Still, the idea that someone could take advantage of the non-Assimilators being grouped together was a possibility we hadn't considered. At least not until after we'd invited them all.

"Well, n-n-nothing left to be done here, I don't think. I'm off to pack!" Ariadna breezed from the hall. I went alone to the arena and practiced using my ax until no light filtered through the trees.

I woke early the following morning. I dressed in the ocala items given to me in the Twilight Grove. While I typically eschewed the cape, I reluctantly put it over the other items, ensuring my marks remained covered. I hadn't fully mastered my ability to temper them with strong emotions, although I'd been able to achieve the opposite. If I willed it, I could make them glow blindingly bright.

I left the forest for the cavern while it was still dark outside. Vanya, Hok, Fell, and his Twilight Grove friend Marx were already there. I supposed they made up most of the welcoming committee, since most of the other trainers had gone to the Hub alongside the delegates.

"Any minute now. Bayard was meeting the Earthers on the Hub side of the Doorway early today to assist them through." Vanya spoke as I walked up. It wasn't long before I heard the sound of shuffling and a line of Earthers, Blanks, and a few other Societals made their way down the tunnel and into the Cavern.

Hale was, not surprisingly, first. I ran to him and enveloped him in a hug.

"I see I've been missed." He grinned as he hugged me back.

"Immensely. Also, are these new tattoos I'm seeing?" As Hale held out his arm for examination, I spotted a large, toothy sea-monster that took up most of his left forearm, and an eel wrapped itself around his wrist.

"I'll give you the stories after today's portion of the meeting." He leaned in closer and lowered his voice. "Anything new for you to share?" I shook my head, casting a glance at the Riftians around us.

While we waited for the others to arrive, I led him to one of the antechambers that had been prepared for the visitors. The Coalition meeting didn't have an exact timeline, but Vanya had mentioned that it often went on for at least a week. The Rift had cleared out enough space for the others to stay in the cavern for the duration. When we returned, I spotted Cassius being introduced to the weapons specialists by Silas.

"I can't show you where we train, but I'd love to spar with you in the antechambers while you're here." Hok scanned his eyes over Cassius's wings as the twin accepted.

"Where are Pim and Sybil?" I craned my neck around his flared, angelic wings. Cassius just shook his head.

"They were personally invited to attend the Hub alongside the Kites' queen. It's considered a great honor and would have been hard for them to refuse. Pim was hoping to use the opportunity to learn more about the Hub's systems." I pulled my cloak tighter around myself as I felt the marks flare. Pim and Hale were the Earthers I most wanted to keep safe. My best friend tapped me on the shoulder.

"Digit went to the Hub as well. She had similar aims."

Su Jin and Thea walked over to our group. I was relieved to see that Thea had finally gained the gelatinous, inky coating that signified her Assimilation to Dagan. Neon swirls and geometric patterns of yellow and pink ran down her arms. My calm was short-lived as I overheard Thea chatting with the other girl.

"I'm upset Sarah isn't coming. We finally seemed to be patching things up. She sent a message that she's representing the Rover Assimilates at the meeting. It's wild, thinking of her with reptilian skin, a poisonous snake and all that. Still, I was hoping to surprise her with my new features. Guess it'll have to wait."

"I was sad Cassia couldn't make it, either. She's been really helpful through this whole process, but something Assimilation-related held her up."

I pulled Hale and Silas aside.

"Half the people we expected to be here haven't shown up. How are we supposed to help them if they're scattered?"

"Not scattered. They're either here or at the Hub. And from what Vanya and Hok have gathered through their communications with the other Societies, we got almost all the other non-Assimilators. So that's something." Silas put a hand on my shoulder. It was reassuring, but even with his words and Hale's presence, I was still on edge. I searched the crowd for Fell, convinced I'd calm down if he were beside me.

He stepped out from the hall, beckoning everyone inside. "The meeting is about to begin."

CHAPTER 31

After we'd entered, a projection flickered to life at the far end of the hall. It was the first time we'd watched a live holocorder event. I felt a mixture of excitement and tension as everyone waited. I knew Juliard was at the meeting somewhere, probably accompanied by Kaiser and any number of task force members. I didn't trust him fully, but I did believe he'd been working on a way to get the Earthers evacuated if necessary. The Societal rulers and delegates sat around an enormous table onscreen, with the holocorder in the center, scanning around to all the faces.

As it scanned past the Kites, I saw Keldrin and Iduna seated at the table. Her grey feathers looked even more washed-out than normal next to his vibrant wings. Standing behind them were several others, including Ryshal and a dragon-winged man with whom he appeared to be holding hands. As the view continued around the table, I saw Kidan, Bayard and a few other Riftians seated with Dagan to their right. The holocorder moved further along its rotation, and I felt elated as it centered on Juliard. Our complicated relationship aside, I was glad to see him.

The moment was quickly overshadowed, though, as a sense of foreboding stabbed me in the gut. My thoughts went back to the library and the film of Earth we'd watched. On that film, too, I had seen a face just like my uncle's. That meeting had ended in disaster. I shook the thought off. After completing the full circle of the table, the holocorder came to rest on Warrick. He was seated in a larger chair than the others, at the head of the table. The chatter both onscreen and around the Riftian hall died down as Warrick raised a hand.

"Delegates ... rulers ... Society members watching from across the planets. This meeting of the Coalition is, as we are all aware, like none we have held before. Even our ancestors planting new Societies were never faced with the scenario of attempting to Assimilate grown members with no knowledge of our history or ways. Tonight, we will begin discussing the role of Earth in the future of us all. We will also be discussing our non-Assimilated Blanks, and what options are available to them, if any. As we hear all views from the delegates seated here, it is my sincere hope we will maintain our respect for the variety of perspectives I am certain we will hear, acknowledging the value of each. Working through our differences together offers strength to all of us." He stopped, hand frozen mid-sweep as lights dimmed on the film.

"Is something wrong with the holocorder?" Hale whispered. A Riftian walked toward the front of the hall.

The delegates on film were still visible, but covered in shadow. Their faces looked strange in the glow of the holocorder in their center. It provided the only remaining light for the Coalition, aside from the Dagan's neon camouflage and several pairs glowing of Riftian eyes. The holocorder whizzed around towards Kidan as the winged delegate asked someone to get the lights back up. From behind him, a figure took shape. As the figure's features became clearer in the shadow, I noticed the mask.

"Hale." My voice shook. His hand reached out and held mine like a vise. He began to pull me up from the table.

A flare of red light caught my attention, and I saw Silas's eyes glimmering with intensity at the end of the table beside Vanya and the other specialists. In the time I had taken to focus on the first mask, more had materialized. The delegates began to turn in their seats, twisting to look at the people in their midst who shouldn't be. As Keldrin looked towards the masked individual behind him, a blade pierced through his feathers, and he screamed. His other wing shot out, knocking away whoever had stabbed him.

At the sound of his voice, everyone in the room with the delegates exploded into action. The masked figures descended on the others, each of their tunics emblazoned with a white spear. The Spear members stabbed and sliced at the others.

More yelling erupted, but from the hall around us. Things dissolved into chaos as people tipped over benches and tables, running for the exits. I wasn't sure what they planned to do, but the same urge to act ran through me.

There was a blur of so many moving bodies on screen that it was impossible to tell who had fallen. It was clear the Spear had the advantage of surprise. I did manage to spot Keldrin's torn wing, with his form slumped into a chair. The holocorder spun wildly as it tried to center on the source of each new noise. It swept over the Earther seats, but they were all empty. Panic swept through me at the thought of Juliard, defenseless against Societals with weapons.

Before I could find Bayard in the crowd, a cloaked and masked figure stepped up, and the holocorder locked in place as he spoke.

"The Coalition has been disbanded. The Societies will fall. We were not meant to live like this. Consider your loyalties carefully. We are coming."

The holocorder clicked off.

Someone laden with weapons sped past, headed toward the cavern. Of course, everyone wanted to get to the Hub. It was the only hope of stopping the madness that had unfolded onscreen.

"We're too late." My words were soft, and I hadn't expected a response.

"Not if we hurry." Fell stood in front of me, his arm stretched toward mine as he offered his hand. He was right. I reached for it, and Hale grabbed my arm.

"What's our play here? What does he want us to do? Kena, we should be fighting!" It was a Crew attitude, and it fit Hale perfectly. He wasn't wrong, either. I needed my ax. I cast a questioning glance back at Fell, who nodded before heading toward the cavern with the others.

"Come with me." I led Hale in the opposite direction of the fleeing Riftians.

"This is the wrong way, isn't it? Shouldn't we be headed toward the Doorway?"

"Not without a way to fight!" I tugged him along, and we exited the tunnel into the main grove. I was pulled backwards as Hale came to a sudden stop. He was wide-eyed, staring up at the foliage.

"No time!" I tugged on his arm again.

I was thankful for all walks with Fell as I raced over the moss and dodged in and out of trees. I took a sharp turn and rounded the corner past a grove of giant willows before I saw my creek and home come into view. I pushed open the door. I threw my cloak into a small pack, not wanting it to hinder my movements. I donned the ax, the strap for it conveniently built into the bodysuit. I strapped the sheath for Vanya's daggers onto a thigh, then realized that Hale needed something. I shoved the weapons toward him instead.

"I really hope you know how to use these."

"I can be very effective using one." He handed me the second back and I strapped it to my leg. We ran back to the cavern.

We met up with the others as we entered. Vanya raised an eyebrow, her gaze lingering on her dagger in Hale's hand, but she said nothing.

"You weren't the first ones through the Doorway?" I shouted the question at her as we moved.

"We went to the weapons shed first, to make sure anyone going was well-equipped. We should hurry, though; we have no idea what level of damage those Spear members have already caused."

Before her voice had faded, the cavern began to quake. I locked forearms with Hale as I struggled to stay upright. The ground shook beneath us as rocks and stalactites rained from above. For once, I wasn't alone in reacting emotionally, as everyone's marks flared brightly anywhere they were visible. The whole room was alight with Riftians, their marks revealed before the Earthers and others. Fell was the only one who maintained an even glow, his cloak still worn over his marks.

As the tremors receded, our group surged across the cavern. Vanya, Hok and Silas veered off toward a few individuals who had been pinned down by rocks. I kept running directly for the tunnel that led to the Doorway, with Fell and Hale close beside. A cloud of dust enveloped me, and I coughed into my arm. The tunnel that contained our Doorway had partially collapsed. I surged forward, determined to get anyone injured out, and get to the Hub.

As I entered the tunnel, small rocks clattered down beside me. The whole area was littered with them. I didn't come across anyone else as I clambered over them and toward my exit. Frantic, I heaved pieces of debris aside. My only thought was getting through the Doorway and back to the Hub. With each piece I moved, I pictured someone different. Juliard, Pim, Sybil, Ryshal, Sarah. None deserved to be at the mercy of the Spear. And no one else would know what they faced until we shared what we'd seen on the film, or the resistance shared their information.

I heard voices, one louder than the others, behind me. I managed to pull something loose, producing a domino effect as several rocks tumbled down. I side-stepped back and flattened myself against the wall. When the dust had settled, I was mercifully uncrushed. I could see the gleam of a metal door through a hole created by the mini-avalanche.

"Almost. There." I urged myself onward out loud.

I lunged for the Doorway's entrance, and my fingers had just grasped one of the spokes when a hand clamped down hard around my right bracer. I was pulled backward into someone's chest. The rocks beneath us gave way, but I felt myself being pulled out. I wrenched around and realized I was facing a chest of intricately stamped black ocala. I stared up into mesmerizing eyes the shade of twilight and stars.

"What are you doing?" I hissed in confusion, pulling myself back toward the rocks.

"You can't! Think for a moment! What is beyond that door?"

"The Doorway to the Hub!"

"Wrong! It *was* a Doorway. Once it's damaged like this, you'd be opening a door to an air-sucking vacuum of space. You would *die,* Kena. We have to leave it closed."

"But we have to find a way back there!"

"And we will. I have a plan." He led me back out into the cavern.

"Let. Her. Go." I turned to see Hale striding through the rubble toward us.

He had one hand on the dagger I'd lent him. Fell stepped in front of me without letting go of my bracer as he stared my best friend down.

"That Doorway isn't functional anymore. It's just a giant hole into space. If she'd opened it she would have died. And everyone in here would have been in danger."

"Kena, what happened?" He looked at me for answers, ignoring Fell entirely.

"I just wanted to get to the others."

"We need to stop and think, here. What did we all see on that film? Those Spear members, who are we certain they went after?" Silas and the others joined our huddle.

"The delegates. They stabbed the one from Kite, and I saw them get another from Dagan. Also, one of the Rovers." Vanya's voice was decisive.

"True, and I know I saw some tattooed Crew members fighting them. Actually, I can think of an example of every kind of Societal fighting, except the Earthers." Marx's gaze turned to Hale and me. As I wracked my memory of it, I realized he was right. By the time the holocorder had swung around to their seats, they'd all disappeared.

"So, were they working with the Spear or against them?" Marx questioned.

"The head of Verkent has been helping us with a plan to protect the non-Assimilators. It's impossible for us to know about the others without going up there ourselves," Fell answered in front of me, and I appreciated his white lie where my uncle was involved. I had no way of knowing for sure what he'd actually done, but I believed he was on our side more than the Spear's.

"I think it's safe to assume the Spear is responsible for the explosion that just rocked the cavern and wrecked our Doorway. What if they're cutting everyone off, not just us? The other Societies could be in this same situation. They said they were coming. It's much easier to control all of us if they're able to keep us separated." Silas had one hand on his chin as he spoke, falling into strategist mode.

"If that's true, it's even more urgent that we figure out a way back as soon as possible." I pulled away from Fell and began to pace. A loud *crack* echoed above me, and his hand grabbed onto mine, pulling me back against his chest. A stray stalactite fell and shattered directly where I'd been standing moments before.

Fell's hand tightened over my own as I stared up at him. I was enthralled by the feel of his skin on mine. In the past he'd always grabbed at my cloak, my sleeve, the ocala items I was wearing, but never my skin. Even when he'd pushed me out of the way of the ixtor, he'd been holding onto my tunic.

I couldn't seem to will my hand away, and he made no move to break the contact. I felt him tense, jerking both our hands. Then he began glowing with the full-force light Riftians revealed only with strong emotions. I saw soft light that matched the color of his eyes emanating from the arm that grasped mine. He must have discarded his cloak when he'd gone after me. As I stared, twilight-colored symbols began spiraling out from his existing marks, moving further down his arm and toward his wrists. We were all trapped together in the Rift, the Spear had reappeared, the others were in danger at the Hub, and I was riveted to the spot by what I saw. Fell's markings ran up his arms, and new twilight lines began racing outward, delving beneath the ocala he wore.

I gasped as I felt my own marks spiral into motion. I felt the new symbols as they moved over each arm and then down my back, between my shoulder blades. I twisted around, straining to see them. I was held in place by the hand that still gripped mine. The cut of my bodysuit revealed opalescent marks everywhere there was space to see them. As I reached my left arm up, my hand falling out of his grasp, Fell's gaze zeroed in on something. The mark Ama had refused to read had been completed. I glanced up and saw that the pupils in Fell's glowing eyes had dilated. He reached up and undid his own ocala attire at the neck, throwing the tunic to the side. It revealed the same thing I'd seen him staring at when my first marks had appeared after the ixtor.

I heard Hale faintly in the background, demanding to know just what was going on, but couldn't bring myself to answer him, any more than I could explain myself to Fell. My gaze was glued to the mark over his chest that he kept pulling on, re-examining from every possible angle as he looked back and forth between it and the one on my arm. Mine glowed a soft opal next to his twilight. They were identical, a symbol I recognized from my lessons with Ama. Her books had provided only one possible interpretation for them. Soul.

The cacophony behind us reached a fever pitch and drew me back to my senses. Fell hastily began to pull his tunic back over his head, tying the neck back in place. As he stepped back and the others rushed in, I felt something akin to loss. The moment broken, I refocused as a pair of boots stomped up next to us and a hand waved between our faces.

"Hello! ... Is anyone going to tell me what the heck is going on here?" Hale demanded. "Because I for one would like to know why we're being treated to a Riftian strip show, and why you two were suddenly holding hands!"

I shot a worried glance at Fell. I had no idea how to explain to Hale exactly what the markings meant. I needed to confirm them with Ama, although I had a good idea.

"Kena has advanced in her Assimilation." Fell volunteered the information with a straight face, giving nothing away. He shot a glance at Vanya and Hok, off to the side. They stood there, tight-lipped and stone-faced. I found myself thankful for the sanctity and privacy of markings. Whether they could read the mark itself I had no idea, but its probable meaning seemed obvious even if they couldn't.

Hale sighed and ran his hand along the back of his neck.

"Well, what about *his* markings, then? You know what, it doesn't matter. Kena, congratulations, or however you Riftians typically acknowledge these things. That being said, I'm still not sure what that has to do with Fell putting his pecs on display."

Fell opened his mouth, probably ready with another lie, but Hale pushed on.

"We don't really have a whole lot of time to linger on this development with several planets in jeopardy. Our former home possibly included." He shot another accusatory glare at Fell, who shot one right back.

"You're right. Of course, you're right. We have to move quickly," I agreed. As I stepped further away from Fell, toward my best friend, I was overcome with a regret I couldn't suppress as the marks dimmed. I caught a similar expression flash across his face before he schooled it once more into his typical mask of composure.

"Our primary focus needs to be getting back to the Hub and helping out our fellow Riftians and other Societals. Who *are* still alive, I'm certain of it. We will protect our family." Vanya's green marks flickered as she spoke. She had to be sick with worry over Ariadna.

A crowd had gathered at the edge of the lake, where we stood. Vanya surveyed them all, casting her gaze around the room before she continued.

"Riftians are considered a peaceful people. We know we are a *just* people. There is a way to get our loved ones back! And we will make the Spear feel our judgment. Anyone willing and able, go gather supplies. Be ready to leave quickly." As she finished, Hok spun on his heel and walked toward the forest, several Riftians following him.

Earthers and other Societals trailed after them. I needed to go, but I had to speak to Fell privately first. I wasn't sure of the best way to separate him from Hale, but Silas came to my rescue.

"Hale, why don't you come with me to the arena? You can get a weapon you're familiar with before we head out to ... wherever it is we're heading out to." Silas swept an arm over his shoulders and hauled him away before had a chance to object.

The others dispersed until Fell and I stood alone in the cavern. As the sound of their steps faded, we were left with the soft lapping of the lake and creaking of loosened stalactites as the only sounds between us.

"Where is Vanya taking us?"

"I know you've been studying with Ama—"

We spoke at the same time. He answered my question first, pulling me toward him as he did so. Our marks hummed with light as he spoke.

"First, we'll stop by your home. You'll need to pack light. After that, the group will need to find Ama. We'll be going to the Mists. And then, the Hub. We have another way to get there." I was relieved. That was one major issue solved. If they had a way back, that meant I'd be able to go after Juliard and the others. It calmed me enough to answer his question.

"I know what our symbols translate to, if that's what you're asking. I'm assuming yours was the other incomplete mark she spoke of?"

"It was. When I first Assimilated, I acquired markings on my left shoulder and upper arm, and the incomplete one on my chest. But that was it. Nothing was added after the initial set. I waited, but for nearly a hundred years, no new marks presented themselves. Until today."

We'd have to circle back to that timeline later. No wonder he'd scoffed when I'd mentioned Silas being out of my age bracket.

"So, all the rest of the marks, they're brand new?" I gestured toward him where I knew they covered his arms, chest, and back. He nodded.

"And if we have time, I'll ask her to interpret them fully for me, but the most important part is that we're connected."

As he spoke, Fell stepped closer and took my hand in his again. Then he pulled his tunic aside and laid it over his chest. Standing in the glow we gave off, I found myself struggling to breathe as he leaned his face toward mine. The question I managed to formulate came out breathy and hoarse.

"And what does that mean?"

I needed to hear the answer before we rejoined the others. All the Societies were in danger, and yet a smile formed on his face, eyes sparking as he answered.

"It means exactly what you think." I didn't even have time to register the meaning of his words before his lips met mine.

Acknowledgements

This novel could not have happened without so many wonderful people. Catherine, thank you for being the first person to set some "editor eyes" on this in its earliest stages. Lizzy, you have the most helpful feedback and have support me on this series since day one. Alyssa and Shelbs, the reactions you texted me while reading the book were both hilarious and helpful. Every author wants some yelling, screaming "what!?" reactions and I enjoyed receiving yours. Ally, you are the reader who has kept me on track with this series! Readers will have you to thank when they get the whole trilogy released in under a year. To my parents and husband, thank you for listening to me provide writing update after writing update and for all your supportive words. To my dogs, thank you for not looking at me like I was crazy when I went through plot points out loud with you. I know you're just in it for the treats, but it was still very much appreciated.

Upcoming Releases

The Trilogy Continues Later This Year With Two Releases

August 2023

Serpentina: A Societies Novella

September 2023

Alliance: The Societies Book 2

Note From The Author

Thank you so much for reading Assimilation! I hope you enjoyed the first book. Reviews are one of the most helpful thing to authors, and if you liked the book I would truly appreciate you taking a moment to leave a review on Amazon, Goodreads, StoryGraph or wherever you prefer to look for new reads! I would love for more people to be able to find and enjoy this book.

For updates on new releases and events, sign up for my newsletter at nightlochpublishers.com or join me on Instagram @reameswrites

Thank you,

S. Reames

Don't miss out!

Visit the website below and you can sign up to receive emails whenever Sydney Reames publishes a new book. There's no charge and no obligation.

https://books2read.com/r/B-A-CRDY-PELIC

BOOKS 2 READ

Connecting independent readers to independent writers.

About the Author

Sydney Reames has long been a lover of all things reading. Each time she's set loose in a bookstore she comes out with several purchases because "this particular book spoke to me." She is often found reading or writing while drinking what might well be considered too much caffeine. She loves swimming and spending time with her husband and two dogs. Both of whom feature heavily in her newsletter, the dogs, not the husband.

Read more at nightlochpublishers.com.

www.ingramcontent.com/pod-product-compliance
Lightning Source LLC
Chambersburg PA
CBHW031333020726
47499CB00005B/1246